Cut and Paste

FIONA BOLSER

FISHER KING PUBLISHING

Cut and Paste

Published by
Fisher King Publishing
The Studio
Arthington Lane
Pool-in-Wharfedale
LS21 1JZ
UK

www.fisherkingpublishing.co.uk

I dedicate this book to the memory of my fabulous mum. She was a truly special woman in every way and I miss her every day.

I'd like to say a special thank you to Corrie and Christian, my kind and lovely sons, for all their encouragement and praise. They believed in me when I didn't believe in myself.

Thanks to my amazing siblings, their partners, my dad and my friends.

Also thanks to all the brilliant colleagues I've worked with over the years and the truly wonderful students that I've had the privilege to teach - you know who you are!

And finally, thank you to all from Fisher King Publishing for their support and help along the way.

Light... one, two, three...

...light... one, two, three, light... one, two, three... fear, pain, darkness. *This can't be happening, this isn't real.*

Trying to speak, her words were thick, indistinct, strange. She was being dragged along, ice digging into her body. She could smell mud and smoke. Nothing made sense. She was naked, her flesh exposed, vulnerable, defenceless. Dark eyes above her. Rough hands. Claws. Again, she opened her mouth to scream, shout, something. Her voice was lost, somehow slurred and inaudible. The thick undergrowth pierced her flesh. Whoever was pulling her was strong and ruthless. She tried to speak, to make sense of this senseless situation. Her brain tried to form words but once again her voice failed her.

Sunday January 1st

When she came around on New Year's Day, Pamela's head was wedged between the wall and her bed. Grisly memories stabbed her brain. She tried to piece together why she was feeling so desperate. Gradually, snippets flashed into her mind.

Oh god, she moaned, her voice muffled, croaky. She had behaved like a crazy lady, she remembered being sick at the foot of Soph's stairs, in front of everyone.

She tried to open her eyes, but they seemed to be glued together. Her mouth was gaping, dry. Her throat ached.

As the room came blurrily into view, she realised she was not alone. On the floor, a large shape was covered in her dressing gown and was obviously still asleep. She reached back into her mind and realised she had no memory of getting into bed or of anything after the midnight fireworks and the sick incident.

She managed to disentangle herself from the crumpled sheets, she was still fully clothed. As she tried to sit up her head started spinning. She lay back down in agony, the hangover headache splitting her in two. *Oh god,* she thought, *how have I let this happen, I'm fifty-six, I'm too old for this, too old to have no memory of getting into bed fully dressed and too old to have drunken strangers on the floor of my room. I can't seem to behave like a normal person, there is something seriously wrong with me.*

Her sister's words came back to her - "Did you forget you weren't fifteen?" Yes, it seemed she struggled to remember she wasn't fifteen anymore. She was a fifty-six-year-old woman, with a house, responsibilities and grown-up children. She no longer had a job, of course. The last week at work had ensured that.

She tried to remember how much she'd had to drink. Her foggy, drunken brain scrabbled backwards to recollect the nights events, unreeling vague, stop-start, slow-motion memories. The evening had started off in a civilised way. They'd had cocktails in a nice bar - dirty martinis, two, three, maybe four. Then back to Sophie's house, she groggily remembered drinking a bottle of red wine there. The taste of sick was in her mouth as memories of disgusting alcohol came and went. Yes, a bottle or two of wine – and – oh bloody hell, now she remembered, an enormous glass of Baileys and some port. Dear god, it was no wonder she'd been sick. She remembered at one-point thinking, *this is great, I can obviously drink what I like and not get drunk!* It seemed fifty-six years of experience had taught her nothing.

She reached for her mobile and, in dread, scrolled through the last texts she'd sent. There were happy new year messages to and from her kids and sisters that she had no memory of sending or receiving.

She looked at the photos she'd taken and sighed, disgusted with herself. They were all out of focus and blurry. She remembered slurrily interrupting their conversations, "Shtand shtill, let me take a photograph," as she'd pointed her phone in their general direction in drunken idiocy. *Jesus.* She squeezed her eyes shut in an attempt to escape from the memories. She flinched as each new thought assailed her muddied brain. Once again, she glanced at the sleeping figure on the floor, she had absolutely no idea who it was.

She realised there was no point trying to move. She would just have to lay there for the rest of her life. What did it matter anyway? A part of her knew that at some point she would have to ring her friends and apologise, try to piece together who she had offended and who'd had to clear up after her. Maybe even who had put her to bed. But right now, she was so befuddled and so disgusted with herself she couldn't face the day ahead. What a way to start the new year.

Flashbacks came and went. At one point she could see herself laughing hysterically at something that in the cold light of day clearly wasn't funny. She re-lived the moment when she dropped a full plate of food and ineptly tried to clean it up, that was when she'd fallen. She vaguely remembered rolling onto the floor in an inelegant, gangly sprawl and, from above her, concerned and horrified faces looked down, shaking their heads. Their voices revolted and condescending; "Typical Pam." "Leave her there." "She's pissed the daft bitch."

She remembered going out into the garden, heels sinking into the mud, she had barged into the twenty-somethings and grabbed a cigarette. She hadn't smoked for at least thirty years. They had laughed at her and walked away. *I'm*

3

fifty-six, fifty-six for god's sake, I'm too old to behave like an idiot.

If only she could stop herself from regurgitating all this, if she could maybe go back to sleep, by the time she woke again perhaps the memories wouldn't be so bad.

Something else was on the tip of her brain, something that she could vaguely remember, grass, pain, something she just couldn't get a fix on. What had happened in the hours between forgetting everything and now? Her mind was muddled, vague. Images rolled in front of her like someone had pulled the lever of a cruel one-armed bandit. She closed her eyes but realised that if she didn't have a glass of water she was probably going to die.

A film trailer went through her mind. It showed her slipping in the mud, legs akimbo, knickers on show, with all the other elegant party goers laughing and pointing at her. The voiceover, shocked and disgusted stated, "This is Pamela, her life is a mess, no man, no job and soon no friends. She may as well be dead."

Maybe her friends had been drunk too, maybe they wouldn't remember her atrocious behaviour. She could only hope. One person who would remember was Sophie. She would ring her soon, but she couldn't face it just yet. For now, she had to stop thinking about yesterday. What was the point anyway? It was over, it had happened and now she just had to get over it and think about the future. What was New Year's Day about if not planning new beginnings. But probably not today. Today she had to lay in bed and recover. She would be able to deal with everything later.

She could hear the person on the floor stirring. She squeezed her eyes shut and prayed, *dear god, please, make them just go away, whoever they are. Please just get up and go. Do. Not. Talk. To. Me.* Pamela didn't want to open her eyes and acknowledge this other human who had obviously seen too much and been involved too much in yesterday's humiliations. If only she could remember coming home, getting into bed, anything, then she might have a clue who was on the floor.

She woke again several hours later, suddenly and in the middle of a crazy dream, sweating, feverish. She had been desperately packing a case, with rising panic, she was going to miss the flight or the train, she wasn't prepared, she didn't know what to take. She had been grabbing handfuls of clothes and was trying to stuff them into a small bag. She didn't know where her children were. Then, the plane crashed, *die quickly, die quickly*, she had shouted at herself in the dream.

The dull grey mid-afternoon light seeped under the blinds into her room and pierced her fragile brain. She groaned, remembered where she was and what had happened the infamous night before. She shakily peered at the floor, her dressing gown was flat, abandoned, strewn across the carpet, arms akimbo. It looked like it was attempting a slow crawl away from it's appalling owner. Whoever had been there had silently removed themselves. Thank god she was spared that conversation. A familiar voice cut into her mind, "Oh Pamela, why did you get so drunk?"

"Not now, mum. Please." Her thought-mum shook her

head and sighed.

"When will you learn?"

"Never." Pamela replied.

She felt just about strong enough to drag herself out of bed and into the bathroom. Sitting on the loo she surveyed the cuts, grazes and bruises on her legs and arms. She felt her head and found a couple of painful lumps. *Oh god, who comes home like this, who does this at my age, I'm such a fricking idiot, I'm such a fricking idiot*, she chanted the mantra quietly under her breath.

Looking at herself in the mirror, a pale red eyed creature stared back at her. Her eyes were tiny scarlet holes in the middle of a white face, black make-up smudged around them. She found some paracetamol in the bathroom cabinet and took three, drinking water straight from the tap. The whole room began spinning and she grabbed the sink for support. As the world gradually slowed and came back into focus, she stumbled back to the safety of her bed. *I should be getting up, doing things, being organised.* But she couldn't face the world just yet.

Darkness enveloped the room. *I have to feel better soon, I must feel better soon*, but her words weren't helping. *Maybe if I get up and have a small drink – the hair of the dog – maybe then I'll feel normal.* The idea came and went, on the one hand it disgusted her, on the other it seemed it could be the only way. Well New Year's Day was a right off, she may as well admit that.

Pamela re-surfaced a while later. She felt a tiny bit better. She had to have a strong word with herself, *listen*

Pamela, you cannot let this entire day go to waste OK, you can't start the year as such a failure. She peered around the room for her laptop, it was probably downstairs. Instead she rummaged in her messy bedside drawer for a pen and a piece of paper. She needed to seriously organise her thoughts and write down all the ways this year was going to be better than last year. With a shaky hand she began the list: 1. Get healthy. 2. Lose weight. 3. STOP DRINKING. She thought, *that should probably be number one.* She put a line through her writing and started again. So, 1. STOP DRINKING. 2. gym. 3. lose weight. Then she thought, *number one should be find a new job, surely.* She lay back down, weak and drained. *I'm probably not ready to write this list*, she realised. Her thoughts drifted back to the last week at work. Probably one of the worst weeks of her life.

Her boss had finally won. Nearly everyone else had left the department, jumped before they were pushed, but she'd thought, 'I'm not going to let him get to me, what's the worst he can do?' She found out in that last awful week. Each day she'd been called into his office for a dressing down, over the flimsiest of reasons. She started secretly recording the meetings on her phone. By the end of the week her boss said that in the new year he was going to get the local authority in to observe all her lessons and check all her planning. Before he'd come to the school she'd always had outstanding lesson observations. He said when he'd observed her year 10 class the teaching had been inadequate, and the books weren't marked.

'I'm not surprised they weren't marked,' she'd replied,

'I don't teach a year 10 class.'

He'd looked confused and checked his notes – he was about to insist that she did teach a year 10 – what a fool. As if she didn't know what year groups she taught.

'Oh, I mean your top year 9.'

Once again she'd replied, 'I don't teach any top sets – my year 9 are a bottom set.' You'd think that would've shut him up, but sadly, his incompetence wasn't going to save her. Someone from the local authority would be coming in from January, to watch her every move and make her life a misery.

After thirty successful years she knew she was a good teacher. Her students loved her, and she was always up to date with marking and planning. She could brave it out, prove she wasn't inadequate, but a great weight seemed to crush her whole being. It would be so hard to prove her worth once the Head of Department had poisoned the mind of the observer. He'd already got rid of so many people, what was one more. She knew, without doubt, that she'd be sacked by February half term. So, she'd collected all her things; three enormous bags of paperwork and books and told her friend Lou, 'I'm not coming back next year.'

This is what new Heads of Department's did, they got rid of the expensive teachers and replaced them with young, inexperienced teachers. She knew this for a fact, she'd overheard conversations where the question was, 'Shall I manage her out?' It wasn't easy, but it could be done. Only this psycho had got rid of the younger teachers too. They'd seen enough of his management style to know they had to get the hell out.

She was dreading the first day of term when she would have to ring in sick. She'd been in touch with the union rep at school, who'd been sympathetic but useless. He told her to ring union head office with all her complaints. When she did ring them, she found that they were not surprised to hear about her boss. In fact, they knew all about him. 'Oh yes – he's well known to us – he's already done the same thing in several other schools.' She was told to ring back in the new year if she couldn't face going back. Knowing that he'd ruined the lives of other people didn't make her situation any better.

She couldn't help going back to that depressing feeling that had been weighing her down since she woke up, the feeling that she was a total failure. She ticked off the list of failures in her life, her marriage had failed, her various diets always failed, her attempts at going tee-total had failed and now her career had failed.

Her marriage - *Ha! What a joke.* She couldn't believe that as of the new year she had been divorced for over twenty years. She'd been divorced longer than she'd been married. She'd had a few dates since her marriage ended, but she refused to try on-line dating like her single friends. She was famous for saying, "You go on-line dating and you know what the prize is - a bloody man."

She got out of bed and put her head between her knees. When everything stopped spinning she stood up and went downstairs. As usual she touched the photo of her mum, *I love you and miss you every day,* she told the image. What she would give to phone her mum and hear her real voice, her sensible words of advice.

Putting the kettle on she peered out of the window, it was dark and cold outside and dark and cold inside. She shuddered. *Winter was endless.* She found a discarded crust in the bread bin and put it in the toaster. She realised she had run out of butter and pretty much everything else. Another resolution – whatever number – keep up with shopping, buy nice things for the fridge so that she would always have delicious food to eat. At least she'd have more time on her hands now. She could go shopping more regularly – well at first – after a while she'd obviously be poor, but for now she would still get paid. She drank a couple of mugs of water, made a black coffee and took that and her dry toast into the sitting room.

The room was freezing and depressing and according to the cheerful weatherman on TV another hurricane was about to hit. She found the thermostat and turned the heat up. She felt too exhausted to light a fire. She sat back on the settee and worried about school. She could still change her mind. But she'd never had a more fixed feeling in her life - she knew she would be sacked by February. It was so clear; she couldn't doubt it for a moment. At least this way she had a tiny bit of control over her own fate.

It wasn't as if she was loving the teaching. Those extra classes had taken it out of her. The last few lessons she'd had with one of the extra year 9 classes had been so awful. Exasperated she'd put on a programme about growing up poor in the UK. People who hadn't cared about school and now regretted that decision, as they had no job, no prospects and nowhere to live. The kids had been unimpressed. "That's a load of shit Miss," she'd been told in no uncertain terms, as they then carried on being little shits themselves.

She felt so sorry for the poor supply teacher who was going to have to take over her awful classes. She'd done her own fair share of supply teaching when she and Derek-the-dick had split up. She'd left her lovely school to move nearer her family. It had been another brand of hell that she never wanted to face again. But at least you could pick and choose the schools you went into. And if you had a horrendous day you never had to go back again.

She'd had two or three awful experiences on supply. Once, in a tiny drama studio, she had completely lost control of the class. The kids had turned off the lights and the room was plunged into absolute darkness. They'd raided the prop room and were flinging heavy objects around the room. She didn't know where the lights were or the door to escape. A crazy mob were laughing hysterically, whilst some were screaming as objects hit them. She was shouting, "Turn the lights on, turn the lights on," but they were having so much fun they didn't want it to end, no matter what punishment they might have to face later. She had crawled on the floor to a wall and sat there in tears, not knowing what to do.

Another time, in a particularly bad school, one of the boys had stolen the window key off her desk, quickly opened it and before she could do anything all the kids had jumped out of the window and run away. She interrupted her thoughts, *what am I doing?* She knew she wasn't allowed to dwell on things that had happened in the past. She had banned herself from going over and over past events and yet, because she'd felt so low today, it was all she'd done. She hated herself for today. She'd been weak and stupid and self-pitying.

It was time to re-evaluate. Time to get better. Time to face the world. Her head had stopped spinning, her headache was gone. She was starting to recover. Right, now to the phone call she'd been dreading. She only hoped that Sophie would forgive her for the sick and everything else she didn't want to remember.

'Hi Soph, so, so sorry about last night.' There was a slight pause as Sophie seemed to collect her thoughts. Pamela continued quickly in order to cover up the silence 'Happy New Year, it was a great party.'

'Thank you,' Sophie managed to reply, 'how are you feeling today?'

Her question was loaded with underlying meaning – what she meant was, "How the hell did you manage to drink so much and still be alive!" Or alternatively, "You are a complete liability and I'm never going to invite you to a party of mine ever again, you were such an embarrassment." In the background she could hear Russ say something inaudible. Sophie sniggered.

Pamela felt a stab of shame and her face flushed, 'I'm fine really, well fine considering... look I'll come over and help you clean up.'

Sophie couldn't help a sarcastic guffaw at this, 'Pam it's six O'clock at night, I cleaned up first thing this morning!'

'Oh, of course, obviously. Look I know I behaved like a complete moronic, alcoholic nutcase, I don't know what I was thinking, I just suddenly thought I could drink as much as I liked. I am so sorry I was sick... I honestly don't know what I was thinking. I've spent all day feeling so bad. Can you actually ever forgive me?'

Sophie had started to get off her high horse and was slowly thawing towards Pamela. 'Of course, I can, honestly it was fine, you weren't the only one. You should have seen Helen and Rob, they practically had to be carried out!'

'Was I carried out?' Pamela asked tentatively.

'No! I think you went home with Tom.' Again, she heard Russ, in the background saying something that Sophie couldn't help sniggering at.

Shut up Russ, she thought uncharitably. 'Tom,' *Who the hell was Tom.* 'Did I?'

'Yes, you got a taxi back to yours after the fireworks.'

'Do I know who Tom is?' She asked, feeling her face flush with horror and embarrassment. What had she done? But, of course, he must have been the lump under her dressing gown. 'I didn't sleep with him,' she found herself blurting out, 'I mean he could have done anything, I wouldn't have remembered – but he was sleeping on the floor when I woke up this morning and a bit later he'd gone, so nothing happened...'

Sophie jumped in, 'Well you were getting on pretty well before the taxi came!'

'Oh my god... what was I doing... no don't tell me... I don't want to know.'

Sophie laughed, clearly enjoying Pamela's humiliation and distress, but softening she said, 'You weren't doing that much, just seemed to be having a deep and meaningful conversation in the corner!'

'Oh god.'

'No, don't worry, honestly it wasn't that bad.'

'Who is he?'

'Just a friend of Russ's from work.'

Pamela felt mortified, 'He's not married is he?'

'God, I hope not!'

'Don't you know?'

'I'm pretty sure he isn't, I mean it was New Year's Eve, if he had a wife, or something, I'm sure she'd've been there.'

This was not the most reassuring of statements. Pamela had to admit to Sophie that she remembered nothing after going into the garden and stealing a cig off the kids outside. 'Honestly, I'm such a stupid cow, how could I let this happen.'

'We all do it.'

'But we're getting a bit old.'

'Yes, let's never drink again!'

'Good plan. Right well I'll let you go, sorry again for... well... everything. See you soon and thanks again for the party and being so nice about it.'

'What are friends for?'

'Bye love.'

'Bye.'

Did she feel better now that was over with... not really.

If anything, she felt worse. How had she let this happen? All her friends must be laughing at her. She needed to ring someone who would fill in the blanks and not make her feel awful. Sophie hadn't been that bad, but the disapproval she'd felt at Pamela's behaviour was unmistakable.

She mentally went through all the friends who'd been at the party. Of course, she'd ring Helen, apparently, she'd been atrocious too! *Hurray!* Someone else with no 'off switch' like herself.

'Hi Helen, it's Pam. Happy New Year! How are you feeling today?'

'Disgusting,' came the weak reply.

Pamela couldn't help laughing in the same evil way that Sophie had. 'Sorry, I don't know why I'm laughing, I was the same. God it's terrible, isn't it.'

'I know, now Rob isn't talking to me. He says I'm a complete embarrassment and he never wants to be seen with me again!'

'What! That's not fair – he was as bad.'

'He thinks he wasn't, so...' Helen's voice trailed off.

Pamela realised that she'd rung the wrong person if she wanted to fill in the blanks of the night, she obviously wanted to cheer herself up by talking to someone who'd been as badly behaved as she'd been. 'What is wrong with us!' She groaned. 'Wouldn't you think we'd know better.'

'I know.'

'I've spent all day beating myself up – and – apparently, I brought a random guy home.'

'Oh my god, YOU DID NOT.'

'Yes, and I've absolutely no memory of it. I woke up today and saw someone asleep on my bedroom floor, so I just closed my eyes and hoped that when I woke up he'd be gone.'

'And was he?'

'Yes, thank goodness. Soph says it was someone called Tom, but I can't remember even meeting him, let alone bringing him home.'

'Bloody hell, you poor thing. How was Soph when you rang?'

'She was nice, but underneath I think she was pretty disgusted with me.'

'She won't be. God after all these years she knows what we're like.'

'I know, it's shocking, isn't it!'

'Yep.'

'Have you spoken to her yet today?'

'Yeah, I called earlier. She was very sweet. I offered to come over and help clean up, but she just laughed.'

'Same here. I s'pose it was a bit late, apparently she'd been up at six am or something!'

'No, she never went to bed, just stayed up cleaning all night!'

'Smug Bitch!' They both laughed. 'No, I don't really mean it. Bless her, she puts up with us!'

'I know. God I'll never live it down.'

'Same.'

'Oh well, another year, let's hope it's going to be productive and sober.'

'Cheers to that.'

'Let's meet up one evening next week.'

'Great idea, in the meantime I hope Rob forgives you!'

'Ha! Thanks! Bye love.'

'Bye.'

Pamela felt a tiny bit better after this conversation. She hadn't been the only one completely out of control. And poor Helen, at least she didn't have an evil, controlling man making her feel one hundred times worse about the night. Imagine some man rubbing it in, telling her she'd been a total disgrace and not accepting that he'd been as bad. And, not for the first time, Pamela felt so relieved and happy not to be in any kind of relationship. Especially as the man she'd married had been a domineering dick, who had made her life hell. How he would have loved to go on and on about what a fool she'd been. He would have taken great delight in recounting, in lurid detail, exactly what she'd looked like when she fell over and who she'd been vile to. And really, she didn't need any help in tormenting herself.

She started to think about this Tom character. She had absolutely no memory of him whatsoever. Maybe he'd just needed somewhere to stay and her house had been as good as any. But it was strange that he'd slept on the floor. Maybe he was some sort of perv who liked watching drunken, out-of-control women whilst they slept. Who cared, anyway it wasn't like she was ever going to see him again. *Thank god.*

She sent her boys a quick WhatsApp, 'Hi Guys - hope you both had a great time last night xx'.

A while later they replied, "Hi mum great thanks xx."

"Hi really cool cheers talk soon. xxx."

She'd ring them when they got back from their respective holidays.

She messaged her sisters, "Hope you both had a fab night last night – love P xx."

She was suddenly starving. She hadn't eaten anything all day except dry toast and there was no way she was going to start cooking, even if there had been any halfway decent food in.

She remembered the Quality Street tin in the cupboard. That would do for now. She took the box into the sitting room and went on her phone to search for the Just Eat App. Thank goodness for modern technology. She ordered what was probably the unhealthiest pizza she could find.

She started scrolling through Facebook. She hated FB but couldn't help going on every now and then. Oh great, Sophie had put up some terrible pictures of her from the party. She looked like a fat, drunken nutter - oh wait, she *was* a fat, drunken nutter.

Her short dark hair seemed to be sticking up at odd angles and the sparkly dress she was wearing had ridden up way past her enormous thighs. Her eyes lost in a sea of black makeup. Sophie, on the other hand, looked beautiful. Happy, composed, slim. Her long blonde hair silky, smooth, her bright eyes shining as she smiled at the camera. *Yeah thanks Sophie,* she thought, *this is how you get your revenge on your drunken best friend.* Everyone else looked fine – well not everyone – Joanne and Phil looked a bit deranged, as did Helen and Rob – obvs.

People loved putting awful pictures on FB, they seemed to check that they looked gorgeous and not care about anyone else. She quickly scrolled through them, wincing every now and then at the awfulness of most of the images. She'd love to pay Sophie back, but as she'd already discovered her photos were out of focus and, anyway, that wasn't a very nice thought. Maybe she should add "be kind" to her new year's resolution list. When she re-worked her list, she must add something like that. But for now, she couldn't help feeling annoyed at the photos.

As she scrolled down she caught site of quite an attractive man standing next to her in the background of one of the photos. They seemed to be deep in conversation. He was tall, well built, smiley. This must be the infamous Tom. Sophie hadn't tagged him, so it could have been anyone. Anyway, she wasn't interested. Whoever it was, she didn't care.

Thankfully the photos came to an end. They weren't as bad as they might have been she supposed. There weren't any of her rolling about on the floor, being sick or smoking, though no doubt if anyone had had a chance, they would have caught those delightful moments. *And maybe one of my friends will upload those photo's in a while*, she thought, uncharitably.

Her sister, Georgie, pinged her back, she'd had a great time, so that was all good. Anne probably wouldn't reply, she rarely did. It was her turn to visit their dad today so no doubt she'd have something to say about that later. She scrolled through FB photo's of her boys. They both seemed to be at fabulous mountain parties. Lucky things.

Her pizza arrived. The young delivery guy eyed her up and down thoughtfully. She suddenly remembered what a fright she must look, still wearing the glittery, though now horribly creased dress from last night. Her black tights were covered in holes and, let's be honest, bits of mud. She'd also not managed to clean her smudged and ruinous make-up off. *Oh well, let him be shocked,* she thought, *yes people over 50 were still capable of going out and having a good time, outrageous as that was.*

'Had a good day?' he asked innocently, as she was fumbling in her bag for a tip.

'Yes, it's been lovely, thanks.' She replied; with all the dignity she could muster. She handed him a couple of quid. He couldn't hide the smirk as he turned away. Oh well, what did she care, she didn't need to impress the pizza delivery guy.

In the kitchen, she grabbed mayo and tomato sauce. She was a tiny bit tempted to open a bottle of red, but good sense prevailed and instead she poured herself a diet lemonade. Back in the sitting room she turned the TV on and opened the pizza box. Oh my god, she loved eating. It was one of the greatest pleasures in life. She'd ordered a super-large veggie supreme with extra chilli and red onions. The crust was stuffed with cheese, she covered the lot with a generous dollop of mayo and ketchup and eat as if her life depended on it.

Pamela had tried to become a vegetarian several times

in her life. Usually when she'd seen something sad, like once she'd seen a lorry slowly drive past and many large, desolate brown eyes had stared out at her. She'd felt so sorry for those poor calves. Another time she'd ordered a pizza bolognese and when it arrived was suddenly and inexplicably disgusted that she was eating dead cow on top of a pizza. But, despite these awful moments, all attempts had failed, mainly due to lack of will-power. That's why it was constantly amazing both to Pamela and everyone who knew her that this last attempt had lasted over ten years. She did have very minor re-lapses, especially when she was drunk, but for the most part she could say she was a proper vegetarian. She did miss meat, but it was lovely to see a field full of cows or sheep and not feel guilty.

She'd been teaching in Dubai when she'd made the decision last time. A gecko had been spotted in the classroom next door to her and her fellow English teacher had run in to tell her that some of the girls wanted to kill it. They were saying that according to their religion if they saw a snake it had to be killed. Pamela pointed out that a gecko wasn't a snake, but they weren't having it. She and Jill were new to the school and knew that they had to be sensitive to cultural differences. She had looked at the tiny gecko and felt so helpless, she desperately wanted to save it, but it seemed impossible. Looking back, she wished she'd grabbed it and flung it out of the window. An Emirati teacher had come into the room and stomped on it. She'd gone back to her classroom and cried.

Later that day, recounting the story to a fellow colleague

he asked, 'Are you a vegetarian Pam?'

She'd felt such a foolish hypocrite and had to answer, 'Well, no.' She decided then and there that it was ridiculous to value one animal over another and had stopped eating meat. That was a hard decision in Dubai, as the meat there had been delicious, and the Friday afternoon brunches completely legendary. When you cut out meat, they were less legendary. After a while she became braver and less worried about upsetting their religious beliefs. She became a hero amongst her fellow teachers for saying to the students, "Step away from the Gecko!" and had saved many innocent geckos from a horrible death.

I must stop thinking about the past, she told herself, *I need to sort my list out.* She found her laptop under a pile of worksheets on the floor. She opened a blank document. She couldn't be bothered to go upstairs and find the list she'd already started. *Number one should be sort out what's going to happen with work.* That was her most pressing problem and it was causing her the most stress. She typed: Number 1. Work. She would have to arrange a doctor's appointment during the first week back and get up early on Monday morning to call school and leave a message, she didn't want to talk to an actual person. It would be hard to tell the doctor the truth, that she was too stressed to go back, that her boss was an out and out bully whose main ambition in life was to get her sacked. She wasn't sure if she was going to say that, but she'd worry about that later.

She carried on typing: Number 2. Give up drinking. Number 3. Go on a diet. (That was always an easy one when you had just stuffed your face with pizza.) *Or at least,* she thought, *start to eat more healthily, more salads, more fruit, more vegetables. Drink more water. Delete the Just Eat App - No, that was going a bit far.* She deleted "Go on a diet" and wrote "Eat more healthily." Yes, she felt this was really making progress. Number 4. Join a gym – no wait - she deleted that and wrote - Research joining a gym. *That only made sense, there was no point joining any old gym.* She needed to go and have a look at a few.

She'd been spoilt in Dubai. The gym there had been luxurious. The weather had always been amazing, and she could sunbathe next to the pool after work. A waiter walked around the pool catering to your every need. It was more like an all-inclusive 5-star hotel than a gym. It wouldn't be possible to get that sort of experience in rainy Yorkshire but if she visited a few she might find a half-way decent one.

Ok, back to the list. She had to improve her life this year. Number 5. De-clutter. *Yes, that was a great one.* She was going to have a lot of time on her hands over the next few months, so that was a no-brainer. She could sort out all her clothes, take most to charity, throw out the complete tat. Go through all the drawers and have only sensible things in them. Things that she used and needed. All the years of never throwing anything away, honestly, it had to stop. Her friend had a good word for drawers full of tat – she called it rubbage, she had an awful lot of rubbage to clear away.

She decided to write number 5 in capitals - BE KIND / BE POSITIVE / DON'T THINK ABOUT THE PAST. Great, this list was totally cheering her up. *Maybe that was enough.* If she was totally honest it was going to be hard to stick to even this short list. *No!* She told herself, *stop being negative. You must believe in yourself. You must believe you can do this.*

Yes, it was all going to be great tomorrow.

Pamela wandered into the kitchen and started rummaging through her rubbagey drawers. She found a couple of packs of salt and vinegar crisps and poured herself a large tonic. She could have a G and T without the G. That was fine. Maybe tonight she could slosh a dash of gin in. After all she was going to start everything else tomorrow. *No,* she walked out of the kitchen, *I'd be crazy to start again.* If she could stop at one small gin that would be fine, but she knew she couldn't. She knew she had no 'off' button. Best to avoid the stuff for as long as she could.

Back in her sitting room she started flicking through the channels. As usual there wasn't much that caught her eye. She settled on some old episodes of Game of Thrones. She was pleased that she'd ignored that first real impulse to have a drink. It wasn't going to be easy, obvs, but if she got her head around it, genuinely tried her best, then surely she could do it.

Pamela woke up several hours later. She felt groggy and weird. She had no idea what time it was. The hurricane promised earlier was now in full swing. Her windows were being lashed by her out of control shrubbery. Sleet was dashing against the conservatory roof in a menacing manner. She was cold and miserable. Her earlier positivity had completely faded away. She went up to the bathroom and forced herself into the shower.

She fell into bed, exhausted and depressed. She woke up half an hour later, feeling confused and dreadful. Her body was burning up, wet and sticky. *Fricking menopause,* she thought. She flung the bedsheets off and lay there listening to the awful weather, twisting about, worrying. Winter was here and the night was dark and full of terror.

Monday 2nd January

The next morning slapped Pamela coldly in the face. She woke to a deep feeling of anxiety. The long, dark month of January stretched before her in an ominous and cheerless fug. Her usual gloomy and despondent thoughts kicked in; *my life is meaningless, everything has gone wrong, I won't be able to stick to any of the positive things I decided yesterday. It's impossible, simply impossible.* She groaned and yawned and felt crap. She couldn't waste today like she had yesterday. She didn't have an excuse for a start. In a minute she'd get up, have a shower and get dressed. Things normal people found so easy. Put clean clothes on. Start the day. *Yes, Pamela, good plan.* She lay down and went back to sleep.

Anne had sent a message whilst she was asleep, "Hi - dad fine yesterday - needs small water bottles x."

Bloody hell. She'd forgotten it was her turn to visit. Why the hell Anne couldn't buy him the water was a complete mystery. It was always a demand to one or other of her sisters. Georgie had made the right decision to get away for the holidays.

She got out of bed and headed for the bathroom. She decided to have a lovely long soak in the bath. It would maybe help get rid of negative thoughts. She put on her most positive music as loudly as she could and immersed herself in the warm water.

There were so many things she should be positive about. She had her own home, a car, enough food to eat, warm clothes, her family were mainly healthy, she was intelligent and articulate. She was fortunate enough to live in the West and wasn't in the middle of an appalling war. She wasn't a refugee fleeing for her life with her malnourished kids and elderly relatives hanging onto her, with a few basic possessions under her arm. So what that work had crumbled into total crisis and she'd drunk too much on New Year's Eve. God, there were so many people much worse off than her.

How selfish to feel depressed. How self-indulgent. For about the millionth time she told herself off for all her negative thoughts, gave herself a mental shake and probably a mental slap or two around her spoilt face. It seemed she couldn't help lurching from one set of thoughts to another. She needed to slow her brain down and concentrate on being normal; if only that was possible.

After fifteen minutes in the bath she was beginning to regain control over her annoying thoughts. Once out and dressed she did start to feel more positive again. *It's important to keep busy, have projects to face,* she told herself.

She went into the kitchen and made a cup of black coffee. She found a pack of porridge oats and made a large bowl with water. It was disgusting, like eating hot, lumpy cement mix. *Never mind, at least it's filling and low-fat.* Right, soon she'd start researching gyms, that would be constructive and help her to tick items off her resolutions list. Then she'd go shopping and buy lots of fresh, healthy food.

Her mobile rang. It was Sophie. 'Hi, how's it going?'

'Good thanks, what about you?'

'Yes, great. Listen, Russ's just spoken to Tom. He wants to know if you want his number?'

At first Pamela was confused, she asked, 'Tom, Tom who?' Then she remembered, 'Oh god, you mean that guy who stayed the night on my bedroom floor.'

'Yes,' Sophie answered, impatiently, 'he asked Russ if you want his number?'

'What do you mean?'

'Well... that. Do you want his number?'

Pamela felt horribly indignant and replied, 'I'm not going to ring him. I actually can't even remember him.'

'He remembers you!'

She could hear Russ making stupid comments in the background. He never left Sophie alone, never let her have five minutes of privacy. Anyway, Pamela was thinking that this was a bit ridiculous, if Tom wanted to talk to her shouldn't he be asking Sophie if he could have her number, not expect her to call him.

Anyway, and more importantly, she had no memory of him whatsoever, so she said, 'No, I don't want his number, I think he's got a bit of a cheek if I'm honest, why doesn't he see if I'd mind him having my number and then ring me?'

'Oh Pam, it doesn't have to be so difficult. You either want to talk to him or you don't.' Sophie couldn't help feeling irritated with Pamela, what was her problem, a nice man wants her to ring him, why be so weird about it?

Pamela could hear the edge in her friend's voice and realised that she was being difficult, but so what, 'Thanks Soph, but no, I probably won't ring him. I can't even remember him, and he seemed a bit creepy. I mean he slept on my bedroom floor instead of going home like a normal person. And there are other bedrooms or what about the settee?'

Sophie sighed, 'I have no idea. So, I'll tell him you're not interested, should I?'

'Yes.'

'Ok.'

There was an uncomfortable silence then Pamela said, 'Sorry if I'm being annoying.'

'Well, he does seem like a nice guy though.'

'He's a catch!' shouted Russ.

'Shut up Russ,' Sophie shouted.

'You didn't even know if he was married the last time we spoke!' Pamela replied, huffily.

'Well, since then I've spoken to Russ about him.'

'He's lovely!' Russ could be heard saying.

'Shut up Russ!' they both shouted.

'And?' added Pamela.

'He's just gone through a horrible experience, his wife just up and left him before Christmas and they'd been together years apparently. He's one of the new managers at Russ's. He's very good looking.'

'Kids?'

'Not sure, anyway you're not going to ring him, so...'

'Yes, no point...' There was an awkward silence then Sophie changed the subject,

'What are you up to for the rest of the holiday's?'

'Well, visiting dad obvs, and, you'll be pleased to hear, trying to sort my life out, give up the demon drink, lose weight, de-clutter, join a gym, you know the usual January madness.'

'God, Russ's the same. Moaning on about being unhealthy and overweight. You can both join a gym together!'

'Well, I've got as far as planning to research a good gym, so I'll let you know how I get on, if Russ finds a good local gym give me a call!'

'Great, will do. Have you made any decisions about work?'

'Well yes, I'm definitely not going back. It's going to be awful though.'

'I know.'

'And, I've just remembered that I'll have to send my planning in every morning, which is going to be a right pain. I feel sorry for my few lovely classes and my friends who are going to have to cover for me at first. But, honestly, I know you think I'm mad, but it's the only way. I just couldn't face all the scrutiny. That psycho has got it in for me and he won't stop until I'm sacked.'

'Yes, I know, but it's not fair that a great teacher like you should be hounded out. Is there no one you could talk to?'

'No, he's the one people believe.'

'But haven't all the other staff left, couldn't they stick up for you?'

'Well that's the point, they've left. And the people who haven't left yet aren't going to get involved if they don't have to.'

'No, fair enough. But it's still a bloody shame.'

'Yes, yes, it is. When do you and Russ go back?'

'Not until next Monday, thank god.'

'That's good, we'll have to have a coffee or something before you go back.'

'Yes, definitely. Ok, well, I'll see you soon.'

'Yeah, thanks for ringing, bye.'

'Bye.'

She wished she didn't have to keep explaining why she wasn't going back to work, no one seemed to understand her decision. And what about this Tom character. He was obviously an arrogant idiot. Why did he think she should ring him. He evidently had an over inflated view of how good looking and irresistible he was! *Ha!* Apart from the FB photo, she couldn't even remember what he looked like!

Talking to Sophie about work had brought back all her insecurities. She felt a blast of horror at the path she was going to take. Her face flushed; a prickly uncomfortable heat crawled under her skin. It was going to be so awful. A rush of all the useless feelings she'd had during that last week of term washed over her. At some point she must start working on an email to send to Dom. He'd had his work cut out last term, there'd been so many absences and this term was going to be worse. It had become such an unhappy place to work.

She wondered if she should maybe re-join weight watchers. There was a class on a Thursday morning that she could go to if she wasn't working. Thursday morning was great because it meant she could eat more-or-less normally over the weekend and then start dieting properly on Monday. It made Wednesday the most depressing and awful day of the week, but it was manageable. She ought to join a slimming club as her will power was so appalling. At least if someone else was weighing her it made it harder to cheat and lie to herself, like she normally did. But that meant she didn't have to start her diet until after weigh-in on Thursday. *Hurray!* She could eat what she wanted for the next few days. It was always easier to lose weight if you'd been binging right up until going. Right, so now the shopping list could be much more exciting. She didn't feel too bad about that. After all, if she was going to give up drinking, she'd need some compensation.

Thinking about eating always cheered her up. She'd probably been feeling so depressed because the idea of her self-imposed diet was weighing so heavily on her.

She slapped a bit of make up on before grabbing her coat, bag and car keys. You never knew who you might bump into in town, no point looking like a total mess.

The town was derelict today, compared to just a few days ago, when it had been manic. It had a kind of crushed, grey feeling to it. The pre-Christmas rush replaced by lethargy and exhaustion.

At least Christmas was over for another year, Pamela felt a rush of relief at that thought. Thank god. She could take down the tree and the cards and all the false Christmas cheer would be gone from shops and ads on TV. She hated everything about it, the build-up, the expectation, the perfect Christmases depicted everywhere. Everyone knew it was a big lie, created by advertising execs. But you had to pretend it was true and spend and spend and spend to create the illusion of perfection.

Maybe next year she could go away somewhere. A Buddhist retreat or perhaps she could volunteer at an overseas charity or something.

She couldn't understand people who loved the Christmas holidays. It was always so expensive, so cold and miserable, such hard work, especially if you happened to be the woman of the house, expected to cook and clean and keep the whole thing jolly and wonderful. And the picturesque snow either never came or turned to rain and slush in a moment, it didn't last or managed to bring the whole country to a standstill.

Maybe she could get a new job in a country that had a proper winter with proper snow. She'd never been a fan of Christmas, but her feelings had deepened now that her mum was no longer around.

The first Christmas after her death had been truly awful. Her dad was still trying to live an independent life in his own home but failing miserably. She and her older sisters had struggled to do as much as possible. They'd been taking it in turns to stay over in those last dreadful months. But it had been so hard. To carry on seemed totally out of the question.

Their dad had never even made a cup of tea for himself, let alone cook a meal. The sisters complained to each other, 'It's bloody ridiculous, mum spoiled him to death.' It didn't help that he was gradually losing all strength in his legs. He was constantly falling over, and he was a big man, it was impossible to pick him up. It was such a distressing time. Soon after their mum's death he'd became totally wheelchair bound. And he was now profoundly deaf, despite wearing two hearing aids.

With their mum gone it was increasingly impossible to get their dad to realise that his daughters had their own lives. They'd tried to get outside help, but it was expensive and totally unreliable. Their dad would ring one of them at work and start yelling that he was on his own and hadn't had a cup of tea for hours. They would shout down the phone as loudly as possible, but he couldn't hear.

'DAD. DAD. PUT THE PHONE ON SPEAKER, DAD. DAD. CAN YOU HEAR ME?'

'I can't hear you, what did you say?'

'DAD. DAD. CAN YOU HEAR ME?'

'No, I'm on my own, can you come?'

'DIDN'T A CARER COME AT 11?'

'What did you say?'

'A CARER, A CARER DAD, DIDN'T A CARER COME?'

'A what?'

'DAD, I'LL BE THERE AT FIVE, FIVE, CAN YOU HEAR THAT? FIVE'

'I can't hear you, I'm on my own...'

And so the conversations went on. It was awful. Pamela couldn't just up and leave, yet she was always the first one he rang. "RING ANNE," she would shout. Anne had her own business and could get away more easily than Pamela or Georgie but, of course, this led to constant arguments and fall outs with each other. Anne thought that as the other two worked for someone else they should rush to their dad; she was far too important and busy to be called away from work. It was exasperating.

Of course, she felt dreadful for him too. She couldn't imagine what it must be like to lose the person you'd loved for over sixty years. None of them had expected their mum to go first, she'd never been ill in her life, whereas their dad had permanent health issues.

That first Christmas Pamela had taken him to Georgie's house and he'd sat and cried throughout the whole meal. They'd all been miserable, but his desolation and wretchedness was just too much to bear. Pamela's boys had both been away, and she had no husband or partner to think about, so it was up to her to look after him over the whole Christmas period. They had tried to get help, but it seemed no one would work over the holidays.

Thank goodness shortly after that first dreadful Christmas he'd decided to go into a home. He said he didn't feel safe on his own. At least he was well looked after now. They felt guilty, of course. If their mum had been alive she would never had allowed him to make that decision, she would have moved heaven and earth to keep him at home. She would have been disappointed that her daughters had let him down.

She was annoyed with herself. Why was she dredging up her mum's death, she had to stop thinking, she had to bring her cluttered mind back to the here and now. *Get on with the shopping and stop thinking,* she told herself. *I must sort out the Christmas decorations before the end of the week.* Why she still bothered with a tree was a mystery to her. *Probably just a bad habit,* she thought.

Later, after a delicious and extremely high fat lunch, she googled, "Nice gyms in Leeds." A few seemed ok. Ideally, she wanted classes as well as a pool and decent equipment, so that narrowed it down. She felt extremely pleased with herself that she was sticking to her plans. Yes, it was good to be making progress.

She clicked onto Facebook and did a bit of stalking and read a few interesting articles. Generally wasted time.

Her mobile rang, it was her dad, 'WHERE ARE YOU? CAN YOU HEAR ME?' He yelled.

'Yes dad. YES' she shouted, 'I'M COMING TO SEE YOU NOW.'

God, how could she have forgotten? She'd just been thinking about him; she must be losing her mind. Her mum's disapproving, sorrowful face flashed in front of her eyes.

'What was that?' he asked,

'I. SAID. I'M. COMING...   I'M. COMING. NOW.

DAD.' She yelled down the phone,

'You say you're coming?'

'YES.'

She grabbed her keys and coat and rushed out of the house. Poor dad, she thought, he lived for their visits. It was ridiculous really. Most elderly parents probably had visits once a week, if they were lucky. So far, they hadn't managed to get their dad to see that that was normal. He was looked after by very sweet, caring staff, yet he felt that at least one of his daughters' must visit every day. Perhaps it was a last link to his wife. Maybe the way he found meaning in his small world. Whatever it was they all struggled to make sure it happened.

Bloody hell, she thought, *I didn't get the water.* Better get to her dad and not worry about water. She'd find a shop after the visit.

Her dad was sitting in his usual chair looking fed up.

'Hi dad, IT'S ONLY ME'

'Hello, only me.' He replied.

'How are you today?'

'What was that?'

'HOW. ARE. YOU?'

'Oh, couldn't be better,' he answered sarkily.

'GOOD.' She said ignoring his tone.

'I haven't had a bath today.'

'No dad, that's Wednesday. WEDNESDAY.' She repeated.

'Oh, is it?'

'YES DAD.'

'What day is it today?'

'It's Monday dad. MONDAY.'

'Oh ok. When's Georgie back?'

'Not 'til Saturday. SATURDAY.'

'Ok.'

'Did you have a nice visit with Anne yesterday. ANNE? YESTERDAY.'

'Yes, she's very busy you know.'

'I know, so she keeps reminding everybody,' she muttered under her breath.

'What was that love?'

'Nothing... I KNOW SHE'S VERY BUSY. IS SHE GOING TO VISIT TOMORROW?'

'She didn't say.'

'Is she still on holiday? HOLIDAY. IS ANNE STILL ON HOLIDAY?'

'What's that?'

'HOLIDAY, DAD, IS ANNE STILL ON HOLIDAY?'

'I don't know.'

That was the difference between her mum and dad. Her mum always asked the right questions and kept abreast of what was going on in her daughters' lives. Whereas her dad always seemed more engrossed in himself. *Oh, that was mean*, she thought, *he did care.* In fact, she knew he loved them all, but he just wasn't interested in their lives on a day to day level, like their mum had been.

Often she woke up and the first thought she had was, "Oh I must tell mum that." Even now she went as far as to reach for her phone before the awful memory came bursting back. There was no mum to ring, no kind, caring, concerned voice at the other end of the phone. Nobody as completely on her side as her mum had been. If she rang that familiar number now, there'd just be silence. An eternity of silence. It was unbearable.

She pulled herself together, now wasn't the time to start wallowing in that grief. Her dad was still here and although he'd been in the depths of despair and wished for death in the months following his wife's death, he now seemed sort of content. His life had more-or-less kicked back to the way it had always been. He had people whose job it was to be at his beck and call, just like her mum had been. Her thought-mum quietly reprimanded her, "Remember your new year resolution Pamela – Be Kind."

"Yes, mum," she silently answered.

She made them both a cup of tea and sat back down. She furtively looked at her watch, she'd spent ten minutes so far. She couldn't leave for at least another thirty minutes. She found him a programme on the history of railways with subtitles and they sat in silence until it ended thirty minutes later.

She stood up and started putting her coat on, 'Right dad, I'll get off now.'

'Are you going?'

'Yes, it'll either be me or Anne tomorrow, ok?'

'What's that?'

'IT'LL EITHER BE ME OR ANNE TOMORROW.'

'Ok, Thanks for coming love.'

And there it was; the overwhelming feeling of guilt.

Guilt and love, in equal measure.

'See you soon dad. BYE.'

'Bye love.'

She spent the rest of the afternoon sitting on the settee watching catch-up TV. At about six pm she started to fancy a glass of wine. *This is ridiculous,* she told herself, *you're probably just thirsty.*

She walked into the kitchen and made herself an elderflower tonic with loads of ice and lemon. This was one resolution she absolutely had to stick to. What was the point if she fell at literally the first hurdle? Yesterday had been relatively easy but today was going to be the real challenge.

What was it that alcoholics anonymous say, *Take it one day at a time*. That's what she'd have to do.

She decided to go for a walk. Although it was wet, dark and grey it would be the best way to get her mind off that delicious glass of wine she could almost taste. It was a miserable walk, misty and bleak.

The town had a flattened wrinkled feeling. Dirty, black, crushed. It was especially hard walking past the pubs. The temptation to go in and order a large Pinot Noir was slightly overwhelming. Though the pubs looked dismal and empty tonight. It wasn't like her younger days when everyone had spent their evenings in a pub and the sound of laughter and drunken merriment rang out onto the dark streets. In those days they'd been inviting, warm places, full of welcome, smoky and atmospheric.

Tonight they were deserted, their coloured lights

twinkling pathetically, incongruous now the festivities were over. The streets were empty. Her footsteps echoed dully, hollow on the cracked pavements, soft, muffled. Struggling up the hill she finally reached her favourite bench.

Looking down she could see the tiny people in their kitchens, cooking, watching TV in their sitting rooms, walking from room to room. It felt strange to be on the outside looking in. *All their little lives. Their petty worries, their small arguments, triumphs, disasters. Their insignificance. Life was so meaningless. So depressing and small. Stop it,* she told herself, *stop being so negative, they're probably, happy, content with their lives. Not spoilt and self-obsessed like me.*

She wasn't sure if the urge to drink had gone but it was so cold and miserable, she had to go home.

There was nothing on TV, as usual. Just bad news from different countries.

She went up to bed at eight-thirty. There didn't seem to be any point staying up.

She lay there, unable to sleep, burning up, sweaty and uncomfortable, praying for morning.

Tuesday 3rd January

She woke up feeling proud that she hadn't had a drink. The day stretching ahead of her seemed a bit bleak without the prospect of a nice glass of wine at the end of it. Chilled Chardonnay or a frozen glass of Sauvignon Blanc. *It's just a bad habit,* she reminded herself. *Stop thinking about it.*

She opened the curtains and peered out onto her bedraggled garden. Another grey and miserable day. But that didn't matter, she told herself, in fact it was a good thing. She wouldn't be distracted from the enormous task of de-cluttering and organising.

She quickly texted Anne, "Hi are you visiting dad today? Forgot water sorry P x." She hoped Anne wasn't going to make a fuss, they both had to muck in when one of them was on holiday.

She took all her decorations down with a sense of joy. *No more Christmas for another year, hurray.* She dragged the tree outside to her small garden, managing, in the process to cover her floor with pine needles and brown mud.

She'd bought a real tree in a pot but had forgotten to get one with dropless needles. It was amazing how you forgot things from year to year, she'd assumed that all trees were now dropless. Wrong.

She vacuumed the pine needles and scrubbed the carpet clean. With her alcohol-free energy, she decided that today would be a good day to start de-cluttering. She went into her bedroom. God, it was going to be a mammoth task. There were piles of clothes everywhere and all the drawers were full of crap. She got a stack of black plastic bags from the kitchen.

There were going to be three piles, one for rubbish, one for charity and one for the things she wanted to keep. She started by dragging everything out of the wardrobe and piling it all on her bed. *It was amazing that one wardrobe could contain so much crap.* She picked up all the clothes that covered every inch of the floor and put them all on the bed too. Every item she owned seemed to be black or grey or a different shade of both. She owned nothing colourful or interesting. Maybe she should start buying some more colourful things.

She was about to empty all the cupboards onto the bed too, but a bit of good sense kicked in. Probably better to see how long this would take before going to that extreme.

Her phone pinged, it was Anne, "I suppose so, but I can't see him Weds or Thurs - will you be ok to do those days?"

What could she say, she couldn't refuse. "Yes, fine x." The water wasn't mentioned.

She emptied the laundry basket and walked downstairs, precariously hanging onto the massive load. She piled everything into the washing machine. She decided to make herself a quick cup of tea and some toast. She must find the new calendar she'd bought before Christmas and fill in the days she had to visit her dad. There was nothing much else to add to it. *God,* she thought, *my life is so exciting. Full of social events and meetings! Yeah right* – but she was supposed to be meeting Sophie this week for a coffee. She sent her a quick message. Sophie replied, she and Russ had decided to go away for a short break before they went back to work. Could she meet today, Pamela replied that that would be great.

She walked into her bedroom and groaned, *oh god, I've just put all my go-to clothes in the wash and now everything normal is under a six-foot pile of rubbish.* She flung a few things back onto the floor, looking for something decent to wear. This just proved that most of her wardrobe was full of utter crap. What was the point of having a wardrobe stuffed with clothes if there was absolutely nothing to wear when you wanted to go out and have a simple coffee with a friend. She found an old, baggy pair of jeans and a crumpled jumper. It would have to do, *but this is why I must sort this lot out as soon as I get back. You can't live like this,* she told herself. *Honestly.* She carelessly applied a bit of makeup, grabbed her coat and walked out the door.

By the time she got to Costa it had started raining and she was soaked, having lost her only umbrella a few weeks ago, probably on another drunken night out. Warm air blasted her face as she entered the steamy café. The Christmas decorations looked wilted and somehow out of place, the atmosphere humid and soggy. She found an empty table in the corner, shook her coat and hung it over the back of the chair. She got herself and Sophie a drink and sat down.

Sophie rushed in, late as usual. 'Over here' Pamela

waved, 'Hi, sorry I'm late.'

'No worries, I've got you a flat white – hope that's ok.'

'Yeah, great, sorry. Russ is having a nervous breakdown about packing. He's stressing out, I nearly couldn't come.'

'Bloody hell, you poor thing. Honestly men, what's their problem!'

'Oh, he's not too bad, just an OCD control freak.' They both laughed. 'So, what have you been up to?'

'Nothing much, I'm just trying to get organised. I'm going back to weight watchers on Thursday.'

'Really?' Sophie sounded a bit sceptical.

'Yeah, I know, the very thought of it is making me want to rush to the shops and buy all the chocolate!'

'I'll bet, it's a depressing thought.'

'You don't need to worry.'

Sophie was probably a size 10 and never seemed to be on a diet. She just seemed to stay the same size all the time. She'd probably never dieted in her life, it was so unfair, Pamela thought, admiringly.

'So where are you going, on your romantic mini-break?'

'Whitby, but I don't think it's going to be very romantic to be honest. Russ is driving me mad actually.'

'Well that's marriage for you.'

'Yes.'

They both sighed.

'What about the kid's, have you heard much from them since New Year?'

Sophie immediately brightened. 'Yes, Laura starts her new job for "Good Morning Britain" next week.'

'Wow, that's great. Is it an internship or real?'

'Internship, but with great prospects. In six months, they should take her on full time. But...' Sophie paused, 'Amelie has decided she's giving up her job and going travelling.'

'Oh god, why?'

'She's just decided that she doesn't want to be dragged down by a boring Monday to Friday. She's also fed up with London.'

'Well you can't blame her for that, London is a bit awful isn't it?'

'Yes, but how's she going to get back onto the work ladder if she leaves? She's not a kid anymore – at her age we were both married with children.'

'Yes, but it's different now isn't it? My boys are nowhere near getting married and settling down, and look at Georgie's twins, they've been travelling since Uni.'

'Oh, yes, I'd forgotten.'

'They turned twenty-seven last month and they're still working as bar tenders in New Zealand.'

'You tend to think that New Zealand is fairly safe, though don't you?'

'Yeah, it isn't too bad, it was very worrying when they were in South America.'

'I bet. It's crazy though isn't it? They get a degree, get into thousands of pounds worth of debt and then go off and work in a bar!'

'I think that's why they go, they can't imagine ever being able to pay off their debts, so they run away to escape it! Where is Amelie going travelling?'

'God knows. She'll probably look at a list of the world's most dangerous places and go there.'

'No, she's not crazy, impetuous, yes...'

'It just seems so silly to give up everything on a whim.'

'Yes, I know what you mean. But as I said it's so different for them nowadays.'

'But what about her pension? And she's giving up her flat, she won't be able to afford to live in London when she comes home.'

'That might not be a bad thing. Maybe she'll move back to Yorkshire?'

'Maybe, if she doesn't meet some unsuitable Australian or something.'

'There's always that! Bless her.'

'I'll just have to try not to worry I suppose.'

'Yes, it's the only way. I mean London isn't exactly the safest city on earth.'

'No, I s'pose not. What about Alex and Jake? Are they still happy in their jobs?'

'Not really, well Jake sort of is. Alex definitely not. He's constantly applying for new jobs, hopefully he'll get somewhere soon.'

'Oh, good for him, at least he's being proactive. Any nice girls in their lives?'

'Well Alex still has his semi-sort of girlfriend, Jen, but there's no one in Jake's life as far as I can tell. As if he'd tell me anyway! What about the girls? Is Laura still seeing that Ollie?'

Yes, but we haven't met him yet, anyway, it's very on

off, you know what she's like.'

'I do.' They sipped their coffees.

Sophie asked, 'Have you heard from Helen?'

'I called her on New Year's Day. I needed to talk to someone else who'd been as bad as me! Rob was making her life miserable.'

'As usual!'

'Apparently he was being awful about her getting drunk!'

'He was just as bad!'

'I know, I said that to her, but he was insisting it was just her.'

'What a jerk!'

'Yep! Thank god I don't have a horrible man rubbing it in. I told her about bringing that bloody Tom home with me, she was horrified!'

'Well you're both adults.'

'I know, but it's a bit mad at my age.'

'Honestly though, he did seem a nice guy, I feel so sorry for him with his wife leaving before Christmas and everything, he's very good looking.'

'I can't remember anything about him, that's the trouble with me and alcohol, I have to stop drinking.'

'Same here.' They sighed, contemplating their coffees. Sophie absentmindedly added a couple of teaspoons of sugar and then asked, 'So, you still not going back?'

'Yep, still not going back.'

'I thought you might change your mind.'

'No. Honestly I just know it's the right decision.'

'Yes, you said.'

'But I'm worried about going to the doctors for the sick note.'

'Don't be daft. You are totally stressed, that terrible man has absolutely torn your confidence to shreds by what he's done.'

'I know, it's just something Joanne said at yours on NYE'

'What did that madam have to say?'

'She said I'd be clogging up the doctors' surgery.'

'What the hell did she mean?'

'I think she was implying that I wasn't actually ill, and I was making the doctor give me a sick note on false pretences.'

'Has she met you! Of course, you aren't doing it for no reason. If you feel that you can't go back then that's a legitimate reason. That man has made you ill. It's not like you've ever done anything like this before. God, that makes me so mad.'

'I know, don't get annoyed, it's ok.'

'Well honestly. You'd think your friends would support you.'

'I know. Mostly everyone has, but she was just getting on her high horse, she does have some very strange ideas.'

'I know, but I wish I'd heard her, I'd 've set her straight!'

'Good job you didn't!'

'Well you know I'm always here for you, if there's anything I can do.'

'I know, thanks so much.' Sophie's mobile beeped, she

rummaged in her bag.

'Bloody hell, it's Russ, he can't seem to do a thing when I'm not there to sort it out.'

'What's the problem?'

'He can't find his case.'

'Of course he can't.'

They both sighed, 'Look thanks for coming, and thanks for the support, hope you manage to find his case!'

'Not a problem. Right I s'pose I'd better go and help the grumpy old git pack!' Sophie finished the rest of her coffee in one gulp and stood up.

'Yep, hope you have a magic mini-break!'

'Yeah right!' Sophie struggled into her coat, 'Bye love.'

'Bye see you when you get back.'

Sophie breezed out of the café to organise her feckless brat of a husband, leaving Pamela contemplating what delicious thing she could eat. She chose a large chocolate muffin and a chocolate brownie.

Scrolling through her phone she glanced at her work emails, oh no, there was one from her crappy boss to the whole department. She'd read it later. It was going to be depressing and she just couldn't face it yet. She finished her coffee and cake and started to organise her coat, scarf and gloves.

The door opened, she glanced up and caught sight of a vaguely familiar face. Bloody hell, was it that man from New Year's Eve, he looked like the FB photo of the man she'd been talking to. Oh no, oh god, he was coming over to her table. She started scrolling through her phone, thinking, *Please, please just walk past, just keep going.* But, of course he didn't.

'Pam is that you?'

She could feel her face becoming hot and flushed. *For goodness sake, he must be able to see I don't want to be disturbed.* She looked up from her phone, pretending to be confused and a bit annoyed as though he'd dragged her away from something important. Idiotically she replied, 'Oh, do I know you?' *What a stupid thing to say.*

'Err... sort of... we met at Russ and Sophie Donaldson's on NYE. It's Tom, Tom Reynolds.'

She had to admit that he was good-looking in a rugged sort of way, but she didn't feel any attraction towards him whatsoever.

'Oh yes, of course, Tom, yes...'

The unspoken hung in the air. Yes, I slept on your floor, you were so drunk you couldn't move. You are an embarrassment to yourself and all women over fifty. Luckily, he didn't say that out loud, but she was sure he was thinking it. She remembered that she must look like a crazy woman, wearing odd, mismatched clothes, hardly any make-up, hair all frizzed from the rain. *But did it matter.* After all he'd seen her look much worse at Sophie's.

'Do you mind if I join you?' He asked.

Of course I bloody do, can't you take a hint, she thought, but out loud she stuttered 'Err... err... no, yes, of course.'

'Would you like anything else?'

She shook her head. 'No, I'm fine thanks.' Oh god, how was she going to escape, what could he do if she just got up and ran out the door? Nothing, that's what. But, of course, she didn't. People had already been openly staring over at them, her bright red face had been noted by all the usual town busy-bodies. No, she would just have to endure this. It was her own fault for drinking too much, yet again. This was her punishment.

He came back with two coffees. 'Just thought you might fancy another one.'

God, what a cheek, she thought. *Typical man, either didn't listen to my reply, didn't care or discounted my wishes.* But she thanked him. What else could she do.

As he sat down he said, 'Look, I just wanted to apologise.' Pamela was surprised, surely, she was the one who should apologise? 'I was a bit worried about you, after, well you know, I didn't want to just go home and leave you, in case you were...' He paused, obviously embarrassed, 'You know,' he lowered his voice, 'sick... during the night.'

Oh, so maybe that's why he'd slept on the floor, maybe he wasn't just some weirdo who liked watching drunken women sleep, or maybe he was making that up to make himself appear less weird.

She couldn't decide, so replied, 'Well that was very thoughtful of you.' She realised that sounded a bit sarcastic, it was his turn to look embarrassed, 'No, I mean really, it was kind of you to worry.'

'I should have left a note or something, I'm sorry.'

Pamela was suddenly struck by two thoughts – one horrendous and one annoying - had she been sick in the taxi and had Sophie set up this meeting when she'd refused to ring him. Both thoughts made her cringe.

She couldn't help blurting out, 'Did Sophie set this meeting up?'

'What?' He looked extremely uncomfortable.

She repeated herself,

'Did Sophie tell you I'd be here today?' If he said yes, she was never, ever going to speak to Sophie again.

'God no, I did ask her to give you my number, but she obviously didn't.'

'She didn't give me it because I didn't want it.' She couldn't help herself - he was such a typical annoying man, with an exaggerated sense of his own attractiveness.

He looked horrified, 'Oh, I'm so sorry, I don't know what to say... I thought we seemed to click, sort of, I didn't realise...' He trailed off, miserably.

'Well the thing is... I can't remember meeting you, if I hadn't seen a photo of us together on Facebook, I wouldn't have had a clue who you were. And,' she went on, unable to help herself, 'I think you were weird to sleep on my floor, whatever your reason, and you should have asked if you could have *my* number, not expect *me* to call *you*.'

'Right! You don't hold-back do you?'

There was a very awkward moment, what the kids at school would have referred to as *hashtag awks*, then they laughed. 'I'm sorry. I didn't mean to be such a bitch; I suppose I'm horribly embarrassed that you came back to mine on New Year's Eve. I can't believe I got so drunk and disgraced myself so thoroughly.' As an after-thought she made herself ask, 'Was I sick in the taxi?'

'No, in fact you seemed quite coherent.'

'Really?'

'Yes. But Sophie told me you'd been sick earlier, so that's why I stayed. Honestly, I'm really not a weirdo, we had a good laugh, we seemed to get on so well, and we...'

She stopped him continuing by quickly adding, 'I'm sorry. I'm sure I thought you were nice, but when I woke up, I couldn't remember anything about you, so there was no point me ringing you...' She paused before adding, 'And I'm not interested in having a relationship with anyone, so...'

'Oh, ok, that's fine. My wife's only just left me, so it's probably not a good time to... to... well you know.' He suddenly looked terribly sad and vulnerable. 'I was married for thirty years.'

'Bloody hell.'

'I know.'

'I must say though, taking me home... I'm glad you didn't take advantage of the situation.' Pamela laughed.

Tom looked absolutely disgusted, 'Well we... well... of course, god I wouldn't dream...'

Pamela had to jump in to shut him up, she didn't want the conversation to go down that track. 'No. Good. So, what happened? With your marriage I mean?' This was a bit blunt, even for Pamela and there was another awkward silence, once again his face had that hangdog, pained expression.

Pamela felt awful, 'Sorry, I shouldn't have asked...'

'No, it's fine, I did tell you at Russ's – but as you said

you can't remember me, so why would you remember what we talked about?'

'Yes, no need to rub it in!'

'She just came home the weekend before Christmas and told me she didn't love me anymore, packed a bag and left.'

'God, no, that's totally awful, after thirty years. Bloody hell.'

'Yes, it was pretty awful.'

'She might come back. Maybe she just needed some space.'

'No, she seemed pretty determined, I don't think she'll ever come back.'

There seemed to be nothing more to say. How could anyone cope with that. Her thought-mum pointed out that, *it would be lovely to have an attractive male friend you could go on nice dates with.* Thanks mum, she silently replied. Her own thoughts suggested that there must be more to this than met the eye. What woman just up and left, leaving everything behind, what woman took a bag of clothes and left thirty years of possessions, of memories behind. His whole break up might have been fascinating when she'd been drunk, but it wasn't now and obviously it was still a painful subject for him.

'Of course it's dreadful for the kids,' he continued.

'Oh, you have kids,' she added lamely.

'Yes, two boys and a girl.'

'How old are they?'

Why am I still talking? She asked herself. She didn't want a male friend and she wasn't interested in him in a romantic way, whatever her thought-mum might think, but she reminded herself, *one of my resolutions this year is to Be Kind.* She should put this resolution to the test right now. She must steer the conversation onto neutral subjects and then, as kindly as possible, extricate herself from this situation.

'Izzy is twenty-two and the boys are twenty-five and twenty-nine.'

'What do they think about it all?'

'I think they're pretty much in shock at the moment. They think there must be more to it, like an affair or something, but there honestly isn't.'

That's what you think, Pamela thought, she wouldn't be at all surprised to find that his wife had found someone else. But she kept that thought to herself, instead she said, 'It's hard for the kids at any age.'

'Yes.'

'Mine were seven and ten, so too young to understand.'

'That is young.'

She desperately needed to get away from this sad, weird man, so she exclaimed, 'You might find it all works out for the best.' What the hell was she saying, he was obviously heart broken and she was telling him to get over it, it'd all be wonderful. He looked like he might cry, she eyed him fretfully, 'No, sorry, I don't mean that how it sounds, I just mean there's no point being with someone who doesn't love you and want to be with you...' Now she was making it worse. He looked even more crushed. 'I mean, it's actually quite brave of your wife... the easy thing would've been to do nothing...' What was wrong with her, she just seemed to be making his misery worse every time she opened her mouth. She almost clapped her hand over her mouth to shut herself up. *What happened to being kind dear?* Her thought-mum wondered.

He frowned and said, 'Well, yes I suppose that's one way of looking at it.' He took a sip of coffee. There was another awkward silence.

Pamela willed herself not to speak, *keep your mouth shut, keep your mouth shut, for goodness sake.* She hated silences and was always the one to fill them with some inane comment. She bit her lip, but couldn't help saying, 'I'm sorry, I didn't mean to make you feel bad,' then she added, 'I'd better be going.'

'Yes, of course, well nice to bump into you again.'

'Yes, you too, and thanks for looking after me. It was very kind.'

He smiled and suddenly seemed to cheer up a bit, 'Look, I know I probably messed up, asking you to call me, but I would like to see you again if you think that's possible?'

Bloody hell why didn't men take the flippin' hint. She'd told him she wasn't interested and now she was going to have to go through the, *Oh it's not you, it's me routine.* Again. She should have been more forceful in the first place, instead of chatting about his kids and wife, obviously giving him some glimmer of hope. *And anyway, what does he see in me*, she wondered, *I look a total fright today and I will have looked worse on New Year's Eve.* But that was beside the point, she wasn't bothered about having a man in her life.

'Well the thing is I'm going through a bit of a bad time work-wise. I don't want to complicate my life with... you know... maybe in a little while... I mean it's still early days for you, so...'

'Oh yes, you told me about your boss the other night, it sounds appalling.'

'It is, yes.'

'Well if you just want a friend to talk to, I'm here. Can I put your number in my phone?'

She couldn't very well say no. But honestly, she had her kids, her family, her friends. She didn't need him in her life when there were plenty of other people she could call. After all she'd only just met him, it wasn't like he was an employment expert, was it. He was one of the managers at Russ's and Russ was a bloody car salesman. But what could she do? Bloody men. *No need to swear dear*, her thought-mum murmured.

She reluctantly gave him her number, and he gave her a missed call. 'There, now you've got my number!'

He seemed very pleased with himself. *Well who cares*, she thought, she wasn't going to call him, so it didn't matter. 'That's very kind, right must dash, Bye.'

She practically ran out of the café. The streets were dark, rainy and depressing. She took a huge gasp of air; she'd felt a kind of suffocation in Tom's presence. *No wonder his wife's left him*, she thought nastily. There was something about him that she couldn't quite put her finger on, something insincere, something that just didn't feel right.

Back at home she glanced in her hallway mirror, bloody hell, her mouth was covered in chocolate muffin, she had looked like this during her whole conversation with Tom, how utterly excruciating. She went into the downstairs loo and washed her face. He'd let her go out of that café looking a total mess, *thanks a bloody lot Tom,* she thought, *what kind of person didn't mention you had something on your face, honestly.* She felt hot with embarrassment. *Maybe he didn't notice,* the familiar little voice asked. *Maybe he didn't mum.* She replied. *Anyway,* she told herself, *just stop freaking out about it, there's no point. It wasn't the worst thing in the world.* She didn't care what he thought about her anyway, so it didn't matter.

She remembered her bedroom. *Oh god.* This morning's energy was completely sapped. Meeting Tom again had drained her completely. Despite him not pointing out her smeary chocolate face, she did feel a bit sorry for him. He was at the beginning of a long and lonely road. All the arguments about the house, maintenance, the kids, it was all about to become a reality. At first, everyone thought they'd try and be civilised, but as soon as solicitors became involved, that thought went out of the window.

Having gone through it all herself she knew the next couple of years were going to be awful. She completely understood the urge to find someone new – she used to call it *cut and paste.* You needed to find someone as fast as possible, cut your ex out and paste the new person in. You tried to make them fit into your life, where the gaping hole of loneliness and sadness festered, raw and painful. But it never worked. The new person wasn't up to the job. Unsurprisingly, they had their own agenda, their own hang-ups, and more importantly they weren't the ex. *And actually, did you want them to be? No. I'm much better off on my own.*

So, Pamela's thoughts ran on, she knew other people thought she was mad. It seemed so hard for people to understand her decision to be alone. Yet, ironically, they all seemed to have appalling relationships. They were always telling her how fed up they were with their respective partners. The guy was crap around the house, didn't help, didn't talk, practically pushed them out of the way if they stood in front of the TV. They went off to the pub, engrossed themselves in a solitary sport, made their wives feel rubbish about everything, questioned every penny they spent, demanded food and were either too interested in sex or showed no interest in sex – depending on who she was talking to! Yet her friends seemed to wish the same fate onto her, it was unfathomable. She liked being on her own, doing her own thing, eating when she wanted, watching anything she wanted on TV, spending money without being questioned. She could make all her own decisions. Going on a diet was her decision - to be healthier - not for some man.

She realised she was putting off going upstairs to face her bedroom. Instead she dragged the washing out of the washer, shoved everything into the tumble dryer and made some tomato soup, checked FB and then settled down to watch some brain-dead television.

Amazingly she hadn't thought about alcohol for most of the day. That was good, yesterday she'd thought of little else. But now the thought was lodged in her mind and refused to go away. She saw herself make a dirty martini, she could taste it, the chilled glass, the fruity vermouth, the harsh tang of vodka tingling on her tongue, the olives... *Stop it. I can't think like this,* she thought, *right, time to go and sort out my bedroom.*

She went upstairs and looked at the huge pile of clothes on the bed. *God.* All her good intentions had gone. She would have to face this later, try to be disciplined, she needed to stick to her plans. What was the point of thinking about de-cluttering if she just made more of a mess. She must concentrate her mind. Get organised.

Her mind wondered off onto thoughts of that idiot Tom. In her imagination he was sitting home alone, listening to old love songs, crying. She shook this image out of her mind. She wondered if she knew any single friends who might like him. *No, better not get involved.* And anyway, he wasn't going to be alone for long. The way he had behaved with her, it was obvious.

Her thoughts went back to alcohol. She could just drink a long, cold gin and tonic. She imagined walking into the kitchen, opening the freezer, getting out the crushed ice, adding frozen lemon slices and then pouring an enormous shot of gin, with a slash of tonic. This was crazy, no one could drink a gin like that. But the more she thought about it, the more she could taste it.

She went downstairs. *If I have a large tonic it'll feel the same.* She could see herself bending down towards the cupboard that housed the alcohol. In a kind of absentminded way, she picked up the gin. *A little one couldn't do any harm.* After all she'd been amazing not drinking for the last week…ok maybe not a week…ok two days…not great. But that proved she wasn't an alcoholic. She poured herself a large gin, added all the other ingredients and took a bag of crisps into the other room.

She realised she didn't feel too bad about falling off the wagon. After all she had to have some pleasures in life. The first few sips were so delicious. She hadn't eaten since the soup, so the alcohol zoomed straight to her head in a rush of ecstasy, a fuzzy joy in her brain. Sadly, that never lasted long and by the time she'd finished the glass, she was feeling appalling. *What is wrong with me, s*he thought, *I can't stick to anything. Well, I may as well have another one.* This time she did just have the gin. Quite a large one. *Why not, what did it matter.*

She staggered upstairs, flung as many clothes off the bed as she could and collapsed in a heap. Her head was spinning her mind was blurred. She fell into a fitful, crazed, guilt fuelled sleep, waking every hour or so, just for good measure.

Wednesday 4ᵗʰ January

She woke feeling disgusted and defeated. Her head hurt, which obviously served her right. *I am such a total waste of space, such a loser, I'm so stupid, so fricking stupid.* She couldn't believe she'd let herself drink so easily and without a thought. As if she'd been dreaming or sleep walking.

It was amazing that you could be so determined to do one thing and end up doing the complete opposite. She hadn't even enjoyed the pints of gin she'd downed, on her own, early evening, topped off by falling into bed, skunkily drunk and unconscious.

She couldn't do this to herself anymore. But she always felt like this the morning after the night before. For probably five minutes of pleasure she'd had an appalling night of unsettled sleep. Waking up every five minutes, either far too hot or far too cold, surrounded by the uncomfortable tangle of lifeless, weird smelling clothes.

Mornings were so different to evenings. Every morning she knew what was right, what was reasonable and responsible, but the evening came around and she found herself unable to stick to the promises she'd made to herself. She'd managed to go two nights without alcohol. That was so appalling. So stupid. And what about her list, she hadn't done one thing on it properly. It was useless.

She got out of bed and had a shower. Thank goodness she wasn't as hung over as she'd been on New Year's Day.

She could get out of bed at least. And there wasn't a weirdo asleep on the floor. But this drinking until you're drunk when you're home alone, surely it wasn't normal. She wondered if her sisters or friends behaved this way. Almost certainly not.

She walked downstairs and into her messy kitchen. It was another grey, disgusting looking day. Thank goodness she hadn't eaten anything at teatime, except crisps, but it probably wasn't the healthiest way to lose weight. Get drunk and collapse. It wasn't something the slimming clubs suggested.

She made herself a black coffee and took three paracetamol. She lay her head down on the back of her hands. She was feeling defeated. Nothing was going the way she wanted it to go. *Maybe I should go to a hypnotist,* she thought, *or a life coach. I obviously can't help myself. I haven't got the will power to stick to anything I start. Look at my diet, I've put off starting it all week. And I haven't even properly looked for a gym and as for de-cluttering...* Pamela would have continued this line of thought for as long as it took for her to feel even more disgusted with herself, but her phone was ringing. It was Alex. Pamela cheered up immediately. Ah bless him, he must be back from his holiday.

'Hello love, Happy New Year, how are you?'

'Good, yeah, Happy New year to you too. How's it going?'

'Same as ever, how was the skiing?'

'Great, thanks, excellent conditions.'

'What was the chalet like?'

'Amazing. What have you been up to?'

'Oh, nothing much, just Aunty Sophie's party on New Year's Eve, standard stuff.'

'Ah good.'

'Are you back at work this week?'

'No, this Monday, I've got quite a lot of holiday to take before the end of the month.'

'That's good, how are you feeling about going back?'

'Same old, same old. I'll be fine. It's just so depressing when you've been away, and you get back to London, to this awful weather.'

'I know, it's bloody grey all the time. I bet it was beautiful in France.'

'Oh mum, it was so nice. Clear blue skies, fresh powder snow, ideal conditions.'

'Oh, it sounds lovely, I can't stand this permanent drizzly grey. I need to emigrate!'

'Yeah, we all do! Have you heard much from Jake?'

'No, just a text on New Year's Eve. What about you?'

'Same'

'He's back on Saturday, I think.'

'Yeah, he is. Have you made any decisions about going back?'

'I don't think I can.'

'Well you know how you feel.'

'Yes.'

That was the nice thing about Alex, he never questioned her decisions, always supported her, even when her decisions were questionable.

Alex interrupted her thoughts, 'Did you make any New Year's resolutions?' he asked.

'Just the usual, what about you?'

'Nah, not really, no point.'

'True.'

'So, I should be coming up soon, Joe's having an engagement party in Feb, so I'll be up for the weekend if that's ok?'

'Of course it is, it'll be lovely to see you, will Jen be coming?'

Pamela had met Jen a couple of times and she seemed very sweet. 'I'm not sure, I'm going around there tonight, so I'll ask. But she's so busy, she's away most weekends.'

'Is she you're actual girlfriend yet?'

'Mum,' Alex complained, 'what's your problem?'

'I just wondered if it had started to get serious?'

'Why?'

'Sorry, you're right, I'll shut up.'

It worried her that neither of her boys seemed able to make a commitment to anyone and seemed miles away from settling down. She knew it must be her fault, well hers and the dick. Seeing their parent's relationship blow up in such an awful way must have made them wary when it came to their own love life. Why would you rush into something that could just fall apart? She quickly changed the subject.

'What about your job applications? Anything come of them?'

'Well quite a large company has seen me on Linked-in and they want me to go for an interview at the end of the month.'

'That sounds exciting – but a long time to wait! Are they a good company to work for?'

'Who knows? I think they're probably all as crap as each other.' He sounded a bit deflated.

'Well I'm sure something will come up soon,' she replied, trying to cheer him up.

'Thanks mum, I hope so, how's grandad?'

'Fine, a bit miserable, you know how he gets. Georgie's away and Anne is too busy, so I'm seeing him today and tomorrow and probably the rest of the week as well!'

'Bloody hell, mum, that's a joke, why is it always up to you?'

'I know, what can I do?'

'You shouldn't be such a pushover.'

'It'll be better when Georgie's back.'

'Yeah, I hope so, well give him my love. I'm just about to get on the tube so I'll say goodbye.'

'No worries, so nice to talk to you, glad you're back safely, give me a ring next week if you get a chance and I hope work isn't too awful!'

'Same here! Love you.'

'Love you, bye.'

She felt the usual pang of heartache she always felt after she'd spoken to one of her boys. She missed them both. But she was proud of them, living their own lives in London, being successful and independent. She knew she'd made many mistakes in her life, but those two were out there in the world, going about their lives, good and kind people. She felt that at least there, with them, she hadn't messed up. Obviously, she worried about them not seeming able to settle down and maybe start families of their own, but all kids started late these days. She was constantly talking to her friends about this. They couldn't afford to for a start. She, and most of her friends had got married in their very early twentys, whereas now it seemed thirty was the new twenty. Even if they got married, they were waiting until forty to have children.

In her day you could buy a house when you left home, but kids nowadays had absolutely no chance of buying a house, especially if they lived in London. Their rents were so high they couldn't possibly save for a deposit. Oh well, it was their choice to live in London. She was always sending emails about jobs in Leeds, but it fell on deaf ears!

Although she worried about her sons' lack of permanent girlfriends, she was glad that they were grown up and could finally understand why she'd had to leave their dad. It had been a different story when they were young. They just kept saying, "Why can't you forgive dad?" They had no real concept of what he'd done, how could they at that age. She had repeated; "You'll understand when you're older." They told her now that they did understand, but for a long time they saw her as the one at fault, which was annoying to say the least. It was easy for kids to grasp the idea of forgiveness, but not infidelity.

By now their dad had four ex-wives and several other

children under his belt and, of course, he lived alone, miserable and lonely, unable to remain faithful to anyone.

She had always told them that if she met anyone important to her, she'd introduce them. But she hadn't met anyone the least bit important. She'd had the occasional fling, but nothing serious. At first her friends had introduced her to single men they knew, but that stopped when she showed absolutely no interest in this odd selection of men. As she wouldn't try on-line dating her options had been limited. And now she was so used to being alone it would seem weird.

She went upstairs and started absentmindedly piling her clothes back into the wardrobe. She'd tackle them another day. By lunch time her bedroom was looking a little more normal.

She turned on her laptop and typed in, "luxury gyms, with pools, Leeds." A few places popped up. She looked at the first one – Cannondale, it was quite near, probably a ten-minute drive. It looked nice, the pool was a good size and it had a sauna, steam room and Jacuzzi. The gym looked enormous. Biting the bullet, she rang them and amazed herself by making an appointment to look around on Friday afternoon.

She felt incredibly delighted with herself. She could tick something off her list! Hurray! And tomorrow, of course, she was going to go back to weight watchers. So, she would be able to tick another thing off the list. If only she hadn't drunk alcohol last night, she'd be doing so well.

Perhaps, after all, it was a totally unrealistic goal to stop drinking completely. Maybe just try to drink in moderation. It was surely counter-productive to feel like an absolute failure every morning. And when she was dieting she wouldn't drink wine, just low-cal tonic and spirits. Maybe she should slowly wean herself off alcohol instead of going cold turkey. The trouble was, she never knew when to stop, one glass of wine or gin or whatever always led to another, then another, then another... *god it's just hopeless.*

She thought about going out for a walk, but it had started to rain. It looked so dismal out, it was probably a bad idea. She decided to tackle one of the drawers in her kitchen. That was obviously the way to de-clutter, just do one tiny thing at a time. She had been far too ambitious with her wardrobe. You had to start somewhere and inevitably, eventually she would have clean de-cluttered drawers, if it killed her in the process, which it probably wouldn't. She always worried that if she dropped dead suddenly it would be awful to leave the boys with all her clutter to go through. Then she thought they probably wouldn't go through it, they'd just tip everything out into the bin. Good idea. But, somehow, she couldn't bring herself to do that.

She tipped everything from one of the drawers into a tray and took it all into the sitting room. There was the usual miscellaneous assortment of old make-up, candle stubs, broken pens, ancient coins, used stamps, corks, a hammer and a screwdriver, a couple of articles, a few old photographs. *If I'd tipped this drawer into a bin, I honestly wouldn't have missed anything in it,* she thought. Underneath it all she found an old notebook. She started reading through it. There was a date on one of the pages – New Year's Day a few years ago. There were pages and pages dedicated to telling herself off, at the end there was also a list of resolutions, six in total. She laughed as she read the familiar details – Join a gym, re-join weight watchers, stop drinking (Especially after last night) she'd written in brackets followed ominously by, "For obvious reasons." She had absolutely no memory of that particular New Year or what she'd done. Probably the usual. But bloody hell, it was depressing. How did anyone ever change the way they behaved. If she carried on clearing out drawers, she would probably find the same list, year in, year out, in each of them.

She started looking at the photos. They were of herself as a young girl. A wistful, clear-eyed, pretty youngster, looked out, beyond the moment, dreaming, yearning, hoping for a wonderful future, planning her escape from the ordinary world she lived in. Sadly, her life hadn't turned out the way she'd wanted it to. It was crazy how quickly she'd got from that to this – this nearly sixty-year-old person. You could warn the next generation as much as you liked, but they would never believe how fleeting your moment in the sun would be, how short-lived your life actually was.

Well, apart from the photos, she could throw nearly everything out, she'd keep the stamps and the coins of course. One of these days she was going to take them to a charity shop. She left them out on the counter – if they were in plain sight, she'd have to take them. But more-or-less everything else could go.

She flung the articles and notebook into re-cycling and put the screwdrivers and hammer back into the drawer, this would be her tool drawer. As she came across other tools around the house, they would now have a home. She felt a lovely feeling of accomplishment as she tipped the rest of the rubbish into the bin. She could start on another drawer. No, one a day was a great decision. It was a nice mindless job.

She opened her laptop. She could start the email she was going to send to Dom about lesson plans for the first day, better not send any more than that, she could build up gradually.

She got her planner and looked at what her classes had been doing in the last week before they broke up.

Nowadays they had to work right up until the last day of term, when she'd first started teaching you could have fun in that last week. Not anymore. No, now you had to pretend that it was like any other week. Which was virtually impossible, as the kids, especially the younger ones, were always so excited before the Christmas holidays. Planning was a relatively easy job as she only had four classes the first Monday back. It was one of the only days she had any non-contact time.

Since the school had outsourced the timetable to a specialist firm their timetables had been ridiculous. When it had been created by a teacher, they had considered how it felt to teach, they were aware of how hard the job was and timetabled accordingly. They would spread your non-contact time over the week. They didn't put three Year 9 classes back to back, if they could help it. These people had never stepped foot in a classroom since leaving school and had no idea how their careless planning ruined teachers lives. But that was all by the by. She wasn't going back. Some poor supply bod would be stepping into her shoes.

When would the powers that be notice how appalling things were in the English Department? How many people had to leave before one of the managers started asking questions? The school was due an Ofsted inspection any minute. How bad would it look when retention was considered? Their department had had more supply teachers than any other, results would be down in summer, how could they not be. But in the meantime, people like Pamela were the victims, fallen, shattered remnants, shadows of their former selves.

At first her boss would think she was only going to be off for a few days, he'd be evilly planning the way he was going to discredit her, enjoying the sadistic pleasure he was going to feel. Then, after a week or two, he might start to get a little bit worried, well maybe, maybe someone might say, "It's so weird that Pam is still off, she never had a day off in the past, I wonder what's going on?" She could only hope.

She wouldn't be able to email her planning to Dom until Monday morning. But at least it was done. She rang Louise, the friend she'd confided in on the last day of term.

'Hi Lou, how's it going?'

'Hi Pam, lovely to hear from you. We're all great thanks, what about you?'

'Good, did you have a lovely Christmas?'

'Hectic, kids went a bit insane and the in-laws were awful, obviously, but we coped! You?'

'Oh, it was all ok, but I'm bloody glad it's over for another year.'

'Yes, I'll bet. How are you feeling about work?'

'The same.'

'Really? Thought you might've changed your mind over the holidays.'

'No, the more I think about it, the surer I am.'

'It'll be weird without you.'

'I'll miss you and my nice classes. You'll have to keep me up to date with everything that's going on.'

'Of course, I will, I'll email you weekly bulletins!'

'I'm so sorry if you end up covering any of my lessons.'

'With my timetable? I don't think I will, I have about one free a week.'

'Yeah, sorry, I forgot about your appalling timetable. But at least the old git adores you.'

'For the moment, he liked you at first and Hannah, Sidrah, Faiza and Charlotte, look what happened to them.'

'Yes, that's true, the poor sods. At least they got out. They were all brilliant teachers.'

'I know, and now he hates Dom.'

'I know, he's probably going to be the next victim. I heard he's already started applying for jobs.'

'We all have!'

'Even you?' Pamela was shocked, she thought Lou would never leave.

'Of course, that man can change his mind in a flipping minute. I don't trust him at all. I honestly don't know anyone who is happy there.'

'Isn't it weird how one person can cause all this? This time last year we were one happy team, then a single person comes along and changes everything. It's the poor kids that suffer.'

'Isn't it always the same?'

'Yes, it's so bloody awful.'

'Well, to be honest, I think you've made the right decision, I heard him say he was 'gunning for you', on the last day of term.'

'You actually heard him say that?'

'Yes, sorry... I should have told you... but I was hoping you'd come back... he is a despicable man, isn't he?'

'I heard him say that about Hannah. How does he get away with it? Fair enough I'm an ancient teacher and he wants to get rid of me, but the others weren't old, he just seemed to hate them.'

'You're not old! But anyway, I think it's a power thing, they'd been in the school a few years and the Head liked them, he couldn't cope with them questioning his decisions.'

'Yeah, you're right, he's an out and out bully.'

'Yes, he is, I read a great article about bullying personalities, I'll send you it. You know I wouldn't be surprised if you aren't the only one-off sick, either on Monday or at some point during this term.'

'Yeah, wouldn't surprise me either. Well I hope you carry on being the golden girl.'

'For now.'

'Yes, watch your back! By the way did you read his latest email?'

Louise groaned, 'Oh no, I haven't seen it. What's he demanding now?'

'I didn't read it either, I couldn't face it, to be honest.'

'I can't say I blame you; I'd better check my work emails. I was so hoping he'd just let us have a decent break.'

'No such luck.'

'Well take care, ring me anytime, I'll fill you in on what's happening.'

'Thanks, love to John and the kids.'

'Bye.'

Pamela ended the call and felt the same wave of sadness and fear that she'd been feeling on and off since the end of term. Truth was, she was absolutely terrified by the decision she'd made.

She peered out of the kitchen window, she'd have to take her garden in hand this spring, it was overgrown and bedraggled. Everything looked messy, drab and underwhelming. It would be so nice to get a gardener in, maybe have it landscaped or something. It was only tiny though; they probably didn't landscape gardens that small.

The weather was brightening up a bit, which was good. She decided to walk into town. She could buy a new set of weighing scales. She had made a conscious decision not to have weighing scales in the house, but then, judging by her clothes, it seemed her weight had just crept up and up. It was a lovely idea in principle, but if she was going back to weight watchers she may as well know the worst.

The late afternoon sun was struggling weakly to climb out from behind a battalion of ominous, gloomy clouds. It had suddenly turned much colder. Pamela's breath came out in billows of white smoke. She was delighted to see daffodils and snowdrops coming through. She longed for spring and summer. But winter would be better for her de-cluttering project. When it was fine outside she couldn't bear to be stuck inside. It was always awful teaching in the summer term. You could only look out the window and yearn to be free. By the time the summer holidays came around the best of the weather had always been and gone.

Again, Pamela wished she lived in a country with proper seasons, real summer, real winter. Maybe such a country didn't exist, but you could dream. She popped into a bakery on the way to Argos. She bought a large slice of pizza and a cream éclair. Tomorrow would be different, so today she was going to make the most of it.

She bought the scales, *now I'll have to lose weight,* she thought, grimly. Passing a couple of off licences she realised she hadn't thought much about alcohol, probably because she knew she was giving up on the idea of being teetotal. Well maybe that's what she should do, drink at home, but not drink when she went out. That might solve the problem. What did it matter if she fell over in an unconscious, inelegant sprawl at home? There was nobody there to judge her, was there. Of course, that totally negated the fact that she should stop drinking for health reasons. And weight reasons. But there are times in your life when you need a crutch, and, after all, she hadn't started smoking again. From what she could remember the cigarette she'd had on New Year's Eve had tasted disgusting, like smoking an ashtray. It had taken her years to finally give up smoking. She'd kept relapsing. It had been so hard. But she had done it, amazingly. So, she did have a modicum of will power.

The sleet began when she was nearly home. It stung her cold face in harsh, malicious slaps. She semi jogged the rest of the way back. She was totally out of breath by the time she opened her front door. She practically fell inside, *I am so unfit, thank goodness I'm actually going to visit a gym on Friday. And weight watchers tomorrow. Two steps in the right direction.* She decided not to weigh herself, why face it right this minute. She'd weigh herself after a week of dieting.

She knew she'd been putting off visiting her dad. She must go now, or he'd be ringing her, going mad. She would tell him it was just a flying visit; he would probably be ok with that.

Later, at home, she felt so guilty. She knew she should have stayed with him longer; it wasn't like she had anything urgent to get on with. He'd been very sweet today, reminiscing about her mum. Guilt oozed from every pore, she couldn't bear to think of him sitting in that room, day-in-day-out.

Your life became so much smaller, the older you got. It didn't help that he refused to have any of his meals with the other residents. He couldn't hear them, so he felt there was no point, she could see that, but it was a shame. Her mum would have been so much more able to cope with this situation, she'd have socialised, made friends, joined the group outings, befriended the staff. It was so unfair. Pamela had always thought her mum would come into her own once widowed. She had been a virtual prisoner in her own home for the past ten years or so. Their dad never wanted to do anything, and her mum had to stay in and look after him and unless one of the girls had taken over, she was stuck. Pamela had envisioned a new life for her mum once she'd been released. How sad that it never came to pass. They always say that it's the carer who goes first. Well, she told herself; you've done more than either of your sister's this week, stop feeling so bad.

The weather outside had seriously deteriorated, the wind had picked up and was wailing around the little row of terrace houses. She decided to light a real fire. She very rarely used the fire, but it always made the house so cosy, it was a shame not to, especially when the weather was so awful.

Later, sitting next to her lovely fire, with a re-run of "The Holiday" on TV, drinking a not too strong gin and tonic, she felt, for the first time that year, quite happy and content. She wasn't beating herself up over everything, she was just living in that actual moment. This was such a strange and rare thing. *Wow,* she thought, *this isn't like me.* Usually she'd be telling herself off for being lazy or for drinking or other miscellaneous misdemeanours. Her inner critic was so ferocious, so angry all the time, finally it was keeping quiet. Here she was, allowing herself to be calm and contented. 'Long may it last,' she said out loud as she sipped her drink.

As usual she didn't sleep well that night. She kept waking up and then she couldn't get back to sleep for hours. The wind was violently rushing around the house, she could hear pots and garden furniture crashing around outside. The night seemed to last for hours. When she did sleep it was fitful, nightmare filled, full of weird places and angry people. She seemed to have finally dozed into a calmer sleep when her alarm went off.

Thursday 5th January

Time to get up and go to the ten am meeting. She sat up and looked outside. The whole of her garden was covered in frost. It would have been pretty if she'd been in a better mood. She didn't feel like getting up, she was nauseous and head-achy. Her whole body ached from top to bottom. One gin had obviously led to two, then three, then god knows how many.

She had to have a very serious conversation with herself. Again. She knew she didn't want to spend another whole week just stuffing her face and if she didn't go, she knew she wouldn't start her diet.

She managed to drag herself out of bed. *Come on, you're fine,* she told herself. *You can go back to bed after weigh in.* This thought cheered her up. She managed to pull herself together and was early for the meeting. She was wearing her heaviest jeans and she'd forced herself to eat some breakfast.

Of course, this time next week she wouldn't eat until after the meeting. She was dreading being weighed.

She greeted the leader, 'Hi, I'm a former gold member.' She told her, with a shameful face. *What will she think of me,* she wondered, *but I suppose this happens all the time. Why else were slimming clubs still running. They are full of people just like me, no will power, no perseverance. Always back-tracking into weight gain, again and again.*

She stood on the weighing scales and held her breath, as if that would help keep the weight down. It clocked a staggering twelve stone and two pounds. *Oh my god, how the hell has that happened, I can't bloody believe it.* Over two and a half stone overweight. She was disgusted with herself. So much for her inner critic shutting up for five minutes. Now it was like a vicious terrier, tearing at her flesh, angry as hell. Well, at least she'd taken the first step. The leader gave her all the booklets and explained how she could go online and use the app to monitor her eating. Pamela just wanted to crawl under a stone and hide. This was surely a personal record. Apart from when she'd been pregnant, she had never been this heavy.

She didn't stay for the talk; she hated the talk. Full of virtuous ladies and a smattering of men, talking about how brilliant they were, what marvellous recipes they'd discovered, how easy they found it to stick to their diets. They were so smug, it made her sick. There was a sign on the door of the slimming club, saying 'going to a meeting and not staying for the talk is like going to the cinema, buying a ticket and then leaving before the film starts.' *Yeah, right, exactly the same - in their dreams!* No, she just needed the weekly weigh in to keep herself on track. That looming deadline was what drove her to lose weight and stick to the diet. And, of course, next week she wouldn't be wearing heavy jeans, and she wouldn't have eaten beforehand. So, she could potentially be much less that twelve stone two pounds.

She knew she needed to go and do a healthy shop, but

she couldn't face it just yet. *I'll just go and visit dad and then buy some fruit, that'll keep me going for now*. She didn't feel like visiting her dad today, she felt heavy and somehow cloggy, her whole body felt sort of submerged in sludge. Every step she took was painful, sluggish. Why couldn't Anne go today? She was so bloody selfish. But almost immediately she felt the flash of guilt. After her visits he always said, "Thanks for coming," which made her feel awful.

'Hi dad, IT'S ONLY ME, YOU OK?' his eyes lit up, as they always did.

'Hello only me.' he replied.

He looked a bit dishevelled today. His hair hadn't been combed and he was still wearing the same clothes he'd worn yesterday.

'I'm really cold,' he moaned.

'That's terrible, TERRIBLE.' she said, although the room felt as sweltering as normal. 'Is the heat on? THE HEAT?' She asked, pointlessly, it obviously was.

'Check, will you?'

She tore off her coat, hat and gloves and flung them on his bed.

'Let's see,' she went to the thermostat, 'Yes dad, it's on high, let me get a few blankets and wrap you up.'

She also found one of his warmer cardigans and with a great deal of difficulty managed to put it on him. She wrapped him up in several blankets.

'I was cold last night as well.'

Her dad had been banned from having an electric

blanket, which seemed a bit mean, but the home thought it was a potential fire risk.

'Yes, it was a very cold night last night, Is that better? BETTER?" she asked,

'A bit.'

'Dad you must get the staff to come in if you're feeling cold, you just press that button on your wrist.' She pointed to his call button on his bracelet, 'PRESS THAT IF YOU'RE COLD.'

'I know, but I don't like to bother them.'

'It's their job dad, you're paying a small fortune to be here, you mustn't be afraid to ask them, that's why you're here, after all, THEY WILL PUT THE HEAT UP IF YOU ASK THEM.'

'I was waiting for one of you girls to come.'

'I know dad, but you mustn't be cold. They honestly won't mind, THEY DON'T MIND.'

He looked up at her sadly. He was so miserable, it was heart-breaking. She couldn't bear it. His eyes became watery and dull. She had to look away, to change the subject she asked, 'Do you want a cup of tea? TEA?'

'Thanks love.'

In the kitchen she met one of the carers, 'My dad's extremely cold today, could you make sure he's wearing warmer clothes and has a few blankets wrapped around him first thing in the morning?'

'Of course love.'

She nearly added, "and make sure he has clean clothes," but managed to stop herself, neither she nor Georgie wanted to alienate the staff, and sadly nor did her dad, who sometimes seemed afraid of them, which was worrying. Anne was a different kettle of fish, she was far more strident than either of her sisters, she didn't care about alienating anyone, but sometimes she overdid it and made her dad more afraid. He'd beg her not to complain, but she wouldn't listen, she would march into the staff lounge and tear strips off people if she thought they weren't doing a good enough job. Georgie and Pamela were often secretly pleased, but you had to be careful, Anne could go too far. Then when he was alone the humiliated member of staff might take their anger out on their vulnerable dad, it was a balancing act and Pamela wasn't sure it always worked.

They spent an hour watching a nature programme, then she got up to leave.

'Well, I'll get going then dad. I'LL GO NOW.'

'Ok love. How are the boys?'

'Oh, they both seem fine, thanks dad. FINE. They've been SKIING.'

'You used to go skiing, didn't you?'

'YES DAD, I DID, BUT I HAVEN'T BEEN FOR A WHILE.'

'Who's coming to see me tomorrow?'

'I think it's going to be ANNE, BUT IF NOT ANNE, THEN ME. OK?'

'Yes, thanks love, thanks very much for coming.'

'It's fine, it's NICE TO SEE YOU.'

'Nice to see you too.' She kissed him on the cheek and left the oppressive room.

She nipped into the local co-op and bought some fruit. At home she crawled into bed. She stared at the ceiling, drained of emotion, depressed and worried. She usually felt a bit better when she'd re-joined weight watchers. But the years of not bothering had taken their toll. She had taken her eye off the ball in a most spectacular way. And now she was paying the price. How long was it going to take to get back to a decent weight. *Well I suppose I don't have anything else to do*, she thought miserably.

When she woke up, it was dark outside. Maybe she'd just stay in bed. She didn't feel very hungry; she didn't feel like doing anything much. Bed was such a great place to be. She realised she hadn't stuck to her plan of de-cluttering a drawer a day. Well, a drawer every other day would have to work. She sure as hell wasn't getting out of this comfy bed to clean out a drawer.

Yes, she'd wasted the day, but at least she wasn't eating and even better, she wasn't drinking alcohol. Half of her knew that if she stayed in bed, she was bound to wake up at two am and be totally wide awake for the rest of the night. Her family had a mantra for that, 'You're turning night into day,' this was very much frowned upon and something you should avoid at all cost. But, for the millionth time she thought, *I live on my own, who'll ever know. Nobody, that's who.*

The night was just as she expected. She tossed and turned, fitfully slept, fitfully woke, she flung herself about the bed, feeling terrible. She couldn't stop thinking about her friends who had died. Their little sad faces peered down from the ceiling. Annabel aged eight, who, one morning, simply forgot to wake up. Prue, who was diagnosed with cancer days after her fiftieth birthday and lived only three months after her diagnosis. Sonia killed on a zebra crossing when she was fifteen. Why were they here, what were they trying to tell her? Their ghostly figures seemed restless, in pain. *Please go away* she murmured, *I miss you all, I absolutely do, now go and rest. Please.*

She shuddered, her breath was visible, it oozed from her mouth, misty and frozen. She clicked on her bedside lamp and the apparitions disappeared. Slowly her breath returned to normal. It was just a dream, she told herself, it wasn't real.

Three am. Her life wasn't normally like this, she was sure of that. Maybe it was worrying about her sad dad or maybe it was because of work, because of the way her boss was treating her. M*aybe he had no idea how he was affecting people,* she thought, *he wouldn't care anyway, he'd probably be pleased.* How could he do this to people. She felt despair and hatred in equal measure. What was she going to do all day, every day, when everyone else was back at work?

She had hoped to carry on teaching until she could draw her teacher's pension at sixty. And now, here she was, lying awake, feeling useless, disgusted with herself and the situation she was in.

There was no point staying in bed. She had to take her mind off things. She walked downstairs in darkness. In the kitchen she got a glass of water and stared out into her garden. A fox was sitting on the patio a few feet away from her, surrounded by glinting ice-white frost, the light from a street-lamp illuminating its little bright face. They both stared at each other. It had a beautiful majesty about it, it's imperiousness and disdain were palpable. It seemed to view her with an aloofness. She sometimes felt that spirits inhabited foxes. Their intelligent eyes seemed to see right into your soul.

'What do you want to tell me?' she whispered to the fox, 'What should I do, am I making the right decision?'

The fox held her gaze for a long time. It seemed to understand her, to look into her heart, it's cool, contemptuous attitude seemed to melt away. She felt such a powerful connection. When the fox answered, she wasn't surprised. It was if it said, "Follow your heart." He then sauntered away. Bloody hell she was losing her mind. She had never mind melded with an animal before. She wasn't an animal sort of person, so it was strange that she'd felt this connection with a completely strange fox, a fox who had seemed to answer her. She must be a bit delirious.

Maybe she was coming down with something or maybe she had just tapped into something deeper, something inexplicable. She remembered that when her uncle had died a few year ago, she'd seen a fox like this – a fox that had sat and casually stared at her - and she'd just thought, for no apparent reason, *Oh there's my uncle*. When she'd told his daughters this strange thought, they said that on the morning before he died, he told them he could see two foxes in his room, tap-dancing.

Friday 6th January

She went back to bed, cold and depressed and finally fell asleep, dreaming of eccentric foxes, dancing and muttering things under their breath. In the morning she shuddered remembering the weird night she'd had. She hadn't thought about Prue and the others for a long time. *Why now*, she wondered, *maybe they were trying to tell me something. Note to self, don't sleep during the day. It's never a good idea.*

She peered out of the kitchen window, it all seemed fine, no talking foxes, just frost, gradually thawing. She laughed at her stupidity; *I'm turning into a crazy old lady.*

She made a black coffee and ate a banana. She peeled and cut up an apple and pear and added pieces of orange. She was determined to stick to this diet. She'd get the ingredients for a very low-fat chilli later today. And some low-fat snacks. From experience she knew that wine, chocolate, crisps and any other delicious food stuff would have to be hidden. *So basically, all the things that make life worthwhile.* But if she was good and stuck to this diet, she would feel so pleased with herself. If her jeans started to fit without piles of flesh hanging over the top, wasn't that a wonderful achievement. *Yes, yes,* she told herself. Depressing, but true. Eating fruit was weirdly and surprisingly filling.

She texted Anne, "Can you visit dad today? x."

Hopefully she'd be able to. *We'll have to wean him off these daily visits,* she thought, *especially when one of us is away,* but how could she even contemplate that after yesterday. He needed someone who was totally on his side, you couldn't rely on strangers, to them he was just an old man, that's what they saw when they looked at him. He'd always be her dad, despite everything.

As an afterthought she texted, "He was very cold when I got there yesterday – I had to wrap him up in blankets x." That would get Anne going, she'd make sure the staff bucked up their ideas.

It took her under ten minutes to drive to the gym, *well that's one thing in its favour,* she thought.

'Hi, I'm Alice,' the pretty young girl eyed her up and down. Pamela tried to ignore the look of disapproval on her face.

'Oh hello, I'm Pam, great to meet you.'

Alice tried to get beyond her first impressions.

'Right, I'll just take you through the paperwork and then we'll have a look around.'

They sat down together and filled in a few forms. When they were walking around Pamela couldn't get the Dubai gym out of her mind. *But remember,* she told herself, *that can't be the benchmark, it would be virtually impossible to find a gym like that here.* The weather was always crap for a start, and the UK just didn't have that sort of culture, especially the Yorkshire part of it. Total luxury seemed to be frowned upon.

She was impressed with the pool and the hot tub, and

the sauna and steam room were ok. The shower area wasn't great and there seemed to be loads of little kids running about, but of course it was still the Christmas holidays, it would be quieter when schools went back.

There were no delicious products, just a soap dispensing machine, also no divine bathrobes and luxurious fluffy towels. The gym itself was on two floors and seemed well equipped. There was a large studio, surrounded by mirrors, *I'm not sure about that*, thought Pamela, the idea of having to watch herself exercise was a bit off putting.

'We have loads of classes in there,' Alice told her, 'Pilates, Zumba, Dance, Aerobics, yoga...'

'Right,' Pamela wasn't convinced that classes were for her. After the tour Alice sat her down and told her it would cost £56 per month for full membership, also you didn't sign up for a fixed length of time, you could cancel anytime.

That appealed to Pamela, she hated being tied down to things, it meant she could un-commit at any point. It seemed reasonable. She'd expected to pay more.

'That's great, right well I've got a few more gyms to see, so...'

'Oh right, where else are you going?' *Yes, Pamela, where else are you going?* She asked herself.

'Err, well there are a couple more, I've, err, forgotten their names,' she racked her stupid brain to remember any others she'd seen, 'Erm, a couple in Leeds, I can't believe I've forgotten... erm... and one on the outskirts of Guiseley.'

'Oh yes, The Heights, that's a popular one.'

'Is it?'

'Yes, I was a member there before I started working here, but it was too busy, at this gym there's just a nice balance.'

Well you would say that, Pamela thought, but out loud she said, 'Right, well I think it's nice here. I'll be in touch.'

Outside it had turned cold and icy. She shivered, wishing once again that winter was over.

As she was getting into her car her phone pinged, it was a text from Anne, "Yes." That was it, short and sweet. Pamela felt elated. *Hurray!* That's great, she was off the hook for today at least. She wondered how people without siblings managed their elderly parents. Even though Anne was selfish she did do her bit, every now and then. "Fab xx." She quickly replied.

By now she was starving. Images of hot buttered toast were playing on a loop in her head. Right, she needed to go shopping before she raided the cupboards and stuffed her face with unhealthy crap. A shopping list went through her mind; vegetables, salad, cottage cheese, baking potatoes, salted popcorn, diet lemonade, diet tonic, low-fat yoghurt, maybe low-fat crisps, or corn snacks. Well she'd see when she got there. This was something she just had to do. She had to feel a sense of accomplishment in something.

This reminded her that she was supposed to be cleaning out another drawer when she got in. *That's fine*, she reassured herself. *No problem. I'll do the shopping and then get on with it.*

As she pulled into the supermarket car park, she noticed

a text from Helen, "Hi a few of us are going into town tonight if you fancy it? Meeting at The Bell 7pm xx." Pamela wasn't sure what to do, on the one hand it was nice to be asked, and it had been a bit of a sad, boring week, on the other hand she sort of had her evening planed. *Eating low fat chilli and cleaning out a drawer isn't a replacement for a social life, though, is it, but can I be bothered?*

She mentally went through what she'd have to do in order to meet her friends. Wash and dry her hair, find something halfway decent to wear, apply make-up, get cash out, generally get up off her arse.

Then she thought, *she's left the invite very last minute.* This annoyed her for a few minutes, but then she thought, *so what, I often don't include Helen in my plans, if Sophie was home, I'd probably be doing something with her anyway.*

She spent a good half an hour in Sainsbury's, it was a bit manic. Everyone was trying to get organised for the end of the Christmas holidays. A worrying thought struck her, if she did go out, they'd all be asking her about her decision regarding work. Bloody hell, how could she cope with that. Maybe she needed to think about a clever, cutting, yet effective way to shut people up, *yes good plan, but what, what would work?* 'Get lost and leave me alone.' 'None of your fecking business.' 'Never mention work to me again.' No, she'd probably just have to have the conversation and get over herself. But it was so hard.

She put the shopping away and tackled another drawer, determined not to think about eating. This drawer wasn't as bad as the other had been. It was mainly full of tea-towels and dish cloths. At the back, though, there was the usual assortment of rubbage; coins, small scissors, nail files, old cutlery that she never used.

She chucked most of the crap into the rubbish and put anything useful with the bag she was going to take to the charity shop. She rolled up all the cloths and tea-towels and put them back in neatly. Right, great, another one done.

She spent the rest of the afternoon making an extremely hot and delicious lentil chilli.

Upstairs, she peered into her wardrobe to see if she could find anything remotely decent to wear. She pulled out great swathes of clothes and flung them onto her bed. She should have sorted everything out the other day. Her black jeans looked like they might fit – just - and she had plenty of nearly fashionable baggy black tops.

Once again, the thought went through her mind that she must buy some more colourful clothes. She knew black was meant to be slimming, but it was also meant to be draining and the older you got the more that was true. Or so she had read in an article on Facebook. *Oh god, can I really be bothered to go out?*

A great wave of exhaustion washed over her. She lay down on top of the piles of clothes. She could maybe have an hour's sleep. It was still only five pm. She could plan when she woke up. She set her alarm for six pm, this gave her about an hour to eat and get ready. That was if she did decide to go out. Anyway, it wouldn't matter if she was a bit late.

She fell into a deep sleep. She dreamt a strange dream.

There were six glass blocks on a stage, on each block lay a dishevelled looking person, surrounded by bits of clothing and rubbish. The blocks lit up from underneath and in turn the person stood up to tell their story, some sang a plaintive, eerie song. Others faced the audience and spoke their monologues in anger or sadness. They all seemed to be homeless people.

She woke suddenly, and looked at her phone, she'd only been asleep for ten minutes. She tried desperately to remember what their monologues had been about, but their words flopped and flipped out of her grasp, like tiny golden fish. She felt a deep sense of dread, w*as this some kind of premonition, some kind of warning, a sign I shouldn't ignore?* She mentally shook these thoughts away, telling herself, *for goodness sake Pam, you had a dream, get over it, think about something else.*

She made herself think about the evening ahead. She couldn't decide what to do. *Should I go out, do I have the emotional energy to meet my friends?* She felt like staying in, but if she did, she would probably eat the chilli and then spend the evening snacking. If she went out, she'd be far less likely to snack, but on the other hand she would be far more likely to drink too much. She had a bad habit of anticipating exactly how any evening would go. Tonight, she was convinced it would be an evening of answering questions she didn't want to answer and other boring conversations. Helen was going to her son's graduation in June and if she had to spend one more minute talking about the dresses Helen had seen, tried on or thought about, she would probably have to kill herself. She drifted back into a calmer sleep.

Her alarm woke her up at six pm. She could feel a strange quiet around the house, she sat up and saw that whilst she'd been asleep it had started to snow. A good two inches clung to her windowsill. Her garden was a complete white out. She couldn't remember seeing any recent weather forecasts, she was sure she'd remember. It seemed to be actual real, heavy, exciting snow. Not the usual pretend snow that looked nice for about five minutes before melting into a slushy, gloomy, murky sort of heap. This was the crispy, cold, deep white snow that England rarely experienced. *Wow, amazing.*

She put on several jumpers and sat by the window, staring out into the white evening. Little paw prints went from her back door to her shed. Poor little fox, she hoped it would find somewhere warm to shelter.

Her phone pinged, "Hi all - too cold and snowy to go out! Next week xx?." Bloody hell, she thought, going out in this weather would have been fab. She loved walking in the snow and a few whiskeys, sitting by an open fire, in a warm pub would have been lovely. *Don't be so contrary,* she thought, *if Helen hadn't texted I bet I still wouldn't have made up my mind.* Well at least she didn't have to think about it now.

She replied, "No worries next week will be fine xx." She got up and put several more layers on, it was so cold she could see her breath.

Downstairs she turned her heating up and set about

lighting a fire. She put the oven on and placed a large baking potato in the centre. She slowly re-heated the chilli. She poured herself a large whiskey. There was nothing like drinking whiskey on a snowy evening. She turned the radio on and listened out for the forecast. It seemed that cold air was coming down from Siberia and the cold snap was set to last for several days. *Hurray! Real snow, how totally amazing.* As long as there wasn't a power cut, well not before she'd cooked her food anyway. How typical and annoying that she'd thrown those candle stubs out. She rummaged about in a few of the still cluttered drawers and found a candle and some matches, just in case.

Later, sitting by the fire, Pamela drew the curtains back and sat staring out at the snow. It was so odd how silent and soothing snow felt. As she watched the wind started to pick up, blowing the snow horizontally past the window. It was becoming a real blizzard. So beautiful. She once again realised how lucky she was, sitting in a cosy, warm room. Poor homeless people, she could only hope they had all found somewhere to stay before this weather hit. *As soon as I'm sorted*, she thought, *I'll volunteer at a shelter. I can't feel sorry for the homeless and do precisely nothing to help.* Maybe she could do some hours at a Shelter shop. There was one in town. Yes, she felt warm and pleased with herself, charitable thoughts tingling through her virtuous body. She poured herself another very large whiskey. She was fancying some chocolate, but instead she got a pack of corn crisps.

She ate them very slowly, one by one, licking the salty

deliciousness off each side, before slowly melting the crisp on her tongue.

She told herself she was doing a fab job, sticking so well to her diet. Well at least today she had. Only five more diet days until weigh in.

Saturday 7th January

The next day Pamela woke, feeling groggy and stupefied. She'd obviously drunk far too many whiskeys. She saw a text from Anne and one from Jake. "Sorted out dad's heating - are you visiting today?"

"Yes, thanks for sorting heat x."

She wondered what Anne had done and hoped it hadn't been too hard on their dad. Jake was telling her he'd got home safely. That was good to know.

She quickly replied, "Great - glad you're home - call me when you get a chance xx."

She drew back the curtains and saw that it was still snowing. Everything looked beautiful. A wintery scene, worthy of a Christmas card.

In the bathroom she weighed herself, eleven stone twelve pounds, obviously she couldn't tell if she'd lost weight, because of all the extra layers she'd worn at weight watchers. She decided she'd only weigh herself on Thursday mornings. If she'd lost weight she'd go, if not she wouldn't. *Great attitude*, she told herself, sarcastically.

She went into the kitchen and started planning today's low-fat food. For breakfast she cut up an apple, some grapes and a pear. She made herself a de-caff black coffee and went into the sitting room to watch TV.

After breakfast she went upstairs and made another attempt on her clothes. She must be ruthless, there was no point keeping clothes she'd never wear again. She started by sorting out the clothes she did think she would wear. She had so many black tops, most of them worn out, baggy and scruffy looking. Why on earth had she clung onto this stuff. She examined her jeans; some were obviously too tiny and even on a diet she was never going to be that slim again. Some were misshapen and were probably twenty years old. Ancient dresses, old skirts, old shirts, old jumpers, old jackets and out of date coats. Dresses that brought back lovely memories; her sons' graduations, Adam and Hannah's wedding, a posh ball she'd been invited to about thirty-five years ago. Summer gear that she should put in a bag and keep under the spare bed until it was summer. There were items that still had their price tags attached, impulse buys that should never have been made.

She sorted out the summer clothes and stuck them in a few bags and crammed them under the spare bed along with a lot of miscellaneous crap. That would have to be another job, for another day.

In the end there were about twelve items that she thought she could still wear this winter. Surely she had more than that, no, that was it.

She bagged up the rest and struggled to carry them downstairs, one by one. All in all, there were ten bags. She couldn't believe it. How crazy. She would have to go into town and buy some more things.

She hated ordering clothes online, they were never what you thought they were going to be and often didn't fit. She couldn't work out how to send things back so she was stuck with even more clothes that she couldn't wear. But she also hated trying things on in the shops, she looked enormous and nothing fit properly. She felt total despair after a shopping trip. But it would have to be done. Her wardrobe was looking crazily sparse. She wondered if perhaps she'd been a bit too ruthless. But she couldn't think of anything in the bags that could be salvaged. It was all tat, tat and more tat.

She stuffed all the bags into her car and then added the bag of rubbage that was waiting in the kitchen. She decided to brave the snow and take everything today before she changed her mind and started bringing things back in. Her drive was quite icy, and her car slipped and slewed its way out.

She chose the Shelter shop to donate to. She tended to alternate between Shelter, The British Heart Foundation and Macmillan. But with this cold snap homeless people needed all the charity they could get.

She couldn't imagine how appallingly awful it must be to be a homeless person. Whenever she came across any, usually in bigger towns than her own, she gave them money. She knew opinion was divided about that, did they go and spend the money on drugs, on alcohol. Some people said buy them food or a hot drink, but that was so patronising. If they felt the need to be drunk or drugged-up, then so what, who wouldn't want to be drunk in that situation, she wanted to be drunk in *her* situation.

The real disgrace was that people couldn't find a home of their own in the first place. It was scandalous that in a country as rich as this one, people could slip through the net. She was also disgusted by food banks. How could a so-called civilised country be ok with food banks. They were even being used by people in work, how could that be right. Wages must be so low for average workers and as for youngsters, they were caught in a terrible trap, paying exorbitant rents, without a hope of ever owning their own homes. When had the world become so unfair? When had the decision been made that people with money could screw over the rest of humanity, only caring about their profit margins and shareholders? It was bad enough that schools were now profit making, private enterprises. When had this all happened? It was now happening to the NHS, gradually privatisation was quietly being allowed to slip in, taking over one service after another, it wouldn't be long before all of it was owned by private companies, who would then start to charge people bit by bit, until the concept of free care had disappeared and become just a fond memory. Why must we always follow the Americans, why must profit come before people?

She sighed, what was the use, there was nothing she could do. She told herself to shut up, to stop worrying, to try to care less.

After dropping off the bags, Pamela felt quite cheerful. She had been putting off clearing out her unwanted clothes for... well... probably years. It felt so good to finally be rid of all that crap. It felt like a noose had been wrested from around her neck.

She could drive straight into Leeds and buy some new

things. *No,* she thought, *better wait until I've lost at least a stone.* If she wasn't working, it wouldn't matter what she wore during the day and it wasn't as if her social calendar was full of evenings out. Jeans and a baggy top would be good enough for anywhere she did go.

She needed to be more organised, not just clear stuff out once a blue moon, she needed to keep on top of things.

Not for the first time she worried about leaving such a mess for her family to deal with. If she dropped dead, then and there, how ashamed would she be about the clutter that her boys and probably her sisters would have to face. *Well, obviously, ashamed was a bit of a crazy emotion to attribute to my dead self, I suppose,* she thought, *when you're dead you probably can't feel emotion.* She didn't believe in heaven or hell. *What do I believe in then?* She asked herself, *well, I hope that when I die that's it, that there is absolutely nothing. Just like before we were born there was nothing, after we die it must be the same.* But a part of her wasn't sure. Anne once said that when you die your body is still there, but you're not in it anymore. So, where had the "you" gone, had you just escaped the confines of your body, was it now free to fly off, unimpeded by the pain of a physical form? Well one thing was for sure, we'd all find out someday. Whatever our own mind-set, whatever we were brought up to believe, one day we would know.

She realised that she was having rather deep and odd thoughts for a normal Saturday morning. *That way madness lies,* she told herself and started, instead, to think about lunch. She'd have something dietful after a quick visit to her dad.

Later, driving home, she resisted the urge to go to the delicious bakery in town. Her dad had at least been a bit warmer today and had looked a little less dishevelled but wasn't much happier.

Once home she cut up some carrots, onion, one potato and a few leeks and made a relatively low-fat vegetable soup. It was lovely, but, of course, it would've tasted better with a big slab of bread, slathered in creamy butter. *Don't think about that,* she told herself, *you're doing pretty well.* She would have the rest of the chilli for tea.

She wondered if Sophie was back yet. She fired off a quick WhatsApp, "Hey - how's it going - are you back today or tomorrow? Pam x."

She then sent a quick message to Georgie, "Hi - how are you - when do you get back? P xx."

She thought about de-cluttering one of the cupboards in the kitchen. No, she'd done enough for the day, no point overdoing it. She'd need to keep some things to do during what was possibly going to be a long-time off work.

She realised she hadn't thought about how long she'd be off. *I mean,* she thought, *if the old bastard died or something over the Christmas holidays, I could, and would, go straight back, but that probably wasn't going to happen.*

She had taught at a school where the head of Science had been killed in a climbing accident over the summer. That had been awful, obviously. But with this new boss, how sad would she be? *Not sad at all, that's how sad.*

But you really shouldn't go around wishing death on

people. It didn't work well with her new year resolutions. She had done once. Her ex's second wife, Shaz. *Shaz, what sort of name was that?* She hated her so much. That woman had pretended to be her friend, whilst shagging her husband behind her back. She'd also lived next door, how handy for the dick. *Didn't he know you don't shit on your own doorstep? Evidently not.*

Pamela had felt so evil towards her. Every night before she fell asleep, she would picture her being pressed into the ground, laying in a pile of reeking mud, she then mentally buried her with soggy obnoxious smelling decomposing leaves. When she'd died at forty Pamela did feel a bit guilty. *But come on,* she thought, *I'm not responsible, how could I be?* Really, she should have kept her hatred for Derek-the-dick, not that woman. After all he was the one who had promised to love her and keep her in sickness and in health and all the other promises you made when you got married.

The woman's crime had been to trust a man who no one should have trusted and, Pamela supposed, her other crime was to pretend to be best buddies with her. Her ex had refused to have children with Shaz, and a few weeks after she died, he was with another woman who got pregnant immediately, so a double whammy. But she hadn't been around to see that, so it was a bit of a hollow victory. She'd never had a chance to tell Shaz that the dick would sleep with anything and that he'd had several affairs before he'd started having an affair with her.

Despite the passing years Pamela still found this annoying. The dick was the world's biggest liar and he'd told Shaz that she was the only one, it was because he adored her so much that he was having this affair, not that he actually slept with anything that moved. She'd heard a description that summed up the dick's behaviour on TV. The female character was describing her boss, "If you threw a ham sandwich across the room, he'd try to shag it before it hit the floor." She had laughed so much, that was the dick to a tee.

Oh well, this was ancient history. *Why am I raking up the past? Let it be, leave it alone, stop thinking.* She reprimanded herself; *you're not allowed to look back. Ha!* She laughed, *it's all I've done this holiday.*

She heard her phone ping. It was Sophie, "Hi yes we got back this morning - do you want to come over tonight - Russ's meeting mates in the pub - we could get a take-away? x."

Pamela couldn't think of anything more appealing than a take-away. She mentally went through what she'd eaten since Thursday. She had been so good, surely she could afford to splurge a bit tonight. As long as she was extra good for the rest of the week.

She replied, "Yes - sounds great - what time? x."

"Any time after 7 - do you fancy Indian? x."

Pamela fancied anything that was full fat and delicious.

"Fab - let me know what you want – I'll order it xx."

"Great - I'll let you know later today x."

She was looking forward to hearing how Sophie's mini break had gone. She was glad that Russ was going out. She liked him, but it was hard to have a good catch up with him around. They were the kind of couple who bickered all the time. They never seemed to agree about anything. You couldn't have a private conversation, he'd be butting in, making comments, Sophie had to divide her attention between them, which could sometimes be very annoying, other times it was quite amusing. But mainly annoying.

She decided she'd go and have a long soak in the bath. Her back was aching from all the bags she'd been lugging about.

It was getting dark outside, she looked out of the bathroom window, it had started to snow again, but quite lightly. It was so pretty. There was no sign of the little fox. She wondered if she'd imagined it. She knew that foxes were quite a common sight in larger cities, but in this small town they were rare. She could put some food out to lure it back. You did hear stories of people bringing foxes into their homes as pets, but she wouldn't like that. It was nice to catch just a glimpse of one, it made them magical and interesting. Also, she didn't want a dog or cat, or any other normal pet, so it would be a bit mad to have a fox.

As she lay in the bath she examined her body, the cuts were healing quite well, but the bruises from New Year were getting larger and darker. That always happened to her, the slightest bang and she had a bruise. It would be nice to see Sophie, have a few drinks and relax. *But I mustn't go mad.* Sophie would probably appreciate a sober Pamela, rather than an insane one. If she was desperate, she could always drink when she got home.

She heard her phone ringing in the bedroom. She hauled

herself out of the bath and struggled into her dressing gown.

'Hi, how's it going?'

'Hi, ok thanks, are you back?'

'No, we get back tomorrow. How was your Christmas?'

'Fine thanks, what about you?'

'Oh ok, I'll fill you in next week. How's dad?'

'He's fine, well, he's being his usual grumpy self. He's complaining about being cold. Are you back in time to visit him tomorrow?'

'Yes, will do. Poor dad, it's been so cold hasn't it? Has it been a nightmare with me being away?'

'Well, not too bad, in fact Anne's been to see him a couple of times this week.'

'Wow, amazing!'

'I know!' They both laughed.

'How are the boys?'

'Both fine, as far as I know, yours?'

'Same!' They laughed again, it's was a running joke whose kids were the worst at getting in touch.

'They did let me know they'd got back safely from their skiing holidays.'

'Well that's something. I've heard nothing so far.'

'Have you texted them?'

'What do you think?'

'Yeah, sorry. I s'pose I'm lucky that mine actually did reply and amazingly Alex called when he got back from holiday!'

'Lucky you!'

'I know!'

Then, the question she was dreading.

'Are you definitely still going on sick next week?'

Bloody hell, couldn't anybody think of something else to ask.

She took a deep breath and said, 'Fraid so.'

The last thing she needed right this minute was a discussion about bloody work. She and Georgie had spent hours before her holiday going over and over all her options. She was sympathetic but it was obvious she didn't understand.

'Poor you, it's so depressing. I thought you might have changed your mind.'

'I only wish I could.' It would be so nice to be able to change her mind. Dripping and cold in the dark bedroom, she didn't fancy a long conversation on this topic. 'Hey, listen I've just got out of the bath, is it ok to call you later?'

'Of course, or shall I call you tomorrow when we're back?'

'Yes, that'll be great. I'm off to Soph's tonight.'

'Ah, that's nice, send her my love, how was New Year at hers?'

'Got drunk, disgraced myself, was sick, the usual madness.'

'Poor you.'

'Yeah right, totally my own fault.'

'Well never mind, she's a good friend, she'll forgive you.'

'Yes, luckily.'

'Any nice men there?'

'Bloody hell, don't you start!'

'What do you mean?'

'Oh nothing, I'll fill you in tomorrow.'

'Ok, great, have a lovely evening tonight.'

'Will do, drive safely tomorrow.'

'Ok love, bye.'

'Bye.'

She wondered if she should get back in the bath, but it looked cold and a bit scummy. She didn't want to run another one. Shivering, she pulled the plug.

She dressed in jeans, with tights underneath, a few warm tops and a fluffy jumper she'd found when she'd sorted the wardrobe out. She put a bit of make up on and messaged Sophie.

"Hey - it's me - what do you fancy?"

Whilst she waited for the reply, she went onto her Just Eat app. She wondered if anything would be low-cal from an Indian take-away. Well, it probably didn't matter tonight. She'd hardly eaten anything since Thursday. But she looked on her weight watchers' app just in case. It looked like she was on the right track by being a vegetarian and if she avoided the nan bread, she was good to go. She was terrible at counting points and tended not to do it. If she stuck to her old tried and tested methods, she would probably be ok.

Sophie texted back, "Chicken tandoori - chicken Balti - 1 nan - 2 chapattis' raita and a portion of rice. Thx x."

Of course, Sophie didn't seem to give a dam about calories, the lucky thing. She wanted to choose either onion bhaji or vegetable samosa, but according to the weight watchers app these were not a good option. *Oh, to hell with it*, she'd have a veggie madras, 3 chapattis and a portion of onion bhaji.

She ordered, adding Sophie's address for the delivery. Thirty mins. Great. She could almost taste the delicious curry. She found her old ski jacket, gloves, hat and scarf; thank goodness she hadn't given those away today. She put on ski socks and walking shoes, maybe she'd walk home later.

She grabbed a bottle of white wine and went out to the car. It was still gently snowing, but all the roads were clear. If it carried on like this school could be cancelled on Monday. *Wouldn't that be typical,* she thought.

She manoeuvred her car out of the slippery drive. The town was empty, unusual for a Saturday night. No one seemed to be out, everyone must be expecting a blizzard or something. Or they were all broke after Christmas. Luckily, Sophie's house was just off the main road, like Pamela's, so her small car wasn't going to get stuck.

She arrived as the Just Eat car was pulling in, *great timing,* she thought. She took the food off the driver and, struggling to hold everything, shuffled up to the door. She rang the bell and beamed as Sophie came to the door.

'I come bearing delicious gifts!'

'Fab, I'm starving.'

'Me too.'

They walked down the hall to Sophie's beautiful kitchen. Pamela couldn't help having flashbacks to Sophie's party, she eyed the bottom of the stairs warily. It was amazing that Sophie could bear to have her back in her house.

'I'm so sorry about last week,' she couldn't help saying.

'Oh, shut up, I've forgotten all about it and so should you.'

'It's very kind of you, honestly I hate myself sometimes.'

Sophie laughed. 'Don't mention it again, ok?'

'Ok.'

Sophie and Russ had just completed an enormous extension on the back of their house. Pamela would have loved a kitchen extension like this. There was an island, an AGA, a boiling water system that meant you never had to use a kettle again, completely luxurious. Sophie put the curry into the Aga.

'We'll give it a few minutes, it's always better isn't it.'

'Your kitchen is just so nice.' She told Sophie for about the millionth time.

'Thanks, you could quite easily extend your kitchen you know. Do you want me to give you the details of our builder?'

'Well, your builder has done an amazing job, but I'd better hang fire for now, what with the work situation and everything, but I don't want to talk about that tonight. And, anyway, I've had enough of builders for a bloody lifetime.'

Pamela had bought her old end terrace at a knock down price because it needed so much work doing, but her builder had turned into a raving maniac.

'Oh yes, you chose the crazy man didn't you!' Sophie chuckled.

'Not on purpose,' Pamela replied, indignantly. 'He seemed ok at first, then he turned into a complete psycho!'

'Didn't he call you a man hating bitch?'

'Yes, the fecking creep, then he tried to apologise, he sent me a grovelling, grammatically incoherent email, which I ignored.'

'Ha! English teachers!'

'I know, I can't help myself.'

'Well our builder was amazing.'

'I know, you were so lucky. Anyway, tell me all about your romantic get-away.'

Sophie opened the wine and poured them both a healthy glass, she handed Pamela one and laughed.

'After thirty years of marriage, nothing counts as a romantic get-away! But we booked a fab Airbnb, overlooking the sea, of course it was bloody freezing out, but we had a gorgeous log fire and Sky TV...' Sophie sighed.

'Living the dream then!'

'Oh definitely, it was lovely. We should book it sometime, me, you and maybe Helen, or Joanne, or both!'

'How many bedrooms?'

'Two good sized doubles, both en-suite and a single room which was actually great because of bloody Russ, snoring for England, I couldn't sleep, so I escaped into the other double.'

'Has his snoring got worse then?'

'No, it's probably the same, but I just find it harder to get to sleep these days, what with night sweats, night terrors, you know, the usual!'

'I know, poor you, I'm not too bad anymore, they've mainly stopped but every now and then I can't sleep because of the sweat pouring down my entire body. Are you thinking about HRT?'

'I'm not too sure, are you still taking it?'

'No, I decided to stop, but I'll tell you something, I absolutely love not having periods anymore.'

'Oh my god, so do I. It's so bloody brilliant. I used to hate them.'

'Same. I can't think of one good thing about them.'

'Me neither.' They laughed, 'Old age does have some perks!'

Sophie got the plates out of the AGA and put one down next to Pamela. 'Be careful, it's hot.' She put the containers on the counter and handed Pamela some serving spoons.

'OMG, I actually cannot wait for this.'

'Oh yes, sorry I meant to ask how your diet was going.'

She laughed, 'Fine until just now, and,' she pointed to the wine, 'the not drinking is going well too!'

'Oh, never mind, you only live once.'

'Yes, or yolo as the kids say!'

They sat down at Sophie's beautiful pine table.

'Flippin 'eck I'm going to have to take some clothes off.' Pamela was sweating. 'I forgot how lovely and warm your house is, especially next to the Aga. I can never get it right in my house, its freezing during the day and then the heat goes on in the middle of the night!' She took off several layers and her jeans, 'Hope you don't mind if I sit in my tights, I dressed for the snow!'

'Don't worry, strip off, there's only us!'

'I won't go that far, don't panic!'

'This curry is bloody delicious.'

'It's so nice to eat non diet food! But apart from tonight, which obviously isn't great, I'm determined to stick to it.'

'One night's not going to ruin it.'

'I know, and I cheated like mad on the weigh in day, I wore heavy jeans, a belt, loads of layers. Next week I'll wear next to nothing!' they both laughed.

'You are crazy.'

'I know, who am I kidding! But once I get into it, I'll be fine.'

'I know you will. But what about the booze?'

'Yeah, that's been less successful. I just know I need to give up, I need to force myself to think about the units, my health, everything really.'

'I know, but the thing is you get into a habit. Me and Russ nearly always open a bottle of wine with dinner, we don't even think about it, or discuss it, and then we'll probably open another later, whilst we're watching telly or whatever.'

'I know and you don't even feel like you're drinking.'

'No, again, like you said, it's just a habit.'

'A bad habit!' they said together.

'Talking of which...' Sophie topped up their glasses. 'This is delicious wine, thanks Pam, and what do I owe you for the curry?'

'Oh, it's fine, you pay next time, I might be broke by then.'

Sophie made a sympathetic face, and was about to speak, but Pamela quickly cut her off, 'Remember I don't want to talk about it!"

'That's fine. You're probably thinking about nothing else, so let's not ruin tonight talking about it.'

'Good plan. Now tell me some more about your trip, did Russ behave himself, apart from the crazy snoring.'

'Well, mainly. We went on some lovely walks, we both love being near the sea as you know. We ate out most nights, which was great. But I thought I was going to kill him on the journey, or he was going to kill us both, he drives like a crazy man. He doesn't pay attention to what other drivers are doing, he speeds, he won't follow the Sat Nav, he knows better than her, obviously. Honestly, he does my head in when he's driving.'

'You're not usually a bad passenger.'

'No, but that's irrelevant, the most laid-back person wouldn't be able to cope with his driving. I insisted on driving home but that was as bad, he kept making stupid comments, pretending to be terrified to pay me back, shouting turn left, turn right, don't follow that sign, why have you turned down there, blah, blah, blah. I think we'll have to get taxi's from now on!'

'There's nothing worse is there, you just feel like throwing yourself out of the car!'

'Yes! But apart from that we did have a lovely time.' They laughed.

'Ah, that's nice. At least you'll feel like you've had a real break.'

'What about you, what have you been doing?'

'I've started de-cluttering, I sorted out my wardrobe and took hundreds of bags to charity!'

'Wow, did you?'

'Yes, I can actually walk into my bedroom and my wardrobe is nearly totally empty!'

'Bloody hell, well done.'

'It felt great. Also, I've been clearing out some of the shit from my kitchen drawers. It's amazing how much rubbish accumulates in them.'

'I know, that's why it was fab to get a new kitchen, it forces you to throw all the old crap away and start again.'

'But I bet you weren't that bad in the first place.'

'I'm not too bad, but I do have to fight the urge to keep things, like champagne corks and stuff.'

'I know, I need to fight that urge a bit more. I'm in danger of being the hoarder next door!'

'No, you're not that bad.'

'I'm in permanent danger of it, believe me.'

'Honestly, I don't believe you.' Sophie laughed.

'Oh my god, to totally change the subject, I forgot to tell you, the day we met in Costa, you'll never guess who came in?'

'Who?'

'Only that Tom person.'

'Did he talk to you?'

'Yes, he came straight over and bought me a flippin' coffee!'

'That was nice.'

'Not really, I was so embarrassed. Remember the last time we were together he was putting me to bed in a completely drunken state! I was mortified.'

'He can't be too horrified with you, he wanted to call you, after all.'

'No, he wanted *me* to call *him*, there's a difference.'

Sophie sighed; she just couldn't understand why Pamela was so adamant that she never wanted another man in her life. Especially someone like Tom, he seemed so genuinely nice. 'But he's attractive, rich, available, what's not to like?'

'OMG are you actually serious! His wife has just left him after all that time, he's at the cut and paste stage, there's no way I want to be that woman.'

'You and your cut and paste! Honestly, not everyone's the same as you, you know.'

'I know, but come on, don't you think he should wait a bit before throwing himself into another relationship?'

'Maybe he just couldn't resist you!'

'Yea, that must be it! I am totally irresistible. But seriously, you know I'm not interested in a relationship. Especially now...' Pamela stopped, she realised that she had alluded to work three times. She didn't want to talk about it, but seemingly couldn't help herself.

Sophie fixed her with a sombre stare and put her hand over Pamela's, 'I know but remember I'm here if you need me. You've decided what you want to do, and I respect you for that. I'm happy to listen to anything you want to say.' Sophie squeezed her hand and went back to her curry.

'Thanks, Soph, I know I can talk to you, but it's just so

depressing, you know?'

'I know, bless you. Right, time for another bottle of wine!'

They both laughed.

'So, is Amelie still going travelling?'

'Oh, don't remind me, yes, she's coming home on the 16th with all her stuff,' they both groaned, 'and then she flies on the 21st.'

'By herself?'

'Yes, this is the girl who never even went camping, either alone or with friends, yet she thinks she can backpack around the globe by herself. They think they can put off the real world, but what about job security, building your pension pot, buying a house?'

'They never think about getting old, it doesn't exist for them, well I suppose we didn't at their age, like you I blame their student loans, they're in such debt anyway, it stops them thinking straight.'

'Yeah, I know but how long can she put off growing up?'

'Don't let her hear you say that.'

'Oh, don't worry, I'm having to pretend I'm delighted!'

'The irony!'

'Tell me about it. But of course, it will be lovely to see her when she comes home, even though it's only for a short time.'

'Ah, it'll be so nice, you'll have to do lots of mother-daughter things.'

'Yes, whilst subtly trying to put her off going away!'

'Good plan!'

Pamela helped Sophie stack the dishwasher and they put the leftovers in the fridge, 'Do you want to take any of this home?'

'No, I'd better be good tomorrow, maybe Russ will have some when he gets in?'

Yeah, he probably will, if that's ok, do you fancy watching a film?'

'Great.'

Later sitting in front of Sophie's wood burning stove, Pamela felt that life was probably worth living after all. Sometimes the idea of her future filled her with such fear. She'd done everything she was supposed to do, gone to college, become a teacher, taught for over thirty years, got married, had kids. But now it was all in the past. Everything she was good for had now come to an end.

Getting old was shit. There was nothing to look forward to. You just got frail, got dementia, got cancer. What was the point. She wasn't one of these women who was dying to be a grandma, she couldn't imagine that happening at all if she was perfectly honest. At least teaching had given her a reason to get up every morning and some sense of purpose in her life. But at this exact point of time, she felt that she could cope. She would get over this horrible moment in her life, maybe even get a job in a different school. The idea of starting somewhere else, where nobody knew her, especially the kids, was terrifying. When you'd been in a school for a long time, you had automatic respect. You didn't have to prove yourself, didn't have to work hard at discipline. But the few times she'd been a supply teacher had proved that you immediately became the lowest of the low. Kids just took advantage of your low status. You often weren't told the discipline policies, who to contact if it all started to go horribly wrong, which it invariably did.

Sophie interrupted her thoughts, yawning she asked, 'Would you like another glass of wine or coffee, tea?'

'Oh no, honestly, I'm fine, sorry, I'd better get going. It's been so lovely.'

'Yes, it's been great.'

'What time is Russ due home?'

'Dunno, that's the trouble with these new opening times, before, everyone was kicked out at eleven and you knew where you were.'

'I know, now there's no knowing when the pubs will close! I'll just see if I can get an Uber, if not I'll call Town taxis.'

'You could've stayed over, sorry never thought.'

'It's fine, I'll walk back tomorrow to get my car.'

'Ok.'

Pamela glanced out of the window, the snow was still coming down, deep and slow. 'In fact, I think I'll walk home. It looks amazing out there.' She was pulling on all her layers, jeans, tops, warm jacket, hat, gloves.

'No! It's late.'

'I know, but we live in the quietest town in the world. I'll be totally fine.'

'No! I'd never forgive myself if something happened to you.'

'It won't, honestly, I promise. Listen I'm a fifty-six-year old woman, I'll be fine.'

Sophie sighed, Pamela was so stubborn. 'But what about the snow, it might be very slippery out there.

'I've got my walking boots. I love walking in snow, especially at night'.

Sophie shook her head, feigning exasperation, she knew Pamela would not be persuaded from her seemingly reckless decision.

'Right, well text me when you get back.'

'Of course.'

As they got to the door Russ was just arriving home, along with, of course, why not? Bloody Tom. To be fair he did look mortified to see Pamela. Sophie held the door open and they came in, shaking the snow from their jackets, shoes and hair.

'Hi, did you have a great night?' she asked cheerily,

'In Town, are you mad? It was bloody dead.' Russ moaned, good naturedly.

'Hi guys,' Pamela said, 'Just on my way home.'

She was hoping she could get away without talking to Tom. No such luck. He stood right in front of her, blocking her way out.

'Hey Tom, Pamela's insisting on walking halfway across town on her own, why don't you walk her home?'

Jesus Christ what was wrong with Sophie?

'No, no, that won't be necessary, I want to go on my own.' She replied in a steely voice, she turned and fixed Sophie a look, her eyes flashing a warning.

'I'd be happy to walk you home,' Tom replied – of course.

'No, Pam's going to be fine, sorry I suggested it,' Sophie back tracked quickly.

'Erm... can I just get out?' Pamela indicated the door,

'Oh yes, of course, sorry, if you're sure you want to go alone?'

'Totally positive, thanks.' They both moved left, then right, performing a little private and embarrassing dance on the doorstep. Pamela could feel her face flush, *what is wrong with this guy?* She felt like shouting, "Get out of my way you fricking moron!" But luckily, she managed to control herself. She took hold of his arm and moved him, firmly, to her left, squeezing through as best she could. He stared at her as she slipped past. Russ and Sophie had moved into the hall.

Tom leant towards her and whispered, 'I've been thinking about you.'

Feck me, she thought, *have we not been here before?* Maybe he was just one of those guys who couldn't believe it when a person wasn't interested in them.

She decided to treat this as a joke, laughing gaily she said, 'Oh yes, I have that effect on men!' She turned to say goodbye to Sophie and Russ. 'Bye guys, see you tomorrow.' She rushed out, leaving a forlorn looking Tom on the doorstep.

'Bye.' Sophie and Russ shouted, ushering Tom inside.

She wasn't sure if they'd heard what Tom said, but it didn't matter. She had escaped. *Hurray!* Thank goodness she had been ready to leave when they'd arrived home, she felt sure that Tom would have insisted on talking to her and out of politeness, in front of Sophie, she'd have had to talk back. And thank goodness he hadn't seen her sitting in her tights and skimpy top.

Tom's creepy voice went through her mind, what was he saying - *I've been thinking about you.* It seemed the worse she treated him, the more interested he was. *Bloody thinking about you, what a creep. Honestly.* Maybe he'd just drunk too much, but still, it was disconcerting.

Pamela decided, not for the first time, to put the weird Tom out of her mind and enjoy her walk. The snow was falling in delicate slow-motion swirls all around her. Her feet made delicious crunching noises as she walked along. The snow was so fresh and beautiful, the night so bright. A tiny sliver of moon smiled crookedly down at her. It didn't feel cold; it was just incredible. It was so unusual to have perfect snow like this. The streets were empty, magical.

At first, she was following the deep imprints of Russ and Tom's footprints, going in the other direction, but these were gradually disappearing as she walked. Town was empty, all the pubs had shut. She trudged along, passing the little terrace houses, their curtains closed, their secrets hidden. TVs glimmered, projecting strange colourful lights onto the street. She imagined the close family groups, huddled around fires. Happy, sad? Just getting on with their lives. Why not?

The wind had picked up and the snow was driving along the street, it was so strangely dreamlike, so wonderful. She thought about Monday. *Bloody hell. Monday was going to be so weird.* But there was nothing she could do. She reached home and, standing in the porch, kicked the snow off her walking boots and shook her hat and scarf. She lived further up the valley than Sophie and there was a lot more snow around her house.

Inside it felt warm and inviting. Ok, so there was no one to shout "Hello, how was your night, did you have fun?" No comforting person welcoming her home. But the person she was inventing, this kind, thoughtful person who asked these nice questions, didn't exist. If there was someone, they'd more than likely be annoyed and bad tempered, asking what she thought she was doing, walking home in this weather, had she a lick of common sense, was she mad?

That was the beauty of single life, you had no one to answer to but yourself. No one telling you that you are stupid, crazy, mental, no one shouting and bawling and making your life a misery. She would hate to give her freedom away, whatever happened. And anyway, she was perfectly capable of making her own life a misery, thank you very much.

She poured herself a nightcap of whiskey and put the outside light on before she went up to bed. She quickly messaged Sophie

"I'm home safely - thanks for a fab night - so lovely to catch up - see you tomorrow xx."

She left the curtains open and got undressed in the dark. Her bedroom overlooked the lighted garden.

Sophie replied. "Thanks – great night – still up talking to Tom! S xx."

Poor Sophie, she thought, *I'm so glad I wasn't staying over, it would have been so awkward.*

She glanced at her bedside clock, it was two am and the snow showed no sign of stopping. She hadn't realised she'd spent so long at Sophie's. She watched the snow coming down from the comfort of her warm bed for as long as she could, but gradually her eyes wouldn't stay open any longer and she fell asleep.

Sunday 8th January

She woke the next morning at six am and couldn't believe she'd slept the whole night, of course it was only four hours, but it had been a deep, dream free, untroubled and contented four hours.

Outside the snow was still gently falling. After breakfast she layered up and went out into the white-scape. It was still early, but parents were already out with sledges and excited children, throwing snowballs and building snowmen in gardens. The gritters must have been out through the night, as the roads were clear. She got to Sophie's at eight am. She hoped that if Tom had stayed over, he'd still be in bed and she wouldn't have to see him. She rang the doorbell. She knew they'd be up; she and Russ were famous for getting up at the crack of doom.

Sophie couldn't help saying, 'Bloody hell, you're up early.'

'Cheeky git, I'm always up at this time!' Pamela replied, indignantly.

'Yeah right! How's your head?'

'Surprisingly good, What about you?'

'Yeah, I feel fine, even though I didn't get to bed until after three! Do you want to come in for a coffee?'

'No thanks, I'll get off, I just wanted to say thanks again for a lovely night.' She'd decided not to say anything about Tom, she'd tell Sophie what he'd said later. She couldn't risk him overhearing their conversation if he had stayed over. Best to keep her thoughts to herself, if he heard her mention his name, he'd probably think he was in with a chance.

'Yes, it was lovely. We'll do it again soon.'

"Yes, that'll be great, see you later.'

'Yes, drive carefully.'

'Will do.'

As Pamela turned to go, Sophie squeezed her arm and said, 'Good luck this week.'

'Yeah, thanks. I'll let you know how it goes.'

'Do.'

Pamela carefully reversed out of the drive. She glanced back at the house and saw Tom staring down at her from an upstairs window. Thank goodness she hadn't gone in or mentioned his name. *What a weirdo,* she thought, uncharitably.

She turned into the supermarket car park and remembered it was Sunday. *Bloody hell.* She parked and rang Jake. No reply. She rang Alex. No reply. She didn't leave a message. Georgie wouldn't be back yet and there was no point ringing Anne at this hour of the morning, there was no way she'd be up yet. It was at times like this that she missed her mum. As usual she tried not to think about that absence in her life. She had been such a lovely, caring person. She would have been totally on Pamela's side about work, she would have been full of reassurance and kindness.

On days like today she missed the solid, sensible and

thoughtful conversation she knew she would've had with her mum. 'Well mum, what do you think I should do about work?' She spoke aloud, her words hollow and flat in the silent car. No reply, her thought-mum had been strangely absent recently. Just a dark void. Her mum loved snowy days like this. A familiar ache spread through Pamela's body and she felt close to tears. Cancer was such a disgusting illness. Her mum should have gone on late into her 90's, like her own mum and grandmother before her. What Pamela could never understand is how someone as healthy as her mum had got cancer in the first place. She didn't drink alcohol, she cooked every meal from scratch, she exercised regularly. It just didn't make any sense. Maybe that's what put her off giving up alcohol and joining a gym, what was the point, you were going to die anyway, so why bother?

She messaged both boys. "Hi - tried to call - nothing to worry about - just checking in - how's your weekend going? xx."

They were much better at answering texts than actual calls. She could go down to London to see them if she wasn't working. She could get the train down and stay in a nice hotel for a couple of nights. If they weren't too busy. Who was she kidding, they were always too busy. But if she said she'd like to come down for her birthday, that might work. Or Mothers' day. Yes, that was a great plan.

She glanced up; another car had slid its way into the car park. Someone else who'd forgotten it was Sunday. She smiled at the harassed looking young woman in the car, she could see several children in the back, giving their mum hell. The woman smiled back, then turned to intervene in a fist fight.

She was glad that part of her life was over. She missed her boys as they were now, not so much their younger needier selves. Although there was always the temptation to romanticise the past, to feel sad that they were grown up and didn't need her anymore. There had been some lovely times when they were younger, but you had to remember the tiredness, the loneliness of being a single working mother, the sheer exhaustion of it all. It had often been overwhelming. Pamela never said to younger mum's, "Enjoy them while you can - they grow up so quickly," because in her experience they didn't. Their childhood years had lasted for about a century.

She turned the radio on and lay her head back against the head rest. The presenter was just introducing the news. Pamela didn't think she could cope with that. She switched to radio 4 extra. A play. She listened for a while, gradually tuning out. Her phone pinged. It was Jake. "Sorry mum - couldn't answer - just got to the gym – call tonight?"

She messaged back, "Yes that's fine no worries - are you with Alex? xx."

"No - seeing him later x."

"Great, talk soon xxx."

She checked her watch, another hour. She should go home and come back, but what was the point. She scrolled through her phone, who could she call? Helen? No. Joanne? No. She decided to ring Lou, she had young kids, she'd probably been up for hours.

'Hi, how's it going?'

'Fine. How are you?'

'Fine, thanks.'

'Have you changed your mind?'

'No.'

'Don't blame you, have you read his latest email?'

'No, not yet, what does he say?'

'Just read it, you'll be disgusted.'

'Is it worse than usual?'

'Yes!'

'How can it be worse? Honestly!'

'I know, but he's managed it.'

'Are you dreading tomorrow?'

'A little bit, not gunna lie, I was praying for a snow day, but it's started to thaw.'

'Ah, bless you. The snow's still quite bad here. But you'll be fine tomorrow.'

'I know, but it won't be the same without you there.'

'Don't say anything to anyone will you?'

'Of course not.'

'Thanks, are you all prepared?'

'Yes, just about, I've spent the last five days planning and marking.'

'Isn't it an awful job?' They both laughed, 'Why would anyone become an English teacher?'

'I know, it's so crap.'

'I wonder how many of the English Department will be off sick?'

'I've been thinking about that. And we've got all the new staff starting.'

'Yes, I'd forgotten. Are there about six new people?'

'Something like that.'

'The poor sods, they've no idea what they're letting themselves in for.'

'True, I'll ring you during the week and let you know everything that's happening.'

'Will you? That's so kind. Thanks a lot.'

'Of course, I'm really going to miss you.'

'I'll miss you too – I know this sounds awful but I'm hoping he's suffered some catastrophic event over Christmas and doesn't come back!'

'Yes, let's hope something nasty has happened to him!'

'No such luck!'

'I agree, shit people don't get their comeuppance, do they? It's poor people like us that suffer.'

'I should be happy that I don't have to go in tomorrow, but I just feel a sense of dread.'

'It is awful.'

'Yes, I wonder who'll be next on his list now I'm not going to be there?'

'Could be literally anyone.'

'True. I still can't believe he said he was 'gunning for me', the git.'

'I know, I shouldn't have told you.'

'No, I'm glad you did, makes me know I'm not just being paranoid.'

'Of course you're not, it amazes me that the head hasn't

noticed what's going on.'

'I know, it's so annoying. Well I'll let you get back to your planning and your family! Take care.'

'Same to you, I'll be in touch.'

'Thanks, bye.'

'Bye.'

Pamela hung up. She'd known today was going to be the worst day of the holidays. She'd felt anxious the whole time, obviously, but today it had finally settled on her, a dark, deep dread, a terror crushing her between its claws.

She shouted at herself, 'For fecks sake Pamela, stop thinking. Stop.'

She opened her eyes and saw five pairs of eyes staring at her from the car next to her. She blushed, turned away and started the car. She may as well go home and come back later. If she was going to scream and freak out, she may as well do it privately.

Her car slid and swerved its way out of the un-gritted car park. It looked like a thaw was setting in. Typical.

When she got home, she saw a car parked outside her house, there was someone sitting in the driver's seat, she couldn't work out who it was as the windows were steamed up. She pulled into her drive and as she got out the person emerged. It was Tom. *Oh hell,* she thought, *what now?*

'Hi, Pamela, sorry to bother you, can I just have a quick word?'

She pulled off her hat and scarf, she was suddenly boiling up.

'Yes, Of course.' She didn't want to invite him in. They

both stood in her drive awkwardly. He obviously wasn't going to speak until she had asked him in. *Bloody hell,* she thought.

'I'll just find my key.' She was so annoyed that she'd left the security of the supermarket car park for this. She fumbled in her bag, playing for time. She mentally went through her house, what sort of mess had she left it in, *oh well, take me as you find me*, she thought. There was nothing she could do now.

As she turned the key and opened the door, she felt his breath on her neck, he was standing too close, breathing heavily. *He'd better not touch me,* she clenched her fists, *I'll bloody punch him.* She walked into the hall, keeping her coat on. He stamped the snow off his feet.

'Shall I take my shoes off?' he asked.

'No, it's fine, don't worry.' Silently she thought, *you're not going to be staying long enough, so don't get comfortable*. He followed her into the hall. Again, another awkward silence.

Pamela couldn't bear it, 'Do you want a coffee or something?' She didn't want him to have a coffee, but what could she do? Social niceties took over.

'That would be lovely, thanks.'

She flung her coat and hat over the banister and marched through the house, silently furious. He followed her into the kitchen. Things didn't look too messy, which was a relief, although she told herself off for caring. *What did it matter what the place looked like?*

She felt weirdly self-conscious as she filled the kettle

and took the cups out of the cupboard. He was leaning back against the sink, his arms folded, just watching her. *What was wrong with him? He was so odd.*

She tried to make small talk, 'So, town was depressing yesterday?'

He just nodded, in a weird, brooding sort of way. Maybe someone had once told him that he looked sexy when he behaved that way. Well, he didn't.

'Milk, Sugar?'

'No, black is fine.'

'Great.' She handed him the mug. She wasn't going to invite him to sit down. The sooner this was over the better.

'How do you do it?' he asked unexpectedly. Pamela wondered if this was a trick question.

'Erm, what do you mean?'

'I mean, you seem to be perfectly happy and sorted on your own.'

'What's the alternative?' she asked.

'Don't you miss being married?'

'I've been on my own for years, it's different for you, everything is still raw and strange. It will get better, honestly.'

'I can't believe that.' He looked so sad that Pamela did feel sorry for him.

'Really, it will. Have you tried to get to the bottom of why your wife left?'

'She won't speak to me, she's not returning my calls, I don't know where she's staying, she hasn't even contacted the kids, it's a real nightmare.'

'Well, just give it time. She'll always be the mother of your children; you'll always have that in common.'

'Yes.' He replied miserably. 'I just don't know how to be without her, I got so used to being part of a couple. Everything has changed so much, we used to do everything together, I just can't seem to function without her...' He trailed off.

Bloody hell, she thought, *what on earth am I supposed to say, why didn't he have any friends he could confide in? Bloody men. Why is he making this my problem?*

She realised he was waiting for her to say something, she took a deep breath and replied, 'I know, it's hard, I'm not going to say otherwise, but, to quote a massive cliché, time is a great healer,' she took another deep breath, she had to try and explain what she thought he was going through. 'I think our first gut reaction is to find somebody else to take the place of our partner, after a split like this you just want to sort of fill that dreadful void, you're wanting the security and comfort you used to feel, but believe me, you need to fight that urge. You need to find out what it's like to be on your own for a while. Try to remember what's important to you, what things you like doing for yourself, not as part of a couple.'

'That's easier said than done.'

'Look, believe me, I do know how you feel. The desire to recreate what you had can be overwhelming, but don't trust that feeling! It's not real. You need to spend some time alone, before you move on.'

He looked more miserable than anyone she had ever

seen. She had to fight the urge to put her arms around him, she knew if she did, he'd take it the wrong way and then everything she'd just said would be forgotten. He sighed a deep, heart wrenching sigh. He was staring at the floor, pensive, wretched.

'You're probably right, I do feel exactly what you've just said, I feel like my life has no meaning, I feel such a failure, it's awful.'

'I know.' She did know, she didn't want to tell him that that emotion never went away.

'I'm sorry I was weird last night,' he almost whispered, 'I feel so stupid saying that stuff to you.'

'You only said you'd been thinking about me; it wasn't the end of the world!' Pamela tried to laugh, but she was feeling miserable on his behalf and the sound came out hollow and strange.

'God, it makes me sound like a crazed stalker.'

'You'd been drinking, it's fine, we all say or do mad things when we've been drinking, look at New Year's Eve for goodness sake.'

'Well that's one of the reasons I was thinking about you.'

He looked at her, properly, for the first time that morning. This sounded a bit ominous.

'What do you mean?' she asked. He paused, she could tell he wanted to get something off his chest.

'You said thanks, in the café, you thanked me for behaving like a gentleman and I didn't contradict you, but...'

Oh, bloody hell what was he going to confess to? Pamela suddenly felt a deathly cold run through her body.

'We actually did a few things.'

'What?' she spluttered, 'I was fully clothed when I woke up and you were on the floor and anyway,' she continued, angrily, praying that he would just shut up, 'whatever did happen, we were both drunk, we're both adults and I don't want to hear anymore.'

He looked stunned at her vitriol. She didn't care. *What kind of total creep was he?*

'I think you'd better go,' she added, turning her back on him.

This was not the reaction he had expected, he spluttered on, 'I didn't mean to, well, I mean, I wasn't trying to scare you or anything, I was just trying to make you...'

She turned around and exploded, practically shouting at him, 'Make me what?' She couldn't believe that a few moments ago she'd felt sorry for him. To be fair he was looking absolutely horrified, which was just as well, or she might've slapped him. 'Whatever happened meant absolutely nothing, do you understand?' She couldn't be any clearer.

'Yes,' he answered meekly. 'I'm sorry, I'll be going then?'

'Yes.'

He put his cup down and walked to the kitchen door, he looked at her once more and was about to speak, but the look on her face put him off, he managed a shaky, 'Bye then.'

She couldn't reply.

She heard the front door close; she waited a few minutes then checked that he had gone. She locked the door and practically fell onto the settee. *He was such a peculiar man, so what if they'd 'done something,' that doesn't make me his flipping girlfriend. Does he think he has some claim on me, how old is he, thirteen? Bloody hell, he was so weird. Was it a sort of power thing, did he feel he had some sort of hold on me because of this?* She wondered what he'd told Sophie and Russ about the night, not that it mattered. They didn't live in the dark ages, they wouldn't care, well certainly Sophie wouldn't and she wasn't worried about what Russ thought, if she was honest. No wonder he thought she'd ring him, maybe he thought he'd made a great impression on her by 'doing some things' to her. He was unbelievable.

But it did give her pause. What was she doing, at her age, getting so drunk that a random and, it now appeared, totally pervy stranger could take her home and do things to her. It was awful that she had no memory of doing anything with him at all. She felt sick and disgusted with herself. This was what happened to inexperienced teenagers, not women her age.

What had they done? Maybe they'd had actual sex. But surely that was unlikely, she had been totally clothed when she woke up. Had she given him a... she could hardly make herself say the words, never mind do it to him. She made herself think the words, *a hand job, a blow job.* She felt sickened by the very thought of it.

She remembered a conversation with her sister Anne about why she was single, she'd told her, "I just can't face the idea of having to give a man a blow job." Her sister had shrieked with laughter and replied, "A blow job – that's a bottle of champagne and a trip to Paris!"

But it wasn't the act itself that was bothering her, it was that she couldn't remember. She had allowed herself to get into that vulnerable position. Men should be taught that if a woman isn't capable of saying no, then she isn't capable of saying yes. But he'd told her in the café that she seemed fine in the taxi. *Is he feeling guilty?* No, if he'd been worried, he would've kept quiet. It seemed it was a sort of power thing, like he'd got something over her. *I wish I'd stayed calm,* she thought, *what did it matter what happened?* They were both adults and single like she'd said to him, but she just felt so creeped out by it. She'd talk to Sophie about it later. In the meantime, she prayed she'd never have to see him again.

She went back out to the car. Hopefully she could get her shopping out of the way without meeting anyone. She walked around the shop in a tired stupor, feeling oddly hollow and rung out, like a discarded dishcloth, stinking on a dirty floor. She felt soiled somehow, unclean to her very core. She avoided the alcohol aisle. Alcohol had a bloody lot to answer for.

Later, as she was lugging the bags in, the thought struck her that Tom had been lying. He was such a creep, he probably just wanted to hurt her.

She wasn't going to think about him for a moment

longer. He was strange and vile and not worth another thought. Except she might tell Sophie about it. See what Sophie thought. Or maybe not. Sophie seemed to like him, no, she'd talk to Georgie about him. She'd probably laugh her head off, which would make all of it seem less awful.

She went into the sitting room and opened her laptop. She'd been putting off reading the email from her boss for days, but after speaking to Lou she needed to know what he'd written. She couldn't put it off any longer, anyway whatever he said couldn't hurt her now.

Hello staff,

Hope you all had a pleasant and refreshing holiday. Now back to work.

Bloody hell, he didn't spend long on pleasantries, did he?

On the first morning back, I'd like to call a meeting in B11 at 7:40.

What an idiot, it was all very well for him, he didn't have children. People like Lou would struggle to get in at that time. *Was he even allowed to call extra meetings?* She doubted it. They weren't an academy yet. But that never bothered him. There were strict meeting times in the calendar, you couldn't just add more meetings whenever you wanted, but he simply ignored any rules that were inconvenient to his demands.

Items on the agenda - 1. 10-minute starters – you are no longer going to let students read for the first 10 minutes of their lesson. Prepare an appropriate starter for all classes.

Stupid man, starting each lesson with a 10-minute quiet

relaxed read was a lovely way to get the students calm and focussed. They'd started their lessons like this for years and now he'd come along and changed it without giving it a chance. She knew many of the Department would be furious about this. It totally summed him up, instead of asking what people thought, instead of negotiating and asking for everyone's input he just laid down the law.

You will design a different 10-minute starter for each class.

No apologies or a time frame in which to do it. The message was clear - DO IT NOW. He obviously had no idea how much extra work that was going to create. Or he did know but didn't give one shit. But that was the sort of man he was. She wasn't sure she could bear to read any more. She got herself another coffee and forced herself to continue.

Item 3. I want a copy of both your short term and long-term lesson plans for each class on my desk by Friday.

Bloody Hell.

Item 4. Also, by Friday, I want 5 workbooks from each class, showing a range of abilities, fully marked and up to date, I will also choose 4 random books from each class.

More work. And yes, again, that summed him up, just in case you thought you only needed to make sure five books from each class were perfectly prepared he threw in the random idea to ensure that every single book had to be up to date.

Item 5. Peter Ronson, from the local authority, will be in on Monday. He will be spending the week observing

Pamela James's lessons.

What a fricking diabolical man. How horribly embarrassing. This email had been sent to the whole department, with the head and deputies cc'd in. He was so obviously trying to humiliate her. Maybe he wanted to scare her off. Maybe she was playing straight into his hands by going off sick. She didn't care, in fact this reinforced her decision. He'd look like a right fool when she didn't show up. Good luck getting all your supply teachers to hand in plans and books! She was so relieved she didn't have to face all this shit. Whether he was trying to get rid of her or not, ultimately it didn't matter. She'd somehow make him pay, maybe not immediately but soon and for the rest of his life. Pamela forced herself to read on.

Item 6 – There will be a series of learning walks throughout the first two weeks of term. These will be conducted by myself, Angela Dawker and Ron Harrison. Regards Mac R.

Poor everyone, Pamela thought. Learning walks were simply code for, 'We will come into any lesson we like, unannounced, and spend as long as we like passing judgment on you.' Angela was the second in department, his trusted side kick, who, at the moment, was right by his side, aiding and abetting his every move. Protecting her own ass. She was pretty dumb, she couldn't even spell properly, her memos were a laughing stock throughout the department. But she'd managed to endear herself to that creep, so she wasn't that thick. Ron was a bumbling old deputy who did as he was told.

For god's sake, the self-importance of the man. This email must have ruined the last week of the holiday for everyone who'd read it. She felt sorry for the staff who'd gone away for the holidays, they'd be coming back to an awful shock. Maybe they'd take a few weeks off too. That email would lower moral and make people sick with worry.

Teaching in an inner-city secondary school was a hard-enough job as it was. The students had so many problems. Most of them were on free school meals, they had crazy, dysfunctional families, mostly unemployed, often suffering from drug and alcohol abuse. Then over the last few years there had been the steady influx of Eastern European children, who struggled to speak English. Her school also catered for visually impaired and deaf children, so the average lesson had to have about five different plans to cater for the different abilities within it.

Class sizes were steadily getting bigger and bigger. In the past there were separate classes for the students who needed help to speak English; but not now. Now they were just thrown in at the deep end. Sink or swim. Invariably they sank. Teachers just didn't have the time or resources to help. Again, in the past you had brilliant support staff in your lessons, often as good as an extra teacher, but not anymore, there wasn't the budget for that. The newcomers were mainly sweet kids, with a much more positive attitude to school than the indigenous population, but they were being set up to fail. She couldn't stand to see their little lost faces as they walked along the crowded corridors, desperate to try and fit in, to make sense of these unfamiliar surroundings.

She was so, so relieved that she wasn't going to have to face that creep tomorrow. For the millionth time it made her realise that she'd made the right decision. She was escaping from a horrible ordeal. *Thank goodness.* Her mobile rang. It was Sophie, 'Hi, are you OK?'

She sounded worried, 'Yes, why what's the matter?'

'We've just had Tom here, he was very upset. What did you say to him?'

'What did *I* say to *him*?' Pamela repeated in shock, 'what do you mean?'

'He wouldn't tell us what happened, but obviously something did.' In the background she could hear Russ say something inaudible, Sophie shouted at him 'Shut up Russ, I'm asking, aren't I?'

'What did he say to you?' Pamela asked,

'He was tearful and weird.'

'Yes, because he is bloody weird.'

'What happened?' Sophie was insistent, which was quite annoying,

'He came around here earlier this morning and insinuated that something had gone on the night he brought me home, as though we had a connection, which we don't. He said, "We did some stuff," which I think sounds horrible.'

'I don't understand.'

'No, neither do I. I can't believe he's gone back around to you and Russ. Last night, when he got back from the pub, he was very strange, he said in a horrible, creepy voice "I've been thinking about you," it was so disturbing. I don't think he's all there, if I'm honest.'

'Why didn't you tell me?'

'I was just ignoring him, I didn't want to talk about it, he's obviously not taking his break-up very well and he's somehow fixating on me, I was hoping he'd get the message and piss off, I've told him about a million times that I'm not interested, he can't seem to take it on board, for some reason.'

'Bloody hell,' Sophie turned to Russ and shouted bad-temperedly, 'I'll tell you in a minute, go away and shut up! So, what happened the night he brought you home?'

'Exactly, I've no bloody idea, and I don't want to know if I'm honest. That was the only good thing going for him, the fact that he'd looked after me and he said he'd stayed in case I was sick, not so he could 'do stuff' to me.'

'Is that what you think happened?'

'I have no idea; I don't want to think about this a minute longer.'

'It's so bizarre,' Sophie went on, 'what does he think me and Russ are going to do?'

'I know, honestly, I just don't need this in my life now. What should I do? How did you and Russ leave it with him?'

'I just said I'd talk to you.'

'Why?'

'I'm not sure, it's like being back at infant school, he's shoved us in the middle...'

Pamela jumped in, 'the middle of what? There's nothing to be in the middle of, are you supposed to persuade me to go out with him? Jesus, if that's the case then it is like infant school!'

'I don't know, god, I'm sorry.'

'Look, can we just forget it? That's what I'm going to do.'

'Good idea, sorry again.'

'You don't have anything to be sorry for, it's my fault for getting drunk and then it's his fault for being a creep!'

'Do you want me to come over?'

'No, thanks a lot, that's so kind, but I don't think he'll bother me again.'

'Ok. I'm so sorry.'

'Don't be daft. Thanks for ringing.'

'Take care, bye.'

Why was he talking about her to *her* friends? It was so strange. She was furious. She was furious and a bit scared. Suddenly her cosy little house seemed exposed, stark. She felt his horrible presence, the house felt sullied, dirty. *Would he come back, had his wife leaving him sent him over the edge? No,* she told herself, *no, he's just suffering and looking for someone to replace his wife.* He was obviously a controlling crazy person, but some woman out there might like that. He'd soon turn his fixation onto someone else.

She was so relieved she'd done her shopping; she could stay home for several days. Oh, except she'd have to visit her dad, she couldn't believe she kept forgetting about him. She got up and made sure that all the doors and windows were locked.

Maybe she should get a locksmith to put a strong lock

on her bedroom door. And a bolt. As a single woman, shouldn't she have a lock on that door anyway. Then she was annoyed with herself. Why should this man change the way she behaved? She shouldn't feel like a prisoner in her own home. But there was a heavy, clumpy feeling in the bottom of her stomach. She felt a horrible sense of dread. *Stop it*, she told herself for the second time that day. Maybe she was the weird one, she was obviously losing it.

Her mobile rang, she jumped, *what if it's bloody Tom?* No, thank goodness, it was her sister, Georgie. She couldn't face talking to her right now. She waited and when it stopped ringing, she texted, "Sorry – I'll call you later xx."

A moment later her mobile rang again, she looked at it, *oh no,* it was a number she didn't recognise. *It was bound to be him.* She shivered, *what was wrong with him?* There was no way she was going to speak to him. She thought, *if I don't answer he may become more fixated, he might get angry.* Then she thought, *so what.* She didn't have to be dictated to by him, he was trying to manipulate her, and it shouldn't freak her out. She didn't answer.

A few seconds later her phone pinged. She was right, it was him, he'd left her a voice message. She didn't want to listen to it. She should just delete it straight away. Then she wouldn't have to deal with his craziness. But he could be just saying sorry. She told herself that she was overreacting and if she listened to the message it would put her mind at ease. If it was a threatening message, she could keep it as evidence, but hopefully it wouldn't come to that. She gave herself a mental shake, he was Russ's boss for goodness sake. She decided to listen to the message. There was a pause, then Tom's voice, 'I'm sorry about earlier, I don't know why I came around. You've made it clear how you feel. I just thought we had a connection, you seemed very keen when I stayed the night. Call me if you want, bye.' That was a very clever message. He mentioned that he'd stayed the night, he said sorry. If he did turn out to be an out and out stalker this message wouldn't help her case. It just sounded like she'd encouraged him to stay the night and that she'd been up for it. Also, he sounded calm and rational. *Well,* she told herself, *he probably was calm and rational.* She was probably just building it out of all proportion.

She went into the kitchen and found some bread in the freezer. She fed it into the toaster. She was going to have something comforting and fattening to eat and then ring her sister. She smothered the toast with butter.

She knew it was bad, but she just needed a fattening fix. *This is the trouble with me*, she thought, *any little thing sets me off kilter and food is my way of dealing with it.* She thought, *I bet Tom's wife put up with loads of this shit during her time with him, I don't blame her ignoring his calls, he'd be constantly bugging her, asking what he'd done wrong.* But it was a bit strange that she hadn't contacted her children. She couldn't imagine ignoring her sons' calls no matter what had happened in her life. As she demolished the buttery toast, she started to feel a bit better. She rang Georgie, 'Hi, sorry about before.'

'No worries. I've just visited dad, he was a bit grumpy,

like you said. He doesn't think he's had a bath all week.'

'Oh no, he mentioned his bath on Monday, but I never thought to check on Wednesday. I'll visit him tomorrow and ask the staff, wasn't there anyone around to ask today?'

'No, it was just the weekend staff - they haven't got a clue.'

'Yeah, you're right, no point asking that lot.'

'Yeah, waste of time. Dad doesn't like any of them.'

'I know.'

'So – tell me what's going on with you?'

'Just tell me about your holiday first and then I'll fill you in on my going's on!'

'Sounds ominous.'

'No, really. Tell me everything.'

'Oh, it's been lovely. Quiet, but lovely. Rach and Jim have the most gorgeous house, it overlooks Lake Windermere, it's just amazing.'

'Wow, I didn't know they lived next to the lake.'

'Yes, they moved there last year.'

'Were their kids' home?'

'No, hence the quiet, but it was so civilised. They had a few friends around for Christmas lunch, and we went to a wonderful party on New Year's Eve, but apart from that it was mainly just us four.'

'Oh wow, what a great way to spend the holidays.'

'Yes, and it snowed! We actually had a white Christmas!'

'It sounds idyllic.'

'It was, I'll show you the photos when we get together.'

'That'll be great. So, it was a much better Christmas

than last year, obviously.'

'Hell yes, no comparison.'

'And did Rich enjoy himself?'

'Yes, he couldn't have been sweeter.' Pamela somehow doubted that, but said nothing, Georgie continued, 'How did the meal go with dad and Anne's family?'

'Oh, ok really, it was a good idea to go out, so no one was stressed, dad was so much better this year.'

'He couldn't have been worse, could he?'

'True.'

'You'll have missed the boys though.'

'Yes, you too?'

'Yes, it was a bit sad, especially not seeing Teddy on his first Christmas, but it was Adam and Hannah's turn to be with her mum and of course the twins are still travelling.'

'Are they still in Sydney?'

'They're actually in Melbourne now, but they're both still working in a bloody awful bar. No sign of a real job I'm afraid. So, tell me, what's going on with you?'

'Well, everything's fine, apart from work, obvs.'

'Oh hell, yes, you poor thing, you must feel sick about it.'

'Yeah, but I've been in touch with Lou and she told me that that wanker said he was 'gunning for me,' at the end of term.'

'No, that's horrible.'

'I know, the idiot.'

'How can he say something like that?'

'I honestly don't know, and he's sent us all the most

appalling email, giving everyone about 100 hours of extra work. But it gets worse...'

'How the hell can this get worse?'

'I know, listen to this - he told everyone that an inspector from the Authority will be observing all my lessons all week.'

'No...' Georgie was horrified, 'he didn't.'

'Yes, he bloody did.'

'He told everyone?'

'Yes.'

'That's absolutely disgusting.'

'I know, can you imagine? I can't even feel upset about it, because I'm just so annoyed.'

'After all these years, it doesn't seem possible.'

'I know.' They both paused, Pamela could hear the shock in Georgie's voice. 'So, you can see why I'm not going back.'

'I can, how awful.'

'And...' Pamela paused ominously,

'Oh no, what else?!'

'This weird guy I met on New Year's Eve is practically stalking me.'

'What weird guy?'

'This man, Tom, he was at Soph's party, he works with Russ, his wife left him before Christmas, he's turning into a complete weirdo.'

'How do you mean?'

'He just won't take no for an answer.'

'Did you do anything to encourage him?'

'No! It's not my fault, well I suppose it is, if I hadn't got drunk at Sophie's it wouldn't have happened.'

'So, tell me everything from the beginning.'

'Well, after Sophie's party, I can't remember coming home, but when I woke up, he was asleep on the floor...'

'Bloody hell.'

'I know, weird right?'

'Well at least he was on the floor.'

'Anyway, I went back to sleep and he'd gone when I woke up, thank god. Then when I called Sophie to say sorry for being so drunk, she told me he'd asked if I wanted his number!'

'Ok.'

'So, I said he should've asked if he could have my number.'

'Good point, and were you interested in him?'

'To be honest I couldn't remember a thing about him, I couldn't have picked him out in a line up! But Sophie said we seemed to be getting along very well, and that he was a nice bloke. He works at Russ's, he's one of the managers apparently. His wife's just left him, after thirty years. Sophie was happy for me to go home with him in a taxi and I was too drunk to care... so... it looked like I trusted him to anyone who saw us together. But it all got very strange this morning, he was just sitting, waiting in his car when I got home, he more-or-less forced me to invite him in for a coffee. Then he stood in my kitchen and intimated that something had happened between us the night he stayed.'

'What do you mean?'

'Well, he said that the night he stayed, 'we'd done stuff.'

'That sounds revolting and is a bloody strange thing to say, but how is that stalking?'

'Well, after Sophie's party, I met him in Costa and he more-or-less asked me out and I had to tell him I wasn't interested. He just can't understand why his wife left him, but I'll tell you what, I bloody can! He's obviously desperate to find someone to replace her... anyway, you know my cut and paste theories.'

'Yes, I do!'

Just like everyone who knew Pamela, Georgie couldn't understand her views on relationships. She'd been on her own for years and it was totally incomprehensible to her sisters. They'd spoken about it on many occasions. 'She might regret her decision when the boys leave home.' Georgie had said,

'She's so stubborn,' Anne had pointed out. Each of them had introduced her to nice single men, but she'd gone out of her way to ridicule all of them. 'No, she's weird,' both Georgie and Anne had agreed.

'Then last night I was around at Sophie's.'

'Oh yes you said you were going – he wasn't there was he?'

'He'd been out with Russ and they both got to the house as I was leaving.'

'Ok.'

'As I tried to get out the front door, he just stood there, right in my way, and then he whispered, 'I've been thinking about you,' in a creepy, bizarre voice.'

'Well, he was probably drunk.'

'That's what I thought, but then, as I said, this morning he comes to my house and stands in my kitchen, talking about the night he stayed over.'

'Bloody hell.'

'I know, I had to let him in, even though I bloody didn't want to, and that's when he started suggesting that we'd done stuff.'

'He sounds awful.'

'I know, right? I mean even if we had, so what? We're not kids, or living in a third world country, it doesn't make us engaged!'

'So, what did you say?'

'I told him to go, which luckily he did, but then Sophie rang me, he'd only gone around there complaining about me!'

'That's so odd. What a strange guy.'

'He also just tried to call me and left a message where he mentioned that I'd seemed keen when he stayed the night!'

'Did he say sorry?'

'Yes, but that's the point, it was a reasonable message, saying he'd stayed the night and I'd been fine with it, so I think he's being a bit clever, if I played it to you or Soph you'd just think it was fine and the police or whatever would know that I'd let him stay the night.'

'You're not thinking of going to the police, are you?'

'No, but if he carries on following me around, I might have to.'

'You don't think it'll come to that, do you?'

'I just don't know. It's weird and annoying, I feel a bit frightened to be honest.'

'Don't feel frightened, he's probably just missing his wife and you've kind of shown that it's going to be difficult for him to move on, he probably thought it would be easy. And you said he's got a good job and that Russ and Sophie like him, so he can't be that bad.'

'Yeah, and Hitler was a vegetarian.'

'Don't bring Hitler into it!' They both laughed.

'I am probably being over the top about it, maybe it's because of work. And it doesn't sound that bad now I've talked to you about it.'

'Could be that you've blown it out of proportion because of work, it's a displacement activity, but listen if you want to come and stay here for a bit that's fine,'

'Ah, thanks, that's kind, but to be honest I'm just going to stay in for a while. Luckily, I went shopping this morning, so there's no need to go out for at least a week! Apart from seeing dad, obvs.'

'Well you can't hide forever.'

'I know, that would be crazy.'

'Look, ring me whenever, ok?'

'Will do. Thanks so much.'

'I hope you don't find this week too dreadful, work-wise.'

'Same here.'

'Right well I'd better get going, we're meeting Frieda and Mike for dinner.'

'Ok, have fun,'

'Will do.'

'Bye.'

'Bye.'

I am over-dramatising the whole situation, Pamela thought, *he is just a weird, sad, lonely man, who's hooked onto me, god only knows why and maybe I wasn't clear enough when I told him I wasn't interested.* That was the trouble, you tried not to hurt someone's feelings – well let's face it – men's feelings - but it was stupid, she needed to be more forceful, she should have looked him in the eye, that day in the café, and shouted 'I AM NOT INTERESTED IN YOU. But, she realised, she could never do that, she wasn't in the business of hurting someone deliberately. But if she'd known how he was going to behave it might have saved a lot of time. *It bloody serves me right for getting pissed and losing control. I must give up drinking. It's just ridiculous. If I'd been sober, I would have seen what an emotional limpet he was.* Alcohol stripped her of all her faculties, including good sense and intuition.

She checked her emails and went on to Facebook for a bit, nothing of interest there. It was boring, she only looked at it to see what her boys were up to. They had both been quiet since getting back from skiing. She checked Instagram. Again, nothing much from her family. The afternoon stretched out ahead of her. She turned the TV on and checked the film channels. She needed something to take her mind off things. Great, '500 days of Summer,' was starting in thirty minutes. She made a cup of tea and thought, *now I've eaten all that toast I can probably have*

some chocolate. I'll be bad today and really good tomorrow.
She lit the fire and settled down to a quiet afternoon, hoping
to stop obsessing about work and Tom.

Later that evening she realised she hadn't spoken to the
boys. She sent them a message to their shared group, 'Hi
guys - sorry we haven't had a chance to talk - hope you are
both doing ok and aren't too worried about going back to
work tomoz - give me a ring some point this week if either
of you get a chance - Love Mum xxx'.

Eventually she received two replies, 'Hi thanks mum
- hope you're feeling ok about tomorrow - talk soon love
Alex xx', and, 'Hi - talk soon Jake xx'.

A Friend request pinged through. Of course, it was
Tom wasn't it. What a prize dick that man was. Well she
wasn't going to reply. As if she'd become his friend. But
she went on his profile, just to see how private he was.
Not private at all, it turned out. She double checked her
settings. Someone looking could only see her profile
picture and nothing else. Relieved that Tom wouldn't be
able to look at her photos she went back to his profile, she
knew she shouldn't, but maybe it would give her a greater
insight into him. There were lots of photos of him and his
wife and family and it still said he was married. Just as
she thought, he was in denial. There were so many photos.
Holidays, various beach and ski scenes, birthday parties,
Christmases. The whole family smiled up at her, looking
cheerful, healthy, prosperous. In happier days, her mum
would've said. The children were good-looking, confident,
pleased with themselves. His wife, though, a little wisp of

a thing, did look a little cowed, a little less pleased with herself than the rest of them. She often appeared to be sneaking a side-glance at Tom. She seemed afraid, seemed to be checking to see what was going on in his dark mind. *Oh, shut up Pam,* she told herself, *stop looking for things that aren't there.* But as she looked more closely, she felt that there was something in his wife's constant expression, something that was hard to define. It did look like fear, the way her eyes didn't quite match her smile, her tilted body language.

She went back as far as she could, all the previous photos looked the same, maybe she'd been planning her escape for years. In all the shots he seemed oblivious to it, obviously. She tried to find his wife's profile, 'Serena Reynolds,' but the search only brought up a couple of Serena's from other countries. She'd probably deleted her account, if she'd had one. Pamela would've loved to talk to her, to get her side of the story. *I'll bet there's a lot that Tom isn't giving away,* she thought.

She put her laptop away. She was in danger of becoming a stalker herself if she wasn't careful. She glanced out of the window; the snow was almost totally gone. According to the weather forecast the snow wasn't coming back for a while and was going to be replaced by rain and high winds. *Great.*

In the kitchen she closed the blinds at the window. Normally she didn't bother, but she had a horrible feeling that she was being watched, not by a benevolent fox, but by an evil presence, not even Tom, but triggered by Tom and his awful despair. It was annoying that she felt so fearful in her own home.

Without thinking she reached for a bottle of wine. She'd had a stressful day, she deserved to wind down, a couple of glasses weren't going to kill her. She chose a nice Malbec and poured it into one of the beautiful crystal goblets she'd inherited from her mum. She took a glug, it was delicious. 'Cheers mum,' she said, as she clinked the glass against the bottle.

That night, she lay in bed, wide awake. She felt sick, her stomach a mound of moaning fat seething under her quilt. She groaned, *why did I have to drink a whole bottle?*

She looked out into the night. There weren't any clouds, the sky shimmered, crystal-clear, decorated with hundreds of shiny white dots. The enormity of it was overwhelming.

She was disgusted with herself, as usual. She had drunk too much. Again. It was so easy to go off track, so much harder to stick to her best laid plans.

She would have to phone school tomorrow and she had written different versions of what she planned to say several times. Some of the things she'd written sounded ridiculous. After all there was nothing, definitively wrong. She couldn't say 'I've got a stomach bug' or 'flu' or 'I've twisted my ankle', because you eventually got over those problems. She was probably never going back. Georgie always said stay as close to the truth as possible. She'd love to say, 'Hi, I'm not coming back because Mac Rutland is a total evil twat, whose one purpose in life is to ruin mine. She finally settled on, 'Hi, this is Pamela James, I'm not well and won't be in today. I'll email my lesson plans to Dom, thanks, bye.' That was ambiguous enough. She wasn't saying what was wrong with her, just that she was ill and wouldn't be in.

She knew she wasn't going to be able to sleep. She lay on her back, staring at the cracks in the ceiling, her eyes wide open, her body tense. Her brain wouldn't slow down. She could see Tom in her mind's eye. He was leaving soggy footprints around her back garden, leering into her kitchen window, evil thoughts on his mind. She had to stop thinking about that fool. He wasn't worth it. He obviously wasn't outside, rationally she knew he wasn't.

Finally, she fell asleep for about five minutes and then was wide awake again. What had woken her up, *did I hear something downstairs?* She lay rigid, listening, *no,* she couldn't hear anything. The house was silent apart from the usual cries and whimpers that always occurred in her old terrace. Usually a comforting sound, but not tonight.

As she lay there, she heard the drip, drip of melting snow and the wind gradually picking up. Gentle at first and then more forceful, rushing around her house, the trees groaning under the force of it. She'd never get to sleep now. Her mind was in overdrive.

She couldn't stop herself touching on memories that were painful, embarrassing. Awful, events from her life that she was not allowed to think about. She couldn't stop. A horrible song was whirling around and around in the background of her thoughts, it just wouldn't be silenced.

She couldn't bring herself to read or go on her laptop or

phone. She didn't want to turn the radio on, it would only be news at this time of night. She could only lay there, at the mercy of her cruel mind. It was two am. Then three am. She got up and went to the loo. She kept all the lights off, again she couldn't help feeling that something evil had started to surround the house. That someone or something was outside staring in. Back in bed she shuddered. Her room was freezing. She was starting to feel heavy headed, *oh no, I'm getting a cold,* she thought, *that would be bloody typical. How long is this night going to last?* She couldn't seem to get warm, her room felt oppressive, a weight was bearing down on her. She hurled herself from side to side, shivering and desolate. She lay there miserable and cold, despising herself. Four am came and went.

Monday 9th January

She finally slipped into a miserable nightmarish sleep, moments later her alarm shook her into a horrible five am dawn. Anxiously she rang work and read out her pre-planned note. She sounded awful, which was quite gratifying. The cold had now totally kicked in, she could barely breathe, and her throat ached.

She emailed her lesson plans to poor old Dom. Bloody hell, what a week he was going to have, sorting everyone's lessons out, assuming other people were off too. There would be others, obviously.

She wondered what the evil Mac would think, he'd probably imagine that she was just avoiding the man from the local authority, he'd be saying to himself, 'Just wait, the second she gets back I'll make her life even worse, she won't know what hit her.' Ha, well at least that wasn't going to happen, not if she could help it.

She was so cold, her whole body felt frozen. She went into the spare bedroom and lugged the heavy quilt off the bed. She lay underneath both quilts, shivering and depressed. Tears stung her eyes. *What am I doing, what am I doing?* The question circled her mind, unanswered, until she finally fell asleep.

At nine o'clock Pamela woke groggily from her belated sleep. Her throat ached, and her limbs felt weak and painful.

She texted her sisters, "Really sorry - can't visit dad

today – full of cold P xx."

Anne would be pissed off, but Georgie would be fine, she'd just had nearly ten days away, so she had a bit of catching up to do. They never visited their dad if they had a cold, if he ever caught it he became so weak. It always went straight to his chest and he was far more likely to fall over.

She looked at her watch and wondered what her stupid boss had said to the Local Authority man. At this time, she would normally have been sitting in the sixth form centre, overseeing private study. She wondered if Louise had told anyone what was going on. Maybe Nicola and possibly Rachel. She didn't blame her; she knew they'd be sympathetic to her plight.

She felt so sorry for whoever was going to take the rest of her classes, especially one group, the year 9 she found so difficult. They were just going to run rings around whoever tried to teach them. There had been no point setting them lesson plans, they wouldn't do a thing.

They were such a weird class, after all these years of teaching she somehow hadn't got to grips with them. Because they'd got rid of five different teachers since September, they felt invincible, no one could cope with them, and they knew it. Kids would just get up and start wondering around the class to talk to their friends, they'd eat sweets, drink pop, drop rubbish on the floor, use their mobile phones. There was no end to how challenging their behaviour was. They'd shout across the classroom, swear, walk out into the corridor and wander off, banging on the doors and windows of other classes, throw things at each other, and more alarmingly out of the window, scribble all over text books and desks, not even attempting the work she set. The list of poor behaviour was endless.

Whatever she'd tried, so far, to curtail this conduct met with blank stares and total disbelief, laughter and derision. But that wasn't the worst thing about the class. The worst thing was, it wasn't *all* the students. Some quieter, well behaved children would just sit there, feeling desperate, knowing that their education was being hijacked and it seemed there was nothing that their useless teacher could do about it. They would look up at her with their big, sad, pleading eyes. They wouldn't dare say anything, as the thugs who were running the class would have beaten them up, but they knew she knew, and it was just awful.

Eventually she would have won, she would have managed to tame them, she just needed time. She'd only just started teaching the class and at the worst time of year.

None of this was helped by the new ethos in the department. In the past you could report this behaviour to the head of department, and the problems would be shared, dealt with collectively. But not anymore. With this new boss the teachers were blamed, not the students. So, you were totally alone. She sighed and turned over.

One good thing; she could recover from her appalling night. If she'd have to go into work today, she'd have been exhausted. She slept for a while, a fitful, anxious, unhappy sleep.

Eventually she managed to pull herself out of bed.

Outside the snow had completely gone, it was a grey,

windy, foul looking day.

She wrapped up in lots of layers and shuffled downstairs. She made herself a Beechams powder and sipped it sadly, feeling sorry for herself. She found a box of tissues and went into the dreary sitting room. She couldn't be bothered to turn the TV on.

She contemplated what her next steps were. She'd have to ring the doctor midweek and make an appointment. She was pretty sure you could have five days off without a sick note. She turned on her laptop and checked her school emails.

Nothing much going on, just a few memos from senior staff about not allowing students out during lessons, telling staff to make sure that they took an accurate register of their class and sent it to the main office within ten minutes of the lesson start. This was especially important in the light of last term's events. The school had been severely criticised when two year eleven and two year ten students had failed to come back to school after morning break. They'd gone into the city and stolen a car, which they subsequently crashed, killing two of the younger boys. It was a total tragedy. The poor parents were devastated. They'd thought their youngsters were safely in school. Questions were raised – how come students could leave school in the middle of the morning and not one teacher had noticed, what safeguarding processes were in place to prevent this from happening? The school had been on the national news - again. No school wants that kind of publicity.

The new head – the one who'd brought Mac Rutland to

the school – had decided that she was going to clamp down on students not wearing the correct uniform. The senior staff had stood at the main gates in the morning and turned away anyone not wearing the exact uniform as stated in the school handbook. Even minor infringements weren't ignored. Parents were in uproar.

The story appeared in all the national newspapers and all the major news channels. The head must've thought she was amazing. 'Look at me, what a tough head I am.'

She'd then made a rule that all the students must stand up when she walked into their classroom. *She was maybe having some kind of breakdown.* Pamela thought. *Delusions of grandeur.*

There was one good thing that happened due to the new uniform rule, several of Pamela's most disruptive students never came back. They were turned away at the gates and either their parents had been so incensed or so unwilling to follow school rules they'd taken their children to other schools in the area. She thought that this was probably an unintended consequence, but it had made her life easier.

There was another email from the creep Mac, sent first thing that morning. He was asking that she attend a meeting with him and the local authority guy after school every night that week. *Ha!* She couldn't help feeling a glow of delight, *sod you, prick face*, she thought with childish hilarity. As poorly and depressed as she felt, the idea that she wasn't going to be there for those awful meetings thrilled her. *In your face, you evil little creep.*

She made herself a de-caff coffee, but she couldn't face

food. Her throat ached. She may as well just go back to bed and wait for the Beechams to kick in.

She lay down under the double quilts and tried to get back to sleep. Her chest felt tight and breathing was painful. *Bloody hell, this is my punishment,* she thought. It served her right; she had planned to be ill and she'd become ill.

Once again, her mind seemed unable to slow down. Her thoughts ranged up and down, around and around, spinning her into near total depression. And she just couldn't find a comfortable position, it was all so useless. She tried to cheer herself up by thinking about her promise to join a gym by the end of the week, but instead it just seemed like a futile and pointless waste of time. She felt pathetic, washed out, sick.

She turned the radio on. It was 'The Archers.' She couldn't listen to that. She had to get up. There was no point lying in bed feeling sorry for herself. She needed to have another Beechams.

Downstairs she checked the post. There was the usual selection of crappy junk mail and letters to the previous occupant strewn on the mat. As she picked them up, something caught her eye, there was a small blank white envelope, no stamp or address. She opened it, inside on a scrappy bit of paper someone had typed, 'You are nothing, you are worthless, stop thinking you are something, bitch.' Pamela practically burst out laughing, *whoever wrote this doesn't know me very well,* she thought. *As if I think I'm something!* It was obviously from Tom, what a fool. He must have nothing better to do than send evil notes to people. He was a weird one, honestly. She'd keep hold of it, just in case. She realised that he must've come around before work, or during the night. Maybe he had been outside, malevolently wandering around her house, like he had in her fevered imagination. Weirdly it didn't feel as frightening as she'd imagined. It just made him more pathetic. She was going to show this to Sophie and Russ, this would prove that he *was* behaving strangely. She realised that they thought she had somehow got it wrong, that someone as seemingly attractive and successful as Tom didn't need to fixate on one person. Honestly, it was bloody annoying.

It was two-thirty pm. Some poor bugger would be standing in front of her awful class.

Thank goodness it's not me, she thought as she went into the kitchen to make another Beechams. She still couldn't face food.

She brought the quilts downstairs and lay on the settee. She flicked through a few channels and left it on some old re-runs of Buffy. She turned the sound right down and blankly stared at the screen. Nothing was going in. So, this was what her life was going to be like from now on, just an empty void filled with re-runs of old TV programmes. She thought she'd be better off dead. And what about that note, what kind of person wrote something like that, anonymously, then risked being seen posting it, it confirmed everything she thought about Tom.

It was annoying that she couldn't talk to Sophie until after work tonight. She felt depressed and alone, he was making her life so miserable. *Don't be so melodramatic,* she told herself. *Don't give him the satisfaction of thinking about any of it. He isn't worth it.* But she couldn't help it, she could see his crazy face staring at her. Despite the Beechams her throat throbbed, and her head ached. She couldn't breathe through her nose. It was awful. But at least she was warm now, it had taken so long to warm up during the night.

She reached for her laptop. She went onto Facebook for a bit, nothing much going on, just some new photos from friends, making snowmen, kids playing in the snow, the usual. Then she looked at her list. She had done some de-cluttering so that was good. She hadn't joined a gym, but she had at least visited one. She hadn't thought about getting a new job but she couldn't apply for anything else whilst she was off sick. It was a strange feeling. If only she'd applied for another job last term, along with almost everyone else.

She thought about all the former English teachers starting their new jobs today. It was going to be hard for them, but at least they'd escaped from the crazy Mac. But going to a new school was also risky. You couldn't be sure there wasn't someone just as bad or worse. But at least they wouldn't have to face Mac anymore. His inconsistencies, his vindictiveness, his cruel, belittling management style.

She went onto the TES website. There were a few English posts in her area, but all at rougher schools. Typical. And anyway, how could she apply for anything when the person writing her reference thought she was totally crap.

She wouldn't have a chance. It was appalling that someone as disgusting as Mac could affect her whole future. It wasn't fair that someone so evil had so much power.

I mustn't think about it anymore; she forced her mind back to her list. She wasn't doing a great job of sticking to her diet, this weekend from Saturday night had been a write off. But at least this cold had robbed her of her appetite, so that might make up for it.

She thought she'd better start planning her lessons for the rest of the week. That at least would be something productive to do.

She managed to find her planner, shoved down the side of the settee. Tuesday was an awful day. Period 1 and 2 Year 9. Break. Period 3 Year 8, period 4 Year 7, lunch. Period 5 and 6 Year 7. It was a miracle that she'd managed a whole term with a timetable like this. Break was a joke, you literally had fifteen minutes and by the time you'd kept one class in the next were arriving. You couldn't leave your classroom, let alone get a drink. And forget about going to the loo, that was a luxury you just didn't have time for.

Lunchtime was no better, you were able to tidy the classroom, clean the board and write up the lesson objectives just in time for the next class to come crashing in. You literally didn't have time to drink, eat or chat to a grown up. In the olden days you could go into the staff room, eat a proper lunch, chat to your colleagues, go to the toilet, all the things normal people expect to do at work.

They'd even re-designed schools without staff rooms, now each department had a 'Work Room.' Thanks a lot.

Also, her school had instigated a new policy where you weren't allowed to sit down after taking the register. Senior teachers would walk past your classroom and peer in, making sure you were following the rules. It felt like a flipping work camp. It was knackering standing up for five hours straight, but the senior teachers didn't know that. They'd managed to get out of teaching altogether.

And now you couldn't retire until you were 68! Bloody hell, how would anyone manage to last until that age.

She realised her planning was going to take her hours. She looked at her watch, it was three pm. She'd now officially been off work all day. She couldn't believe how quickly it had gone. She wondered what the local authority man had been doing. Mac had probably found someone else to pick on. She hoped it wasn't Lou, but that was unlikely, he seemed to adore her.

She sent a quick text to her, "Hi - hope today wasn't too bad - thinking about you love Pam xx."

She worked on planning for several hours. It was crazy how long everything took, but she forced herself to continue, and finally she had plans ready for the rest of the week.

At five pm she made herself another Beechams, double checked her work and saved it. She wouldn't send it until tomorrow morning after she'd rung school again.

She had about an hour to kill before Sophie came home from work. Her front doorbell rang, *there's no way I'm answering that*, she thought, *whoever it is will just have to go away.* She was still in her pyjamas and ill and she certainly didn't fancy answering her door in that shape. If it was someone she knew, they'd call her on her mobile.

Luckily, she hadn't bothered opening the curtains, so they couldn't see her through the sitting room window. Even if she'd been dressed, she wouldn't have answered the door, she had a phobia about anyone calling on her unannounced.

She hoped it wasn't that stupid Tom. No, he'd posted that note as a parting shot, she was pretty sure of that. The bell continued to ring. Bloody hell, couldn't they take the flipping hint? She then heard knocking at her back door.

She lugged herself upstairs, hoping not to be seen. She peered out from behind the curtains. She couldn't see anyone, thank goodness, whoever it was must have gone.

She sheepishly went back downstairs. When she was sure the coast was clear she looked into her porch to see if they'd left a note. No, there was nothing there. A horrible thought struck her, *what if it was my evil boss?* No, she couldn't imagine him calling around, it would look very bad for him if he did, but he was renowned for doing unconventional things. This might be right up his street. Now he might think she wasn't home. Well, so what, what could he do? For all he knew she could be staying with family until she was well again. But her mind went into paranoid overdrive.

She remembered that recently a teacher had rung in sick on a training day and then went to the airport to fly off on holiday. She was seen by a lunch time supervisor, who was also going on holiday. She got reported to the authority and was promptly sacked. Now she wished she'd answered the stupid door. It would have been obvious to anyone that she was in a bad state. She was such a bloody fool. She hated herself. *Why can't I be like a normal person, someone who doesn't cower and hide when something this simple happens?* She felt weak with annoyance. She hated herself so much. She lay back on the settee and wished for death.

Later that evening she got a reply from Lou, "Hi - hope you're feeling ok - Mac freaking out you not being in - he got me to one side and asked if I'd heard anything! Course said no - acted innocent - he was not amused! Ha! Serves him right! Take care - call anytime Lou x."

So, he must be thinking he'd frightened her, maybe he realised he'd gone too far with all the emails about being observed and so on.

She texted back, "Thanks Lou - what a dick he is! Glad I've worried him – the least I can do - were many others off ill? xx."

She replied, "Yes! Sabira, Janet and Rowanna! He's chasing all the girls away! Poor Dom was running around like the proverbial – 6 new staff too – it was outright bedlam! X."

"So sorry - I hate to think of you guys suffering x'.

'Forget it - let's hope the stupid senior staff finally see how incompetent he is, and he gets sacked! x."

"Fingers crossed! xx."

She felt a bit strange, what did it mean, was he worried? Probably just angry. She'd made him look bad, that was the thing. He'd been embarrassed in front of the local authority man.

He probably knew it didn't look good to the senior staff. Pamela was never off - hadn't taken a day off in years, and the powers that be knew that. He must know that too, despite being new. So, he had assumed she'd be there and was amazed when she wasn't.

Also, he was probably looking forward to lording it over her, making her look like an incompetent idiot in front of the whole department.

He'd easily be able to poison the inspectors mind. She'd seen him do it, just a sad shake of the head after a lesson observation. A comment like, 'Yes I know that looked ok, but you haven't seen the whole picture.'

She couldn't fight the unease and dread that was beginning to seep into her body. She felt sick. She had embarked on a frightening path that would lead who knew where.

She'd always worked, right from the age of sixteen. She'd gone back to teaching when both her boys were just a few months old. Now she was becoming one of those people whom she'd despised as a younger teacher. *Well, what can I do?* she thought despairingly. She always knew she was going to feel dreadful at the start of term. And she did.

She thought about what she was going to say to her doctor, she was dreading the conversation. She should just tell the truth; that a vile new boss was making her life a misery and was trying to get her sacked. She just needed to tell the doctor how she felt. She literally felt unable to face work, that was the absolute truth. It wasn't the badly-behaved kids or the bureaucracy or the hours and hours of marking and planning, she'd coped with that for years. No. It was just one evil man.

Maybe the doctor would think she was going mad, that she was having a psychotic episode. Well fair enough. If that's what it took to get time off, so be it. Anyway, she knew enough teachers who were off with stress. Doctors must have at least one teacher a week come to them and say, 'I can't go back, please don't make me.' Like a child pleading to their mum. It was awful, it really was. Right now, Pamela couldn't see one positive in the whole situation.

Sophie would probably be home. She quickly texted her, "Hi - give me a call when you get a chance P xx."

She was sure this note would prove to Sophie and Russ that Tom was a complete nut-job. *But what if they don't think Tom sent the note? Don't be ridiculous,* she told herself, *who else could it be from?* She didn't think she had any enemies. It wasn't likely to be a student or her boss. No, it had to be from him. If only she could talk to Tom's wife, *I bet she wouldn't be the least bit surprised at this weird behaviour.*

Sophie texted back, "I'll be free in about an hour – shall I call then x?"

"Yes, great xx." She added a smiley face emoji for good measure.

She still didn't feel like eating but forced herself to have some tomato soup. Just as she finished eating Sophie called, 'Hi, how did today go?'

'Pretty awful actually.'

'You sound dreadful, are you putting on being ill or are you really ill?'

'Why would I pretend to be ill to you, you numpty!'

Sophie laughed raucously, 'True! So, you've really got a cold?'

'Yes, I feel appalling, typical isn't it? I think I wished it on myself.'

'Don't be daft, that's impossible. So, today was as bad as you thought it was going to be.'

'Probably worse.'

'Bloody hell. Have you heard from anyone at school?'

'Just Lou, she said that Mac cornered her and asked about me, not sure how to take that to be honest.'

'Well it might mean he's feeling a bit pressured, I mean you never took a day off in the past, did you?'

'Only on very rare occasions, remember when I had shingles? I still went in and had to be sent home! I so hope the senior staff realise that it's not normal for me to be off, oh and it wasn't just me, there were another three English teachers off today. And with six teachers leaving the department last term, surely alarm bells are ringing?'

'They probably are, but maybe they don't know what to do?'

'I s'pose. Oh well, I'll just have to take it one day at a time and hope for the best.'

'What, like hope he gets the sack?'

'That would be perfect.' They laughed. 'Well enough

about me, how was your day?'

'Fine, nothing much going on. It's like we'd never been away.'

'It's always the same after Christmas, isn't it? You have all that hype and then it's back to earth with a bang.' Pamela hesitated before saying 'By the way, I got a strange note through my letterbox today.'

'Oh yes, what did it say?'

'Let me just find it, right, here it is.'

'Ok.'

Pamela read the note to Sophie, keeping her voice neutral, trying to underplay it. 'OMG, what kind of a weird note is that?

'I know, it's bizarre isn't it?'

'Who do you think it's from?'

'Well, I think I've ruled out ex-pupils, for a start I live nowhere near school, and even the most committed and angry kid wouldn't bother to come all the way here, and, to be honest, I don't think I've ever pissed a student off that much.'

'What about Derek?'

'No, he's a wanker as we both know, but, after all these years, why would he send me a note like this? I haven't spoken to him much since my mum died. Also, it's not his style.'

'No, I don't suppose it is. Have you annoyed your neighbours recently?'

'Not that I can think of, I don't have much to do with them, we all just keep ourselves to ourselves.'

'So, who could it be?'

Bloody hell Soph, Pamela thought, *wasn't it flippin obvious,* but she said, 'I'm not too sure, someone with a grudge for some reason.' There was a pause before Sophie said

'You don't think it's from Tom, do you?'

At bloody last, Pamela thought, but she feigned a slight note of surprise as she answered 'Tom? Well he has been behaving slightly unhinged, I mean, you know him better than me...'

'Not really, we never had that much to do with him, until he split up with his wife.'

'Well obviously Russ works with him, maybe he has a better idea about what he's capable of?'

'Maybe, when he gets in, I'll ask what he thinks.'

'Ah that's good, thanks Soph, it is a bit unnerving, nothing like this has ever happened to me before.'

'No, well why would it?'

'I know, it's just so awful.' Pamela felt a catch in her throat, *don't cry,* she thought, *for god's sake don't cry.* She'd managed to shrug it off all day but talking to Sophie made her feel sad for herself, she didn't deserve to get notes like that. 'I'm sorry, I s'pose I'm feeling so emotional with work and this horrible cold.'

'Look, try not to worry. I'll ask Russ what he thinks and then maybe ask him to have a word with Tom?'

'No, don't do that. Russ works with him; you never know what might happen.'

'I'm sure he could find out what's going on in a tactful

way.'

'No, honestly Soph, just leave it. It's not worth it, if it was Tom, I don't think he'll do anything else, he was just annoyed I suppose. I'm sure he'll back off, I mean I've not shown him the least bit of attention, well apart from New Year's Eve, obvs, that'll teach me to get so flippin drunk!'

'Don't beat yourself up, shit happens.'

'Yes, it bloody does!'

'Look are you going to be ok, do you want to come up here for a bit?'

'Ah thanks, but no, I don't want to give anyone else this awful cold and it's probably not a good idea to go out for a while, except maybe to the doctors and to visit dad.'

'Don't be daft, you are allowed to leave the house, even when you're off sick.'

'I know, but it doesn't feel right, somehow.'

'Anyway, it's bloody freezing out, so for now stay at home, stay wrapped up well and enjoy the peace and quiet.'

'I will. Thanks, Soph, it's been lovely to talk to you.'

'And you. Take care, ring me if you need anything, I'm only minutes away.'

'I know, thanks again, bye.'

'Bye my love.'

Honestly, I'm such an idiot, why am I letting this upset me? She made a final Beechams and was about to go up to bed when she realised, she needed to put the bin out. She put her boots on and went out in her dressing gown, hoping no one would see her.

It was dark and wild outside, the wind cut through her,

freezing her to the bone. She struggled to push the bin into place, finally propping it against the wall, sure it would be blown over by morning.

She went to bed, feeling totally wretched. *Things would be brighter in the morning, they had to be,* she thought. She lay awake for a long time. Her mind wouldn't calm down. She was worried about school, about Tom, about her shitty life. When will things get better, when can she start living instead of simply existing? Going into work with that awful man every day was bloody awful, but it beat this feeling.

Tuesday 10ᵗʰ January

She woke up at four am, cold and shivery. She felt hopeless and alone. The outdoor light flashed on and off beneath the bedroom curtains. She could hear someone walking around downstairs, quite clearly, quite distinctly. She sat bolt upright. Her skin tingled with terror, she felt clammy and weird, her heart beat crazily.

She grabbed her mobile, she should ring 999. *Don't be stupid,* she told herself, *you're just hearing things. It's an old creaky house, and very windy, that's all. But what if someone's down there? If only I'd bought a lock for this wretched bedroom door.*

She thought she could hear someone creeping up the stairs. *Fuck this,* she thought, she stood up and went to her bedroom door, flung it open and shouted, 'Who's there?' Silence. She shouted again, 'Who's there?' Silence. Then, faintly at first, she heard a banging sound that got louder as she crept downstairs. The hairs stood up on her arms and neck, she had to force herself to keep going, ever instinct told her to turn and run back upstairs.

As she approached the kitchen, she saw that her back door was swinging crazily in the wind. Her heart stopped and her stomach seemed to plunge onto the floor. *Oh my god*, she thought, *has someone been in the house, or did I forget to lock the door when I put the bin out?* She hadn't checked before she'd gone to bed. *Why was it open?* She was sure she'd closed it *and* locked it. She must have been so distracted, not thinking about what she was doing. Nothing seemed out of place. No one had been there. She must have left the door partially open. *Just stop being an idiot*, she told herself, *just calm down and stop freaking out.* She peered out into the garden. The outdoor light was switching itself on and off again in a demented dance. Distorted trees lit up and shut down, their long arms reaching for her. Branches flashed and faded.

Jesus, she shuddered, everything felt so terrifying at night. She slammed the door and locked it. *It's just the wind,* she told herself, *just the wind.* She went back to bed, and lay under the covers, sweating and shivering in turn.

She may as well stay awake until she phoned school. She wondered if maybe Tom had been downstairs and when she'd shouted, he'd run away. *Don't be crazy,* she told herself, y*ou're just being ridiculous. Obviously, he wasn't down there. Why would he be?* She remembered that this had happened before, last summer in fact, she'd gone away for the weekend and when she got back, she'd found the back door wide open. She couldn't understand it; nothing was missing and there was no evidence of anyone coming into the house. Another time some friends had stayed over and when she came downstairs the door was open, swaying gently in the breeze. She thought that maybe one of her guests had been sleep walking, but again maybe she'd forgotten to close the door properly. So, it was entirely possible that she'd done the same again last night.

Thank goodness I didn't ring the police, she thought,

they'd probably lock me up. It was five am. Time to ring school. After leaving the brief message she set her alarm for eight am. She lay down and prayed for sleep.

When she woke, she felt blurry and strange. The events of the night already slipping into a haze of unreality. A feeble sun struggled through the clouds.

She sent her lesson plans to Dom, then phoned the doctors surgery. Engaged. She dialled another twenty-five times. Eventually, she got through to the automated message. She hung on for another fifteen minutes. *Good job it's not an emergency,* she thought.

Finally, an aggravated human voice barked out, 'Yes?' *Bloody hell talk about customer service,* she thought.

'Hello, my name is Pamela James, I'd like to make an appointment with one of the doctors please.'

'Is it an emergency?' The voice asked irritably.

'No.'

'Right well we've nothing left for today, it'll have to be Friday.'

'That's fine.'

'Four pm?'

'Yes.'

'That'll be with Dr Banerjee.'

'Ok.'

'What's the appointment for?'

'Erm, well, I'd rather not say, it's personal.'

'Fine, goodbye.'

The phone went dead before Pamela could say another word. She wondered why people went into that job when they clearly hated other humans. Why work in a place where you had to interact with others when you couldn't stand interaction, maybe it gave them power over people, they had license to be completely awful and that's what made their job worthwhile.

Although she was feeling a bit better, she made herself another Beechams and went back to bed. She wondered if last night had even happened, had the back door been open, had she heard footsteps downstairs? Maybe Tom had taken some of her keys and made copies and was now able to enter her house whenever he wanted. *Don't be ridiculous*, she told herself. *You are just being crazy, of course he hasn't taken the keys, what a stupid thought.* Nonetheless she decided to ring a locksmith and get a lock on her bedroom door, it was probably a bit over the top, but it would make her feel safer.

It was annoying that she was feeling so insecure. She'd obviously left the door a bit open when she'd put the bin out. It was as simple as that. She just had to stop worrying. Her fretful thoughts gradually subsided, her body finally relaxed.

She woke feeling disgusting. Lifeless, stupefied. She didn't have the strength to get out of bed. She felt confused, lost. Her sickly walls were closing in on her, hot, stale, suffocating.

The usual ghosts surrounded her, palms pressed together, fearful. She was delirious, burning up. She was wet and sweaty and couldn't seem to shake this awful pathetic feeling.

A dark shadow loomed around her, claw-like hands pressed down, pinning her to the bed. She tried to move. A high-pitched note was splitting her ear drums. Someone flung her bedroom door open and stalked into the room. It brought with it a hot stink of foul air. She tried desperately to move. She was paralysed, terrified, her whole body was being pressed to the bed by an intense force. She tried and tried to move. She could feel her heart beating, frenetically, out of control. She must be dreaming, she had to wake up, she desperately tried to open her eyes, tried to move, to become part of the real world again.

Time seemed to stop; it had lost all significance in this semi nightmare state. Her life was slowly sinking away. A different sound suddenly stabbed her brain, gradually her mind surfaced from the deep void, it pieced together a feeling, a sensation, then a thought, *my mobile*, she was wrenched back into the real world.

'Hello,' she murmured.

'Hi Pam, it's me, bloody hell, you sound dreadful.'

'Yes, I'm still full of cold.'

'Are you taking anything for it?

'Just Beechams, but they're making me bit delirious.'

'Oh, you poor thing. I was just ringing to see if you were able to visit dad tomorrow, but you can't, obviously.'

'No, I'm sorry, if he got this cold it would be the death of him.'

'You're right. If you don't get any better, you should go to the doctors.'

'I've got an appointment on Friday, but it's about being

off work, not having a cold. They'll just say it's viral anyway, you know what they're like.'

'I know but if it goes to your chest it could be nasty. What do you mean you're delirious?'

'I've been having that horrendous experience where you think you're awake but you're actually not, do you ever get that?'

'I don't think so, what happens?'

'You feel like there's somebody in the room, a horrible evil presence, it's crap. And last night I thought someone was creeping about downstairs and when I got up and went down my back door was wide open.'

'Oh no, that's terrifying.'

'I know, but to be honest, I think I can't have closed it properly when I put the bin out.'

'Look, why don't you come and stay with us for a bit, I can look after you.'

Bloody hell, people were constantly asking her to come and stay with them, everyone around her must think she was a feeble idiot, it was a bit insulting to be honest. She was grown up, not a kid. She was about to say something to that effect but managed to stop herself. Georgie was only being kind. She had to stop seeing the worst in everyone.

'That's so sweet, but I'll be fine.' She resisted the urge to tell Georgie that she was going to get a locksmith in to fit a lock on her bedroom door, it would only panic her and make her more insistent that she come and stay.

'Well you don't sound fine, you're having mad delirious dreams, you're ill and you're forgetting to lock and close doors!'

'I know it sounds bad, but honestly, truly, I'm fine!'

'Well I'm glad you're going to the doctors on Friday, especially if you aren't any better.'

'But I'm panicking about what I'm going to say.'

'Just tell the truth, you won't be the first person stressed out by their boss.'

'It just seems so pathetic though, doesn't it?'

'No, don't be ridiculous, of course it doesn't. Believe me, the doctor will have seen it all before.'

'Yes, I know. But I feel like a total, utter failure.'

'Well stop thinking like that, you're my sister and I know you're not a failure. It's just your stupid boss, he'll be caught out soon enough, believe me.'

'I hope so.'

Georgie sighed, 'It's an awful situation isn't it? if only that blasted man hadn't come to your school.'

'I know, but he did, there's nothing any of us can do.'

'True, but we can still be furious about it.'

'Lou texted and told me that he's freaking out about me being off and there are three other people off sick, so thank goodness it's not just me.'

'That's good at least.'

'Yeah I think he must've looked stupid in front of the local authority guy.'

'Good, serves him right, evil creep.'

Pamela sighed; she didn't want to waste another breath on her stupid boss. 'How's dad?'

'Mainly fine, but his bloody underpants keep going

missing and do you know the last time they changed his trousers?'

'Not sure, why?'

'Well he was wearing that grey pair; they were dirty and I'm sure he was wearing the same pair when I went on holiday.'

'No, that can't be right. But I'm not great at noticing things like that, now I think about it, he did look a bit unkempt last week, his hair hadn't been combed and he did look a bit grubby.'

'Well it's awful for him. Mum would go mad.'

'Yes, she would. Have you said anything?'

'No, I was going to talk to the manager, but she'd gone.'

'Does he seem bothered?'

'Yes, about his underpants, but I don't think he's noticed how grubby his trousers are.'

'Poor dad.'

'It's not bloody good enough, the money he's spending to be there, you'd think the least they could do would be to change his trousers and put his flipping underpants back after the laundry.'

'I know, they don't seem to have any system in place.'

'Exactly, also today he had a completely different duvet cover to the ones we bought him. This one was ancient and grotty; it makes me so mad.'

'Yes, but it's always going to be a compromise isn't it?

'I know but these are simple enough things to get right.'

'True.' Pamela started to cough,

'Bloody hell, you do sound terrible, right I'll let you go.

Get some sleep and call me later in the week, don't worry about seeing dad, me and Anne will sort it.'

'Are you sure? I just feel so bad...'

'Of course I'm sure, stop feeling guilty and get better.'

'Oh my god, I forgot to tell you I got a horrible note yesterday.'

'A note?'

'Yes, I'm not sure where it is now, but it said something like - you're worthless - bitch you think you're so good - you're nothing...' Georgie interrupted her,

'Just a minute – you got an actual note saying that?'

'Yes, it was typed on a scruffy bit of paper and posted through my letterbox!'

'That's awful, it's obviously from that appalling Tom isn't it?'

'Who else?'

'That man is deranged.'

'I know.'

'Have you told Sophie?'

'Yeah, she was annoying though, when I told her about it, she suggested it had come from anyone else but him, she seems to think he's a great guy, I don't understand it.'

'But it's bloody obvious it's from him, who else would be so weird?'

'Exactly.'

'How do you feel about it?'

'Well at first I thought it was funny but later I got upset, it was a bit of a shock if I'm honest.'

'What is wrong with him? Has he nothing better to do

with his time?'

'He's not coping that's for sure, his ego has had a big fat kick in the balls and he's chosen to pick on me for some reason and let's face it, I'm the last person he should've chosen! But I'm sure he got the message on Sunday; I think this'll be the last I hear from him.'

'I bloody hope so. You poor thing.'

Pamela sighed, 'It'll be fine, at least he's showing his true colours.'

'Yes, you saved yourself from a bloody nutcase!'

'Thank god!'

'Right well you try and get some rest and stop worrying about everything.'

'I'll try.'

'Ok love, see you soon, ring me anytime, bye.'

'Thanks, I will and sorry again about dad, bye.'

She googled local recommendations for locksmiths. A couple of names came up. Right, she'd feel a lot better when she had a lock on her bedroom door. Even though part of her felt stupid, *what will my boys and sisters think? Shut up*, she told herself, *stop worrying about what other people think.* She rang the first number and left a message on the answer phone. She got through to the second person, explained her situation and arranged for them to come over on Friday at two pm. She added a reminder on her phone. She knew she was probably just being paranoid, but better safe than sorry. She was always hearing about poor old pensioners being broken into and beaten up. So far she'd been lucky. *Imagine leaving my back door wide open. What a silly cow. And I wasn't even drunk last night.*

She went into the kitchen, she probably should eat something, but again she felt too ill to bother. The weak winter sunlight had gone and the kitchen was dreary and dark.

She went upstairs with her quilts and got back into bed. She couldn't even be bothered to watch anything on her laptop. But her mind couldn't, wouldn't shut off, she started to panic. *Have I left the doors unlocked, or worse - open?*

She dragged herself out of bed and staggered downstairs. All the doors and windows were locked. She stared out of the kitchen window into the gloom. The outdoor light had burnt itself out. Suddenly she could see a red pair of eyes staring at her. She went cold, the hairs on her neck prickled and she was burning up. She closed her eyes and willed the apparition to go away. *It's just my mind being ridiculous,* she thought, *for goodness sake, what is wrong with me? Maybe I am going mad, maybe this is it, finally it's happened.*

When she opened her eyes, the vision had gone. She took a sharp knife from the cutlery drawer and put some chairs in front of the back door, if anyone tried to get in she'd hear them.

Back upstairs she lay down, feverish and weird. She lay the knife down on her bedside table. *If only I had somewhere to hide, a panic room of some sort*, she imagined a locked room, padded and safe. *Wasn't there a film about that?* She tried to remember, but her frenzied mind was too confused to focus in on anything.

She woke several hours later; she could hear the chairs in the kitchen scraping along the tiled floor. *Jesus, this is it, I'm going to murdered in my own bed.*

She fumbled for the knife and slowly crept downstairs in the dark, she thought *I'm not going to shout this time, I'm not going to warn them I'm coming.*

She crept through the sitting room; her knife dramatically held out in front of her. Even in her fear she realised what a comic and crazy person she must look. She leapt through the kitchen door, brandishing the knife in front of her. She possibly screamed, later she couldn't remember if she had or hadn't, she turned the light on - the chairs hadn't moved. She practically fainted with relief.

What the hell is wrong with me, why am I hearing these things? Pamela couldn't understand it; it made no sense.

Back in bed she went on her phone and opened YouTube, she found eight hours of thunder, rain and wind. So what if someone came into her room and murdered her, she wouldn't hear them coming and that felt more like a choice than staying awake half the night worrying. The sound was soothing and intense at the same time.

She fell asleep and dreamt about being in the war. She was with her boys and they were hiding in a large warehouse, overhead planes droned by, dropping bomb after bomb. They were hit, and she was suffocating. They were joined by other people who turned out to be zombies. They ran away as fast as they could, but she kept falling and the boys had to keep coming back to save her, 'Leave me,' she was screaming at them, 'Save yourselves.'

Wednesday 11ᵗʰ January

She woke up, soaked and terrified. It was five am, she rang school and left her message, then hit send on the email with all her work for the rest of the week. May as well, they'd have got the message by now that she wasn't going to rush back in, also Lou might have privately told Dom her situation. He was a good friend and wouldn't tell anyone.

She lay back, exhausted, inert and feeble, asking herself when this was going to end; this sick, delirious, disgusting feeling. If only nights would go back to normal.

She felt weak and fevered. She couldn't shake off the feeling that she had wished this illness upon herself.

If only she was a child again, her mum would walk in, put her hand on her head and utter soothing words. She would bring her a cup of warm rosehip syrup and stay with her whilst she slowly sipped the thick soothing drink.

Pamela's eyes filled with tears at the memory of her lovely mum. Just knowing that she would never see her again was more than Pamela could bear.

Her mum had had an unhappy childhood and she'd been determined to make sure her own children didn't suffer the same fate. She had always put their needs first. They'd been spoilt, she supposed, but she would always be grateful for the love and kindness she'd been showered with. They had all grown up strong and independent women. Or at least Pamela used to be strong and independent, maybe losing her mum was the reason her life was trailing off into misery.

She slipped in and out of a feverish and uncomfortable sleep. She finally came around. It was eight am. It was only at times like this that she realised how alone she was. *But that's a choice I've made,* she reminded herself.

The chairs were exactly where she'd left them. She shuddered, the house felt cold, hostile. She turned the heating on and made herself another Beechams.

She sat in the sitting room. Feeling vacant. Strange. Fearful. Her life seemed to be spiralling out of reach, nothing made any sense. Her mind was soggy, despairing. She could hardly breathe. Her lungs were painful and weak. If only this was a normal day, if only she was about to set off for work. If only she didn't have so much time, alone, to think about everything. Work was never something she'd loved, but it had given her a purpose, a shape to mould her days around. Without it she was lost.

She flicked through the TV channels. There was nothing on. She opened her laptop. *Can I be bothered to look at Facebook? No.* She looked at her phone. No messages from anyone.

The day stretched ahead of her, endless, aimless. She'd had no idea how much work had grounded her, given her a reason to be alive.

Her phone pinged, it was Sophie.

"Hi - hope you are ok – Tom was around last night – we had an interesting convo re you – will call later x."

For goodness sake, what now? Why are Sophie and Russ talking to Tom about me, what was the point? It was so infuriating. She'd thought that note had been his final nasty act, but no, no, *he had to go around to Sophie's and be a big bitch.* She thought she'd finally got through to Sophie the last time they spoke about Tom, but obviously not. She would have to tell her all over again, it was ridiculous.

She finished her Beechams and tried to think about something else. It was weight watchers tomorrow, she hoped she'd feel well enough to go. She must've lost weight; she'd hardly eaten anything over the last few days. There was always a silver lining. *But what if someone sees me?* She didn't think that was possible. She lived miles away from school and anyway she was allowed to go out, she hadn't said she'd broken her leg or something, she hadn't lied, just said she wasn't well and wouldn't be coming into work. She hadn't signed up to be a prisoner. But it felt wrong somehow.

She checked her school emails; she'd been avoiding looking at them until now. It was all the usual crap. Then she noticed an email from the Head of sixth form, Anwara, asking for her private email address. She answered immediately. She got on well with Anwara, who had given her a gifted and talented group as her form.

Sixth form tutor groups were in demand and you had to be interviewed to see if you were suitable. It made morning and afternoon registration pleasant, instead of a battlefield. After years of horrible lower school tutor groups, she'd finally risen to the dizzy heights of being a sixth form tutor.

Pamela had been feeling awful about abandoning her lovely tutor group and she was feeling guilty that she was letting Anwara down, betraying the faith that had been shown in her. Almost straight-away Anwara sent her a private email

"Hi Pam, hope you are ok, sorry to ask for your private email – but I think all our school emails are being monitored (the times we live in!) I'm pretty sure I know why you haven't come back, your HoD is mental! I've spoken to the senior staff about him, I keep asking them why everyone in the English Department is leaving or is on sick leave, but they aren't doing anything about him. All the English staff I've spoken to are feeling the same way as you must be. He is so evil! He's making so many people's lives miserable, I can't believe he's getting away with it. If you want to talk to me, please call me on my mobile – I'd be happy to chat anytime. Cheers Anwara X."

Pamela felt such a rush of relief. Of course, she knew it wasn't just her, but the fact that Anwara could see what was happening and wasn't furious with her for being off was so amazing. Especially as she wasn't even in the same department, she taught Business studies. Thank goodness other people could see what was going on. Why didn't the senior staff do something, maybe they couldn't, maybe they were being bullied too?

The ethos of the school had become so toxic, everyone seemed to be afraid to speak out. It felt so nice to know that Anwara was on her side and understood why she wasn't back. At least she had tried to talk to the powers that be, maybe that would do some good.

She replied, "Hi, lovely to hear from you. It's such a

relief to know that at least one SLT can see what's going on in the English department. I feel so guilty about not coming back, especially letting you and my lovely form down. If and when the senior staff realise what's going on, I'd be so happy to come back. Do you think that is totally unlikely? Anyway, thanks so much again – if people like you can see it maybe the powers that be will eventually take note! Thanks so much, Pam xxx."

She'd thought that other departments didn't know what Mac was like, so it felt good to know that Anwara could see what he was doing. But it was typical that most of the senior staff were just ignoring it.

She needed to contact her union and see if there was anything she could do.

She noticed another email from her head of department, addressed to everyone, she felt sick but forced herself to open it.

It was full of his usual bullshit, more-or-less accusing everyone of disobeying his demands. He was just such a vile and disgusting person.

In all her years of teaching she'd never once received an email like this. All the senior staff were cc'd in too, so they could see what he was doing. She couldn't wait to talk to Louise about it. It was probably one person doing something a bit different, but instead of dealing with that lone person he'd sent everyone this email. It made her so mad.

Sickened, she went back to bed. She was woken by her mobile ringing. She was tangled up in her bedsheets, hot and dripping wet. She managed to press the right button. It was Louise, she answered groggily 'Hello.'

'Are you alright? You sound shocking.'

'Yeah, just got the most appalling cold. How are you?'

'Fine, just wanted to touch base. Have you looked at any of your school emails?'

Pamela tried to unscramble her brain, 'err... yes... sorry... just woken up,' her mind gradually un-fogged, 'oh you mean that disgusting lecture from Mac about written warnings and stuff?'

'Yes, the stupid prick, could you believe it?'

'I was pretty shocked and appalled to be honest. Who was he getting at?'

'We think it was one of the supply teachers, but none of us are totally sure.'

'He's such an idiot, why couldn't he just have a chat with whoever was doing it and leave it at that?'

'I know, but that would be far too easy wouldn't it?'

'The bit I don't get is why he cc'd all the senior staff into it, I mean you'd hope they'd be a bit stunned, you just don't talk to members of your department like that, do you?'

'Well no one normal does, anyway.'

'How long can the head turn a blind eye to all of this?'

'I know, she brought him into the school, though, didn't she?'

'Yes, and it would be admitting she's got crap judgement to find fault in anything he's doing. Bloody hell, what a nightmare.'

'I know, also he's constantly sending hand written

messages around, asking for impromptu meetings – every break, lunch, after school and it's not like it's about anything important, just some petty misdemeanour he's noticed in someone's lesson, like Rachel, she's carried on letting her classes read for ten minutes at the beginning of each lesson, oh my god, you'd think she'd stabbed a small child the way he went on about it.'

'That's dreadful, he's not allowed to call extra meetings, is he?'

'He does exactly what he likes.'

'And the ten-minute reading thing was brought in under Jo for very good reasons and he didn't even give us a chance to argue for it, did he?'

They both sighed remembering the lovely Jo.

'Why did she have to leave?' Pamela moaned.

'I know, I can't believe how great the department was when she was in charge.'

'Has anyone told her about Mac?'

'Not as far as I know, we don't want her to feel bad!'

'She bloody should feel bad, leaving us with that man.'

'I know.'

'Has he said anything else about me?'

'Yes, he has actually, he made some sarcastic comment to Dom about the lessons you were sending in.'

'Well he can get lost, they're as good as they're going to get.'

'I don't blame you, honestly it's actually getting worse, if you can believe that.'

'Course I can! Why do you think I'm stuck at home?'

'I know, poor you, try not to worry about it though, there's nothing you can do and let's face it, the longer people are off the worse it looks for mad Mac.'

'I hope so.'

'Oh, and bloody Angela is as much up his bum as ever.'

'Course she is, that way she's shielded from his evil eye.'

'And obvs we're constantly being threatened with Ofsted.'

'When do they think it will happen?'

'Any minute if stupid Mac's to be believed.'

'It's just their way of keeping you on your toes, isn't it?'

'Oh definitely, but it's no way to work, in continual terror!'

'I'm so sorry this is happening; I feel like I've let the department down.'

'Don't be crazy, it'd be the same if you were there, wouldn't it?'

'I s'pose. But I promise I haven't been enjoying my time off!'

'No, I know, plus you're obviously ill!'

'I know... the irony! I've been meaning to ask you - what happened to the guy from the authority, without me to harass?'

'He went off to the maths department!'

'What poor person is he looking at there?'

'I think it's the two teach first kids.'

'Poor sods. I thought they were being trained by school; how can he interfere?'

'Not sure, but he's another one who can probably do what he likes! By the way have you been in touch with the union yet?'

'I'm going to call them today, I just hope they can somehow sort this out for me, I mean I can't even apply for other jobs, can I?'

'I don't think that the school can give you a bad reference though.'

'Really?'

'Well check with the union, but I think they have to look at your work record up until now.'

'Yes, but remember who'll be giving me my reference.'

'Bloody hell, of course, that idiot.'

'He thinks I'm inadequate, what school will touch me now?'

'But it's not true is it? Have you thought about applying to Jo's school? She knows how good you are.'

'That's not a bad idea, I'll give her a call, after all I have genuinely been off ill!'

'Yes, you wouldn't have been in anyway.'

'Well knowing me I probably would've dragged myself in.'

'Yes, I know. Look give Jo a ring and I'll be thinking about other people I know in different schools who can help. I know you'll return the favour when it gets too awful for me!'

'Will do, thanks Lou, it's so lovely to talk to someone normal from that bloody school!'

'No worries, that's what friends are for.'

'Thanks, bye'

'Bye hun.'

If she could get a job with Jo, life would be worth living again. As quickly as her spirits rose, she slapped herself down - there probably wouldn't be a job. What were the chances of a job coming up at Jo's school? Why would there be?

She had nearly told Louise about the private email from Anwara, but thought better of it, it might have caused trouble for her if Louise mentioned it to anyone.

She slumped back into her tangled bed. If only she could start to feel better. Her brain fogged over again, she knew she should get up and phone the union, but not just yet.

She slipped back into sleep. Her fevered brain skidded nightmarishly into half dreams, half nightmares.

It was dark and cold when she finally came around several hours later. Her bedclothes were heaped around her like tangled vipers.

Was she ever going to feel well again? Her head throbbed, and her lungs felt thick and heavy. She sat up and put her head in her hands. She needed something to help her chest. She thought that there might be a tub of Vicks in her bedside cabinet. She peered in, typically the drawer was rammed with all kinds of incongruous crap.

If only I'd started on the upstairs cupboards first, she thought despondently. She rummaged about, then started flinging things out, books, papers, pens, needles, thread, paper clips, old iPods, several ancient mobile phones, various charging cables, packets of paracetamol, Vaseline, old diaries, photos, packs of tissues, a hammer. *For God's sake,* she thought, *what the hell is wrong with me, why can't I either throw things out or sort things neatly, so that when I need something, I can find it easily?* By the time nearly everything was on the floor she realised that there wasn't any Vicks. She found some Olbas oil and put that onto a tissue. She tried to breathe it in, but her nose was completely blocked. She sprinkled some on her chest and hoped for the best.

She lay back, defeated. *If only I'd organised my life when I was well*, she thought. *Why do I always put everything off?* She had a horrible stabbing feeling in her lungs. She took shallow breaths and tried not to move. Her head felt like a stuffed toy, her limbs were weak and trying to breath was torture. *Maybe this is how it ends*, she thought, laying here, surrounded by superfluous odds and ends, rubbish that she'd simply had to keep, as though it was somehow valuable. Once again, the picture of her boys finding her like this filled her with dread. *What would they think? Dear God, let me survive this for long enough to de-clutter my bedroom cabinets.*

Somehow, she didn't think God would care about her problems. She had a pretty poor relationship with him at the best of times, calling upon his help every now and then, but being completely agnostic the rest of the time. She knew she wasn't alone in this, but that didn't stop her from feeling a hypocrite. She felt her chest burning up where she'd dripped the Olbas Oil. It must be doing her some good. She ought to get up soon. *But why, what was*

the point? I must get up and take some more Beechams,
she told herself, but her body was unwilling to co-operate.
Come on, her brain begged, forget it, her body answered.

She'd missed her chance to talk to the union. But
anyway, it would be stupid to call when she felt this poorly,
she'd never be able to take in what anyone said to her. She
would need all her wits about her to make that call.

She wondered what time Sophie would ring. She didn't
want to talk about bloody Tom. *Why the hell is he going
around to my friends?* She thought, *he was obviously
insane. And what did she mean they'd had an interesting
convo, what sort of language was that anyway? Convo –
how weird.*

She picked up her phone and texted the boys, "Hi guys
- how's your week going so far xxx?."

She hadn't talked to either of them this week, but that
was quite common these days. Sad though. She had a fear
of bugging them, seeming needy. Every now and then she
gave in and called one of them, but she would rather wait
for them to call her. That way at least she knew they wanted
to talk to her, and she wasn't interrupting them at important
moments. She'd rather not talk to them when she was
feeling so ill and vulnerable. She always tried to put on a
brave face with them and pretend that everything was fine.

She forced herself to get up. It was freezing. She
wondered if it was going to snow again. The wind was
howling around the house and the windows were being
lashed with debris. She shuddered and quickly put on
woolly tights and several jumpers, topped with pyjamas

and her thick dressing gown.

Downstairs was dark and miserable. She turned the heat up and put on all the small lamps to try to make the house feel cosy. She made some tomato soup and another Beechams.

She felt too ill to light a fire, instead she found an old electric fan heater tangled up with all the other junk under the stairs. She sat on the settee and felt sorry for herself.

As usual there was nothing on TV. She opened her laptop and found a show on Netflix, but she couldn't concentrate. The wind was getting worse.

Her phone pinged, "Hi mum - hope everything is ok with you - all good here Alex Xxx."

She responded, "That's good - call this week if you get a chance m xxx."

"Will do - love you xxx."

"Love you too xxx.."

That cheered her up for a moment. Hopefully he would ring at some point. She wondered if she had any lemon, if she did, she could mix a whiskey and lemon with lots of sugar, but after the Beechams it probably wasn't a good idea. Maybe, if she was still awake in a couple of hours, she could make it then. It would probably help her sleep through the night. Her throat and chest were starting to feel better, the drugs were kicking in, thank goodness.

Her phone pinged again, "Hi - all super fine here – hope you good J xx."

"Yes - call this week if you get a chance - love m xxx."

There was no point telling them about being ill, there

was nothing they could they do. They may have forgotten that she was off work, it wouldn't surprise her. It was so strange to go from being the centre of their world to the very furthest tip of it. Gone were the days when they needed her approval for anything, when they'd rush home with their news or call her immediately. But that's just the way it was. Being annoyed at that would be like being upset that the world turned or that the tide came in and went out. But still, no matter what, no matter how hard she tried to tell herself that that was just the way it was, it wrenched her heart, like a physical pain, her dried up uselessness.

Her phone startled her out of her self-pitying thoughts. It was Georgie.

'Hi, are you any better?'

'Not really, how are you?'

'Worried about you, are you going to the doctor?'

'You know I am, on Friday.'

'But you sound so bad, you might need antibiotics for your chest.'

'We'll see, how was dad today?'

'A bit low, he said 'I'm just sitting here in this room, surrounded by the same four walls, it's like a life sentence,' I asked him where he'd rather be, and he said 'DEAD."

'Bloody hell.'

'I know.'

'Poor dad, that sounds dreadful.'

'I know, but what can we do?'

'I feel so sorry for him, he's right, he is stuck in that room, just waiting to die.'

'I reminded him that he just used to sit and watch TV at home, but he said, "yes but mummy was there." And she was.'

'I mean, he's probably getting the best care in the world, but it's just not his own family doing the caring.'

'I know.'

'It's not like its cheap, is it? He's spending every last penny in there.'

'I know.'

'And he hates his catheter.'

'Who can blame him?'

They both sighed and were silent for a while. Who could have foreseen this? That their dad would outlive their mum, it was just crazy.

'Oh, by the way, I'm waiting for a call from Soph, she texted earlier saying that that stupid Tom had gone around last night and they'd had an interesting 'convo' about me!'

'Convo!'

'Yes, I know, how annoying is that?'

'What, the word 'convo' or that he'd gone around?'

Pamela managed to laugh, even though it hurt, 'I'd say both!'

'What the hell is he doing, going to your friends behind your back and talking about you?'

'That's exactly what I thought.'

'It's so weird.'

'Oh well, I can't get too worked up over it can I?'

'Well you've every right to be a bit pissed off.'

'I s'pose so.'

'Have you heard anything from work?'

'Yes, meant to tell you, I got a nice email from the head of sixth form, Anwara, you won't believe this, but she asked for my private email!'

'Bloody hell is that because she thinks the work ones are being monitored?'

'Yes, isn't that awful? Anyway, she sent me a lovely private email saying she knows why I'm off and that she's spoken to the senior team to ask them why everything is going so wrong in the English Department.'

'That's good news isn't it?'

'Well it does mean that people from outside the department can see what's going on, I honestly thought he was blaming individuals and getting away with it.'

'It's going to be pretty obvious though isn't it, if everyone is leaving or off sick?'

'He's so cunning though, he'll be spinning it to make himself look blameless.'

'Yes, that's how these people get away with things like this.'

'He also sent the most appalling email saying he's going to issue a written warning to anyone who doesn't do exactly as he says!'

'No!'

'Yes, it's actually preposterous. He even cc'd senior staff into it, he just doesn't give a toss. I'll send you it – you won't believe it, honestly.'

'Blimey!'

'I've genuinely never met anyone like him. Lou called

me and said he's just becoming a total megalomaniac, constantly calling extra meetings and victimising people.'

'The more I hear about that creep, the happier I am that you haven't gone back.'

'Same here, being trapped at home is crap, but it's not as crap as being back in that place!'

'True. Listen as I said before, you know you can come and stay here anytime, if you want.'

'I know, thanks for the offer, but I'm fine, just a bit pissed off with the whole situation.'

'Well let me know if you change your mind.'

'Thanks, will do.'

'Well I'll let you go; you sound so ill.'

'Bye love talk soon'

'Bye.'

It was kind of Georgie to ask her to stay, and although it made her feel like a useless child, she might have been tempted, but then she thought about Rich. He was such a horrible person, he pretended to be so nice when Georgie was around, but he showed his true colours whenever she was out of the room. He constantly made nasty digs about Pamela's weight or her drinking or whatever else he could think of. He seemed to hate teachers and made every effort to say something awful every time they met. He drank far too much and then had a go at Georgie, which she couldn't stand.

It was getting late; Sophie probably wasn't going to call tonight. Obviously, she wanted to know what this conversation had been about, but it was up to Sophie to ring her.

She decided not to have the whiskey, it probably wouldn't mix with the Beechams. She was still feeling achy and bunged up and couldn't face food. Hopefully she'd feel up to going to weight watchers in the morning, it'd be such a waste if she didn't go.

She double-checked that the doors and windows were locked and dragged her sorry self to bed. She gathered all the crap she'd flung out of the drawer and crammed it back in, another job for another day.

The wind continued to howl, battering the windows mercilessly, trees flung themselves violently from side to side. She felt like she was in a Ted Hughes poem, the house did feel as though it was out at sea, with booming hills and crashing woods. The windows were threatening to break, and she could hear the stones cry out under the horizons. Whenever she taught that poem, the kids would say, 'Was he from Yorkshire, Miss?'

Thursday 12th January

She was awake for hours, her mind probing all the worrying things she wasn't allowed to think about. She sank in and out of sleep, delirious, confused. Her body was burning, she couldn't get cool.

She thrashed about, feeling useless and weird. The thought fox was stalking crazily through her head, snuffling around the debris scattered there.

If only I was normal, she thought, *if only I could be like other people, then my life wouldn't be so deranged and unhinged.* She looked at her bedside clock, it was five am.

The storm had subsided during the night and the dark morning was quiet and peaceful.

She rang school and left the usual message and finally went back to sleep. Her alarm pierced through her strange dreams at eight am. She forced herself to sit up. The world was spinning at a strange and alarming rate. She gripped the side of the bed and waited for everything to come clear. She fixed her eyes on one spot and gradually the spinning stopped, she could focus again. Her breathing was almost normal, and her throat wasn't hurting at all. It looked like the worst was over.

I must get up and go to weight watchers, she told herself. She couldn't be bothered to shower and tried not to look at herself in the mirror. She didn't need to weigh herself; she knew she had lost weight.

Her jeans agreed with her, they slipped on easily with room to spare. Yes, there was still a muffin top, but it wasn't nearly as huge. She wouldn't take a Beechams yet, she'd rather be weighed on an empty stomach, old habits die hard.

She felt disoriented and peculiar as she got into her car. *I hope I don't see anyone I know*, she thought, *but so what if I do, there's no point worrying.*

She'd lost 6 pounds. The leader was a bit nonplussed, 'You shouldn't have lost so much weight in a week.' Pamela could feel the disapproval in her voice, she felt like a naughty schoolgirl.

'I know, I've been ill.' She replied weakly.

'Oh, I see, but it is important to eat healthily, not starve yourself.'

Pamela nearly laughed out loud, she was the last person to starve herself. 'Yes, I know.'

'Really you should lose one or two pounds a week.'

'I know.' Bloody hell would she ever shut up for goodness sake.

'And you are staying to the meeting today, aren't you?'

'Uhm, probably not.'

'It helps with success if you stay.'

'I know, but I've got to get back...' Pamela's voice trailed away, the leader glanced at the queue, which was stretching out of the door, otherwise she was sure the lecture would have gone on. 'Well try and stay next week, ok?'

'I'll try.' She replied, knowing full well that was never going to happen. 'Right bye.'

Pamela rushed out of the meeting as quickly as she could. It felt cloying and claustrophobic in that village hall, she was so relieved to escape. Again, she thought; *what the hell is wrong with me, why can't I sit and play nicely with all the other dieting people, why can't I listen to their moronic drivel, do I think I'm better than them?* There were no answers to her stream of internal lectures. *Stop thinking about stupid things,* she told herself, *concentrate on the good news, try to be happy that you lost six pounds, you're now eleven stone ten pounds!* That sounded so much better than twelve stone two pounds. The fact that she was now under twelve stone was amazing and even though she knew the first week she'd worn heavier clothes and obviously she hadn't had an appetite because of her cold, it still felt a bit of an achievement. *Now I mustn't go back to my old ways,* she reminded herself, *I must promise to be good.*

She stopped off at Tesco and bought fresh fruit, vegetables, salad, lentils, cans of mixed beans, cottage cheese, and low-fat mayo. She avoided the bakery section, ignoring her usual haunts beside the wine, cakes, biscuits, crisps and freshly baked bread. If it wasn't in the house, she wouldn't be tempted. She bought bottles of mineral water and fruit teas. She may as well try to be as healthy as possible.

She realised she was darting about, keeping her head down, terrified that she might meet someone from work. *So what if I do?* she reminded herself, *it's not illegal to go shopping when you're off ill.* But Pamela had never left the house before when she'd been ill – to kind of make a point to herself, she supposed.

In Dubai one of the women had been sacked when she'd taken a couple of days off ill and then posted pictures on social media of herself on a mini break in Oman. She was pictured grinning from a hot air balloon. Her dismissal notice had been handed to her the moment she'd walked back into work. But how stupid, like the teacher at the airport. You needed to be smarter than that. But she still felt horribly guilty. Some poor person was teaching her worst year nine class. She should feel delighted about that, but she couldn't. She'd never shirked from appalling classes throughout her whole teaching life.

She remembered, early in her career, a whole year when she'd had the worst year 8 class in school. It was only for an hour, once a week, but every Monday at 11 am, straight after break she would find herself trudging down the stairs from the staffroom, coffee in hand - you could in those days – to face this lesson. She had never taken a single Monday off; it never occurred to her.

Around November she made a chart to see how many lessons she had left until the end of the year. Whooping for joy when she discovered there was a training day or a bank holiday. After every lesson she ticked the chart and was then happy to face the week, but Sunday nights were more abysmal than usual that year.

It was strange that she still remembered that feeling as she approached the class, even after all those years. Luckily the lovely classes had nearly always outweighed the terrible ones.

She got home, put the shopping away and texted Sophie.

"Hey - hope work's going well - call me when you get a chance xx."

She wasn't surprised that Sophie hadn't called, she'd have her work head on, which meant that she couldn't focus on much else. But she could've texted to ask how she was feeling about everything.

For the millionth time she reminded herself that people only care about themselves. She had spent the whole of the last three weeks obsessing about herself and her own worries, nobody else had got a look in. *Why should anyone else be any different?* Obviously, her family cared, and her mum would have been genuinely concerned. What she would give to be able to call her mum right now. If only she was here. '*I love you and miss you every day*' she muttered the mantra aloud. Her mum might hear her from wherever she'd gone.

Thinking about her mum brought back a dream she'd had. Her mum had been alive, and they were walking through the countryside.

'What was it like?' she'd asked.

'Ok really.'

'Where were you?'

'It was dark.'

'So, no heaven or anything?'

'No, just dark.'

Bless her. When they cleared out their mum and dad's house, they found their mum's address book. (She'd lost it a couple of years before and had been completely distraught.

It was an old book that she'd managed to keep hold of over the years, even though she misplaced nearly everything. It was extremely precious, containing all the addresses she needed every Christmas. Pamela and her sisters had spent hours going through all the drawers and boxes searching for it, but it had disappeared completely.) So that day, it suddenly turned up underneath the cooker. They all stared in surprise and sadness.

'If only we could tell mum we've found it.' Pamela sighed. Just then all the doors slammed shut throughout the whole house.

'I think she knows!' Anne replied and they all laughed hysterically.

During those first few awful weeks, she'd often felt her mum was with her. Before they'd sold the house, she'd walk through the desolate rooms and tell her mum what was going on in her life and where their dad was and what he was up to. It was the strangest feeling walking through the nearly empty house. Heart breaking to see the bare bookshelves, the old photos and letters piled up, in the wrong place. Boxes and boxes of books, paintings, letters. A lifetime reduced to a mass of worthless objects. The years of a life scattered carelessly throughout the house.

Her mum used to say; "I'm worried about all the clutter in the house, what will happen when I die?"

Pamela had replied, "Don't worry, it won't be your problem mum."

Clearing that house had nearly killed the sisters and their relationships, so in a way their mum had been right to worry. They didn't fallout over who should have what, that was sorted very amicably. No, it was just the sheer hard, back breaking, emotional slog. Going through each room, the memories, the sadness. No one can prepare you for how that's going to feel. She was filled with such an overwhelming feeling of sadness. *How was it possible that someone so vibrant and full of life could go away forever, where does the brightness go?*

Her poor mum, she was always saving for a rainy day, never spending a penny on herself, probably looking forward to a long and healthy old age. Who could blame her, she'd been so well all her life. There was a lesson in it all, there had to be. We must live life to the full, grasp opportunities when they arise. Probably her mum's death was what made her so sure she couldn't go back to work. Why struggle when your situation was intolerable.

You had to do what felt right, live for the moment, not for the future. Pamela sighed, it was easy to know this, but so easy to get side-lined, forget what is important in your life. She had to count her blessings, be thankful her dad was still alive, even though he could be bad tempered and irascible, be thankful her sons no longer needed her, after all it meant she had done a good job with them.

She absentmindedly made some porridge. At least she could make it with milk. She added a spoonful of sweetener. Her appetite still hadn't fully returned, but she thought she'd better eat. She had to plan her lessons for next week. Get them out of the way. It was a bit of an impossible job as she had no idea what they had managed to complete, but it is what school expected, so she had to do it.

She finished several hours later, feeling drained and stiff from sitting over her computer for so long. She opened the TES website. Nothing for a teacher in her area or her subject. She knew she was putting off ringing the union. But she did need to speak to someone.

Finally, she made herself call the union main line. She got through to a very supportive and helpful man. He told her they saw this sort of thing all the time, he said schools were always trying to sack older teachers as they could bring in two inexperienced teachers for the same price. She told him she knew that; she'd just never thought it would happen to her. He couldn't have been nicer, and she was annoyed with herself for putting the call off for so long. He said he was going to ask her local branch to email her in the next few days. That was good.

This was happening to so many other teachers. It was so unfair. These schools should respect the experience that older teachers brought with them. It was a disgrace. One of the most galling things about her situation, when she thought about it, was the fact that that creep Mac had never formally observed her. He'd just wandered into her lessons a few times, sat down, looked disgusted and left. He'd never made official notes, he hadn't done anything properly, yet she was the one being penalised. He was such a liar and people didn't expect that from someone in his position. It was so frustrating. She felt so sorry for herself. It was awful. In all her years of teaching she had tried to be totally professional. She never lied, she marked all her books, she never took time off, she kept her planner and mark books up to date, she followed all the new initiatives, even when they were plainly ridiculous, she dressed smartly, jacket and skirts, nice shoes, tights. She'd been a bit of a goody-goody, truth be told. *And what good has that done me?* It had all gone so horribly wrong.

She forced herself to stop wallowing in this crazy self-pity. She decided to go for a walk, get her mind away from these self-destructive thoughts. She didn't bother with a hat or gloves, she didn't care.

The wind had started up again as she left her house. Outside everything was dull and dark and miserable. The wind smashed into her face and was quickly followed by lashing sleet. *So what, let me get wet and frozen and die of pneumonia. What else do I deserve?* she thought.

She walked towards the moors, ignoring passers-by who stared after her. They had never seen a more dejected looking figure and it worried them for a moment or two, before they went back to their own thoughts.

Trudging up towards the tarn, she shivered. It was cold enough to snow. Everything looked so brown and wretched. She once again yearned for summer. This winter seemed to have gone on forever. She could hardly remember what summer felt like.

She was always depressed at this time of year, but it felt worse without a job - nothing to take her mind off the remorseless, unrelenting awfulness of it all.

She sat on a bench with a sweet plaque, "June and Harold loved to sit here in life, in death they are together again at last."

How could they possibly be together? Pamela pondered. *And sitting in their favourite spot, but if that's what the family thought, surely that was ok?* She wondered if she should get a bench for when she died. "Here sat Pamela, she was a bit crap in life and is still a bit crap in death." Yes, that should do it.

She watched a lone dog walker hurry around the tarn, eyeing her suspiciously. If she had a dog with her she might look like she fitted in but sitting on her own in the freezing cold for no apparent reason made her look totally deranged. *So what?* She couldn't bring herself to care. She looked at her watch, the bell would have just gone, signalling the start of period 4. She thought about the poor supply teacher. She'd made a point of always being friendly to the supply staff, remembering her own awful experiences in strange new schools.

She was frozen to the core, but she couldn't bring herself to get up and face her empty, cold house. She remembered that she was going to join a gym tomorrow. That would be better than this aimless wandering, both physically and emotionally.

It was getting dark when she finally got up to go home. Her body was stiff and achy, her cold seemed to be back. She realised she was crying. *For goodness sake,* she told herself, *stop being such an idiot.* But she couldn't stop.

She was half running, half jogging, stumbling towards her house when a large figure stepped out from the bushes and grabbed her. Her heart stopped for a moment, she looked up in horror. She could hardly see through her bleary, teary eyes.

Tom stared down at her, he was holding her by the shoulders, 'Bloody hell, what's the matter?' He asked, as though he had every right to be there talking to her.

She wrenched herself from his grasp, 'What the shitting hell are you doing?' she screamed, 'skulking around my street? Jumping out of bushes.'

'Hey, it's ok, stop panicking.'

'Panicking – are you fricking joking?'

He looked alarmed, 'I was just walking into town. I live at the end of this road!'

She was gasping for breath; her nose and eyes were streaming. He handed her a handkerchief but she waved it away in disgust and rummaged around in her pocket for some tissue.

'Has no one ever told you not to leap out of bushes and grab people?' She yelled, 'What the hell is wrong with you?'

'I saw you coming, and I thought it would be funny, sorry, I didn't mean to frighten you.'

'What could possibly be funny about a stranger leaping out of a bush and grabbing someone?'

'When you say it like that it is a pretty stupid thing to do.'

He looked down at his shoes. He'd never met anyone like Pamela, she refused to be interested in him. It was disconcerting. He'd never had this problem before. She was such a stubborn, annoying woman, she interrupted his thoughts.

'Look, you just can't go on like this, hanging around my house, sending me horrible notes, talking to my best friend about me.'

He seemed to physically reel at this new outburst, 'What are you talking about?'

'I'm not stupid, you've been practically stalking me!'

'I bloody well have not, I don't know what you're talking about. What note?'

'Look, let's forget it, ok? I just want to get home; I'm fricking freezing in case you haven't noticed.'

'I'm sorry, honestly,' he stepped away from her, 'I haven't sent you a note, I haven't been hanging around your house, I admit I've talked to Soph about you, but nothing bad...' He paused before delivering the final blow, 'You should be flattered.'

A cold blade seemed to twist violently into her heart, *how fucking dare he?*

'Well that's the problem isn't it?' Pamela fixed him with a withering stare and continued coldly, 'That's what you think, you think a single woman of my age would lap up any attention, that I'd be so grateful for any tiny crumb of affection, well you are wrong, you are totally wrong. I don't need a man in my life to feel complete and if that doesn't fit in with your pre 19th century views there's nothing I can say is there?'

She stormed past him. She was furious. He exasperated her, always turning up unannounced and expecting her to be pleased to see him, to be flattered! What a fool. She shakily let herself into her house, leaving a stunned Tom on the pavement.

She texted Sophie, "Hi - call me as soon as you can – love Pxx."

She went into the kitchen and put the kettle on. She made some toast and a cup-a-soup, took two paracetamol and went to bed.

She was woken from a distressed shard of a dream by her phone. She glanced at her bedside clock it was five pm, 'Hello' she uttered, blearily.

'Hi Pam, it's me, just got your message, sorry I didn't ring earlier, work, you know... is everything alright?'

'Not really, I just met that idiot Tom person, he jumped out of a hedge and frightened me to death, what is going on with him?'

'Bloody hell, that's a weird thing to do.'

'No bloody kidding. He's so odd, honestly Sophie, can you tell him to leave me alone?'

'I'm so sorry, I thought you'd eventually come around to liking him.'

'Why?'

'I don't know,' Sophie answered with a tinge of sarcasm, 'maybe because he's rich, very good looking, got a great job. And wouldn't it be nice to have a man in your life?'

'Bloody hell, you sound like my mum. How long have you known me?'

'I know, but with work going so badly, I thought it might help.'

Pamela couldn't believe what she was hearing, she

continued coldly, 'So, you've been encouraging him?'

Sophie paused, before replying, quietly, 'Well, not really, well encouraging would be a bit strong, but I did think, you know, given time, you might give him a chance. He has been so sad, I thought you'd be good for each other.'

'Soph, I've got to be honest, that is so annoying.'

'I know, I'm sorry.'

'Bloody hell.'

'Look, I felt sorry for him.'

'I'm supposed to be your best friend...'

'I know, honestly, it wasn't like that, he was on his own, you were having problems at work...'

'So, you thought you'd palm me off with some psycho to make you feel better?'

'It honestly wasn't like that.'

'Really?'

'I know you're pissed off, but I was thinking of you.' Pamela felt like screaming, but instead took a calming breath and said, 'I know.'

They both paused then Sophie added, 'I am so, so sorry.'

'I know.'

'You don't need to ever speak to him again, I'll tell him you're not interested.'

'I thought you were going to tell him that ages ago.'

'I know, he's just so persuasive, it's hard not to get sucked in, I'm really so sorry.'

'Look I know you think there's something wrong with me and maybe there is, but if Tom had been a bit more normal it might have worked, but fuck me, he is a fucking psycho.'

'I can't believe he's been acting so weird.'

'Just tell him to back off.'

'I promise I will, I just thought...'

'I know...'

'Right, well next time he comes around being all pathetic I'll tell him I'm not going to talk about you, ok?'

'Thanks.'

'Ok, see you soon.'

'Yes, bye.'

'Bye.'

Pamela ended the call. She immediately called Georgie, as she waited for her to answer her mind was racing, she didn't know what to think. It seemed that Sophie had been partly behind all the unwanted advances from Tom. She'd encouraged Tom to pursue her, made him think she could be interested, even though she couldn't have been any clearer about how she felt. An unnerving thought struck Pamela, *maybe Sophie fancied Tom? No, that was crazy. She was probably just thinking about me, worried that I'm having a bad time.*

He did seem to be genuinely shocked when she'd accused him of sending her that note. She thought, *well maybe he was a good actor or maybe there's another deranged and deluded man following me around?* But it didn't seem likely. No, Tom was the most likely suspect. Her sister answered sounding flustered, rushed, 'Oh, sorry, is this a bad time?'

'No, not at all, just cleaning up cat sick.'

'Pleasant!'

'Very!'

'Shall I call back in a bit?'

'No, no, I've just washed my hands, it's fine, how are you?'

'Well you'll never guess what that twat's just done.'

'Your boss?'

'No, that bloody Tom.'

'Go on.'

'Well I was out on the moor...'

'In this weather?'

'Yes, it seemed a good idea at the time'

'Ok.'

'And when I was nearly home that freak leapt out and grabbed me.'

'No, he did not!'

'Yes, he bloody well did, he was only hiding in the bloody bushes.'

'Oh my god, hiding in the bushes? What is wrong with him?'

'I know, who does that?'

'No one, well, no one sane anyway.'

'But the worst bit is I spoke to Soph and she's been encouraging him.'

'Bloody hell, why?'

'She thinks I secretly like him, or I secretly want a deranged, newly separated man in my life.'

'Has she met you?'

'Exactly what I said, and the other worst bit is they both

think I should be flattered by his crazy attention.'

'No! that's ridiculous.'

'I know, I went mad with both of them.'

'Even Sophie?'

'Yes, I was absolutely furious. She thinks he's an ok person, but she knows how I feel, so it was stupid of her to encourage him.'

'True, but I'm sure she wasn't being malicious, just a bit over enthusiastic. How annoying though to say you should be flattered did they honestly both say that?'

'He actually said it and it was obvious that Soph thought it.'

'As if you need this right now, with your boss and everything - how are you feeling about the work situation?'

'The same, and this cold hasn't helped, how was dad today?'

'The usual, quite down again, you know, the same as ever.'

'Poor dad. I'm sure I'll be well enough to see him soon.'

'I hope so, for your sake as much as anything, I'm glad you're going to the doctors, it's tomorrow isn't it?'

'Yes, but I'm still worried about what I'm going to say.'

'Just tell them the truth.'

'Won't they just say what do you want me to do about it?'

'No, stress is a real condition, you'd be back in work if your position wasn't so unbearable.'

'True, well listen, you get back to your poorly cat, how is she by the way, sorry should have asked.'

'Oh ok, every now and then she just gets sick, no idea why, I'll probably have to take her to the vet.'

'Poor Poppy, she must be getting on a bit now.'

'She's twelve.'

'Is that old?'

'Not really, remember Rafty, she lived until she was eighteen.' They both smiled remembering their childhood cat, 'She was a cantankerous old bitch, at least Poppy is a sweet little cat.'

'Yes, she is. Well I'll call you after the doc's tomoz.'

'Great, good luck and don't worry about it all, everything's going to be fine.'

'If you say so!'

'I do, bye.'

'Bye.'

She was glad she'd spoken to her sister, but instead of feeling better her underlying fear and depression seemed even more intense. Just having a normal conversation made her situation feel hopeless. Her cold was back in full force. She felt weak and awful. Her bones ached from sitting in the cold. She wished she hadn't sat on the moors for so long. Her life was so meaningless, empty. *What was the point of anything, when would it all end?*

She fell asleep. She dreamt she was falling deeper into a blackness that was unimaginable. Her whole world swirled and skittered around her. She was falling off the edge and nothing could help her. She woke feeling disgusted with life.

It was freezing when Pamela finally heaved herself

from her bed. Her throat had started to ache again, and her head felt muddled and woollen. It had started to snow in a half-hearted, feeble way.

She lumbered downstairs and made herself a Beechams. It was seven pm. *Where had the day gone?* She wondered. She turned the heat to high and made some toast. She couldn't be bothered to follow her diet today. Maybe when she felt a bit better, *anyway it's Thursday, I've got a whole week until weigh in,* she reassured herself.

Sitting in front of her TV she clicked through channel after channel.

She checked her phone – no messages. She found a hot water bottle, *I must buy an electric blanket, especially if winters are going to be this bad,* she thought, making a note on her phone. She set her alarm for five am, although there was probably no point, she'd been waking up at five or earlier every day since Christmas, or so it seemed.

Lying in bed her mind wandered back to Sophie and Tom. *How had he managed to manipulate Sophie so cleverly? It wasn't like her to be so easily conned.* Every time she thought he must have got the message something happened, like him grabbing her today. *What a creep.*

Through her open curtains the streetlamp illuminated the trees, silhouetted against the steely brutish sky. It was snowing. The soft flakes cascaded delicately past her window. The night was hushed and still. She couldn't believe she'd been off work for nearly a week.

She was worried about seeing the doctor tomorrow. *What if they just tell me to buck up my ideas and get on with it? What if they just say, 'Why are you coming to me? What do you think I can do about your problems? Get your fat-arse back to work.' That would be so awful.*

She backtracked from these terrible thoughts and asked herself what the best scenario would be. Well they'd be sympathetic and write her a sick note for at least a month. *Did they do that?* She wondered. Hopefully, after all she didn't want to, 'clog up the doctor's surgery' as her friend had suggested. *What a mad system,* she thought, *I'm going to have to go in there and give the performance of my life and hope they're sympathetic towards me.*

She lay awake, worrying for hours. *At least I'll look bloody rough,* she thought. *I mustn't forget to mention that I've been so stressed I'm not sleeping. What else, anxiety, nightmares, panic attacks, constant dread.* These were all things she had been and was *still* experiencing. *It's not going to be a performance,* she thought, *it's completely true. I won't go in there acting like a deranged maniac, I'll go in there **as** a deranged maniac.*

Friday 13ᵗʰ January

Her alarm seized Pamela firmly be the heels and smacked her ample bum. *Fuck,* she thought, *Fuck.* 'Pamela!' her thought-mum spluttered, shocked,

'Sorry mum.'

Her bedroom window was half covered with drifting snow; it must have snowed all night. The usual early morning sounds were muffled, hazy. She rang work and left the message. At least when she got her sick note – if she got her sick note – she wouldn't need to call in every morning. She lay back down and enjoyed the calm that snow always engendered in her. She wondered if school might be closed. Probably not, the new head would see it as a failure. She worked so hard to appear in control, *I bet she's as terrified as the rest of us deep down,* Pamela thought.

She didn't need to get up for a while. *Why can't I enjoy this time, didn't it feel great not to be getting up and facing work?* No, she couldn't enjoy it. Her future was so uncertain. She would probably never get another job now. What school would take her after this, her references would be awful and the longer she stayed off the harder it would be to go back. Maybe she could go and work in a supermarket. She reached for her laptop and googled, 'Best supermarket to work for.' The top answer was 'Aim higher.' *Bloody hell, that's ridiculous,* she thought. *How demoralising.*

She scrolled down and came across a forum for workers

from various supermarkets. It looked bad. No one seemed to rate the place they worked. The comments were very worrying.

She then searched, "Courier work." Driving around delivering things would be ok, surely, but again the comments from actual couriers showed that it wasn't a great job. She wasn't qualified to do anything but teach. All these years in the classroom meant she'd buried herself away from the real world, she wasn't fit to do anything else. *But come on,* she told herself, *you haven't done a lot of research, you've googled two stupid options.* She'd have to do a bit more research, obviously.

Surely ex-teachers were suited to loads of jobs. But at that moment she couldn't think of any. Her friend had re-trained as a midwife a few years ago, but at fifty-six, she was surely too old. And anyway, being a midwife would be horrifying. She was scared of blood and seeing all those poor women in agony would be so depressing.

If only she could think of a business plan, the rich people she knew all seemed to have their own businesses. She needed to make money, but she had left it too late; she was too old to re-train and start again, yet she felt too young to retire.

Life was awful when you weren't working. There was no reason to be alive, no reason to get up, no purpose. She racked her brain, there must be a decent job out there for her.

Maybe she could foster. They were always advertising for foster parents. But it would be awful to never have a moment to yourself. These were damaged, needy children, they wouldn't sleep at night, they'd have emotional problems, they'd be hard to control. They might take drugs, self-harm, be aggressive or abusive. You'd never have a day off or be able to go out at night, and surely you couldn't drink when you were in charge of someone else's children. No, Fostering was terrifying.

Maybe she could become a private tutor, that could be less demanding. But you'd have to tutor loads of kids to make any money.

She'd have to investigate her future properly. She needed a suitable plan, not just these ramblings.

It seemed that the worst of her cold was over, although her body still ached. At least she wouldn't be contagious anymore.

She texted her sisters, "Hi – feeling much better – I'll go to see dad today P x."

She'd go after her doctor's appointment. Her sisters must be feeling fed up with her. She looked tired, pale and pretty poorly. That was good. It would make today easier. Her hair was floppy and dirty.

Not going to work meant she had got out of the habit of a daily shower. Even though she wanted to look terrible she couldn't possibly see the doctor with filthy hair. Her mum would've been horrified. "Get into that shower now," her thought-mum demanded. It did feel good. *I must try to keep up with my personal hygiene,* she thought. It was soothing to feel the warm water running down her body, the soap rinsing away the dark thoughts that seemed to constantly plague her every waking moment. Her cuts and bruises had faded, thank goodness, she couldn't wait to get back to normal. She couldn't be bothered to get dressed just yet, so she wrapped her hair in a towel, put on her dressing gown and went downstairs.

As she made breakfast, she turned the radio on. "Woman's Hour." She listened absentmindedly, at least it wasn't the news. *I've stopped paying attention to the news,* she realised, *ever since mum died.* Part of her relationship with her mum had been to discuss news and current affairs. When she'd died there was no longer any reason to be aware of what was going on in the world.

Knowing about all the appalling things going on just made you feel unhappy and powerless. What could you do to help - mainly nothing - except possibly donate to the various appeals. There always seemed to be some terrible war happening, some awful natural disaster, what was the point of knowing about it. The news should just be called "The Horror" not "The News," that would be more realistic.

She'd also stopped reading since her mum died. She'd always read the books her mum had recommended. Apart from at college, she very rarely read a book that her mum hadn't read before her. One of their great delights was to discuss a book after they'd both read it. Her mother had never recommended a single book that she hadn't enjoyed. Now she couldn't imagine reading a book without then discussing it with her mum.

When her mum had been dying, she'd asked her daughters to read to her. She could no longer focus on the words. Pamela had tried to read their old shared and much-loved novels, but she'd had to stop. Remembering the times they'd read these books made her so sad, all she could do was sob and sob. "I'm sorry mum, I'm sorry," she'd said, tears streaming down her face, "I just can't."

Her mum had understood. The only thing she could just about read to her was poetry, but even this could be horribly upsetting. The last poem she'd read to her was "Stopping by Woods on a Snowy Evening" by Robert Frost. It was the final verse that made her cry and cry. She'd read it at her mum's funeral and managed to be composed until the last verse:

The woods are lovely, dark and deep,
But I have promises to keep.
And miles to go before I sleep,
And miles to go before I sleep.

The sadness and power of those words, making her think of the journey her mum was about to go on, all alone, no one to talk to, no one to take care of her, just crushed Pamela's soul. She'd tried to hide her tears the last time she'd read it aloud to her mum, tried to be brave for her mum's sake, but internally her heart was breaking. She forced herself to stop thinking about her mum and those last few dreadful weeks. It was pointless, nothing would ever bring her back. Death had stolen her away, swallowed her whole and there was nothing she could do about it.

She found her lap top and looked on Facebook for a few minutes. Boring. Instagram was just as bad. She played a game of solitaire. It was so odd not to be rushing about, organising things. Nothing to do but sit and think.

She remembered that she had been going to join the gym today, but it wouldn't be safe to drive up those hills in this weather. She'd probably walk to the doctors. It was still only eleven am. She had hours before her appointment. She sent a WhatsApp to her boys. "Happy Friday – hope you've both got a lovely weekend planned – snowing like mad here - m xxx."

She turned the TV to the Syfy channel and found some re-runs of Buffy. She was bored rigid. *If only it was summer,* she thought, *at least then I could sit outside and enjoy being off work.* Snow was beautiful but when you didn't have small children to play with there wasn't much you could do. She'd been skiing a couple of times when the boys had been little, it had been fun but since they'd left home, they obviously didn't want to go with her anymore and none of her friends skied.

Her lap top buzzed, she'd got a personal email from Dom. They seemed to be so paranoid, not going through the school system. They must think that Mac was somehow reading them.

Hi love - hope you're ok - Lou has told me a bit about your situation - Poor you - but I totally understand - Don't worry about sending me your lesson plans - from now on I'll sort it - Look forward to hearing from you soon - Take Care Dom.

That was great news, it was a bit of a crazy exercise planning lessons when she had no idea what the class had got up to. Also, at this time of year lessons were often interrupted by exams, talks and so on. Or maybe her lessons had been so crap Dom didn't want them anymore. Well she'd been following his overall planning, so that was unlikely. And she had worked hard on them, whatever freaking mad Mac thought. That was the trouble, her confidence had been so badly knocked it was hard to imagine that she'd ever been a competent teacher, although she knew she had. She had to keep reminding herself that before Mac had started, she'd always got outstanding observations.

Jake sent her a reply, "Hi - all good here - weather wet and dull - lucky you getting snow - going to Geneva for the weekend - what are you up to? x."

"Nothing much - just seeing grandad - have a great time in Geneva - Love you xxx."

"Will do - love you too x."

It was nice to hear from him. Both boys seemed to lead such hectic lives, always dashing off to some lovely place over the weekend.

"Send photos xx," she added as an after-thought.

"Will do x." Came the reply.

A few minutes later Alex added, "Hi - all going well here - hope you're both ok – wish we had snow - come to London soon mum – xxx."

That was sweet of Alex, she would go down soon, she promised herself. Maybe when she'd lost a bit more weight.

She answered, "Yes – great idea – would be lovely to see you both – send available dates and we'll arrange something m xxx."

She didn't hold out much hope of seeing both of them

at the same time, but if it was planned in advance it might happen.

Her phone pinged – it was a reminder – shit, she'd forgotten the locksmith was coming this afternoon.

She took herself upstairs and dried her hair. She didn't bother with any make-up, when she went to the doctors she wanted him to see her looking pasty and unwell.

She hadn't given the locksmith much thought since she'd made the appointment. If she had a Yale lock fitted to her bedroom door the danger was she'd lose the key, which wouldn't be great. *Maybe just a very big sliding bolt. Bloody hell.* She'd gone off the whole idea. She decided to cancel.

'Hello, this is Pam James, you're due to come around today but somethings come up, can I ring you later to rearrange.'

There was a slight pause, then he replied, 'Yes, that's fine. Look forward to your call.'

She felt a bit bad; business was probably slow and now she'd cancelled at the last minute. She hoped she wouldn't regret this spur of the moment decision. *This is so typical of me,* she thought, *I should have just got a lock on the door and be done with it,* but part of her was relieved that she'd cancelled the guy. It was crazy to be scared in her own home. She didn't want to live her life like that.

Walking to the doctors, she enjoyed the bright sunlit day. The snow glistened, making everything appear clean and fresh. She sat in a corner and prayed that she wouldn't meet anyone she knew. It reminded her of when she'd come to the doctor, secretly, at sixteen. She was arranging to have the contraception pill. Of course, she'd met one of her mother's friends, who outright asked her why she was there, at the top of her voice, in front of the whole waiting room. She'd gone bright red and muttered something inaudible and thank goodness her name had been called and she was able to rush off, praying the woman wouldn't mention the meeting to her mum.

That was the trouble with growing up in a tiny town, everyone knew everyone, and busily nosed into your life. Then the doctor had been appalled at her request, it was so embarrassing and awkward. He'd been her doctor all her life and was stunned that this obviously immature sixteen-year-old was asking for the pill. She probably looked so young to him. He told her off and said she must tell her mum. *Like that was going to happen!* she thought. Her mother would have gone mental.

She remembered saying to him, "Well I'd rather come here and ask for this then the alternative."

He did a double take, inhaled deeply as though he was truly shocked, then said, "I'm going to put in your notes that you want the pill because of heavy periods."

Honestly, that's what it had been like in those days, so stupid.

She stared dismally at a huge fish-tank. The fish swam aimlessly around, trapped in their pointless little world. They were only supposed to have a few seconds memory, but how could anyone tell. She wondered why people thought it was a soothing thing to look at. It just made you more aware of your own futile life. It forced you to confront the reality of your own being and made you question everything.

She wondered if she'd ever walk into a classroom again. The way things were going in education she was right to start looking into doing something else. But she'd only ever been a teacher her whole adult life. It was all so depressing.

Her body was slumped against the chair, she didn't have the energy to sit properly. "Don't slouch Pamela, sit up straight for goodness sake." Her thought-mum insisted.

She made herself sit up, *come on Pamela,* she told herself, *it's all going to be fine.*

"Mum, am I doing the right thing, should I just go back to work and face whatever that horrible man throws at me, am I being totally cowardly?" Her thought-mum had become, suddenly, very silent.

Her name was called. *Here goes,* she thought, *stay focused on what I want, the doctor must see the pain I'm in and understand and agree to a sick note.* She timidly knocked on the doctor's door.

'Come in.'

She gently pushed the door open, feeling sick with worry. She took a deep breath and sat down. She immediately reverted to that anxious sixteen-year-old. Thank god Dr McGregor wasn't still here. She didn't know where to start, her silent fear hung in the air.

'Talk to me.' He waited. Griping her hands together she forced herself to speak,

'Well, I've been having a very stressful time at work.

I've been having panic attacks, not sleeping, feeling sick. I just can't face going back.' Her voice was cracked, weak. She was wringing her hands and sniffling, she was genuine, everything she said was true, but she knew she must look like an actor in a 'B' movie.

'Has this happened suddenly or has it been building up for a while?'

'It's ever since my new boss started, he's totally got it in for me, he hates me. He's trying to get rid of me and I just can't face it.'

He asked her to continue and she tearfully poured out the whole sorry tale. She hadn't planned to tell the doctor everything, but she couldn't help it now she was face to face with him.

He listened attentively, then said, 'This seems to be happening a lot to teachers.' Pamela could've cried with relief,

'I feel like a total failure, but I just can't face going back.'

'Look, give yourself the weekend to think about it, you don't need a note for this week, if you're still feeling like this by Monday ring reception and say Doctor Bannerjee has arranged a sick note for you.'

'Ok, thanks very much doctor.'

She didn't dare ask how long the note was for. She would have to keep ringing school until she saw the actual note in black and white.

As she walked away from the surgery, relief washed over her. Thank goodness. She could hardly believe it had gone so smoothly. But, she had to keep reminding herself, everything she'd said was true. At least he'd seen other teachers with similar problems. She knew she wasn't the only one, but it was good to hear it from him. She felt like she'd been set free. The doctor was totally on her side, he completely understood what she was going through.

It was weird that he hadn't offered her any drugs, she would have said no, but it was surprising that he hadn't looked for a chemical solution. Despite her relief, Pamela wondered how long she could keep going to the doctor and throwing herself on his mercy. *I must chase up the local union person,* she thought.

She knocked on her dad's door, 'Hi dad, IT'S ONLY ME.'

'Hello, only me.' He replied. Their usual greeting.

He seemed ok, a little fed up. Who could blame him. She tried to talk him through it, but probably didn't help.

She sat directly in front of him and spoke clearly and slowly, 'Can you hear me?' She asked, he nodded, desolately. 'Look dad, you've had an exciting life, you've worked abroad, you've had children, grandchildren, great grandchildren even! You were very lucky to be married to a lovely person for over sixty years. Your life has just changed that's all.'

He looked miserable, 'I'm just shut up in this room, but for how long, how long do I have to sit here looking at these four walls?' She felt dreadful, her poor dad.

'Well dad, you just have to look on the bright side, you're being very well looked after, the food here isn't too bad. I'm just so relieved you're here, being taken care of, if you fall over there's always someone here to pick you up. You know you were struggling on your own at home. None of us are carers. Remember you asked to be put in a home.'

'Oh.' His face crinkled into a worried frown.

'Yes, you were worried about being left on your own'

'Oh.' He repeated, looking away, he clearly didn't want to listen to this, it was too depressing.

Pamela felt she had to go on, 'Look, everything changes, you had a great life, but things change. No one foresaw that mum would die before you, it's awful that it happened, but it did. I don't know what to say, maybe you need to be on anti-depressants.'

He shook his head, but said, 'If it made me feel better...'

'Look we'll get doctor Janet to come and see you.'

'I've just had enough; I don't want to carry on.'

'You don't mean that dad.'

'I do.' They stared at each other; her mum would've been so sad to see him like this.

Pamela felt miserable and helpless. She made him a cup of tea and left when his small evening meal arrived. What a horrible situation. She couldn't imagine what it must feel like to be him, with nothing to show for his life but one small room and a few photographs. Life with his wife had meaning, he'd felt safe and loved. Now he was alone and diminished, just one more old man on the scrap heap of life.

Leaving the overheated, stuffy home, she saw the shadowy outline of a man across the street casually leaning against the wall. He seemed to be staring at her. She stopped in her tracks, wondering whether to go back inside. Don't be so stupid Pamela, she told herself, no one is staring at you. She fumbled in her bag, pretending to be looking for her car keys, she glanced back and the figure seemed to melt into the wall. There was nothing there, she told herself, just your crazy, over-active imagination. She shuddered and braced herself for the chilly winter evening. The twilight winter sky was ominous, grey and foreboding. It wasn't long before the heavens opened around her. The sleet and wind slammed into her face, numbing her nose and cheeks.

She wished she'd brought her car, she felt alone and vulnerable. Weak. Exposed

The sleet was turning to snow, it swirled and skittered across the pavement in front of her. There was no one about, the streets were empty and cheerless. January was such a dismal, depressing month. The street lamps in this part of town were ancient and unreliable. They flickered an orange glow casting distorted shadows around her. She felt like the only person in the world. She began to hear footsteps behind her, echoing faintly through the deserted streets, fragments of a mans voice, muttering, indistinct. Her heart missed a beat. It was Tom, he'd followed her and waited outside her dad's so that he could... could what Pamela? she asked herself, for gods sake stop being so melodramatic. She stopped walking and stood underneath the feeble light, waiting. The noises had stopped. There was no one there.

She finally arrived home chilled to the bone, her jeans were soaked through and her so-called winter coat hadn't kept the worst of the weather out. She turned on all the house lights and made sure that both the doors were properly locked. She had to shake off the feeling that something awful had been following her home. She wearily walked upstairs and stripped off. She ran a hot bath and sank into the bubbling warmth.

Wrapped in her warmest dressing gown, she lit a lovely fire. She realised she was starving; she hadn't had anything since breakfast. She made herself some veggie sausages and a jacket potato with loads of veg. *This can't have many calories,* she thought, feeling pleased with herself. She couldn't resist the urge to open a bottle of red wine. Argentinian Malbec, delicious. *It was Friday evening after all,* she reassured herself.

As soon as she'd eaten, she started wondering what sweet thing she could eat. Fruit wouldn't cut it. She rummaged about in her freezer and found some old ice cream right at the back. It was chocolate, her least favourite, she must have bought it years ago for one of the kids. It was as hard as rock. She left it out for a bit and kept cracking its hard exterior with a spoon. Gradually it turned back into something edible. She ignored the voice in her head that warned her about the calories and took the whole dripping container into the sitting room and eat the lot.

When she'd eaten that she still felt a nagging urge to eat something else. She found the tin of Quality Street left over from New Year's Day and eat what was left, an unappetising selection that she'd previously discarded. The strawberry, orange and coffee ones that she would only eat in desperation, when their more delicious friends had been eaten.

Later that evening she rang her sister, 'Hi Georgie, can you talk?'

'Yes, just finished tea, what about you?'

'Yeah, I can't stop eating and drinking.'

'I know the feeling!'

'So, it went amazingly well at the docs, he was so lovely.'

'Of course, I meant to ring to see how it had gone. You must feel so relieved.'

'Yes, it was great. I'm ringing on Monday for a sick note.'

'Why didn't he give you one then and there?'

'He hopes I'll feel better by Monday!'

'Like that's going to happen!'

'I know, but I suppose it's fair enough to want me to wait.'

'Yes, oh well done, I know you were dreading it.'

'Yes, I totally was. But I actually thought about how it would go in an ideal world and that's more-or-less exactly what happened!'

'Bloody hell, that's good!'

'I know, shame that doesn't work all the time.'

'Yes, annoying! How was dad?'

'He was depressed.'

'Still?'

'Well yes, it's not like anything has happened since yesterday.'

'True.'

'I told him I'd call Dr Janet.'

'Good idea. I've invited him over for lunch on Sunday, do you want to come?'

'That sounds lovely, what time?'

'About 2-ish? Adam, Hannah and Teddy are coming up, so it should be nice.'

'Really? You must be delighted. How long are they up for?'

'Just Saturday evening until Sunday afternoon, so not long, sadly, they're going to visit Hannah's mum's tonight.'

'It'll be lovely to see them, can't wait to see Teddy, how old is he now?'

'He'll be one next month!'

'Bloody hell, that's gone fast'

'I know, I can't believe it.'

'Are you inviting Anne?'

'Not sure if she's around this weekend, I think she said something about going away, I'll check though.'

'Yeah, good idea, it'll be nice for dad to have us all there'

'Yes, it's been a while. Have you heard any more from that idiot, Tom?'

'No, thank goodness.' She decided not to tell Georgie that she'd thought Tom had been following her earlier. It would only worry her and she didn't want to sound any crazier than usual.

'Good, he needs a good kick up the butt by the sound of it!'

'Yes, he bloody does!'

'Right, are you sure you're ok to make dad that appointment with Dr Janet?'

'Yes, it's not like I'm doing much else with my time, at the moment.'

'I know, how are you feeling about everything?'

'Pretty pissed off, I never thought I'd be in this position... well, you know how I feel, I'm not going to go on about it again, I've talked about nothing else, you must be fed up listening to me.'

'Don't be silly, I'm happy to talk about it.'

'I know, you're a very good sister!'

'I try!'

'Honestly, I'm not going to bore you with it, but I have phoned the union, and I think someone from the local office is going to email me, so I'll let you know how that goes.'

'Ah, I'm glad you called the union, you do need expert advice.'

'True, especially as I know I'm not going back.'

'Yeah, well, let me know what they say.'

'Will do, is there anything I can bring on Sunday?'

'No, I've got everything, I think.'

'Well call me tomorrow if you think of anything. Shall I collect dad?'

'No, I said I would, you always end up ferrying him around, it's only fair.'

'Ah, that's very kind, thanks.'

'No problem. Ok my love, I'll let you go, but remember, call me anytime or come over anytime if you want to chat.'

'Ok, take care, bye.'

'Bye.'

She opened her laptop and checked her personal emails. There was one from her local union man. He gave her his number and asked her to phone him as soon as possible. Bloody hell, she should have checked earlier. Oh well, she'd ring him on Monday. She poured the last of the Malbec into her glass. She thought about opening another bottle but wandered into the kitchen and poured herself a large whiskey instead.

Pamela fell into a drunken sleep. She was boiling and freezing in turns. The night seemed never-ending. Every few minutes she was shaken awake by fear. Weird black dreams wracked her brain, her mouth frozen open in a deathly grimace, immobile, painful. She had to melt her mouth back to normal with the water that, thank goodness, she'd somehow remembered to bring to bed. Her body ached, sweat poured from her.

She couldn't believe she was still going through the menopause, it seemed to be going on forever, or maybe it was just the remnants of her cold, or the quantities of alcohol she'd consumed.

Saturday 14th January

When morning finally arrived, she felt sick, her mouth tasted of alcohol, a damp soggy feeling ran through her body. She groggily remembered her evening; she was appalled with herself for drinking and eating so much ice-cream and chocolate. What was the point of dieting all day and then stuffing her face *and* drinking all night? She was a horrible person. *I'm so crap, so useless, it was unbelievable,* she told herself. She forced herself to stop thinking, *what was the point.* She would do better, she had to.

She called her dad's doctor and made an appointment.

She sent a message to both her sisters on their What's app group, 'Hi – I've made a docs ap. for dad on Mon afternoon re his depression - I can be there when she comes – Anne are you visiting today?'. Georgie replied a few minutes later 'Thanks for that - Anne I've asked Pam and dad around for Sunday lunch – can you and Pete come? 2-ish xx'.

Whilst she waited for Anne to reply she dragged herself out of bed. *I must stick to my diet today,* she told herself. *And not drink.* It was madness, how could she face her weigh-in on Thursday if she was so easily led astray.

Her phone pinged, Anne replied, she'd visit dad today. That was a relief. And she and Peter were going to come to Georgie's for Sunday lunch. She responded a few minutes later 'Great - see you all tomorrow xx'.

Georgie was a fabulous cook, which was bad as she was hoping to stick to her diet and she wouldn't be able to tomorrow. She was about to privately message Georgie to ask that her meal could be low-fat, then thought better of it. It might sound a bit ungrateful. At least she would be driving so she wouldn't be able to hit the bottle.

She started absent-mindedly sorting out a drawer. It was supposed to be the cutlery tray, but it was also stuffed with lots of miscellaneous crap.

Later she checked the TES website for anything remotely interesting. There was one job in a Leeds school, but it was part-time. It might be nice to work part-time. She read the details. Typical, it seemed they wanted someone to do a full-time job, but to pay them on a part-time salary.

She made some veg soup and left it simmering. It looked particularly unappetising. Oh well, it would probably taste ok. But without butter and cream it was a poor imitation of real soup.

She turned on the TV and flicked through the channels absentmindedly. She came across 'Midsomer Murders,' what a dreadful programme that was, as if, in a tiny village like that, someone got murdered every week. *What were the writers thinking, honestly.*

Then with a sudden flash of horror she thought, *Tom murdered his wife*. It was suddenly so clear, so obvious. She couldn't believe she hadn't realised it before. That would explain his wife's posture and fearful appearance in the photos on Facebook, it would explain why she wasn't contacting her kids. It would also explain why Pamela permanently felt uncomfortable in his presence. He was always trying so hard to come across as this wronged man, someone people should feel sorry for, and he'd certainly fooled Sophie and Russ and probably everyone else he knew. He was doubtless sizing her up for victim number two, perhaps he'd got a taste for murder.

Bloody hell, what should I do now, she thought, *I can't just ring the police.* She got as far as grabbing her mobile and punching in 99... then, of course, sanity kicked in, *don't be so stupid, he hasn't killed his wife,* she told herself, *that's just plain ridiculous.* How could she have jumped to such a crazy conclusion. *But it did happen. Maybe his wife had wanted to leave him and when she'd told him he'd killed her by accident in a sudden fury. Then he'd buried her under the patio. For god's sake, stop having such ludicrous ideas. What the hell is wrong with me,* she thought, *I know you feel awkward when you're with him, but that doesn't make him a wife murderer.* But the thought that he was capable of murder kept going through her mind.

Once this thought was out of the bottle, try as she might, she couldn't squeeze it back in, it became solid, permanent. It stood behind her shoulder, this sad genie, in the form of poor old Serena, pleading with Pamela to help her. 'No one is even looking for me,' the apparition said, 'Everyone believes that evil man, please help me.'

She decided to ring Sophie, maybe find out a bit more about his wife. *People don't just disappear into thin air. Most mothers contacted their kids, but seemingly Serena hadn't. I wonder if she has parents, brothers, sisters,*

Pamela thought. She could hardly talk to Tom. Now she was regretting being so awful to him, she could have got a lot more information from him about his wife, but that might make him suspicious. She didn't want that. What about his kids, they must be concerned that their mum had just vanished without a trace, supposedly taking one case of belongings with her.

But she had to admit Tom was very plausible, he'd played the loving husband for so long, no one would think him capable of murder. *Yes Pamela,* she told herself, *because he isn't a murderer, stop trying to build this out of all proportion. You've obviously gone a bit crazy, bloody calm down.* But she found herself calling Sophie, she couldn't help herself. She mustn't tell Sophie why she wanted to know about his wife, she had to pretend it was for another reason. Luckily Sophie's phone went straight to voice mail. Good, that was just as well, she mustn't leap into this, she should be cautious, careful. She didn't leave a message.

She rang Georgie instead, and blurted out, 'Hi I think Tom killed his wife!'

'What?!'

'Look, I know it sounds incredible, but she seems to have disappeared without a trace, she's not contacting anyone, even her kids.'

'I can't believe you think he's killed his wife, honestly Pamela, you need to stop obsessing about stuff.'

'But don't you think it's weird?'

'Pam, there could be loads of reasons.'

'Like?'

'Well, for one, maybe she needs a bit of space without people asking her all sorts of questions, two, you've said yourself how strange Tom is, well he'd be begging her to come home every five minutes wouldn't he? And I'm sure there's a three, four and five.'

'What woman packs ONE bag and walks away after so many years?'

'Well everyone's different aren't they, maybe possessions aren't that important to her?'

'Doesn't the whole situation sound a bit suspicious to you?'

'Well not really... well, maybe a bit... but I'm sure there's a perfectly reasonable explanation, you don't like him, fair enough, but that doesn't make him a murderer!'

'Ok, so I know it sounds crazy, but it does happen, doesn't it?'

'Yes, I suppose so, but honestly, I think you're putting 2 and 2 together and making 5, you've had too much time on your hands recently!'

'Maybe, but I'm sure his wife deserves someone on her side, how can I find out if she's ok?'

'Do you actually need to? Shouldn't it be up to her kids or other family?'

'The kids just think she's being awful, which of course, Tom is encouraging, and I don't know if she has any other family.'

'Look, I think you'd be best to stop all this speculation, concentrate on you, not that idiot Tom.'

'I know you're right, of course you are, but now it's in my head, you know?'

'I do know, but try to think about other things, like talking to the union, sorting out your job, rather than imagining crazy things about that man. You're becoming fixated with how horrible he is!'

'I'm not fixating thanks very much. I'm just worried about some poor woman lying in a shallow grave.'

'Bloody hell Pam, stop being so over dramatic.'

'Ok, sorry, I am probably jumping to conclusions, but what if... what if, you know?'

'I know, but there's not a lot to go on and I'm sure she'll contact her kids, maybe she actually is talking to her kids, but she's told them not to tell their dad?'

'Yes, I suppose that makes sense.'

'In the meantime, keep away from him, he's turning you into a crazy lady!'

'Believe me, I'd be happy never to see him again!'

'Ok, well I'll see you tomorrow.'

'Are you sure you don't need me to bring anything?'

'No, just you will be fine.'

'And are you sure you're ok collecting dad?'

'Yes, it shouldn't always be up to you.'

'Great, well I'll see you tomorrow, bye.'

'Bye love see you later.'

Georgie was right, of course, she had to stop over-thinking everything. She was just being melodramatic, as usual. She remembered her soup and ran into the kitchen, luckily it wasn't burnt much. She scraped out as much as she could, trying to avoid the burnt bottom and flung the pan into the sink to soak. She added some hot sauce to hide the taste and took it back into the sitting room.

As she ate, she mulled over the reasons that made her think that Tom was a murderer. 1. He was not as nice as he pretended to be – she always got the feeling that something else was going on when she was with him, something unsavoury and worrying. 2. He was trying to rush into something with her, which was weird. 3. He was always going around to Soph's house and complaining about her, which was annoying. 4. He'd hidden in a bush and jumped out and grabbed her, no normal person did that. 5. He'd followed her to her dads place, waited for her and then purposely frightened her on the way home. She realised that none of these reasons added to her theory and as for number 5 she had absolutely no proof that Tom had been there.

Ok. Start again. Stick to the actual, true facts, not just her gut feelings. His wife was gone, but everyone only had his word for how it happened. He was the one who said she came home one day and announced she was leaving for no apparent reason and taken one suitcase. As far as everyone was concerned, she hadn't contacted a soul, including her kids. This seemed like very strong proof that Tom was indeed a murderer. Maybe she had said she wanted to leave, and he'd locked her in the cellar. Maybe she was a prisoner. Pamela wanted to ring the police, but she was worried that they wouldn't believe her. They would think she was a manic woman, with an over-active imagination.

Well maybe she could make an anonymous call, a tip off. That would make sense. Then leave it up to the police to sort it out. She should tell Sophie what she was thinking. *No, I should do it through the police.* But she couldn't quite bring herself to make that call. She made herself wait, give it a few days, what difference would that make. If poor old Serena was dead, then it didn't matter and if she was alive then there was nothing to report. But what if Tom *was* keeping her a prisoner somewhere. *Oh shut up Pam,* she told herself, *stop leaping from one crazy idea to another.*

The dead Serena ghost disappeared, howling expletives as she was sucked through the floor, 'Bye, sorry,' Pamela waved. *Dead Serena is only in my imagination,* Pamela told herself, *alive Serena is probably on some deserted desert island, with no phone reception, hand in hand with someone better, drinking cocktails and congratulating herself on escaping the angry, needy Tom.*

Sophie texted her, "Hi - sorry I missed your call – been so busy – this is going to sound a bit strange but if Russ asks, I'm at your house tonight – I'll explain later! Sxx."

What was Sophie up to? She and Russ were usually a pretty solid couple, what could make her lie like this? She couldn't help feeling annoyed, it was mad to make someone else lie on your behalf. But she was probably arranging some kind of nice surprise for him.

Pamela forced herself to be kind, and texted back, "Yes - of course - sounds intriguing though x."

"No - nothing too interesting – I'll fill you in tomoz xx."

A weak sun was straggling through her sitting room

window, she could hear the constant drip of thawing snow. It would probably freeze over later and make driving treacherous. Well she didn't have to go out anywhere, so it hardly mattered. She set about cleaning out the fire. At least she could make her house warm and cosy.

Her phone rang, it was Jake.

'Hi, love, how are you?'

'Hi mum, fine thanks, sorry I didn't ring earlier this week, I've had so much to do at work, it's been totally crazy.'

'That's fine, I know what it's like. Aren't you in Geneva, shall I ring you back?

'I am but luckily I've got roaming so don't worry.'

'Are you there for work?'

'Yes, I had a few meetings yesterday and I've got another one this evening.'

'Bloody hell you're working all weekend?'

'It's not as bad as it sounds, I'm mainly taking clients out, so ok really. How about you? Alex said you weren't going back to work?'

'Sadly, that's true and to be honest I can't see myself going back.'

'Oh god mum, that's so bad.'

'I know, I feel awful.'

'I'll bet, you poor thing.'

'Oh well, let's hope it all turns out ok in the end!'

'Do you see yourself going to a different school?'

'Maybe, anyway, hopefully the union can sort something out. How's your job going?'

'Fine, very busy as usual, but all good.'

'Any girls in your life?'

'No, still playing the field, what about you?'

They both laughed, he knew what his mum was like regarding men, 'What do you think?' she replied.

'Oh mum, you are a very strange person!'

'I know, the only person who's shown any interest in me is an evil wife-murderer!'

'Bloody hell, what do you mean?'

'Oh, don't worry, he probably isn't a murderer, but he's a weird guy I met at Soph's at her New Year's party. He can't seem to get the hint that I'm not interested and keeps calling around and being annoying.'

'That doesn't sound good, but why do you think he's a wife-murderer?'

'Oh, I'm just joking, he reckons his wife just left and that she hasn't contacted anyone since, even her children, so I've just decided he must've killed her!'

'Logical conclusion! Well keep away from him just in case!'

'Don't worry, I'm doing my best.'

'What a shame he turned out to be such a nutter!'

'I know, typical!'

'Have you still got loads of snow?'

'It's melting a bit now, but it's been amazing, you'd have loved it.'

'I would, but it's beautiful here.'

'Snowy?'

'Yeah, so pretty. Just a shame I've got to go back to

London, it's so miserable.'

'I know, you must come home for a visit soon.'

'Yeah, you must come down soon too, especially now you're off work.'

'I'll try to organise something.'

'What are you up to for the rest of the weekend?'

'Nothing tonight, but we've all been invited to aunty Georgie's tomorrow for Sunday lunch, Adam and Hannah are visiting with Teddy!'

'Ah, that's lovely. I haven't seen Adam since I don't know when.'

'Well it must have been when we all went down to visit, just after Teddy was born, his birthday is next month.'

'Is Teddy a year old? Bloody hell, that's gone fast.'

'I know, I can't believe how quickly it's gone.'

'Well give everyone my love.'

'Will do, can't wait to see you soon.'

'Same, love you mum.'

'Love you, don't forget to send photos!'

'Ok, bye.'

'Bye.'

Pamela folded herself into her sofa. She found she couldn't move. She felt exhausted. She was appalled by this lethargy. She'd had a sweet conversation with Jake, *so why am I feeling so depressed? Stop. Stop this right now. Stop feeling so sorry for yourself, you need to get on with things, stop dwelling on stuff you don't have any control over.*

She forced herself to get up and at least finish cleaning

out the fire. She'd feel so much happier when that was finished.

When the fire was ready to be lit, she looked around her, the house was becoming distinctly grubby. She grabbed a duster and polished all the furniture and the blinds. She then started to vacuum the sitting room, the hall, the stairs, the bedrooms.

She was sweating and shattered by the time she'd finished. She would reward herself with a nice gin and tonic.

She opened the freezer and realised it was absolutely revolting, everything was just shoved in, willy-nilly, thick ice covered everything, making it nearly impossible to open the drawers. *When was the last time I cleaned this out?* She wondered, she'd moved into this house over four years ago and she realised she'd probably never defrosted it in all that time. She had no clue what to do.

She googled 'how to defrost a freezer.' The advice was to wrap everything up in newspaper and turn the fridge off. Well she wasn't going to wrap everything up, that was a mad idea. She turned the fridge off and opened the freezer door. She took everything out and crammed them into black bin bags and put them out the back door. Everything should stay frozen in this weather. *What have I been shoving everything into the freezer, why am I keeping all these bags and containers of crap? I'm such a freaking hoarder. Why can't I throw anything away?* Instead of chucking leftovers away everything was just shunted into the freezer, making it overcrowded and nearly unusable.

She read that you could put containers of hot water into it to speed up the process. She boiled the kettle and put a tub of hot water on each shelf. Her kitchen was now looking like a bomb site.

She made herself the promised gin and went back into the sitting room. At least everything else was looking tidy. After she lit the fire, she realised she was starving, but she couldn't face the kitchen. She stared longingly at her Just Eat app. *What harm would it do to order a small pizza?* She had been so good today and she'd had loads of exercise, cleaning up, *surely a small pizza would be ok?*

She ignored the tiny voice of reason in her head that was trying to be heard, 'What about your diet?' it screeched, 'You promised you were going to stick to it.' *Sod it,* she thought, *one little pizza should be fine.* She fed a few more logs onto the fire and snuggled down on her settee.

She thought about Sophie's text, *why was she being so strangely secretive? It wasn't like her to behave like that. Oh well, she'd find out soon enough.*

It had started to snow again as the pizza delivery guy arrived. At least tonight she was looking a little more respectable, not that he'd remember or care. Women of Pamela's age were more-or-less invisible to the younger generation. *So what?* she thought, *it was quite nice, you didn't have to worry about looking good or making a good impression. You were finally free to be yourself, whoever that was.*

She didn't bother with a plate or cutlery, she wanted to spend as little time in her disorganised kitchen as possible.

The pizza was delicious. *What was life about if you couldn't indulge now and then?*

Later she went into the kitchen, poured herself a neat whiskey and tackled the freezer. She managed to prize off most of the ice. It was looking like a real freezer by the time she'd finished, not some sort of crazy icebox that served absolutely no purpose. She sorted out the frozen bags. Everything in there was vegetarian, so she wasn't going to die if things had partially defrosted.

She forced herself to throw away all the random bags and containers of leftovers, most had probably been in there for four years, so definitely past their sell by date. Finally, it looked a normal person's freezer. *Thank goodness I'm finally getting organised, hurray!*

Whiskey in hand, she stared into the embers of her fire. Earlier she had tried to concentrate on a Scandi drama but reading the subtitles had become a chore and anyway the earlier gin and current whiskey made focussing nearly impossible, the words danced and blurred in an annoying way.

She turned the lamps off and watched the beautiful snow fall gently outside her window. Once again, her thoughts turned to the scared little face of Serena, a montage of random pictures flashed across her mind. *Can I just sit back and do nothing?* She wasn't feeling in the least bit tired. She wondered if she should walk along the road towards Tom's house, but maybe he'd been lying when he said he lived on her road. She didn't have his actual address, but she'd probably recognise his car. She could maybe have a look around the garden, but in this weather would she be able to see anything. It was a crazy idea, she knew that, she clearly was not thinking straight.

She googled 'find an address' It turned out she could find his address by keying in his mobile phone number. It was only eleven pm, not that late, really, she'd often been out on her own later than this. *But am I going to wander about the streets at this hour for no good reason?* As she put her boots and coat on, she realised that the answer was yes, yes, she was.

It was a wonderful night; the snow was coming down in giant, soft globes. As the cold air hit her, she began to sober up. She was the only one out, unsurprisingly. She crunched along, enjoying the feel of fresh snow underfoot. She wondered what she could possibly hope to achieve by walking up to his house. *Do I think I'll be able to see into the cellar, where, no doubt the imprisoned Serena will be in full view?* It made no logical sense, she just felt she ought to be doing something, no matter how ridiculous. She could always turn back, obviously.

She started counting the house numbers. Her road was a bit like the opening to the sopranos, you started at the cheap busy end and ended up at the posh detached, gentrified end. Number 98, 100, 102, 104, then finally at the very end, the largest and poshest of them all - number 106.

It was massive, set back, down a long tree-lined drive. *Bloody hell,* she thought, *this is amazing.* It was a good job she'd googled the address; she'd never imagined that he lived in a place like this.

There were relatively recent car tracks leading down to the house. She wondered what to do, she couldn't just march down the drive, anyway a house like this would be bound to have automatic lights and probably CCTV, it was amazing that the imposing electric gates were open.

She slipped through them and turned left, following the hedge. The garden seemed to go on forever. The hedge stopped, taken over by a wooden fence, beyond which open countryside rolled away down to the river. The snow was quite deep, and she was struggling to keep upright. Finally, she was near enough to approach the house from the side. Suddenly she saw the front porch light switch on, *Oh God, have I tripped some sort of burglar wire?*

She could hear laughter, *shit,* she flung herself behind a small bush. She could see two figures on the porch, and she could hear two familiar voices. She squirmed around on her bottom to try and see what was happening and dared to peer around the bush. On the steps in a deep embrace were Tom and *oh no,* she couldn't believe it, Sophie. *What the hell? Why was Sophie kissing Tom, what was going on?* She nearly stormed out from her hiding place to confront them both, to ask what they thought they were doing, but thought better of it.

She managed to twist away from the bush, crawling on her hands and knees. Bloody hell, the gates were probably only open to let Sophie out.

She got to her feet and ran as fast as she could through the thick snow, keeping close to the fence and then the hedge. What a terrible, embarrassing situation. How long had this been going on? Was Soph encouraging her to go out with Tom to hide her own affair with him? Did that make any sense? Or had it just happened? Bloody hell, Sophie, what are you doing?

She thrashed through the dense snow, disbelief and anger flooding through her. She got to the gates just as a pair of car lights illuminated her way. She flung herself against the hedge as Sophie's car slid and slewed its way past. It was incredibly slippery, luckily Sophie was concentrating hard on not losing control, so she didn't look up from the road. As soon as the car pulled out onto the street the gates started to close. Pamela flung herself forward and managed to get through them with a fraction of a second to spare. She was panting, wet-through and disgusted. She saw the car slip and slide its way down the long, deserted road.

Pamela trudged home, she couldn't focus, couldn't make sense of what she'd seen. *What did it mean? How could Soph do this to poor Russ? How could Soph do this to me? How long had it been going on?* She was furious and frightened in equal measure. *It's all my fault,* she thought, *I should have* **made** *Soph realise how horrible Tom is, I should have warned her that he's an evil, potential wife-murdering weirdo. What were they thinking? Precisely, they weren't thinking. They were just putting their own selfish needs and desires before anybody else.*

She was right about her cut and paste theory, Tom simply couldn't bear to be alone, so he was prepared to tear someone else's marriage to bits, to ruin his so called "friends" life. *Should I tell Russ? Of course not, Soph is my friend, and after all Russ is an irritating idiot. Yes, but he is a saint compared to bloody Tom.* She had to think carefully before rushing into anything.

Firstly, she would text Sophie tomorrow and ask why she had to pretend she'd spent the evening at her house. See how far Sophie was prepared to go with this deceitful behaviour. *Oh Soph, Soph, what are you doing?* Pamela's eyes were streaming, she felt so confused, foolish really.

She and Sophie had been friends since primary school and had shared everything from secrets to boyfriends. They'd been each other's bridesmaids; they were godparents to each other's children. It just didn't seem possible, the Sophie she knew was just not like this. She was straight as a die. *Why hasn't she confided in me?* She seemed to love Russ. She'd seen first-hand how awful divorce was. She was the person Pamela had turned to when she'd finally had enough of the dick. Sophie had helped her through those first few awful months. She'd seen the pain an affair could cause. *And how the hell had she fallen for someone so revolting as that blasted Tom?*

The weather had taken a turn for the worse, the wind was coming down from the valley, whipping her face and cold drenched body. The snow had changed from delightful soft and gentle flakes to spiteful, sharp, stinging pellets. She was miserable and alone. The world was full of hateful, lying, devious people.

At home she stripped off her wet, soiled clothes. She was shivering; bitter and nauseated. She turned on the shower, she had to heat up. *Maybe things would look better in the morning*, she wandered. *But how, how?*

It was 2 am when Pamela finally fell asleep, but she was plagued by awful dreams. She kept waking up and remembering what she had seen. She couldn't get it out of her head.

Sunday 15th January

At five am she realised she wasn't going to get back to sleep. Desolately she got up and went downstairs.

The snow had finally stopped, and it was looking like a perfect day, sunny clear blue skies, crisp fresh snow. Normally she would have relished a morning like this, but not today. None of it could bring her any joy.

Am I just jealous? She asked herself, *am I jealous that Tom has moved on so quickly?* No, she hadn't wanted him anyway, she was worried about her friend, her friend and her friend's marriage and on top of that the fact that Tom could be a wife murderer. She could hardly discuss that with Sophie now. But of all people, Sophie needed to know.

What if he killed Russ? If he was capable of one murder, surely he was capable of two? She made herself stop thinking these ridiculous thoughts. She'd get a chance to talk to Georgie and Anne today. They would probably make her see sense. She wondered if Sophie would contact her. *I bet she doesn't text me,* she thought. *I'll have to text her, but then again, I don't want to hear her lie, she's hardly going to tell me where she spent the evening.*

She made some cereal and sat and stared into the murky bowl. Nothing made any sense. The contents of the bowl swirled, turning brown and grimy. She emptied it all into the bin. Her stomach felt upside down.

She dressed and sat downstairs waiting, still and cold,

until it was time to set off to Georgie's, her head pressed back against the cushions. She felt that strange infected feeling she had felt as a child, a worthless dread, depression licked at her feet, her body was full of worms, crawling and writhing inside. She mentally wrung her body from top to bottom until all the filth was squeezed out, it collected in dark, murky pools around her feet.

She couldn't bring herself to turn on the radio or the TV, her laptop lay on the floor, untouched. Her mind was just a fuzzy blank, partly due to lack of sleep and partly because she just didn't want to think. But every few seconds she couldn't stop her mind trying to go back to the awful picture of Tom kissing Sophie on the doorstep. Tormenting her by flashing the image again and again onto her mind's memory screen.

She had to keep shaking her head, thinking of anything other than that moment. She still couldn't understand why she felt so desperate about it. She needed to get some perspective; she was being ridiculously over-dramatic. *New thoughts, new thoughts, how can I see this differently?* She made herself re-think. *Ok, Soph's having an affair with the awful Tom. People have affairs all the time, don't they? And wasn't Russ an infuriating and frustrating husband, snoring his head off, always butting in when she was on the phone, telling Sophie off for driving badly, selfishly following his own needs and desires and not caring enough about keeping his wife happy? But they'd just had a lovely holiday and they had two beautiful daughters. They'd made a lovely life together. And what about their beautiful home, they'd just made it perfect, how could Sophie walk away from that? But then again Tom's house was a billion times better and he was probably far richer. If he isn't a murderer shouldn't I be happy for Sophie? It's so complicated.*

Her mind restlessly whirled from one idea to another. She asked herself again, *am I jealous? Do I think that Tom is stealing my best friend away?* Maybe he'd started the affair to get back at her for being so awful to him. She had to admit she had been horrible to him, but it had been his own fault. No wonder he'd kept going around to Sophie's house, he was pretending to care about Pamela, whilst secretly trying to get Sophie. She wondered when it had happened, *maybe last night had been their first night together?*

Cut and paste, cut and paste, snip, snip, snip. Your marriage is over, done and dusted, so ruin someone else's. Bloody hell. Well there was nothing she could do; it had happened and there was no going back now. She had to stop thinking about it. It was none of her business. Sophie and Tom were grown-ups, they could do what they liked.

But she couldn't control the awful feeling of dread in the pit of her stomach, the feeling that something terrible was going to happen. She'd had the feeling since her realisation that Tom had murdered his wife, she remembered it hadn't been just a suspicion, she had felt it was a fact. Her best idea had been to wander along in the middle of the night and look how that had turned out.

She was probably going to lose her best friend, she just had to accept that. If only she hadn't gone out last night, she'd still be blissfully ignorant of the whole thing. Now that she knew, she could never go back to not knowing. She simply couldn't un-see what she'd seen. She would never be able to see her friend in the same light.

She chose a bottle of wine, wrapped herself up in warm coat, gloves, hat and thick winter boots and reluctantly went out to her car. She cleared the windows, it had really come down in the night, but luckily it wasn't frozen, and the snow slipped from the car quite easily.

She drove to Georgie's, although every fibre of her being wanted to go back to bed and forget the world. She knew she would tell her sisters everything, even though she didn't want to. She didn't want them to see her best friend in this shabby light, she didn't want their theories, thoughts, idle speculations. She felt numb and frightened.

The roads were less slippery than the night before and the pretty snow was turning to muddy slush. Dark banks of mud-spattered snow fringed the roads, *why did this always happen, why did nothing beautiful last?*

She arrived at the house just after two. Georgie's drive was clear, but she left her car on the road at the bottom in case it started to snow again.

Her dad was in the hall when she walked in, 'Hi dad. It's only me." She bent down and kissed him, 'How are you?'

'Hello only me, I'm ok,' he replied.

She stripped off her boots and coat, relishing the warmth of Georgie's house. *Why are other people's houses so much cosier than mine?* She asked herself.

Georgie breezed over to her and kissed her cheek, 'Hi

love, how are you? You look a bit tired.'

As she handed the bottle of wine to Georgie she replied, 'Oh, I'm fine, just not been sleeping too well.'

Georgie looked concerned and was about to speak when their dad interrupted them.

'I've been freezing.'

'Oh, that sounds dreadful.' She turned to Georgie, 'Why has dad been freezing?'

'We're not sure are we dad?'

'What's that?' He said.

Georgie raised her voice, 'WE'RE NOT SURE WHY YOUR ROOM IS SO COLD?'

Their dad shook his head sadly. Pamela and Georgie exchanged glances.

'Have you said anything to them?'

'Yes, they're getting maintenance in to check it.'

'And does it feel cold?' she asked Georgie, they both knew what their dad was like, he could sit next to a blazing fire with six jumpers on and still complain that it was cold.

'Yes, I think there's something wrong with the thermostat.'

'Well he can't stay in a freezing room.'

'I know.'

Poppy came slithering towards her and rubbed her gentle face against her ankles, she bent down to stoke her, 'Hello Poppy, how are you?' She picked her up and snuggled her under her chin, 'How is she now?'

'Oh, she's fine, just terrified of Teddy!'

'I'll bet!'

Georgie wheeled their dad into the main sitting room and put him next to the fire. She turned the television on to a sports channel and handed him the remote. 'I'll just get you a drink dad,' she told him with a motion to her mouth.

'Thanks love.'

'Cup of tea?'

'What's that?'

'TEA?'

'Thanks.'

Poppy jumped onto the settee, where she stretched her legs luxuriously and began to purr. Pamela followed Georgie into the kitchen.

She looked around admiringly, how organised everything was, if she'd been doing a dinner party for eight people everything would be totally chaotic.

She washed her hands in the kitchen sink.

'Everything will be ready in about twenty minutes.' Georgie was saying as she put the kettle on.

Pamela dried her hands and said, 'Lovely. Where's Rich?'

'He's just popped out to get some more wine.'

'I could have brought more wine.'

'I know, but you know what he's like.'

Pamela knew that he didn't like any of her family, although Georgie never acknowledged this sad fact. He would always make an excuse to be somewhere else whenever there was a family occasion. It was obvious to all of them, but Georgie seemed oblivious to it.

'Where are Adam and Hannah?'

'They're just upstairs changing Teddy.'

'I bet it's been lovely to have them here.'

'It has, Teddy is so adorable... but listen...' Georgie lowered her voice and continued, 'I don't think Hannah is doing too well, don't say anything will you?'

'What do you mean?'

'You'll notice immediately, but just keep quiet, ok?'

'Of course.'

Georgie made their dad his tea and poured Pamela a large glass of wine.

'I can't wait to see Teddy. Hey, that's too much, I'm driving you know!' But she took it anyway. She was dying to launch into her story, but she made herself wait. She wanted to be able to tell her sisters together, when they were less likely to be interrupted.

'Do you need any help?'

'No, everything is more or less organised. Just take dad his tea, would you?'

Pamela went back into the sitting room, just as Adam walked in, holding little Teddy in front of him, like a prize.

'Hi Aunty Pam.' He kissed her cheek.

Poppy leapt off the settee and ran out of the room.

'Hello Adam, how lovely to see you, hello little Teddy.'

Teddy squirmed and wriggled away from her, looking miserable and horrified.

'Ah bless him, is he shy? Are you shy little Teddy Top?' She patted his head,

'Say hello to your aunty Pam.' But Teddy just writhed further away, wanting the floor to eat him up, 'He'll come around!' Laughed Adam, 'Eventually!'

'He is so cute.' She said as she tried to get a glimpse of his little face, great brown eyes stared coldly at her, from underneath a mass of blonde curls. 'His hair is getting so long!'

She put her dad's tea on the small table next to him and left Adam trying to coax little Teddy into being sociable.

'Say hello to great-grandad, let's have a little smile, come on now,' she glanced back at Teddy, whose mouth was forming a perfect circle of horror. He started to wail, 'Come on now, smile, smile little Teds.'

Fat chance she thought.

Back in the kitchen Georgie was putting the finishing touches to the large dining table.

'I wonder what time Anne will turn up.' They both laughed, she was a terror for turning up two hours late to everything.

'Well I told her one pm.'

'You should have said twelve!'

'Yes, I wish I had. Did I hear you talking to Adam? Did you see Teddy?'

'Yes, he is adorable, a bit freaked out by me and great-grandad though! Adam's looking well.'

'Yes, I think he's taken to being a father very well.'

'He looks very relaxed with him.'

'He is. Was Hannah down?'

'No, not yet.'

Georgie walked a bit nearer to Pamela and whispered, 'So, as I said, I don't think she's doing too well at the moment.'

'How exactly?'

'I think she's suffering from post-natal depression.'

'Oh, that's awful, has Adam said anything?'

'He doesn't have to.'

'I'm so sorry to hear that.'

'I know, and she's supposed to be going back to work soon.'

'Bloody hell, that's awful.'

'Anyway, don't say anything, will you?' She repeated.

'Of course not.' Just then Adam walked into the kitchen, with little Teddy clinging limpet-like to his dad.

'Is your grandad ok?'

'Yes, he was just watching the football, I think we were getting in his way!'

'Where's Hannah?' Georgie asked brightly.

'She's just having a little lay down; she didn't get much sleep last night. She'll be fine by the time dad gets back and before Aunty Anne arrives.' They all laughed.

'We'll have eaten by the time Anne arrives!' Pamela quipped, uncharitably.

'Yes, especially these days, dad can't be kept waiting a second, he gets so cantankerous if his lunch is late.'

'Not just these days, he was always the same. Cantankerous is his middle name!' Pamela said.

'Yes, that's true.' Georgie agreed.

Adam was trying to stuff Teddy into his high-chair, his little legs kept sticking out in any direction, in order to avoid the dreaded seat, he was screaming and kicking.

'Don't you want to get into your high-chair, little Teddy top?' Pamela coaxed, 'Come on it's not that bad.'

He flung his head back and cried as though he'd been beaten. Adam gave up and sat down at the table with Teddy on his knee.

Georgie gave him a few pieces of bread and butter, 'There you go little Ted.' He smiled for his granny. At last a few moments of peace descended on the kitchen.

'So, how's fatherhood treating you? Pamela asked.

'It's amazing, but bloody hard work,' Adam laughed, 'I think we'll stick at one kid; I don't know how you all had more than one!'

'It is hard at first, but you kind of click into another gear, you know?'

'Well I'll be happy with just one.'

'We'll see,' said Georgie, looking a bit disappointed, 'you might change your mind.'

'Never say never!' Pamela agreed.

'So, how are Jake and Alex? I haven't seen either of them since just after Teddy was born.'

'I know, it's crazy, we need a family reunion! They're both fine, working hard, hating London though, I think.'

'Really?'

'Well maybe hating is a bit strong, anyway they're certainly showing no signs of wanting to move back to sunny Yorkshire! What about you and Hannah, might you move nearer home now that you've got Teddy? Free babysitting with the grans and devoted great auntie's after all.'

'Yeah that would be nice, but my job is going so well, it'd be a shame to leave it, I doubt that I could find something better up here to be honest, much as I'd love to live nearer family.' He smiled at his mum,

'Yes, we'd love to have you closer.' She smiled back.

'And Hannah goes back soon?'

'Yes, next month, poor kid.'

'It's so different to our day, we got three months if we were lucky.'

'Yes,' Georgie agreed, 'but I think that made it easier to go back, a year is too long if you ask me. At three months the baby didn't mind as much, at a year they're so much more aware, and sorry to say this Adam, but I was bloody delighted to go back! I could finally finish a full cup of coffee!'

'Yes - and go to the loo without an audience!' Pamela agreed.

'And finish your lunch!' Georgie added.

'God, I get it, no need to apologise, don't tell Hannah, but...' he covered Teddy's ears, 'I love escaping, work is nothing compared to looking after this little chap.'

Teddy wriggled out of Tom's grasp, he let him down onto the floor. He bottom-shuffled towards his gran.

'Come here, little Teddy.' She picked him up and squeezed him, kissing his plump, pink cheeks.

'I wonder if I'll ever get to be a gran, the rate my boys are going I'll be too decrepit to enjoy it.'

Just then Rich came dashing into the kitchen, arms laden with wine, 'Sorry I'm late,' he breathed, as he put the wine into the fridge. 'How are you Pam?' he kissed both her cheeks.

'Fine thanks.'

'Hello Teddy,' he grabbed him and swung him around.

'Be careful,' all three of them shouted.

'Oh, don't worry, you'll be fine, won't you little man?'

Teddy was half inclined to be disgusted, but half inclined to enjoy himself, his face wavered between the two emotions, before settling on disgust, and he began to cry, Rich handed him back to the waiting arms of gran, 'I think your dad is getting a bit fed up in the other room.'

Georgie handed Teddy back to Adam, 'Bloody hell, how do you know?'

'He was shouting for you as I came in, I popped my head around the door, and he wants one of you girls!'

'I thought he'd be happy watching the football for a few minutes,' Georgie moaned.

'Never mind, I'll go.' Pamela took a glug of wine and went to see what her dad wanted. It went straight to her head with a rush and she remembered she hadn't eaten anything, *I must be careful,* she warned herself, *don't go crazy.*

As she went into the hall, she saw Hannah emerge from upstairs, 'Hello Hannah, how are you?'

Hannah's little pale face and wide eyes answered the question, she murmured, 'I'm fine thanks, nice to see you Pam.'

'And you, I've got to go and check on my dad, they're all in the kitchen.'

'Thanks.' Hannah's thin frame shuffled away from Pamela, towards the kitchen.

She looked terrible, Pamela thought, *bless her, what a change.* She'd always been a beautiful, well-built, joyful person. Now there wasn't a bit of flesh on her spiky bones, her hair was thin and dishevelled, her face hardened and old before her time. She hoped her dad wouldn't say anything, tact was not his strong point. She didn't dare warn him not to say anything as the chances were he may not notice the change in Hannah, but if she pointed it out and said don't mention it, he may blurt something out. She chose to say nothing and hoped for the best. 'Are you ok dad?'

'What's that?'

'ARE YOU OK?'

'Yes, when are we eating? I'm starving.'

'WE'RE JUST WAITING FOR ANNE.'

'Ok.'

'SHALL I GET YOU SOME BREAD AND CHEESE OR SOMETHING?'

'Ok.' He sank back into himself, shrivelled and alone.

She went back into the kitchen, Hannah was sitting listlessly at the dining room table, shredding a napkin, staring into space. Adam, Georgie, Rich and even little Teddy were looking at her with similar anxious expressions. She seemed oblivious to their concern.

Pamela interrupted their reverie, 'Err, sorry guys, dad says he's starving, can I just make him some bread and butter or something?'

Georgie snapped, 'Jesus that man, can't he wait five

freaking minutes?'

Adam and Rich turned away from the lonely figure at the table and fussed over Teddy.

'I know, but no, he can't!'

'Look we'll just bring him in and give him a bowl of soup, that should keep him going until Anne turns up.'

'Good idea.' Pamela replied, turning to go back and get him.

'Do you want any help?' Adam shouted after her.

'No, I'll be fine.'

She was quite relieved to get out of the kitchen - the tension in there was palpable. Poor Hannah, she looked so sad and far away. *Bloody hell, I wonder how long she's been suffering,* Pamela thought. She prayed her dad wouldn't say anything. *And what about Anne, should I text her and warn her? No, she wasn't an idiot, it would be obvious the moment she came into the kitchen.*

'Ok dad you're going to have some soup,' he looked at her, 'SOUP' she shouted,

'Good.' She wheeled him into the kitchen and put him at the head of the table.

'Are you ok to stay in your wheelchair?' She pointed to another chair and mimed him sitting on that.

'I'm fine in this.'

That was a relief, it was so hard to get him up, seeing him struggle was awful. When he was in his wheelchair, he didn't seem so vulnerable.

Adam sat down next to Hannah. 'So, how's it going in the home grandad? Are the people still nice?' He asked, then repeated, 'THE HOME, GRANDAD, IS IT OK?'

'It's the same old, same old,' his grandad replied, 'me and four walls...'

Pamela knew what was coming and tried to head him off, 'Would you like cream on top of your soup dad? Salt?'

'Shall I butter your bread dad?' Georgie mimed the actions.

Rich looked at the sisters, his cold judgemental eyes flickered, then flashed away, revolted.

Pamela wished she hadn't seen his expression, but Adam and Georgie were oblivious to it.

'Isn't anybody else eating?' Their dad asked, with uncharacteristic concern for those around him.

'We're just waiting for Anne, dad... WHEN ANNE GETS HERE.'

'When will she get here?' He asked, sadly.

'Good question,' said Pamela as she and Georgie exchanged glances, but replied 'WE'RE NOT SURE DAD.'

She handed him his creamy soup and bread and butter. He slowly started eating. It broke Pamela's heart and she had no idea why. She could have cried for her dad at that minute. *Stop being so stupid,* she told herself, *he was perfectly happy, so what if Rich was a prize twat. Ignore him.*

'Hannah would you like some soup?' Georgie asked, but Hannah just looked up blankly,

'We may as well all have the starter,' Adam quickly interjected, giving his mum a warning look.

'Great idea. Anne and Pete won't mind.' Pamela added.

Georgie placed the large tureen in the middle of the table and served it out. Creamy leek and potato soup, *can I face it?* Her stomach was still feeling strange. She managed a few mouthfuls. As she ate the warm soup, she began to feel a bit better.

They eat for a while in silence. Pamela sat opposite Hannah and tried not to stare. She toyed with her soup but didn't manage to eat anything.

Teddy had had enough of his dad's knee and tried to fling himself onto the stone flags, Adam grabbed him, alarmed, 'Careful there, bud.'

Hannah didn't seem to notice while Adam gently let him down onto the floor, where he shuffled under the table.

Adam got some toys and put them under with him. Teddy seemed relatively content, for now anyway.

Her dad was eating as though the home starved him to death, she caught Rich looking disdainfully at him. What a shit. Well, all wasn't rosy in his perfect little world. She wondered how he felt about his daughter-in-law. *No, that's not a kind thought,* she reprimanded herself, she could hardly look on that misfortune in any light other than sadness.

The door opened, and a windswept Anne came rushing in, 'Sorry we're so late, the roads have been dire, Pete's just parking the car.'

Pamela was about to say, "The roads are the same for all of us and I managed to get here on time," but bit her tongue.

Anne dashed from person to person pecking them on the cheek.

'I hope you don't mind us starting without you?' Georgie asked pointedly, but her tone was totally lost on Anne.

'God no, it's fine.' She plonked herself down next to Hannah. 'Hello Teddy,' she called under the table, 'He's grown such a lot, hasn't he?' she addressed her comment to Hannah, who smiled tragically and didn't reply.

Anne exchanged a glance with Georgie and seemed to get it instantly. Georgie was serving soup as Peter came in,.

'Hello everyone,' he smiled and shook hands with the men and kissed the women, he too shouted a greeting to the child under the table, but this was just too much for Teddy who was very insulted and started to scream.

Adam dragged him out and walked off trying to calm him down.

'Sorry I seem to have that effect on small children.'

Peter laughed, then turned to Hannah, 'Sorry,' again the pathetic smile, the dead eyes, he looked at Anne, who imperceptibly shook her head, he flushed a little and then turned to Pamela, 'How are you, I hear you are having a nightmare at work?'

He can't help putting his foot in it, poor Pete, she thought.

'Yeah, it's pretty awful, I'll tell you all about it later.'

He may have sensed he'd managed to upset everyone and replied, 'Of course.' He looked down at his soup, not sure who he had offended and who he could safely talk to.

Peter seemed to like everyone, and, in the wider world,

was generally very popular, but his wife's family hadn't made their mind up. They were reserving judgment, constantly waiting for him to reveal his true self. *After all he had married Anne and stayed with her all these years. How odd was that?*

Hannah suddenly got up and walked out of the room.

Everyone stopped eating and looked, there was a full three seconds of silence, then they immediately looked away and carried on eating. Adam waited a few moments, then he and Teddy soundlessly followed Helen out of the room.

Glances were again exchanged, only their dad didn't seem to notice what was going on, 'More soup love?' he asked Georgie, who was glad to have the opportunity to bustle about the kitchen again.

Typically, Rich ignored what had happened. 'Right, Pete, Anne, what can I get you both to drink?'

'Am I driving, or are you?' Peter asked Anne,

'Well I'd rather you did in this weather.'

'Yes, fine, I'll have one small glass, if that's ok?'

'Fine'

'Red or white Pete?'

'White, thanks'

'Anne?'

'Yes, white's great thanks.'

'Would you like a drop more Pam?'

'Ok, just a tiny bit though, I'm driving.'

'I can give you a lift home Pam,' Peter interjected.

'Hmm – not sure – I'm supposed to be being good.'

'Well it's not like you have work tomorrow is it? Pete joked.

'That is true, thanks for pointing that out' she replied sarcastically.

Rich filled everyone's wine glass to the brim, including his own.

'Well there's always an upside isn't there?' Anne quipped.

Georgie flashed her a look, turned to Pamela and said, 'Sorry love, it must be a nightmare, what are you going to do?'

'Not too sure, it's not great, you think I'd be happy, but I just feel dreadful.'

Anne looked sheepish, 'I'm sure it's awful for you, but you need to sort it, surely you can't just not go back?'

'What's that?' their dad asked Anne,

'Nothing dad' they both replied,

'NOTHING,' shouted Pamela.

Their dad looked offended, but luckily his replenished soup had arrived, so his attention turned away from his girls.

Pamela added quietly, 'let's just change the subject, please.'

Everyone looked miserable. Georgie sat down, and an uncomfortable silence ensued, she eyed the empty seats at the other side of the table. 'Rich could you just go and see what's going on with Adam and Hannah, see if they're coming back to eat?'

Rich sighed, took a massive gulp of wine and

ostentatiously left the kitchen.

'Sorry everyone,' Georgie sighed, in a hushed voice,

'Don't be ridiculous,' they answered in unison.

'It's just one of those things, isn't it?' Pamela said.

'Yes, true, but it's a bit of a strain, obviously.'

'Yes, poor kids.'

'How long has she been like this? Anne asked, quietly.

'I'm not too sure, Adam's been very cagey about it, which is bloody annoying, I wouldn't have done this lunch if I'd had any idea what she was like.'

'You should have cancelled.' Anne interjected, sourly.

'Of course I couldn't,' Georgie hissed.

They contemplated this in silence.

Pamela couldn't help saying, 'It's so sad to see her like this.'

'Yes, terrible.' Peter agreed.

'Have you spoken to her mum?' Anne asked,

'No, we're going to ring her after they've gone.'

'Does Adam mind?'

'I don't care if he does, he isn't dealing with it is he?' Georgie snapped.

Again, the mumbled, sad agreements. What could anyone say? It made Pamela's news about Sophie pale into insignificant gossip.

Rich came back into the room. 'Hannah's gone for a lay down and Teddy is having his afternoon nap. Adam's going to join us again in a few minutes.'

Georgie got up and collected the soup bowls.

'Do you need a hand?' Peter asked,

'No, I'll be fine, Rich could you get the plates out of the oven please?

'I was just about to,' he answered, tipping the last of his wine into his mouth. He refilled his glass and took it into the kitchen.

The guests sat silently, wishing that Georgie *had* cancelled the lunch. The only person vaguely enjoying himself was their dad. *At least that was something,* Pamela thought.

She realised that she had finished another large glass of wine. She looked across at Anne and indicated her empty wine glass, 'Well it looks like I'll need a lift with you and Pete, Anne, if that's ok?'

'Yes, obviously,' Anne replied, sharply. 'He wouldn't have offered, would he?'

Peter lent over and poured her another glass.

'Thanks Pete.' She tried to smile, but the whole event had become so tense, it was hard to even pretend she was enjoying herself.

Rich put their plates out. 'Be careful they're very hot.'

Georgie put two casserole dishes on the table, followed by a large tray of roast potatoes.

'This looks amazing,' enthused Peter, trying to salvage some happiness from the ruined afternoon. 'You must have been cooking for days.'

It was well known in the family that he and Anne never cooked and that they lived on takeaways and ready cooked meals. Anne stared at him coldly. He stopped talking and sipped his wine.

Georgie pointed to the first dish, 'That's a beef bourguignon and that's a haricot bean and mushroom cassoulet. Help yourself. I'll be back in a minute.' She walked out, leaving them to it.

Pamela shouted over to her dad, 'DO YOU WANT SOME BEEF STEW DAD?'

He looked up and smiled, 'That would be nice, love, yes.'

As she began to serve her dad, Rich also left the room,.

'Bloody hell,' Anne whispered under her breath.

Pamela ignored her and continued to serve the others.

'Thanks, that's lovely,' Peter said as he helped himself to the roasts, 'This is delicious isn't it?'

They all murmured agreement.

'It would be better if the rest of the family could join us,' Anne added nastily.

'So,' Peter began, trying to lighten the mood, 'How was your New Year Pam?'

'Oh,' she groaned, 'I drank far too much and spent New Year's Day wishing I was dead!'

'So, the same as ever.' Anne replied coldly.

Pamela ignored this and trying to be cheerful asked, 'What about you guys, you were at home weren't you?'

'Well that was the plan, but we ended up going around to the neighbours, didn't we Anne?'

'Yes.'

'Was it a good night?'

'It was ok.' Anne replied dispassionately. They slipped back into silence.

Pamela emptied her glass and helped herself to more wine. She may as well get completely drunk, she didn't have to take her dad back, for once, and Pete was right, she didn't have work tomorrow. Her stomach still felt a bit weird, but drinking seemed to be numbing the feeling.

Georgie came back into the room. 'Sorry everyone.' She sat down and helped herself to a tiny amount of the beef casserole. They each politely looked down at their own plates.

Pamela, of course, couldn't bear the silence. 'This bean cassoulet is so nice, Georgie, where did you get the recipe from?'

'I think it's a Delia or Nigella, not sure which.'

'You must give me the recipe.'

'Yes, I'll send you it.'

'Thanks.'

Peter tried to join in. 'This beef is so tender, it just melts in your mouth.'

'Thanks.'

He looked at Anne, raising his eyebrows, Anne shook her head. She wasn't about to try. Typical, Pamela thought.

This was awful, Pamela felt crushed by the oppressive atmosphere. She knew Georgie was worried about Hannah, but did she have to make this whole lunch so unpleasant? And where the hell had Rich gone? He was being even ruder than usual.

Adam came back into the room and sat down wordlessly to join his silent family. He helped himself to the beef casserole.

'Give me that I'll heat it up for you,' Georgie took his plate away and put it in the microwave. Nobody could think what to say to Adam, he was looking so despondent and forlorn, his eyes red rimmed, suddenly lifeless.

Pamela wanted so badly to make him feel better, 'It was so nice to see little Teddy, he's so adorable, is he having a nap?'

'Yes, he gets horrible in the afternoon.'

'They all do, it's only natural.'

No one dared ask about Hannah, but not mentioning her made the whole situation so much worse.

Georgie handed Adam his meal, 'Thanks mum,' he tried to smile, but all he could manage was a miserable, crooked little twist of the mouth.

Their dad suddenly looked up and said, 'Where's the baby?'

'HAVING A NAP, GRANDAD, 'Adam shouted. Rich walked into the room.

'For god's sake Rich your food is going cold,' Georgie snapped.

'Not to worry I'll put it in the microwave.' He gave her a sickly-sweet smile, that was anything but kind.

Pamela wasn't going to eat the roast potatoes, but they looked so lovely, she couldn't resist them. She helped herself to some. As she ate, she became aware that Rich was staring at her, 'How's the diet going Pam?' he asked, feigning interest.

She immediately felt her throat close and she couldn't swallow.

'For goodness sake Rich, shut up.' Georgie looked at him warningly.

Pamela took a large gulp of wine and managed to force the potatoes down. 'It's going fine, thanks,' she spluttered.

What a fricking creep he was, he always managed to make her feel stupid and greedy. He wouldn't have dared say something like that to Anne. *It's always me,* she thought. She would've loved to say something equally cutting back, but for Georgie and Adam's sake she just pretended they were having a normal conversation. She should have obeyed her first instinct and not eaten anything. Peter caught her eye and smiled sympathetically, but she wished he wouldn't, that would wind both Anne and Rich up.

She carefully placed her knife and fork down; *how can anyone eat in this atmosphere? Well done Rich,* she thought, *you've been so unbearable, you've made everything a hundred times worse.* Her eyes stung with tears, *please don't cry, please don't cry,* she repeated to herself. *Don't be such a baby. Stop feeling sorry for yourself.* She always felt the same when she was with her two older sisters, somehow, she reverted straight back to the baby of the family. She was never given a chance somehow to be a fully-grown person in her own right.

Their dad had finished his meal. 'Would you like any more dad?' Georgie mimed spooning food from the casserole.

'No thanks love.'

'Shall I get you some pudding, PUDDING?'

'What is there?'

'STICKY TOFFEE PUDDING AND ICE CREAM,'

'Thanks love.' Georgie gave their dad a large portion.

'I can't eat all that, I've got no appetite anymore.'

The girls looked at each other in exasperation. This was his constant refrain, but from what they could see he managed to eat the same as ever. 'JUST EAT WHAT YOU CAN DAD.'

'Ok.'

'WOULD YOU LIKE ANOTHER CUP OF TEA?'

'Yes please.'

Rich started to fill everyone's wine glasses.

'Not for me,' Peter shielded his glass.

'Yeah, I'd better not as well,' Adam said. I've got a long drive ahead.'

Georgie got some sparkling water out of the fridge and gave everyone a tumbler. 'Rich, not everyone is an alcoholic you know.'

'Oh, sorry for trying to be a good host, just chillax won't you.'

'Chillax? Chillax? What are you, sixteen?'

'Oh my god, what are you saying, it's a perfectly reasonable word, you don't have to be sixteen to...'

Pamela sighed, if these two started bickering all was lost. She interrupted, 'So Rich, did you enjoy your quiet lake district Christmas?'

He turned his cold blue stare on her. 'Did we enjoy it?' he mused, 'did we enjoy it Georgie?' he asked menacingly,

'Of course we did, Rich, just shut up and eat your bloody food.'

Adam looked miserably at his parents. He knew the tension was because of Hannah, but he was powerless to do anything about it.

Pamela realised that Rich was a bit drunk. He'd obviously been drinking something – probably a secret stash of whiskey - every time he went out of the room. She looked over at Georgie, who seemed totally unaware of the state he was in. He wasn't going to get any kinder, that was for sure.

Pamela felt the need to somehow salvage this dire lunch, her dad was fine, he was oblivious, tucking into his pudding, but she needed to steer Rich away from the cruel path he had embarked on so she found herself blurting out, 'Well I've been stalked since New Year by a horrible man who probably murdered his wife!'

They all turned to stare at her, appalled.

Oh no, she thought, *I'm obviously more drunk than I thought,* but she couldn't help going on, 'Yes, he's called Tom, his wife has disappeared, and he's been coming on to me, but actually that was just a front, he's been secretly sleeping with my so-called best friend.'

'What the hell?' from Anne.

'Sweet Jesus,' from Georgie, then, 'Don't be ridiculous...'

'I know it sounds crazy, but...'

'Which bit, the wife murdering bit or the having an affair bit?' Rich asked, sneeringly.

'Well probably the murder bit, but the other thing is definitely true.'

'Are you sure?' Georgie asked incredulous.

'How do you know Pam?' Peter asked as kindly as he could, he felt that she must be ever so slightly unhinged, but he understood the urge she'd had to avoid a Georgie-Rich stand-off.

'I went around to his house late last night.'

'No, you did not.' Georgie was aghast, 'What the hell possessed you to do a thing like that?'

'I thought I might see something, I dunno, a clue or something to show that he'd killed his wife.'

'What, like her body parts spread across the lawn?' Peter asked, amused.

'Yeah, something like that!'

'Fuck me, you have lost the plot woman, there was a blizzard last night!' Rich weighed in.

'I know, I know, it was a crazy idea, anyway I got down to his front door just in time to see Sophie leaving.'

'Maybe she was with her husband... what's-his-name?'

'Russ... no, I somehow doubt that, she wouldn't have been snogging Tom if Russ had been there.'

'Bloody hell,' said Georgie.

'Bloody hell is right.'

'And did they see you standing there staring at them?' Rich asked callously.

Pamela gave him a look, but continued, 'Thankfully they didn't, I was hiding behind a bush.'

'Naturally,' said Rich.

Sod you, she thought.

'Oh no, that's awful, what has Sophie got to say for

herself?' Georgie asked.

'Well that's the other annoying thing, she'd texted me earlier on Saturday to say if Russ asked, she'd spent the evening with me, and, of course I agreed without thinking about it, and she hasn't got back to me today.'

'What are you going to do?' Anne wondered.

'I don't know. I mean, I know I'm probably being over-dramatic thinking he's murdered his wife, but what if he did, you know?'

'Why do you think he's murdered his wife?' Peter asked.

'Because she's got an over-active imagination, that's why,' Anne said, unkindly.

'Anne's right, Pam, sorry,' Georgie added, giving Pamela a regretful shrug of her shoulders.

'Look I know it seems unbelievable that a perfectly normal man, who lives in our little town, going about his everyday business actually murdered his wife, but it's so suspicious, nothing about it adds up.' Pamela stated gravely.

'Right, can we please talk about something else?' Georgie entreated.

Then Peter asked, 'Why don't things add up?'

Pamela looked at Georgie, who shrugged again, the lunch had gone to hell anyway, how much worse could it get, and at least they were distracted from thinking about Hannah, and Adam and Rich seemed intrigued, 'Oh, go on then tell them your theory.'

'Well, he said she disappeared just before Christmas, she only spoke to him, none of her children or friends, or family, he said she took just one small suitcase of stuff and she hasn't contacted anyone since.'

'Not even her kids?'

'No one.'

'Well that does seem strange.' Peter had to agree.

'Yes, but there are still a million other conclusions to jump to, surely?' Rich pointed out.

'That's more-or-less exactly what I said,' added Georgie.

'True, but it *does* happen doesn't it?' They all had to agree with Pamela on this,

'So, have you phoned the police?' Adam asked.

'No, do you think I should?'

'Yes!'

'Does everyone else agree?'

'Yes,' from Rich and Peter

'I'm not sure,' from cautious Anne,

'Neither am I,' from equally cautious Georgie.

'Why not, mum?' Adam asked.

'Well, I just think Pam should keep out of it, it's nothing to do with her and now Sophie's involved...'

'You don't think she had anything to do with his wife's disappearance, do you?' Peter asked Pamela.

'No, I don't think so, she was trying to get me to go out with him, so I think it's unlikely.'

'Maybe that was just a front, to hide her relationship with him?'

Thanks Rich, she thought, but had to say, 'I must admit that had occurred to me, but they'd both have to be pretty evil to plan that, I don't think Sophie is that sort of person, but then again I didn't think she was the kind of person to have an affair, so who knows? She did seem to genuinely want me and him to get together, I think he's played a blinder though, constantly going around to her house asking her about me, whilst all the time wanting to get off with her!'

'Having an affair's one thing, but murdering your wife, that's a whole new level of crazy.' Rich put in.

Their dad looked up, he'd finished his pudding, 'What was that?' he asked Pamela, 'Who's been murdered?'

They all burst out laughing, he heard nothing all day, but could suddenly pick up on that. 'NO ONE DAD, JUST A FILM WE ALL SAW.'

'Ok,' He finished his tea and asked, 'Can someone take me home?'

'Of course, dad,' Georgie replied. They all got up and kissed him goodbye.

'Can you clear the table and get everyone some pudding Rich, please?'

'It will be my pleasure.' Rich replied condescendingly, if he had his way they'd all be leaving.

'Thanks for taking him back,' Pamela whispered, above her dad's head.

'No worries, thought I'd give you a day off!'

'One of us will see you tomorrow dad, TOMORROW.' Anne added.

'Ok'

'Bye Grandad,'

'Bye dad.'

When they'd gone Rich busied himself in the kitchen.

'Do you want a hand, dad?'

'No, you sit and entertain your mad aunties.'

'Thanks a lot, Rich.' Anne replied, but Pamela couldn't be bothered rising to his drunken bait.

'So, Pam, what do *you* think you should do?' Asked Adam.

'What would you do?'

'I'd definitely call the police, I mean it does sound a bit weird, who leaves someone just before Christmas?'

'Someone very cruel, and she doesn't look cruel'

'How do you know?' Peter asked, 'Did you know her?'

'No, just done a bit of FB stalking!'

'Well, I'd speak to Sophie anyway.'

'Would you Anne? What do you think I should say? I can't imagine having that conversation with her.'

'I'd be absolutely furious that she was using me to cover up her affair, what kind of friend does that?'

'Yes, but how do I know she's having an affair? I can't admit that I was creeping around Tom's house in the middle of the night, spying on him, that'll make me sound totally deranged.'

Rich sniggered and added sarcastically, 'Yes, we wouldn't want people to think you were deranged, would we?' Peter gave him a look,

'She's got a point though, Rich, how can she admit that she was in his garden at that time of night?' Peter agreed.

'And I don't want to hear her lie to me, she's not going to admit this is she?'

'Probably not, but I think you should ring the police

if you think he has murdered his wife.' Adam added reasonably.

'How old are his kids?'

'He did tell me, but I've forgotten, they're grown up, anyway.'

'You'd think they'd have started to worry, wouldn't you?'

'Georgie thinks that they probably are in touch with their mum, but they're not telling their dad.' Pamela pointed out.

'That could be true, but how could you find out?' added Peter.

'The thing is, I think you're all missing the point here, my friend could be in danger.' Pamela slurred, in danger of becoming a drunken emotional mess.

Rich snorted with laughter. He was loving this.

'Oh for god's sake Pam, you are being ridiculous.' Anne blurted out, 'Ring Sophie and tell her you know everything, she'll be so shocked she won't ask how you know, and then just tell her you think he murdered his wife.'

'Just like that?'

'Yes.'

They all stared at Pamela. She hiccupped and downed her glass.

'I'll make you a black coffee,' Rich said nastily.

The family sat in silence. Rich collected the plates. 'Pudding anyone?'

Pamela wished she'd kept her mouth shut, *what is wrong with me? Why do I always have to be the centre of attention?* She thought it would have been far better to have

Rich and Georgie bicker and argue than to have shared this with all of them. She'd never intended to tell anyone other than her sister's. What a bloody fool she was.

Rich put a coffee and a bowl of pudding in front of her. She pushed the bowl away and ignored the coffee, instead she helped herself to another glass of wine.

The conversations carried on around her, she sank into a muddled drunken oblivion, letting other people talk for once.

'Whiskey, brandy, port?' Rich was asking everyone when she focused back on the conversation.

She would not have another drink, she would not, she'd had enough, but she found herself slurring, 'Great, I'll have a whiskey.'

Anne looked sternly at her, 'We'll be going as soon as Georgie gets back.'

'Then I've got plenty of time to drink this whiskey, haven't I?' she replied nastily.

She could see that Anne was furious with her. Rich, on the other hand, was enjoying himself. He looked like he was thinking of something unpleasant to say, when Adam interrupted, 'Hey dad, can you come and help me check the car? There was a weird noise coming from the engine towards the end of the journey, yesterday.'

'And you've waited 'til now to tell me,' his dad moaned, but his eyes lit up, he loved messing with engines.

As they left the room the remaining three drew a sigh of relief. Pamela knocked back the whiskey and poured herself another glass of wine. The peace was short-lived,

Anne was watching her, with a sour little expression on her face, 'Listen Pam, I think you've had enough.'

'Thanks Anne, so kind of you to point that out.' Pamela replied caustically.

'I'm not trying to be nasty; I just think you need to know when to stop.'

'Like you, you mean?'

'We're not talking about me, honestly, you make yourself a laughing stock, Georgie told me about New Year's Eve, you need to grow the fuck up.'

'Oh, do I?' The sister's glared at each other.

Pamela stood up, 'Say goodbye to Georgie for me, I'm going home.'

'Oh my god, you are not driving in that state.'

'Who said anything about driving? I'll walk home, thanks very much.'

'It's bloody miles and anyway you're too drunk to walk home.'

'That doesn't make any sense. What the hell do you mean?'

'I mean you'll probably get run over or something.'

'I've lived to this age and managed not to get run over, thanks,' she pointed out, then added, 'bitch,' under her breath.

'Look we're going soon, wait until Georgie gets back and we'll all go together,' Peter added kindly, hoping to calm the situation.

'I don't want a lift with you two, is that so hard to understand?'

Peter looked shocked, she hadn't meant to shout at him, but Anne wound her up so much she couldn't help herself.

'Right well fuck off then.' Anne said spitefully. She stood up and started collecting plates from the table, huffily keeping her back to Pamela, who looked at Peter and raised her eyebrows, he looked away, he'd tried his best, he didn't want to take sides. He started to help Anne.

Pamela stood up shakily and sarcastically slurred, 'Bye and thanks for all your shupport.'

'Yeah, whatever,' Anne spat out, 'bye.' She added.

She was such a bitch, Pamela thought as she unsteadily left the room. In the hall she grabbed her coat and gloves. When she sat down to put her boots on the room began to spin. *I hope I sober up soon,* she thought, *this is dreadful.*

She staggered out of the front door. It was dark and freezing, the shock of outside air hit her like a great weight. Her breath came out in huge white clouds. *Bloody hell,* she thought, *can I walk home in this state?* Too late to go back in, she wasn't going to speak to Anne ever again, *that little bitch,* she muttered repeatedly.

She shouted goodbye to the two men bending over Adam's car in the garage. Adam looked up, 'Are you going home Pam?'

'Yesh.'

'Are you walking?'

'Yesh.'

'Will you be alright?'

'Yesh.' Adam stared after her, then went back to helping his dad, she was halfway down the drive when she realised she had been rude. To redeem herself she shouted to the bent figures; 'Say thanks to Georgie. And give Teddy a kissh from me.'

Back in the garage Adam asked, 'shouldn't we give her a lift?'

'You know your aunt Pam, she's a crazy lady, best leave her alone. Besides, it's only half past four, it's not late.' Then he added, 'she seems to like wandering around by herself in the dark.' He chuckled nastily to himself.

Adam shrugged,

'Well as long as you're ok with it, mum might be annoyed though.'

'When is your mum not annoyed by something or other?'

'On your head be it, when she gets back.'

Pamela got to the bottom of the drive and stood at her car door, she fumbled for her keys. *Should I get in?* She was sure she'd be able to drive home. There wouldn't be any police around at this time in the afternoon and it wasn't far. The snow on the road had all but melted, so that was fine. But Georgie and Anne would see that her car was gone, and they'd know she'd driven home. She couldn't face them going mental with her. Well, Georgie anyway, she didn't give a shit what Anne thought. *Has she said one kind thing to me today?* No. She'd pretended to care about her work situation, but only after Georgie reminded her. And then it was just to say she should go back. What did she know? She'd always worked for herself; she had no idea how hard teaching was.

She was one of those people who always bitched about teachers having long holidays and finishing at three pm. She didn't believe Pamela when she told her the realities of the job. *Stupid bitch,* she thought, *horrible, mean, little cow.*

The sky ahead was dark and ominous. She tried to work out how long it was going to take her to walk home, but realised she had no idea. There were a few small shortcuts she could take, so maybe it wouldn't be too bad.

She slushed through the dirty crumbling snow, her winter boots turned out to be totally useless in these conditions and her feet felt like lead, wet, icy and numb. *Why didn't I call a taxi? What is wrong with me,* she thought, *why do I never do the sensible thing? I'll probably fall over and die in a pile of slush and it'll serve me right for always drinking too much and behaving like a fricking idiot.*

She felt her mobile vibrate. *That's probably Anne,* she thought, *saying she's sorry and begging me to come back, yeah right, like that was going to happen!* She fumbled in her bag and looked at the screen. It took a while for her bleary eyes to focus. It was Russ. *Bloody hell, what did he want?* She couldn't possibly talk to him right now. She pressed reject. If it was important, he'd call her back. As she was closing the case, she noticed that there were several missed calls from him, her phone had been in her bag during the meal, and she hadn't felt it vibrate, which was just as well, she didn't want to talk to Russ. *Was he checking that Sophie had been with her last night, that was unlikely, wasn't it? He didn't have any reason to suspect anything yet, did he? Bloody Sophie dragging me into this. What am I supposed to say to Russ if he asks me outright? Well,* she supposed, *I'll just have to lie.* But it felt wrong and annoying, why should she stick up for Sophie when she was being so deceitful and hadn't even bothered to let Pamela know what she was up to. Keep everything from Russ, fair enough, but not your best friend.

Sleet suddenly began to pelt down, icy, sharp pellets bit into her face. She kept her head down and wished for the zillionth time that she hadn't got so drunk. She wouldn't have fallen out with Anne and she'd now be in her lovely warm car driving home. *I must stop drinking,* she chanted to herself as she lurched and staggered her way home. *My life would be so much better. I'll have to ring Georgie when I get in and apologise, I'm not going to say sorry to Anne though, she's a nasty piece of work, she told me to fuck off, I didn't swear at her, she was the one who totally over-reacted, typical.*

Her drunken thoughts rumbled on as she walked, gradually getting soaked to the skin. She wished she'd not talked about Tom to her family, she was just being ridiculous, of course he hadn't murdered his wife, Georgie and Anne were right. She was a melodramatic fool. She should just take a vow of silence or something. She drunkenly promised herself she'd stop over-sharing everything. Nobody cared, after all. And it made it look like she had over-dramatised how her boss had treated her. It made her look like a complete liar. *Yes,* she told herself, *stop over-thinking, stop being weird and keep your crazy thoughts to yourself.* Images of a hot bubble bath kept her going on the freezing walk home.

Arriving on her street, she looked at her watch, half past five, it had only taken an hour, but it had felt like ten hours to Pamela's befuddled brain.

She was shaking with cold and the after effects of too much alcohol.

As she turned towards her front door she rummaged in her bag for her keys, when she looked up, she saw Russ sitting on her front doorstep, 'Jesus,' she almost screamed, 'you gave me a shock.'

He'd been sitting with his head in his hands, he looked almost frozen to the spot, wet through and dejected. When he looked up, she saw fear and distress on his face.

'What's happened?' she asked, feeling her skin crawl, prickly heat piercing her body, despite the cold.

'Where is she?' he asked, simply, hollowly, a man bereft of all emotion.

Pamela didn't know what to say, she stuttered something that sounded deranged. He slowly stood up, she had never seen him look like this, his face pale, hollow, gaunt. She'd only ever seen him as a happy, easy going sort of person, it was hard to see the real Russ behind this shrunken figure.

'C..c..come in... I... I...' she couldn't seem to speak. Her voice was lost, drowned out by the blood pounding in her ears. *Use your words,* Pam, she told herself.

He stepped out of her way and waited in silence as she tried to unlock her door. She grappled with her key and finally managed to open it. He followed her in.

The house was warm for a change, for once her heating must've turned on by itself. Pamela stripped off her wet coat. She sat down on the stairs and yanked her boots off and carelessly peeled each wet sock from her frozen feet and flung them aside. Russ took his boots and coat off and waited. She grabbed both their coats and flung them over the banister, where they mutely dripped and steamed. Luckily the long cold walk and the shock of seeing Russ had more-or-less sobered her up.

She didn't know whether to invite him into her sitting room or just continue the conversation in the hall, 'Do you want a coffee or tea, or something stronger?'

'Look I don't want to be rude, but can you just tell me where Sophie is?'

'I'm so sorry Russ, I have absolutely no idea.'

Well that wasn't strictly true was it? She reprimanded herself.

'She came back from yours last night in such a weird mood, then this morning she was gone when I woke up, I've been worried sick all day, what happened between you two?' the question hung in the air.

This was the moment... this was the actual moment where she had to decide whose side she was on. If she told Russ the truth, she would let her friend down and Sophie would be furious with her. But she'd only asked her to cover for last night, not today, today was a whole new kettle of fish. She couldn't possibly see him suffer like this. *Bloody hell Sophie,* she thought, *what was your bloody problem?* Russ was waiting for her to speak, he was shaking, pale, murderous. His hands tight fists, white knuckled.

'Look Russ, I'm sure everything will turn out for the best,' what the hell was she saying?

'What the fuck are you saying?' Russ asked incredulous, reading her thoughts. 'What happened last night?'

'Look Russ just come in and sit down.'

Pamela walked away from him so that he had no choice but to follow her. She indicated a chair, for him to sit on.

'Pam, I don't want to sit down, I just want to know where my wife is? Is that so hard to understand?'

Why the hell did he think she had anything to do with it?' She felt aggrieved, if only she hadn't walked to Tom's house last night, then she genuinely wouldn't have had a clue. She took a deep breath, she had to tell him the truth, even if it cost her her friendship.

'Please sit-down Russ, I think I might know where she is.'

'Well?'

'Look, Sophie didn't come to mine last night.'

He looked stunned, she may as well have punched him in the face.

'What do you mean?'

'She texted me and asked me to tell you she was here... if you asked.'

He sat down heavily, before replying, 'I don't understand.'

'Listen, I just thought she was planning something special, you know, for you as a couple, that's what I thought she was doing, I kind've shrugged it off.'

'Ok.'He was sitting forward, tense, hands clasped together, 'And...' he prompted

'And... and... look I better put this in context...'

Russ interrupted her, grim, cold, 'Just tell me what you know, please Pam, I'm not interested in the context.'

'Well I just need to tell you how I think I might know where she is, I know I'm not making much sense, but just listen, please.' Pamela rushed on, 'I had the mad idea that Tom had murdered his wife.'

Russ interjected, sceptically, 'What the hell are you talking about?'

'Look, let me just finish, ok?' She pleaded. He indicated for her to go on. 'Well anyway, I had this mad idea and last night I walked along to his house and...' how on earth was she going to tell him what she'd seen?

'And?' he asked,

'And, I saw Sophie coming out.'

'Well maybe she was talking to him about his wife again, she's been supporting him through this, you know?'

Pamela paused; did she have to tell him what she'd seen?

'Well they looked a bit too close for that I'm afraid.'

'What do you mean?'

Did she have to fricking spell it out? Why couldn't he get what she was saying? She was finding this totally unbearable, she found herself saying, 'Well, they were... they seemed to be... kissing...'

'Seemed to be... seemed to be kissing? Are you fucking joking?'

'No.'

'Oh god,' Russ's face crumpled, there was no other way to explain it, it simply crumpled. He put his head in his hands, 'Oh no, that can't be true.'

'I'm so, so sorry Russ, I'm just as shocked as you, I had absolutely no idea what was going on, the last I knew Soph was trying to force *me* into a relationship with him.'

'All those times he came around, I thought he was a friend, you know. We were giving him support, staying up 'til all hours talking to him and all the time... all the time... I can't believe they've done this to me. How could Sophie be so cruel Pam?'

'I don't know, I can't believe it myself.'

'Why didn't she talk to me, tell me she was leaving?'

'It's awful, it totally is.' Pamela didn't know what else to say, Russ stood up,

'Pam, will you come with me to his house?'

'What, are you crazy? You want to go there, now?'

'Please, I need to hear it from her own mouth, and she isn't answering my calls, I've got to see her, I've got to try and make sense out of this, this... madness.'

'Russ are you sure that's a good idea? Tom is your boss, isn't he?'

'What's that got to do with it? That's irrelevant, I'm going to kill him, I just can't believe this is happening, please Pam, please come with me to his house.'

Pamela stood up. 'Shall I try and ring her? Maybe she'll talk to me?'

Russ was pacing around the room, his knuckles were

white, his hands balled into tense fists.

Pamela got her phone and pressed Sophie's number. It went straight to voicemail.

'Sorry, Russ, it's her answer phone, shall I leave a message?'

'No, just come with me, please.'

Pamela was sure that was an incredibly bad idea, but Russ was so determined. She was furious with Sophie too, what a horrible thing to do, after all these years, how could she just leave Russ without a word, not even a note or anything. She was being so selfish; it wasn't like her at all. And she'd left her so-called best friend to pick up the pieces.

'Look Russ, I just want us to think this through, what do you hope to gain by going around there tonight?'

Russ answered her as though she was a five-year old, 'What do you mean? Why is this so hard to comprehend I just want to talk to *my* wife, I want to try and understand what is happening, she can't do this to me and just get away with it,' he grabbed Pamela by the shoulders and stared crazily into her eyes, 'listen to me, I have to see her, do you understand? I have to.' He turned away, his whole body was tense, shaking with fear and dread.

She realised she wasn't going to be able to talk him out of it. She also knew she had to go with him, she couldn't let him face that awful Tom by himself.

'Ok, Russ, ok, we'll go, but promise me you won't do anything crazy? Promise me you'll try to stay calm.'

He looked at her, disbelievingly, he shook his head, 'I

can't promise anything Pam, I'm sorry.'

She stared at him, there was nothing she could say. His wife had been stolen from him by a so-called friend, she of all people knew how that felt.

Even though she wasn't a violent person she regretted that she hadn't punched Shaz in the face when she'd had the chance.

'I'll have to change; my jeans are absolutely soaked.'

'Ok.' Russ replied miserably.

'And you're wet through.'

'I don't care,' he answered through gritted teeth.

'Ok,' she shrugged, 'I'll be two minutes.'

She walked wearily upstairs, bloody hell, did she have to go too. *I don't want to face Soph and bloody Tom,* she thought, *it's a stupid idea to drive over there and confront them. It would be so humiliating for Russ, but he obviously wasn't in his right mind.* She changed into a pair of jogging bottoms and some dry socks.

Downstairs she and Russ put their wet boots and coats back on. They got into his car and sat in silence. She realised she'd left her bag and phone at home, but she didn't dare ask Russ to go back.

Dark snow clouds were gathering ahead of them. The gates were open when they arrived. Russ fearlessly drove down the intimidating drive. 'Bloody hell' he muttered under his breath. There was no sign of Sophie's car and no lights were on in the house.

Russ jumped out of the car and marched up to the front door. He rang the bell, then began banging on it in desperation. Pamela reluctantly joined him.

'There doesn't seem to be anyone home,' she said, lamely pointing out the blindingly obvious. Of course she was secretly relieved.

He began to walk around the front of the house, intermittently banging on windows. 'What the fuck,' he was shouting, he turned to Pamela, 'Where the hell are they?'

'I don't know.' She replied despondently. By the time they'd walked around the whole house it had started to snow again. They got back in the car. The snow skittered and swirled around the miserable couple, huddled and wretched.

Russ turned on the engine and cranked up the heat.

Finally, Pamela spoke, 'What shall we do?' He turned to look at her,

'I have no idea, I can't believe this is happening, it's a nightmare.'

'Should we go?'

'Can we wait a bit?'

'Yes, of course, if you think they're coming back.' What else could she say?

'They have to come back at some point, don't they?'

Pamela shrugged, she was hoping they wouldn't, she could think of nothing worse than seeing the ghastly Tom and her ex-best friend.

'You said something before about thinking Tom had murdered his wife, what did you mean?'

'Oh, don't worry, I was just being over-dramatic, of

course he hasn't killed his wife.'

Russ looked concerned, 'No, tell me why you thought he had?'

'I'm an idiot, I just get these ideas in my head, it's stupid, honestly I don't think he did, now.'

Russ stared ahead, anger and fear flickered across his face, 'But you thought it, so you must have had a reason.'

'I just never liked him, you know. I always thought he had a hidden agenda, he was so false somehow, I couldn't explain it, now it's obvious what his agenda was.'

'Yes, to take my wife off me, what a fucking bastard, coming around to my house, getting all that sympathy from me and Soph and all the time he was trying to steal her.'

'What a fricking creep, honestly.'

'You could see right through him from day one, couldn't you?'

'Well I wouldn't exactly say that, but I thought he was strange, especially when he slept the night on my bedroom floor, then intimated that we'd had sex or something. And he never took no for an answer, I couldn't have made it plainer that I wasn't interested in him.'

'Yeah, that was weird. I wish me and Soph had seen through him.'

'Well, hindsight and all that.'

'Yes.'

They sat side by side, gloomily waiting for something to happen. The car windows fogged up around them. They were cocooned in a little vibrating shell, alone and yet together, breathing softly, resigned to the stillness and isolation. Russ's body hunched and desperate with fear. Pamela felt that they could have been anywhere, waiting for anything. Time had become unimportant. The snow continued, impersonal, cold, caring nothing for the two motionless passengers.

There was something spiritual, unworldly in this moment, something Pamela couldn't put her finger on. Russ may have felt the same, encased in his grief and disbelief, she couldn't read his emotions, he was unreachable.

She thought about the last two weeks. *When had Sophie turned from decent friend and wife into this selfish person and what would her daughters think about it all?*

Then she thought about her suspicions – she had told Russ that she didn't think Tom was a murderer, and she had almost convinced herself that he wasn't. *But,* she thought, *what if he has murdered Sophie, shouldn't we be treating this as a missing person rather than a runaway wife? We've both jumped to the same conclusion but what if it's the wrong conclusion?* She had to say something to Russ.

Finally, she broke the silence. It felt irreverent somehow, like talking in church. She cleared her throat. 'What if Soph hasn't run away with Tom?' Her voice was rasping, hoarse, as though she hadn't spoken in a long time.

Russ stared at the steering wheel and quietly asked 'What are you saying?'

'She might not be with him. I know it seemed the most logical conclusion, but what if we're wrong?'

'Where else could she be?'

'I don't know, but maybe we should call the police?'

He turned to stare at her, fear once again etched upon his face, replacing the hardened anger. 'You think he's hurt her?' he managed to stammer, disbelieving, yet overwhelmed with the horror of that thought, chased almost instantaneously by another less charitable thought - was it better to have a dead wife, a murdered wife, or one that had carelessly fallen into the arms of another man? How much more acceptable would that be? He shook off those appalling thoughts, how could he see her death as preferable to an affair? But deep down he knew it was true. He knew he would be able to go on with his life as the tragic figure whose wife had been murdered and not as the stupid sap whose wife had run away.

Pamela could see the myriad thoughts flash across his face and realised she didn't know Russ at all.

'I don't know, no, of course not, well, probably not, anyway.' She garbled. 'Should we maybe wait? Should we just go home now and hope she rings one of us, but if we haven't heard anything by morning, call the police?'

He shook his head, grasping the steering wheel with both hands, 'I don't know what to do.'

He looked at her and she had to look away, she couldn't bear the look in his eyes. Again, there was nothing she could she say. They sat in silence, both contemplating the enormity of the situation.

Something seemed to snap in Russ's mind, 'I'll take you home,' he said.

Thank god, she nodded, murmuring, 'Thanks.'

Bloody hell this was just so horrific. What a ghastly

situation. She could barely breathe, worried sick that Tom's car would suddenly turn up. She silently prayed that they'd get back to her house without seeing either Tom or Sophie.

The untreated roads had become treacherous in the short time they'd been waiting. The journey felt excruciating. When he finally pulled up outside her house, she could have cried with relief. She turned towards him and patted his arm, a feeble gesture. There were no words.

She got out of the car, but before she closed the door he said, 'Pam, if she contacts you any time tonight, will you promise to call me and let me know, it doesn't matter what time, even if she tells you not to tell me, will you promise to call me?' She nodded miserably.

'And you'll ring me if you hear anything?'

'Yes, of course.' He tried to smile, but his face was frozen.

'Ok, bye.'

'Bye.'

He drove away. Pamela watched his brake lights until they disappeared. She stood in the snow, wishing this wasn't happening. Her heart was breaking for Russ. *What can I do? Nothing, nothing at all.* She let herself into the house. Normally she'd be straight on the phone to Georgie, but she didn't think it was a good idea. Georgie was probably upset that she'd just walked off without waiting for her to come home and Anne would have been bitching like mad about her. She'd have to face a telling off and she couldn't cope with that.

She couldn't see herself telling anyone about this.

Georgie would be so disgusted with Sophie; she was disgusted with Sophie herself. It was bad enough that she had lied and then spent Saturday evening with Tom, but to just up and walk out on Russ this morning without a word, to leave him worrying all day, causing so much pain to people she was supposed to love. Her behaviour was incomprehensible.

She went into the kitchen and put the kettle on to make a soothing camomile tea. Where was Sophie, what was she doing? Had Tom attacked her or were they selfishly out somewhere having fun? It was so annoying, not knowing whether to be furious or afraid. She wondered if Russ would let the girls know. Maybe not tonight, but if she was still gone tomorrow, he'd have to let them know.

She realised that it was only seven o'clock. It felt so much later. She fished her phone out of her bag, there were ten missed calls from Georgie, bloody hell, she'd have to ring her.

'Hello,' it was Rich.

'Can I speak to Georgie please?'

'Oh, you're home are you?' he asked caustically. She heard him call out, 'Hey Georgie, it's your mad sister.'

Georgie replied, 'Which one?' which made him laugh and Pamela cringe.

'Hello, sorry about just leaving earlier.'

'I should bloody think so, honestly, I've been worried sick, your phone just keeps going to voicemail, and you left Anne in the mood from hell. I was just about to organise a bloody search party.'

'I'm so sorry, I forgot to take my phone with me. I know I should've waited for you to get back, but Anne was such a fricking bitch, I couldn't stand being in the same room as her.'

'Well she says you were totally drunk and behaving like a crazy woman.'

'Well, to be fair, I was drunk, and I am sorry I fell out with her. She's just such a madam at times.' Pamela paused, she knew she was in the wrong, there was nothing more she could add. 'I just wanted to say thank you so much, it was a lovely lunch. Have Adam and Hannah gone?'

'Yes.'

'I'm so sorry about Hannah. It must be awful.'

'It is, yes.'

'Is there anything you can do?'

'No.' Georgie was furious with her. Selfishly she gambled that telling her about Sophie would take her mind off everything else.

'When I got home, Russ was waiting for me.'

'Oh?'

'Yes, we think that Sophie has either run off with Tom or... maybe...' Pamela felt a catch in her throat, she forced herself to continue, 'if he has murdered his wife... well maybe he's hurt Soph?' It felt unimaginable. Saying it out loud to Georgie brought home the enormity of this awful situation.'

'What the hell?'

'I know, she left this morning before Russ woke up and she's not answering his calls. It's dreadful, he made me tell him everything and we went to Tom's house.'

'Oh my god, what happened?'

'The house was empty and there was no sign of either of them.'

'Jesus.'

'I know, poor Russ is beside himself.'

'How dreadful.'

'The worst thing is she hasn't bothered to tell Russ anything, she just lied to him about coming to me, he said she was in a peculiar mood when she got home and then nothing, it's so strange.'

'That isn't like Sophie is it?'

'That's what I keep thinking, but obviously, even after all these years, I can't know her at all. I mean how could she just run off and not have the guts to face up to Russ? If that is what happened.'

'Did you ever get a chance to tell her you thought Tom had murdered his wife?'

'No, I wish I had told her, it might have made her think twice, but I told Russ and now we're both worried that Tom has done something to her. I said he'll have to ring the police tomorrow if he hasn't heard anything by then.'

'Do you think she'll ring you, assuming she's ok?'

'I just don't know, it's so weird.'

'Bloody hell, what a terrible situation.' Pamela's bet had paid off, Georgie was completely enthralled, 'How did you leave it with Russ?'

'It was awful, he was so unlike himself, so cold and frightening actually, you know what he's usually like, always joking about everything, I've never seen him like this, it was terrible.'

'I just don't understand why she would go without saying a word, I mean why didn't she talk to you?'

'I know, I'm pretty shocked with it all truth be told, if it turns out that she has just run off with Tom she's treated me and Russ like crap.'

'I can't believe it.'

'Me neither.'

'Have you tried to call her?'

'Yes, when Russ was here, and I'll keep trying tonight. It's awful, half of me is furious with her and the other half is terrified that something has happened to her.'

'Well if you hear anything let me know.'

'Will do, and again sorry about before. I don't know why I drank so much.'

'It's ok, you have got a bit of an excuse, you're very stressed about work, but you should try to stop drinking, that's why you and Anne fell out, normally you go out of your way not to fall out with people.'

'I know. I'll try.'

'Ok. Well I'll let you go.'

'Bye then.'

'Bye.' Pamela was mortified. Georgie was disgusted with her. She was disgusted with herself. *What is wrong with me, why can't I just have a couple of glasses of wine like everyone else?* It was so awful to have her own sister feel embarrassed because of her drinking. Giving Rich ammunition against her, and god knew he didn't need much to be a complete bitch about her family.

Her thoughts turned to Sophie. She tried to call her, but it went straight to voicemail again. This time she left a message, 'Hi Soph, it's me, hope you're ok, Russ's been around and we're both very worried about you. Please, please call me as soon as you get a chance.'

She was numb with fear. She felt so helpless. She opened her laptop and went to Facebook, Sophie often added updates, but there was nothing. She looked at Tom's page, again nothing. A status flagged up from Amelie, 'Goodbye London town, I'll be seeing you!' *Bloody hell*, Pamela thought, *when was she supposed to be arriving in Yorkshire?* She had obviously left London already. That was the kind of thing a mum remembers, but not necessarily a dad. She quickly rang Russ, he answered in seconds, 'Yes?' his voice sounded drained but hopeful,

'Hi, sorry just me, no news, sadly, but I've just been on Facebook and isn't today the day that Amelie comes home?'

'Christ, no, I don't think so, fuck, I'm not sure, what's the date?'

'I think today's the 15th?'

'Shit, she's due back tomorrow, not sure what time, wait a second, I'll just grab the calendar,' there was a pause as Russ checked. 'Yes midday tomorrow, Sophie's taken the day off work to collect her.'

'Fuck.'

'Fuck.'

Pamela and Russ were silent for a moment, she could

hear her heart beating and her breathing felt sharp, painful.

He broke the silence, 'Listen I'm going to call the police, I'm too worried to wait all night.'

'I don't blame you, Soph would never just disappear like this.'

She felt a bit awful implying that Sophie might leave him but wouldn't do something like this to her daughter, except it was true. Sophie had been looking forward to seeing Amelie since she'd planned her trip.

To make Russ feel better she said, 'Maybe she forgot Amelie was coming?'

'No, we were talking about it yesterday, it went out of my mind today, for obvious reasons. The police might want to talk to you tonight Pam, would that be ok?'

'Of course.'

'Bye.'

'Bye.'

Pamela felt awful. Poor Amelie, coming home to face this. Sophie wouldn't do something like this to her kids, she adored them. Tom must have done something to her, it was the only logical conclusion.

Pamela wondered whether the police would want to talk to her. If only she'd rung the police and told them her suspicions about Tom when she'd first thought about it, if only she'd confided in Sophie.

She sat, rigid, on the settee, fear gripping her body. *Bloody hell, Soph, what was going on?* She sat, motionless, groggy thoughts swirling around her head.

Finally, she lay back on the settee, she was totally

exhausted. It had been a long day of emotional roller-coasters, both real and imagined.

She wanted to stay awake, but despite herself she couldn't help falling asleep.

She dreamt that Sophie was running down a long dark tunnel and she was chasing after her, screaming, 'Where are you going?' but Sophie ran on, ignoring her. She woke up, sweaty and panicked.

There was a firm knocking at her door. *That must be the police*, she thought. She ran to open her front door. Looming on her doorstep was Tom.

'What the hell...' she began to shout, trying to close the door, but Tom shoved her out of the way and slammed the door shut behind him.

'Don't say a word.' He muttered menacingly.

She backed away from him. 'Don't come anywhere near me,' she managed to splutter.

He looked at her in disgust. 'Shut up for Christ's sake, I'm not going to hurt you, just sit down.'

'No, I'll stay standing, what the hell do you want with me?'

She was surreptitiously looking around the room for anything she could use as a weapon, there were some logs around the fire, she could possibly grab one of those and whack the little prick on the head if he came any closer to her.

He stood his ground. 'Listen, me and Sophie have become very good friends recently, and she's decided to leave Russ...' he waited a few moments for that to sink in, then continued, 'we want you to come over to my house, she wants to tell Russ everything, but she needs your support.'

'No, she doesn't, why are you lying? If Sophie wanted my support, she'd have answered my calls and she wouldn't have sent you around, she would have come herself. What have you done to her?'

'What do you mean? I haven't done anything.'

'Sophie's not the kind of person to do this to Russ.'

'That's what you think. You know their marriage was a complete sham.'

'What the bloody fuck, no it bloody well wasn't.'

'Look, will you come with me or what?' He was red faced, angry.

She felt confused and disoriented. She didn't believe him, but what if he was telling the truth. If her friend needed her, surely she should go. But a niggling voice kept repeating, "He's lying, he's lying."

Pamela took a deep breath, 'Listen Tom, I will come with you, but first I need to change into warmer clothes.' She was saying anything, desperate to stall him,

'Why?'

'Because it's so cold out there, I'll only be a couple of minutes.' Surely he couldn't argue against her putting warmer clothes on. She began to edge towards the door, wishing she'd had the stupid lock put on her bedroom door.

He took a step towards her, 'STOP. We haven't got time; she needs to see you now.' He looked demented, crazy-eyed, *fuck,* she thought, *this is shit.*

'Ok, Tom, that's fine, just calm down a bit, of course I'll

come, you just took me by surprise is all, I'll just grab my phone... it's only in the kitchen, that's ok isn't it?'

She began to edge away from him towards the kitchen door.

'You know I can't let you do that don't you Pam?' His mouth was twisted, menacing, terrifying.

I'll have to try and pretend I think everything's ok.

'That's fine, Tom, not a problem, I think it's dead anyway,' she tried to laugh, holding both her palms out in front of her, trying to calm him down, trying to show him she wasn't a threat, she was just a simple, weak woman, 'There's absolutely no need to get upset Tom. I'll come with you. I do want to see Soph and help her with this.'

He wasn't stupid, he must know she was playing him, but he did seem to calm down a bit, *bloody crazy man*, she thought.

A part of her somehow knew that if she got in the car with him it would be the last car journey she ever took. If she lunged towards the logs, he might get there first and god knows what he'd do to her. *Why did I answer the stupid door?* She thought uselessly. *I never answer my bloody door.*

She'd seen scenes like this in films, but never in a billion years did she think something like this would happen to her. In real life. In her little house. In her little town. She had been right about him all along, but that was no consolation right now. She had no choice but to agree to go with him. She would play along with his stupid charade, pretending that she believed that Sophie wanted her, but they both knew it was a total lie, otherwise he'd let her get changed, let her get her phone. *God is this how it ends for me?* She thought. She felt sad for Alex and Jake. *How awful to have a murdered mother.*

He waited for her to walk past him.

'I'll need to put my boots and coat on.' He nodded.

She sat down to put her soggy boots back on, desperately trying to work out how to escape this horrendous situation. She stood up and went to the front door. She knew she had to do something, it wasn't like he was holding a gun to her head or anything, but he was much bigger than she was, he could easily knock her to the ground. *And what if I am over-reacting, what if he and Sophie do need my help somehow?* But she knew that was ridiculous. That wasn't what this was about.

She walked out onto the snowy path. The weather had got much worse, a snowstorm surrounded them, bludgeoning their bodies. He was standing right next to her, breathing heavily. His breath was disgusting, evil smelling, foul. It smelt metallic, sour somehow. She felt sick.

'I'll just have to lock the door,' she spoke as reasonably and normally as possible, desperate to lull him into a false sense of security.

Again, he nodded. She turned away from him and locked the door. She clutched the front door key between her fingers. She knew she mustn't get in the car with him, if she did all would be lost. She gripped the keys in her clenched fist, ready to strike.

Once again, he waited for her to walk past him. He

stood uncomfortably close as they walked down the path towards his car. As they got closer to the vehicle, she made her move. She turned around rapidly towards him and stabbed him in the face with the key as hard and as fast as she could. He looked astounded and for a split second they both reeled on their feet, neither sure of the next move. She was as stunned as he was, but then she turned and ran, slipping and sliding in the dreadful icy conditions.

Amazed, he grasped his injured jowl and snarled as he came lunging after her.

The pavement was treacherous and the road nearly as bad. She ran screaming down the street, 'Help me... Help me.'

A few curtains twitched, but no one came to her rescue.

'Come back here, you fucking bitch,' Tom was yelling at her.

The roads were so slippery, neither of them could pick up any speed. Jesus, she thought, this is madness. The streets were totally deserted, 'Help,' she screamed again, 'Help me.'

She had a fleeting thought that she could rush up to someone's door, but no one would have time to answer the door before Tom grabbed her. And they'd probably be too afraid to open the door anyway. *Maybe someone would ring the police?* But she knew from her own experience that people would just think they were a pair of drunks, who'd fallen out. Her only hope was to get to the small corner shop further down the road.

She ran, desperation and despair in her every step, her

breathing painful and laboured as she sucked in the thin, frozen air. He was gaining on her, overcome with fury at her actions.

'Stop running,' he was shouting.

She rushed away from the road towards the pavement, in doing so her foot caught the curb and she fell heavily, crashing her head on the hard stone.

All is lost, she thought as she slipped into unconsciousness. Time slowed down, she had a vague, intermittent sensation of being dragged along a cold, snowy passageway. Pain and loss seeped through her mind, making no sense. She couldn't understand what was happening. She tried to speak, but her words leaked from her mouth, watery, weak, unformed.

"This is what death is," a voice said.

"Oh, I see," she replied. Her thought-mum had finally come back.

"This is death is it mum?" This was the answer to the question she'd been asking her mum in all her dreams. Lights began and ended. Time began and ended. Sporadic pain, consciousness, unconsciousness all blurred into one.

Monday 16ᵗʰ January

Pamela felt the cold ground beneath her. She was lying face down, unable to move. She tried desperately to piece together what had happened. The last thing she remembered was being in her house with Tom, *did he chase me, did I fall?* She couldn't make sense of anything. She tried to open her eyes, but they seemed somehow glued together. She was beyond pain, her whole being felt numb, crushed. It was all inexplicable.

She could hear footsteps in the distance. The footsteps got louder. Then a person was leaning over her, feeling her wrist. She felt icy breath on her face, the breath of a devil.

She lay still, silent, trying to regulate her breathing, even though every fibre of her being wanted to scream. The person turned and she heard their footsteps disappearing. She had no idea how much time she had before that freak came back.

Her wrists were tied behind her back. She moved her legs a little, they also seemed to be bound together. She tried to rub her eyes with her shoulders. *Why wouldn't they open, Jesus, what has happened to my eyes?*

For the first time the enormity of the situation hit her like a punch to the stomach. Everything came back to her in a stink of memory. *That bastard*, she muttered under her breath, she was filled with rage. She found herself praying, *Dear God, please let me escape from here, I promise I'll be a better person, I promise I'll do whatever you want, I'll stop drinking, I'll be good, I'll be kind to Anne, I'll go back to work and face that man, just let me escape.*

She was silently sobbing, terrified. She was alone and about to face death. "What shall I do mum?" she asked, but her thought-mum had deserted her again. She was on her own, like always.

She had to calm down, crying wasn't going to help. She had to try to find a way out of this. She couldn't just wait here and accept whatever fate that man had in store for her. She had to be brave, *you are a strong, resourceful woman,* she told herself, *you are not going to die like this. I have to sit up; I must open my eyes.* She mentally went through her body, *is anything broken?* She wasn't sure, she was beyond pain.

Gradually she began to rock herself onto her side, pulling her legs up, inch by inch. She realised she was almost naked, *that disgusting pervert, what has he done to me?* She shut those thoughts away, now was not the time to dwell on what had happened, she had to concentrate on this moment, nothing else.

She managed to sit upright. Her head was spinning, throbbing, and a sudden stabbing white pain pulsed through her. She felt like she'd been hit on the head with a hammer.

Slowly she bottom-shuffled across the floor, until she felt the smooth wall on her back. She began to slide along the wall, desperate to find something sharp to cut the ties around her wrists.

She had never been so afraid in her life. But within that

fear she felt a cold calm, an inner voice that said, *I am going to escape, I will live to talk about this, I must.*

She reached the corner of the room without encountering anything that could help her. She began to slide along the next wall. She came across something that felt like a steel cabinet. She leant her shoulder against it and bit by bit she managed to heave herself up. She began to rub her bound wrists against its sharp edge.

She knew she didn't have much time; the footsteps might come back any minute. She felt the restraints give a little, then suddenly her arms were free. She felt down to her legs and desperately pulled at the binding. It came away quite easily, her captor obviously hadn't expected her to try and escape. She felt her face, and realised her eyes were covered with a thick blindfold, as she pulled it off, she could see again.

Looking around she realised she was in a darkened cellar. She turned to the cabinet to see if there was anything in it she could use as a weapon. It was screwed to the wall and its metal doors were closed and locked. She limped painfully to the door; thank goodness it was unlocked. He's underestimated me, she thought triumphantly. She closed it carefully behind her. Creeping along the corridor she came to the bottom of the stairs. She had to go up, she had no choice, if she stayed in this room she was going to die.

If only I'd found some kind of weapon, she thought, *a screwdriver, anything that might help.* Once again she felt a murderous rage towards Tom, a violence that she'd never felt before towards anyone, not even her useless ex-husband. She knew there was no doubt now, he'd killed his wife and probably Sophie. And possibly countless others. *Maybe his wife had found out? Maybe that's why she'd been dispatched? I refuse to be his next victim. Not without a fight anyway, I'm not going to make it easy for him.*

There was a small alcove at the side of the stairs, she could push herself against it and when he walked past, she could make a dash to the top of the stairs. Or she could creep up the stairs and try and rush towards an outside door before he realised what was going on.

She was thinking about the practicalities of each of these ideas when she heard footsteps approaching. *Oh God,* she thought, pressing herself against the alcove. It was smaller than she'd imagined, *he's going to see me, and if he doesn't see me, he'll hear me,* she was finding it impossible to breath quietly, her chest felt like it might explode.

The footsteps began their descent. Just then she heard a phone ringing from inside the house. Miraculously the footsteps turned and went back up the stairs. She breathed a sigh of relief.

She started to creep up the stairs, shit, there was a door at the top, she carefully tried the handle, it was locked. *Jesus, what should I do now?* She had no choice but to go back to her hiding place. She crept back down the stairs.

Why hadn't Russ called the police? Maybe he had. Surely they would've come to Tom's house and searched it. Or at least taken him in for questioning. Wouldn't they have gone to my house by now and realised I'm missing. Maybe we did have to wait twenty-four hours before the police did anything. The police might not take it seriously, they might just think that Russ was a jilted husband with a grudge. She knew she had to rely on herself. She couldn't hope that the police would just turn up and save her in the nick of time, this wasn't a film, this was real life and it was dreadful.

She tried to calm her breathing, she couldn't let him hear her, he mustn't know she'd escaped from his pathetic attempts at tying her up. He'd underestimated her and that was an advantage she must make use of.

She mentally went through what she would do when he next came down the stairs. Maybe wait until the last moment and stick her foot out and trip him up. No, that would take careful, calm timing and she was in no position to be calm. She could possibly wait until he walked past and shove him from behind. Or back to her original idea and rush up the stairs behind him before he realised she was gone. *If only I'd found some sort of weapon,* she thought again, *I'd be in a much better position.*

She felt alone and vulnerable, standing, shaking in the dark, wearing torn and tattered underwear. As her eyes became more used to the dark, she saw that her body was covered in blood. *What had he done? Maybe this was part of his psychotic ritual, maybe he was some kind of Satanist. Oh god,* she silently moaned, *how the hell did I get myself into this?*

She went back along the corridor to see if the cellar door had any sort of lock on the outside, she could wait until he walked into the cellar and then close and lock it behind him. It had a bolt at the top, but it was too much of a risk, he'd realise she was gone the second he opened the door, he wouldn't even need to walk in. The only thing she could do was make a dash up the stairs and hope against hope that he hadn't re-locked the door at the top of the stairs.

I must be brave, I must be brave, she chanted.

Thoughts flashed through her mind, her boys, her mother's death bed, her father's sad, lonely little room, her unfaithful, inadequate husband, her sister's and their families.

Myriad memories floated through her brain. *If only I'd lived a more fulfilled life, if only I'd been happier,* she rubbed her stupid face, anger surged through her. *I've spent my entire adult life not feeling satisfied, drinking too much, eating too much, being a selfish, greedy, waste of space. If I get out of this, I'll do something meaningful, something to help people. I promise.*

She thought of her little terrace house, her tiny world, it seemed so far away, she didn't know if she would ever see it again.

When the inevitable footsteps approached, she was ready. She pressed her body against the wall, waiting, waiting. Her fists balled, ready, *flight or fight, fight or flight,* the words danced and buzzed in her brain. She could hear his heavy breathing as he made his way down the stairs, she tried to minimise her whole being, tried to merge into the wall.

His bulking figure loomed past her, he had an axe in his hand. *Jesus,* she thought, *fuck.* The moment he reached the closed cellar door she turned and fled, rushing up the stairs as hurriedly and as noiselessly as possible.

She got to the top as she heard a roar from downstairs. Thank god the door at the top was unlocked, she flung herself through it and slammed it behind her. Yes! He'd left the key in the lock; she quickly locked the door. She grabbed the biggest knife from his knife block, then hobbled down the hall to the front door.

As she staggered along the hall she glanced into the open door of his front room, a movement caught her eye, she stopped. It was Soph. She was obviously semi-conscious, tied up and gagged. She spoke to her limp and bloodied friend, 'Soph, Soph, Jesus what the hell has he done to you?'

She couldn't leave her friend, she had to stay and fight, but what chance did she have against an enraged Tom and a fricking axe.

She stripped the gag from Sophie's mouth and cut the ties to her hands and feet. They could hear a crash from the cellar, Tom was smashing the door with his axe, 'Go get help Pam, please.' Sophie rasped, weakly.

'I can't leave you.'

'Please, you have to escape, it's the only way.'

Pamela nodded; Sophie was right. She couldn't take on the crazed Tom. Their only chance was for her to get help. She gave Sophie the knife and then turned and stumbled out the front door.

In her mind's eye she could see the axe smashing the door down, she could see him running down the hall after her, but as she snatched a look behind her there was no sign of him yet. She couldn't feel the cold, but her shoeless feet were slipping and sliding up the drive. Then she saw the high, electric gates, how could she possibly get through them. She turned and limped to the right, down towards the fence that led to the river. She could climb that fence, but then what, there'd be no one down there for miles. No wonder he wasn't rushing out to get her, he could just take his time, he knew she wouldn't be able to get through the gates and he could follow her stupid footsteps in the snow wherever she went.

She carried on, he'd underestimated her before, he'd maybe underestimate her again. She got to the fence and clumsily climbed over it, flinging herself to the ground on the other side.

If only she could find somewhere to hide. She shambled down the hill towards the river, falling and tearing her body in her dishevelled attire. She had to get away, she had to find a place to hide, a place where she could have the upper hand. *I'll kill him,* she thought, uselessly.

She looked back and saw Tom striding inexorably towards her. She tried to run, cursing her weak and useless body. The river was her only escape, she had to get there before he did.

He had almost caught up with her by the time she approached the river. She was inches away, she flung herself towards the violent torrent, but too late. He grabbed her by the hair as she crashed into the brutal icy water, he lost his grip on the axe and it fell to the ground with a sickening thud.

He began to hold her head under the water. She was writhing and gurgling, muddy sickening water drenching her lungs. His eyes were cold, murderous. She kicked and struggled, but she was no match for his brute strength. Her hands desperately clawed at his arms, but her strength was failing, she couldn't fight anymore, she was slipping into unconsciousness, her arms flopped into the water, she had nothing left. A smile spread across his grim and evil face.

A dark shadow loomed behind Tom. Suddenly she saw the axe crash into the side of his head. Sophie was standing above them, looking horrified at what she'd done.

Pamela tried to scrabble out of the river, but the recent rain and snowstorms had made it treacherous. She was swept away from the frozen figure of Sophie. The dark icy torrent crashed against her semi-drowned, semi-naked body; she was immediately swept along by the current.

Her body tossed and tumbled. She was being held under the water, then thrown up, then scraped along the bottom, like the rivers plaything. She couldn't get a breath, the river was merciless, freezing. She fought with all her strength to get her head above the current, to snatch a breath. She desperately tried to cling onto the frozen rocks, but it was hopeless, her fingers slipped away, useless against the might of the river.

She had no strength left. She surrendered to the water. She had to accept her fate. She was going to drown. As her body relaxed, as she stopped thrashing and fighting and became at peace with her impending death, the river seemed to slow, it's vicious current ebbed and stopped. She was no fun anymore. It was bored with her.

She was washed up alongside the beautiful snow-covered lawns that led down to the river from the posh houses. She was so cold, so close to death, blood pouring from the jagged cuts to every inch of her body so cruelly inflicted by the river.

It would be just fine to curl up here and die, so easy to just give in. Instead she found herself crawling on hands and knees through the snow, leaving a ragged red trail in the pure white. A small fox looked out at her from the bushes, its wise eyes seemed to smile and in her mind she heard it say, "You're going to be ok." She nodded, weak and frozen, bloodied and pathetic.

Nearer the house she could hear children laughing as they played in the snow. Their laughter turned to screams as she approached. She was saved.

A hush of murmured voices echoed below her. Pamela seemed to be floating through the galaxies. She was warm and happy up there. She didn't want to go back down, she wanted to stay up amongst the stars, where all was peaceful and calm. She could hear a strange, beautiful music, suffusing every part of her. Her soul was finally free. Beyond pain, beyond anxiety, happy. Little Annabel was floating beside her, she reached across to hold her hand. Annabel looked unhappy, "No," she shook her head, "no."

Suddenly she was falling, hurtling back to earth, she felt a crashing agony in her chest, someone was beating her. 'Leave me alone,' she whimpered before slipping into unconsciousness.

Tuesday 17ᵗʰ January

Pamela heard voices, strange and familiar. She couldn't move. Her whole body seemed trapped, thick bloody hands were pressing her down, she was tied and bound. She tried to open her eyes, but there was no point. She slipped back under. She felt herself drifting away, on a calm blue sea. She wasn't in any pain. *Am I dead?* She wasn't sure. She could feel nothing, no emotion, no fear, no happiness, just a strange numbness. She seemed to be in a dream world, peopled by bizarre voices and sounds, the hands holding her became benevolent, strangers surrounded her, touching her. She heard her own heartbeat and somehow, deep inside, knew she was still alive.

Sometimes she felt herself surface, her eyes blurry and unfocussed, before the waves took her again. One time she could make out two figures sitting in a room, but they seemed to be far, far away, as though she was looking at them through a long dark lens.

She was in the shadow and they were encircled in a round, harsh white light. She tried to speak, but no sound emerged from her lips. She could hear their voices, but no words formed in her mangled brain. Her eyes closed again.

Later she heard two familiar voices. *Are my children here? That was impossible, they'd be in school, wouldn't they?* She drifted in and out of reality, nothing made any sense. *Why am I here, why can't I move?*

A part of her shattered brain thought she might be in a hospital room, but another part was languishing in a deep dark lagoon, water lapping at her icy, wet body. She couldn't piece anything together. *Did I fall? Did I crash my car? Is this a dream?*

She tried to sort out her shattered memories, she probed her brain, tentatively like a tongue touching a throbbing toothache. Gradually fragments came back, she could remember who she was, she remembered her sisters, her dad.

Images came and went, she saw herself walking somewhere, it was snowing. The last thing she could picture with any clarity was being at a house, something had happened there, but she couldn't remember what it was. She vaguely remembered having an argument with someone, she remembered walking away from the house, but that's where her memories ended.

Again and again she resurfaced, trying her best to keep her head above the swirling swamp water and again and again she was sucked under, drowning, choking, unable to breathe.

Rational thoughts mingled with absurd, troubling ones. The devil was leaning over her frozen body and she couldn't move, couldn't escape his grasp.

She felt a little fox walking on her broken body, sniffing and inspecting, its delicate paws leaving little dark prints on her skin. Finally, it lay down next to her and went to sleep.

Time and reality had become insignificant. Around

her, doctors and nurses tended to her broken and shattered body. Her sisters sat and waited, talking in hushed tones, tense, distressed.

She had arrived at the hospital her body in strips, half drowned. They'd stitched the cuts and ragged holes in her flesh. They'd done what they could for her body, but for now, her mind was locked shut.

Pamela felt her chest tighten, she could feel herself slipping deeper and deeper into a strange labyrinth. She was walking along an ice-covered corridor; she could see her small children in the distance. They were running away from her, hand in hand with Sophie, giggling and laughing at her attempts to call them back, their long blond hair flashed every now and then as they rushed around the darkened corners.

Sophie's face was suddenly staring down at her, blurred, hazy. Then she was gone again. Pamela was terrified, they had to come back. She shrieked, 'For god's sake, stop running,' instead of coming back they seemed to run faster, she started running towards them, slipping and sliding on the ice. She wasn't getting any closer, it was impossible to get any closer. She sat down and started to cry. A strange presence was looming over her, the air filled with a deep, dark-red smell of blood. She had failed, failed again, she couldn't save her children, she couldn't save her friend. All was lost. She put her head in her hands. Suddenly a tidal wave of filthy, black, nauseating water rushed towards her from the furthest end of the cavern. She stood up and was immediately washed away, her body scraping and sliding, crashing against the walls and the floor, 'RUN,' she screeched to the disappearing figures of her babies and her friend. She was sobbing, she knew the water was going to catch up with them all. They would all die.

Wednesday 18ᵗʰ January

Late Wednesday evening Pamela finally came around. Her boys were sitting by her bedside. She tried to smile at them.

'Hi.' She murmured, and feebly held out her hand, they gently covered her hands with theirs.

'God mum you gave us such a fright,' Alex spoke softly.

'Yes, mum, so good to see you awake.' Added Jake.

'Is Sophie ok?'

'Yes, she's home.'

'Oh thank goodness for that,' Pamela said, 'is Tom...'

'He's not dead, he's here, in intensive care.' Jake replied.

'At this hospital?'

'Yes.'

'Do the police know what happened?'

'They've got a good idea, but they'll want to talk to you when you're feeling better.' Alex replied. Pamela lay back down on the pillows. 'I can't believe he's here; I want to go home; he's going to kill me.'

'Mum, you're going to be fine. You'll be able to come home in a couple of days. Believe me that man won't be going anywhere for a long time. Get some rest mum, you've been through a hell of a lot.'

A nurse arrived and administered a drug through the canular in her hand.

'Yes,' she murmured, sinking once again into a seemingly endless, troubled sleep.

She could see Tom strip the tubes and breathing apparatus out of his body, he picked up the bloodied axe and headed for her room, he was swinging the axe above her head when she woke, screaming in fear and agony.

'Pami, are you ok?'

Someone was standing over her. It was Georgie.

'He's here, he's going to kill me.' Pamela was sweating, heart racing, her breathing laboured and strained.

'There's nobody here except me, Pam, you're ok. Believe me that creep is in no fit state to get out of bed.'

'Are you sure?' Pamela whispered.

'Yes, I promise.'

'But why is he here? Why am I in the same hospital as him? I need to go home Georgie, please take me home.'

Georgie held Pamela's hand. 'You're just not well enough; listen we're never going to leave you alone. One of us is going to stay with you all the time. The boys are coming back to stay over tonight.'

'They should be at work.'

'They'll go back as soon as you're well enough.'

'Thanks.' Pamela whispered and once again slipped into a drug-fuelled sleep. She re-surfaced hours later. She could hear familiar voices.

'Things like that just don't happen, it's mad.' Alex was saying.

'Mum told me she was trying to get rid of a mad wife-murdering man, but I thought it was a joke.'

'When did she tell you that?'

'When I was in Geneva.'

'Bloody hell.'

'I just thought it was the usual over-dramatic thing mum say's, you know, I never thought it could be real.'

'Typical mum.'

'Yes.' Alex looked at Jake then they turned and looked at their mum. 'I can't believe she managed to escape from that nutter.'

'I know.' He took hold of Pamela's hand, 'You did good mum,' he told her.

She wanted to reply but she couldn't wake up enough to talk to them, there seemed to be a thick fog surrounding her, from under which she couldn't emerge. It was easier to drift back, beneath the murk, helpless, safe in the certainty that her family were watching over her.

They lapsed into silence. A nurse silently arrived and took Pamela's pulse, then left.

The room was dark and stuffy. Lights flashed and a soft susurration of sound suffused the air. They were in a peculiar, protected little world, where real-life didn't exist. Suddenly all their important meetings and commitments faded to nothing.

They squirmed, uncomfortably on the inadequate hospital chairs. It was going to be a long night.

They didn't talk much, there seemed to be nothing to say. They tried to sleep, but it was impossible, they just couldn't get comfortable and it was so hot and stuffy.

Around midnight Alex got up and went for a walk, in order to stretch his cramped body, He saw signs to Intensive Care, but turned and went in the other direction, he didn't trust himself to go anywhere near that man.

He wandered around the darkened hospital corridors, aimlessly peering into rooms, where dials bleeped and flashed and strangers lay, unprotected and remote.

Hospitals were such strange places at night. He shuddered, lonely, isolated from his real life. He felt like he was on a dark cruise ship sailing off into the night, towards an unknown, distant land. Saddened and depressed he came back to his brother and his mum.

'Has she been awake?' he whispered.

Jake shook his head. They sat glumly scrolling through their phones until the early hours of the morning. At some point during that long night they managed to snatch a few moments of sleep.

Thursday 19th Jan.

At around seven am Alex woke up. He saw one of the nurses staring into the room. It was a guy he remembered from school. Jonnie or Jamie, something like that.

He stuck his head around the door, 'Hiya Alex.'

'Hi.'

'Sorry about your mum.'

'Thanks.'

'You know the guy that did this?'

'Yeah.'

'He died last night.'

'Bloody hell.'

'I know.'

The nurse gently closed the door. Alex shook Jake awake. 'Hey, sorry to wake you.'

Jake peered at Alex, 'What's up?' He looked over at their mum, 'Is it mum?'

'No, she's fine, well you know, not exactly fine, but anyway, one of the nurses... you remember Jonnie something or Jamie something, from my year at school?'

Jake shook his head, still half asleep.

'No, not really, why?'

'Well he just told me that that Tom creature died last night.'

'Oh God.'

'I know.'

They both sank into silence. It was awful, but they were glad.

Pamela felt his dark presence looming along the corridors, trailing blood, his fingers stretching down, misshapen. Sharp fingernails scraping along the floor. He was looking for her. He would find her. She would not escape this time. The fingers inched their way around the door. She felt his breath on her face, smelt the hot stink of his desire. He leant down towards her, leering, evil-eyed, crazy.

She was back in his house, running through the endless rooms, looking for Sophie. There was no escape. His long arms were surrounding her, choking her, she struggled and fought, but he had her. She was going to die. He was holding her head underwater, she couldn't breathe. His red eyes fixed, inhuman.

Something clicked inside her mind, 'Fuck you,' she screamed at the top of her voice. She twisted her body so that he was in the water, she wrenched his arms away from her, she kicked him with all her strength. He was squirming on the floor, he was helpless.

'Mum, mum, wake up.' It was Jake. 'It's ok, you're safe.' She opened her eyes,

'He was here,' she stuttered.

'Mum, that's impossible.' He looked at Alex quizzically. Should they tell her? Alex shrugged; he wasn't sure.

'Mum, that dreadful man wasn't here,' he hesitated, then went on, 'mum, he died last night.'

She couldn't believe what Jake was saying.

'I killed him.'

'You didn't, mum,' Alex said, 'he died in intensive care. You had nothing to do with it.'

Pamela looked from Alex to Jake, they seemed to be sure, she relaxed a little. But she still didn't know how to feel; this information didn't seem to make any sense. The events of the last few days were just so surreal, so mind-alteringly weird, it was hard to focus, hard to adjust to this new reality, hard to pin down how to react. This new world was so totally alien to anything she'd experienced before.

Georgie arrived a few hours later and the boys went back to their mum's house to get some sleep. Pamela was half awake but groggy and still quite heavily sedated. Georgie wondered what the death of Tom would mean for Sophie. She'd killed him defending her friend. She was pretty sure you didn't go to jail in those circumstances. She'd spoken to Sophie that morning, before she knew about Tom. Sophie told her that she and Russ were going away for a while to try to sort things out. She thought they'd probably be fine.

When Pamela woke up later that day, she was a little more with it.

'Thanks for being here, Georgie.' She murmured.

'No worries, you seem a bit better today.'

Pamela smiled weakly. 'You've heard then, about that man?'

'Yeah. How do you feel?'

'Not sure.'

'Hmm. Well it's bound to take some time. I spoke to Soph today, she said to say hello.'

Pamela let this sink in. 'She saved my life.'

'I know.'

'But she's a stupid cow.'

'I know.'

'I don't think I want to be her friend anymore.'

'Well, see how you feel later. It's early days isn't it?'

'I don't think I can forgive her though.'

'Well, we'll see.' Georgie patted her little sister's hand. She was transported back to their childhood. Pamela was constantly falling out with one or other of her little school friends and Georgie was always trying to make it ok again. But of course, this was different, Georgie thought, Sophie had nearly got them both killed, it wasn't surprising that Pamela wasn't sure if she could ever forgive her.

'When can I go home?' Pamela interrupted her sister's thoughts.

'I'll go and ask a doctor.'

The boys had brought Pamela's phone into hospital, it was charging next to the bed. She leant forward and struggled to unplug it. She turned it on and several voice messages blinked at her. She listened to the one from Sophie. It was full of apologies and regret. Pamela was unmoved.

Then there were a couple of messages from Helen and Lou. She listened to the first message: "Hi Pam, it's Helen, so sorry to hear about the awful time you've had. As soon as Georgie says it's ok, I'll come and visit. Lots of love and kisses."

Then she listened to Lou's message: "Hi hun, just heard

about your accident. It sounds so dreadful. Everyone sends their love and hugs and we all hope you get better soon. This might cheer you up though – Mac has been suspended! When you're well enough they want you to come in and give a statement to an independent enquiry person. I know work is probably the last thing on your mind, but can you believe it?! He's gone and we need to make sure he doesn't come back!"

Pamela knew she should feel something at this news and maybe in time she would. But for now, that part of her life didn't seem important. So much had changed in the last three weeks. She wouldn't go back into teaching. That part of her life was over.

It was time to start healing, time to re-evaluate. Time to stick to the promises she'd made to herself. She felt a new strength, a new belief in herself. Everything was going to be ok.

She had faced death and now. At last, she could face life.